I0653869

Virtual Gandhi

Pacifying Warmongers by the Dozen Since 2062

KRIM FAUSTINO

Sure, the world is rushing toward another global conflict, in the Balkans, in the Straits of Taiwan, on the battlefields of Chechnya and along the Pakistani-Indian border – yet can we do anything other than shake our fists and fulminate?

— Justin Raimondo

...unless there is interference from what may be called by many the supernatural forces and influences, that are active in the affairs of nations and peoples, the whole world—as it were—will be set on fire by the militaristic groups and those that are "for" power and expansion in such associations...

— Edgar Cayce (416-7)

Part 1 – AND ONLY!

"A vicious hit job funded by communistic foreign elements hellbent on destroying our democracy." — John C. McMaster, SLDB

"The people behind this insult should be investigated and stripped of their citizenship." — Marketta Fellows, Ph.D.

"Claiming to be against violence while urging violent acts against peaceful politicians and captains of industry." — Darwin Lancelot, M.D.

"Biased beyond belief!" — *The Lusteus Review*

"A threat to our national security." — Senator Gavin Ra

"Terribly unfair to the defense industry." — Brigadier General Garfield "Barki" Bordogonne, JSC, Ret.

"I've heard rumors the author is into despicable, deviant acts. That alone renders unda's book an exercise in mendacity." — Anonymous

FALLING UP

. . . switching to The EavesDrop Portal™, Posting the World's Every Hack!

[Live Transcript - SunnyNews Interview Show™, with host Albert Relayant]

Albert Relayant: The Real Peace Dividend Party, or RPD, as it is commonly known, has only one candidate, Robert Gandhi. No major media company wants to talk to him, so his staff has arranged back-to-back interviews on smaller streamcasts to get his message out. Robert Gandhi has been kept from participating in official debates in past elections because of not being, quote, a candidate of consequence, as critics have put it, even though the RPD Party is on the ballot in all 51 states. Mr. Gandhi has gathered enough signatures to run as an independent candidate again and again.

. . . switching Dimensional Portal to The MeSez Network™, Expertly Bot-sorted and Curated to Make Sense

we're the majority now—the young, the overburdened by debt, pushed to the limit, with few prospects for things to ever get better for us. that's us. the majority. [posted by ignacius barros]

That's me, and I'm voting for Jenni Patel [posted by Annie Bora]

Jenni's young. She gets us. [Mariko Spanking]

She had to go out and form a new party of her own—the BJP-America, as a branch of the American Hindu Party, to finally address the herd of elephants in the room [Lodi Sketcher]

plus the thousands of asinine asses who were all talk and zero action! don't forget the asses! [landedGentry]

INFOPOST: SOURCE: World-O-Pedia™: Jennifer Patel:
Political figure and candidate. Founder of the BJP-America
Party. Known for unda's sublimely short and to-the-point
speech titled "Vote the Rascals Out!" in which und doesn't
mince words and speaks self-evident truths that have been
ignored for decades:

"We think the experiment has had its chance," Patel begins,
"with the Democratic and Republican parties, year after
year, decade after decade continuing to make the world safe
for hypocrisy. You see it now, with mayoral candidates of
both parties campaigning to, quote, 'get rid of the blighting
hordes' from their cities—and by hordes they mean us,
human beings. These hordes are people who have reached
the ends of their ropes.

"For whatever reason, they have lost all hope, lost their jobs,
their dignities, the means to make a living and support
themselves. But in the process, they have become completely
free. These so-called hordes are free to roam the downtowns
of our major cities, to set up shop on sidewalks and try to eke
out a living, by begging or by doing odd jobs, by engaging in
the business of surviving.

"But the Republican and Democratic candidates and mayors
hate this kind of freedom. Poor people in America have
gradually become freer and freer. They've lost everything,
but they are free from loan payments, from mortgages, from
building codes, from the mountains and mountains of
regulations that government agencies pile on us, one on top
of another, to harass and burden the general population—
and the poor are free from it all simply because they don't
have any money, so they have nothing to lose.

"Oh, but the politicians running against the poor hate that
freedom. They want to remove the truly free Americans out of
sight, because they don't want the rest of us to see what true
freedom looks like. We say, NO! Give me freedom or give me
death, as Patrick Henry is said to have uttered once. Give us

the freedom to walk the streets of downtown Washington, where tens of thousands now make their homes.

"Why shouldn't a cardboard shanty be placed right next to a high-end jewelry store selling watches priced north of sixty-thousand dollars? Where in the U.S. Constitution does it say that being poor is a crime, and that setting up shop in a public space is illegal? Or where in the 14th Amendment? 'No State shall make or enforce any law which shall abridge the privileges or immunities of citizens of the United States; nor shall any State deprive any person of life, liberty, or property, without due process of law; nor deny to any person within its jurisdiction the equal protection of the laws.'

"If the jewelry store owner in downtown Washington is free to walk up to that store and sell watches for sixty thousand dollars, why not the poor citizen, with equal protection of the laws, be allowed to set up a cardboard stand, right there on the sidewalk, and make a living selling whatever?

"Because the poor are the truly free citizens, so the politicians want them out of sight, all the tens of thousands of street dwellers removed far away because mayors and their cronies refuse to share their cities with ALL citizens. In their minds, every city must be clean and orderly, so the rich don't have to smell the poor. Truly free citizens aren't welcome.

"And I'm here to promise you, right now, that, in my administration, everyone will be expected to live in true freedom. Seattle, Des Moines, Boston, Palm Beach—everywhere—might not end up looking as spotless and tidy as they have in the past, but they will be FREE, open to ALL citizens, not just those who can afford to live there.

"This is the true face of freedom, not the selective hodgepodge of hypocrisy that the political duopoly has been trying to sell us for over a century. It's time to vote the rascals out!"

heard bout dis candidate jenni. we're all hearing more n more bout und. [posted by jung'N'pourful]

reminds me of episodes of "old romans" last season. like a mirror, eh? same road map. corrupt senators? check. unnecessary foreign invasions and occupations? check. expansionism? check. world's military bully? check. rotting from the inside out? check. jenni has my vote. [posted by hotSmoke]

jenni's a carpetbagger from india. don't fall for her snake-charming tricks. [marcia kokette]

all the fault of the haley-gabbard immigration act, allowing that south-asian refugee travesty that blew up our population out of control! last straw. the camel's back is broke, spewing its guts out as we speak. [power fister]

melting pot has melted! [moloko90]

no one asked india and pakistan to use tactical nukes on each other, so why couldn't they live with the consequences OVER THERE? why did hairy-gabbard have to invite them all here? [Xie Zedong]

they were not true refugees. they brought it onto themselves, including jenni the carpetbagger. don't care if she was born in the united states. she woudnt have if her parents had not been refugees of a situation their government itself created over there. [marcoPoloPlayer]

she wasn't born here [fakerSimple]

jenni talks freedom like there's no tomorrow, but she's an ardent subscriber to the federalists' 1818 stratagem, and, once in power, intends to apply it to the hilt, to force our supposedly free population to do her bidding. [gun-distracted]

> *INFOPOST: SOURCE: Know-it-All-eBook™: The Federalists' 1818 Stratagem: A plan cooked up by Alexander Hamilton to gradually and surreptitiously give power to a*

central government by trumping everything else in the legacy U.S. Constitution.

He and his likeminded politicians did this with "the 1818," a reference to Article 1, Section 8, Sub-Section 18, which states that Congress shall have the power "To make all Laws which shall be necessary and proper for carrying into Execution the foregoing Powers, and all other Powers vested by this Constitution in the Government of the United States, or in any Department or Officer thereof."

The stratagem was opposed by Patrick Henry, James Monroe, George Mason, and other anti-Federalists, but Hamilton won the day, and his so-called "Elastic Clause" tailed Section 8 like a caboose of subterfuge, becoming the 18th and last statement of the section, and, to Hamilton's delight, a dormant clause for unlimited power that could be activated at any time in the future, when a central government saw the need to activate it.

. . . switching Dimensional Portal to the iRiver Network™, the world's never-ending stream of comment, opinion, and thought

BREAKING: Malsain Smith, Secretary of Defense since replacing Berkley Oomajan—when the latter had a stroke a little over a year ago—has ALSO had a stroke undself![*] Smith was in the middle of making good on unda's threats to Belize, working with President George Marshall-Patel to send a fleet of drones down to the small Central American nation and "teach them a lesson," in Smith's words. But now that und is incapacitated, just like unda's predecessor, Washington is scrambling to quickly fill the position again.

[*] Required Federal Disclaimer: Per the 2039 Americans Free of Gender Act (AFGA), this publisher does not discriminate on the basis of gender self-classification. Thus, except in direct quotations, where the individuals quoted refused to observe the law, for political reasons or otherwise, this book adheres to the pronouns required by AFGA, adopted, without prejudice, by publishers and academics

across the United States of America, and further enshrined in the 2040 U.S. Department of Education's "New Word Manual of Style." The pronouns thus adopted—und, undself, unds, etc.—originally evolved from the word "underline," used at the beginning of the gender-free movement in the late 2020s as a placeholder for gender-based pronouns. But because underlined spaces became too visually unappealing to readers, the underline was replaced by AFGA with the handle "und"—short for "underline"—taking the place of he/she/it. Likewise, unda's for the possessive pronouns his/her/hers/its; and undas' for their and theirs; oundas for ours; unda for the direct object him/her/it, and undahas for them; undus for us; undself and undselves for the reflexive himself/herself and themselves; and unduselves for ourselves. To complete the set, unds took the place of they, and also the popular alternatives undas, undadem, and undis, revised to undisem by the 2047 amendment due to hate-speech implications. The publishing industry thanks Senator Ricannstrip for marshaling the AFGA.

good riddance smith and oomajan! [ramba23]

servs unda rite [love goo]

thats what u get when u pander to the military industrial complex [lester the molester]

bring on the next sec of defense warmonger. god will take care of the asshole toot sweet! [Bismark Zambrano]

. . . switching Dimensional Portal to the Juicy News Network™, Keeping Americans Alert to All Threats

BREAKING: 20G wireless technology has run into mounting opposition now that a noticeable number of sudden-tumor cases have begun to hit virtual emergency rooms across the ether. Telemedicine bots have been overwhelmed with cases streaming in through the feed. "Something is rotten in the Empire of Gotham," said NYC Mayor Loquacious Restogar, an ardent opponent to 20G deployment. "After the fiasco with 18G, which ended up being scrapped, and for good reason, now we have this," und added. The

Center for Humane and Sensitive Technology™ echoed Mayor Restogar's sentiments by posting a 200-word exposé about an industry, und said, "bent on getting rid of what elitists call 'the surplus population,' by dint of technology-induced brain tumors. This is not what a kinder, gentler, humanist society is supposed to be doing to its citizens. #Stop20Gnow!"

BREAKING: Secretary of Defense Malsain Smith, famous for unda's quip, "Beautiful day to depose somebody," is being forced to resign by President Marshall-Patel, who said, "Malsain was a tremendous public servant—still is—but we will let unda rest and try to recover unda's motor skills, and we won't burden unda with any of unda's former duties."

BREAKING: In other news, President Marshall-Patel announced that the National Freedom Tax will go up again next fiscal year, by five percent, "so we can be in a more stable financial position to combat terror and defend the homeland," und said.

there it goes again, *dastardus amerikanus* [joy-too-lil]

warrior of the species [mikadu2020]

secretary of war crimes [candleman]

BREAKING: New political scandal surrounding Democratic candidate for president Flori Jankar, who, during an interview, indicated that "some women prefer to stay home and have children." An eyewitness reported on the EavesDrop Portal™ that there was a sudden quiet in the studio, and Jankar "instantly knew und had put unda's two feet in unda's mouth—thick wool socks, Doc Martens, and all." Jarintza Marchetti, who was conducting the interview, smiled at Jankar, who said, "Interviewer Marchetti, I didn't mean..." It was too late. The interview was over.

. . . switching to the EavesDrop Portal™: Posting the World's Every Hack!

BREAKING: Jankar DESTROYED! . . . within minutes of the end

of the Marchetti interview, ether-media platforms were burning up with #destroyJankar and commands to "Unfollow the asshole!" Editorial boards across the country were asking undselves, "How can anyone be married to this monster? We all need to save the spouse immediately! Run, Rammie, run! Give Rammie a call. Here's unda's number @202-318-####. . ."

Even Flori's father, Senator Agar Jankar, posted advice for Flori on the VoxPopuli Stream™: "Apologise, son. It's not a big deal. Let them emasculate you in public. It's just symbolic. You'll still have your dignity."

"But politicians say sexist things all the time!" replied Flori. "Why are there no repercussions for them?"

"Politics, son. We have special privileges. You're allowed to call people names and undermine their electability. It's part of the democratic process. Apologise and be done with it. Or why are you running for president? If you're afraid of someone punching you, don't become a boxer!"

Flori Jankar, an elementary school teacher until announcing unda's bid to get the Democratic nomination, has used unda's lack of Washington experience as a primary feature of unda's electability. Jankar's campaign slogan, "No Political Past = Great Leadership for the Future," has not convinced a significant number of the electorate. The current scandal won't help. Nevertheless, thousands of persons with real uteri have flooded the streets of the nation's downtowns with pickets announcing, "Flori, I want to have YOUR baby!"

> *INFOPOST: SOURCE: World-O-Pedia™: The EavesDrop Portal™: An anonymous network administered by AI Bots whose purpose is to either hack or facilitate real-time transcripts of conversations, be them on the phone, the set of a studio, a private chat in a restaurant, or a board meeting somewhere. The Bot Transcripts or "bottrans" are automatically dumped by the bots on the iRiver Network™, the VoxPopuli Stream™, and many other public platforms for anyone to read.*

. . . Welcome - you're entering the VoxPopuli Stream™

Check out candidate General LaRose's interview on The Normal Network™. The journo skewered unda's retrograde views. Excerpts:

Journo: General, you've been accused of genderizing your prejudices, a serious offense under AFGA that could bring on criminal charges and a complete disruption to your presidential campaign. In one of your speeches, you used the long-discarded term LGBTQ...., which is considered not only offensive, but also a candidate for inclusion in the list of national hate-crime epithets. What do you have to say in your defense?

Chase LaRose: Look, of course I wasn't thinking when I said it. The moment the term came out of my mouth, my assistant—who is a non-gender person, by the way—pointed out to me the mistake I had made, and I immediately apologized. I posted on Contrition Net™ a full statement denouncing my act, and I will be posting there again.

Journo: Genderizing human beings is a character flaw this country cannot accept in a political candidate running for office. Are you willing to repeat your apology, right here, right now, on national PureVision™, to all citizens? Or, better yet, are you prepared to denounce all gender supremacists and their hateful organizations and religious biases, and PLEDGE that YOUR administration, if elected, will prosecute, to the full extent of the law, all gender supremacists engaged in hurtful and offensive genderizing?

Chase LaRose: I pledge to treat all citizens equally and to follow the spirit of the 36th Amendment and of the AFGA.

Journo: I'm afraid that's not good enough. We would like you to denounce gender-supremacist organizations.

Chase LaRose: Look, I will not be singling out any citizen. All I can do is pledge to treat everyone equally before the law.

Journo: Failed attempt, General. You've proven yourself incapable of being inclusive, and you are clearly incapable of redressing wrongs. We'll be right back after this commercial pause.

. . . iRiver Network™

> *INFOPOST: SOURCE: World-O-Pedia™: General Chase LaRose: Born in Greeley, Colorado, to descendants of French Huguenots who migrated southwest from Nova Scotia. He attended Fork Union Academy in Virginia and later earned a four-year Military Excellence Degree from The Virtual Star and Stripes University™, after failing to be admitted to West Point. Anecdotal evidence places him near the top of the list of youngest generals in the history of the United States.*

candidate's trending, obviously. put his dick in it with hate talk. [honey trap]

personally, i rather let bigots be free to express their bigotry so i know who undas are. Otherwise, undas'll be seething in private, nourishing resentments and planning undas' revenge—with us none the wiser. [bowling with ballz]

LaRose walked the talk. Now we know who und is. So, und's deprecated. [bow 2 ur prez]

forget the gender stuff. he's pro-war, and that's where he needs to be brought down [loco locavore]

Saw LaRose the other day spouting nonsense about military alliances and the need to "invest" in the weapons industry when other countries refuse to buy our shit. "We have this military product we need to sell," he said. "If our industries can't sell it, the least we can do, as a nation, is find a use for it somewhere. We can sell it to Uncle Sam! That's a big win for the American economy!" That's the candidate we want, for sure. He cares about the military and, right now, he's also caring about "our persons in uniform." [loud barker]

. . . switching to the EavesDrop Portal™

Live Transcript - SunnyNews Interview Show in the Morning™ with Electra LoganPine interviewing presidential candidate General LaRose

General LaRose: You're damn right, Lectra. We need better pay for our persons in uniform and military loved ones. My campaign calls it Heroi Funding, and I'll make damn sure that our persons in uniform get the pay they deserve for protecting our country. We're in a global race against evil actors everywhere, and I will not apologize for being the hawk who looks after Americans and American interests.

Electra LoganPine: That's alright, general, but I want to bring back our conversation to what matters to voters, to your incapability of being inclusive regarding differently-gendered citizens.

General LaRose: Oh, boy. Here we go again. I'll give it to you straight, Lectra, so there's no equivocation on where I stand on this matter. It is my goal to protect the innocent once I'm their commander-in-chief. Back in the dark ages, we used electroshock therapy to treat the homosexuals, right? Today, everyone recognizes such treatment as ineffective and inhumane. Instead, we've turned to hormonal therapy, not to treat homosexuality but a host of other made-up categories of sexual morbidity. We're at 38.6% now, Lectra. Did you know that? It's well over a third of the U.S. population deciding they don't want to be the gender biology that came with their birth. They say they don't identify with their bodies. They wanted to be the opposite ever since they can remember, etc. That's fine. Be whatever you want to be. But to start taking hormones in massive quantities to grow boobs or facial hair . . . how is that any more natural or acceptable than applying electroshock therapy in the belief that it will achieve some barbaric outcome?

Electra LoganPine: But electroshock therapy was forced on people who did not want it, General. Hormones today are taken willingly by individuals who WANT to better themselves.

General LaRose: Willingly willed by unscrupulous doctors who push hormones like the drug peddlers they are, taking advantage of people who are so lost in their lives they can't think of anything other than how to chemically change their bodies to a supposedly heightened state—just like taking heroin, cocaine, eXe, Kandy B, or any other drug.

Electra LoganPine: Then you're a bigot.

PUBLICITY!: Binge the fourth season of "Sexy Tots" starting tonight! Don't miss Amanda and Shakirita's descent into a vicious catfight in their bikinis at Amanda's slumber party, with new tot Lilly joining the cast!

BREAKING: The saga goes on with the trial against the Newman's Own Foundation for continuing to use the image of a smirking, middle-aged white male on its labels. That image has been deemed insensitive and hurtful to individuals of that gender, age, and demographic.

The foundation's attorney, Ulrika Fapritti, has justified the use of the image based on its likeness to one of the founders of the charitable organization, decades ago. The prosecution, representing the State of California and the Center for the Defense of Human Dignity in Advertising™, is not buying it.

"Hateful, demeaning imagery has no place in public discourse, let alone when it is used for marketing a product," a spokesperson for the Center said. "Times change, and if it was OK to caricature that old person decades ago, that's no longer the case," added the White Senior Citizens for Justice™ nonprofit in its amicus brief, siding with the plaintiffs. "The Honorable State of California will prosecute this crime to the full extent of the law, and we intend to seek damages and have the defendant pay steep fines to the plaintiffs," the document added.

old folks no longer command or deserve any respect. [Guadalcanal Diarist]

think about it, every fuckup mess we're in now is because of these people who're trying to have their retirements on OUR backs! [fauxgatha]

it's not the old folks who fucked us up, it's the indians [DNA doctor]

yeah, and it's those old folks who were young and in charge when they let the indians in, so it IS them to blame! [carter's avatar]

A little history lesson for those blaming us Indians and India for the current state of things in the United States: DON'T! We didn't start the wheels that turned towards mass migration and a refugee crisis. It was American president Japleen Gupta who fanned the nuclear embers and egged India on to "defend itself, nuclearly," against "foreign aggressor Pakistan." You, of course, didn't count on the Pakistan-Russia-Iran-China (PRIC) coalition retaliating immediately. Poor India found itself outgunned and completely abandoned by treacherous America! So, all that was left for America to do was to accept responsibility, take the hundreds of millions of refugees fleeing radioactive India, and settle them in the United States. Now, legacy Americans have the nerve to complain and point fingers at us because Indian immigrants have become dominant in tech, finance, publishing, real estate, education, and myriad other corners of the American economy. Losers will always lose when they overreach. The winners from America's warmongering activities in the last four decades? The PRICs, and us Indians who migrated and started new, successful lives in America. If you don't like it, tough! For the rest of us, Vote Flori Jankar, y'all! [another patel]

you know what? bullshit! mi casa is NOT su casa! we never wanted you here, and now you can go back! [bidonville mogul]

shut up. it's no longer your house. you irresponsibly lived high on the hog and got deep in debt, so we foreclosed on you. it's OUR house now. be thankful we haven't evicted you yet. [stanley shankar]

indians being indians, so what's new? [mielduh]

Don't knock war. All human progress has come to us thanks to armed conflict. All significant technological advances, from the early stages of human interactions, were due to the necessity to come up with something that would give one group of people an advantage over their opponents. [captain grape juice]

advanced societies arise through war [Mitzu Arrabal]

the fertilizers that grow your food today were developed from poison gases used in a world war over a century ago. [OchoCuartos]

airplanes, too. pods. virtual machines. we'd have nothing advanced today without the wars of the past. [mollusk of the sky]

Nonsense. China's golden age (618 to 906 A.D.) was the most stable and peaceful of its history, and great technological advances came out of it, without war. [lemming du jour]

all those advances were developed earlier, during armed conflict among tribal chinese. the fact is, if it weren't for war, we'd still be hunter-gatherers. that fact alone qualifies war—all wars—as being just and necessary events for the sake of human progress. antiwar fanatics are anti progress, anti sharing the wealth of technology with every human alive. [mollusk of the sky]

What's needed is a war on warriors and warmongers [paz da jelly]

yes, and all incumbents are warmongers by default, by doing NOTHING to change the status quo. [alice in wonderbread]

incumbents are such shits. not one of them should ever be reelected. when they ask you for your vote to keep them in office, it's like your roommate who leaves a "Don't use the toilet!" sign on the bathroom door. "I haven't finished my poo!" [ivy snuff]

shit-o-crats and merdepublicans [garden mole]

its a big cuntree. there's room for everyone, including the indians [california nightmaring] gotta stir that melting pot every once in a while, eh? [suave predator]

too late, the cook's already poured a mountain of curry and ruined the stew [colonist638]

Here we go again, spreading hatred based on resentment of Indians' success. [another patel]

perennial angry-victim wannabes [soft-core philosopher]

We Indian immigrants worked hard to achieve our dominant status in this country. In most cases, our parents or grandparents arrived in the United States with no money and little education. [another patel]

haa, and as members of a non-white ethnic group, we have proven that success has nothing to do with skin color, and though we have suffered racial discrimination like any other non-whites, we don't use it as an excuse to justify our staying in place without social and economic mobility. [american atman]

hard work, perseverance, and focusing on our efforts, y'all, rather than wasting our lives blaming everything on the Und. [988plum]

whites no longer a majority in the united states anyway. we browns and blacks and the melting pot of ethnicities are the majority [main theek hoon]

haa, and because the whites are no longer numerous enough for people to keep accusing them of racism, it's us successful indians who receive the wrath of the underachievers who refuse to take responsibility for their own destinies. [american atman]

our super successful tamil brothers are as dark as they come, and they don't hide behind the excuse of racism to not get ahead. [Guarav Sathiyamoorthi]

yes! even dalit immigrants hit it big working hard, creating the dalit café chain. how's that for being proud of your past? [soft-core philosopher]

PUBLICITY: Celebrate Dalit History Month with authentic Dalit cuisine! Get the most delicious Goat Blood Fry in the Americas, delivered to you in minutes by ChowDrone™! Celebrate Dalit culture!

i thought it was brahmin history month [Fabrikator]

both. we can share. not enough months for everyone. [Chetan Lodha]

if legacy minorities insist on holding grudges against us indians, there's nothing we can do about it but pocket the cash and keep on getting ahead. let's lose the losers! [mumbai rose]

PUBLICITY: El Tocino de Cochino se Hace Saborear™. Order your bacon-curry burrito today! Yell "Tocino de Cochino!" at your listening device whenever your mouth starts watering. Enjoy the best multi-cultural taste this side of the Atlantic has to offer to discerning palates. Tocino de Cochino!

. . . Switching to The Contrition Net™, Where Wrongdoers Set Things Right

We regret that, in an article dated 5 June 1838, certain individuals were referred to as "Asiatics" in a tone unworthy of our publication. We deeply apologize for any harm or suffering this may have caused to living persons at the time and to any of their descendants since. Note: The publication of this notice does not in any way qualify it to be used as a claim for financial reparations for either psychic or economic suffering from past actions. [The Far East Explorer Weekly]

I, Swifty Johnson, Mayor of Indianapolis, Indiana, would like to apologize to the Indian-American community and to the members of the Indians from India Living in Indiana Association. I did not mean to make fun of or belittle their demands to call for a referendum on renaming the City of Indianapolis "New Gujarat." Note: The publication of this notice does not in any way qualify it to be used as a claim for financial reparations for either psychic or economic suffering from past actions. [Swifty Johnson]

I, General Chase LaRose, deeply apologize for using the long-discarded and demeaning term "LGB..." I was not thinking when it came out of my mouth, and though that is no excuse, I will definitely strive to do better in the future. I denounce my callous act and apologize and beg for forgiveness from those who were affected by my action. Note: The publication of this notice does not in any way qualify it to be used as a claim for financial reparations for either psychic or economic suffering from past actions. [Chase LaRose]

PUBLICITY: Get your baby llama today! 100% legal, and llamas make excellent sex partners! We at ErosPets™ are at the vanguard of this human revolution! Reserve your baby llama at MyLlamaMyLife@3546! Our production lines are humming as fast as they can!

I am 42 years old and supposed to be modern, having been born in this century, but can't get used to this filth. It may be legal, but that doesn't make it right. [humbrella20]

you missing out, bud! i bought me a baby llama and, man, fantastic! wouldnt do nothing else. [life fantastic]

there's a store in new york selling trained gerbils. [robespierre raspberry]

NOW weer talking! [life fantastic]

just ordered a couple for me and my son [justin in training]

you f**king degenerates. going to hell. [eliseo renn]

hot and cozy down there, right? like you know what [justin in training]

. . . Switching to ClassyNet™

Warning: This portal is owned by the National-Security Intelligence Services Corporation™ of the United States of America. If you have no business being here, exit this logon screen IMMEDIATELY. All visitors without permission, even if no attempt is made to illegally log on, may be subject to cyber-terrorism charges that carry prison sentences from twenty years to life, plus fines.

Enter your network identifier: *******

Enter your biometric algorithm: ********

Enter your Dispatch PIN: ****

Enter your National Security Number: **-****-***

. . . Switching to The MeSez Network™, Expertly Bot-sorted and Curated to Make Sense

A new crop of lawsuits is being harvested right now against SpaceX and Ariane, folks. The fact that another condo was wiped out by falling space debris in Oregon this morning won't help the defendants. Fifty-three residents dead. [space kadet504]

add to that the 248 killed in korea last week [bored house pet]

19 en Argentina antes de ayer [cacique22]

government agencies will bail them out. they always do, in the name of national security. [honest klepto]

the u.s. and china are organizing space debris removal missions as we speak, not to mention the ruskies and froggies. [star-struck bambi]

sweetening the deal with documentaries and movie offers about "the courageous spacepeople trawling the universe to save our planet." utter bullshit [space kadet504]

first mission will air live next month, just about the time some of these lawsuits will have their day in cybercourt. they'll make it look like the feds are taking care of the problem. [london mandy]

just a distraction to bury what's going on in belize! [monkey smoker]

. . . The iRiver Network™

TRENDING: Belize: Central American Country, a popular tourist destination for Americans over several decades, until the Belizean People's Freedom Front (BPFF) took control of the government, removed the British monarch as the head of state, and began a systematic, Marxist dismantling of the rule of law and democratic institutions. The current United States administration has strongly condemned Belize's "departure from freedom, honor, and good-neighborly behavior," said Secretary of State Raja McKenzee, who has bowed to impose new sanctions, including a total economic embargo against the government of Belize if the country does not return to "the sphere of good nations," und added, "within the next six weeks." [Know-it-All-eBook™]

The BPFF announced yesterday it will start executing foreign nationals who insist on interfering in Belize's internal affairs. "If you come as a tourist, you stay a tourist," said president and former footballer Charlie Zabaneh. [cow pose]

followed by a private reply from raja mac, leaked on eavesdrop this morning, something like "we'll beat the shit out of your little shithole country!" presumably if any such executions take place. [carib381]

wasn't leaked but broadcast on purpose to scare and let zabaneh know that some 18 year old kid in a bunker in nevada is training satellites on belmopan. [punta chick]

> *INFOPOST: SOURCE: The Know-it-All-eBook™:*
> *Belmopan: Capital city of Belize but now a term more*
> *commonly used to describe the expansive, 64,000-square-foot*
> *presidential palace recently completed by the administration*

of President Charlie Zabaneh, a former footballer often accused by critics of "wasting the country's treasure on flashy symbols of opulence." See Belmopan Palace.

BREAKING: The Hate in Speech Act (HISA) has passed the Senate and has been signed by the Prez! Article One of the HISA says it all: "No entity that is in a position to communicate with the public, including individuals who communicate with other individuals or groups, be it via speech, writing, sign language, sound, light, vibration, or any other form of possible communication between sentient beings, shall have the right to use hurtful and offensive vocabulary that can be perceived—by the receiving end of the communicating participants, or anyone else—as a threat, a form of intimidation, an offense, malignant intention, or even unintended psychological damage." The HISA contains a "Compromise Clause" to allow for the First Amendment, stating that VoxPopuli Stream™ will be the one and only venue exempt from the Act. [Free America News]

marshall-patel's signature on the HISA made vox's stock shoot to the stratosphere! got me 300 shares right before it reached 618%. It's now at over 3009%, folks! can't believe morons are shorting it! [square deal]

just gonna keep going up [leezard_5]

only place in merika where yul be able to say whatever the fuck without getting yur social points shot to hell and yur crypto turned off by the feds [bunker 14]

relax, children, the hissing act doesn't take effect until six months from now, even if already signed. in the meantime, hate away anywhere you want, if you can do it anonymously, of course, or they'll still get you. [nature boy]

imma hisssssss and keep on hissssssng whereever i want. free country. free world, free universe. fed asssholes can hissssss the hisa act up their hass [kola nut] voxpopuli will be it. all other platforms will utilize technology to scrub posts clean, or even delete them automatically, if too offensive. even if you start using your "hisssss" as an epithet, they'll ban that too [cindy chan]

. . . Welcome - you're entering the VoxPopuli Stream™ - buy our stock!

fuck fuck fuck fuck fuck! [kola nut]

HISA is trending, so no one's paying attention to new developments at the Social Assets Stock Exchange. [BarbieCon]

yeah. saw that. sase's tightening them screws big time. [framematick]

Have you seen Fitzy Jamahl's FJA stock price lately? [3rd_musketeer]

king of porncoms one day, pariah the next. his 49% stake on fja now nearly worthless. [austinwood]

Everyone's #shortFitzy and selling [3rd_musketeer]

da sheeple have spoken. fitzy's nearly bankrupt, and sase will for sure delist fja by the end of the week. cancelled. [so-so life]

was never a good actor anyway. just the bod. [albertz2027]

but WHAT a bod! [salt licor]

BREAKING: Fake Mars colony revealed. Jeff Bezos™ has been arrested in an underground compound in Arizona after 7 years in hiding. Best known as the founder of now defunct Amazon, an online distributor, and from the biopic "Egghead to Mars," Bezos tantalized the world with unda's live-streamed "Departure from Earth" documentary in 2054, followed by the supposedly Mars-produced "Into the Void of an Eternal Journey." [Mara News] bunk. bezos's been dead for years. [popculturist]

debunked. he lives! [Lanzalot Martinez]

wouldn't he be like over a hundred now? is that possible? [dirty kimono]

age don't matter. had a SoulTransplant™ done [carey-oh-key]

amazon always a c.i.a. front. changed its name after bezos was offed. [kumar in heaven]

didn't they report about his death on mars years ago? i'm confused. [fountainHeader]

wasn't mars. und was in california. [Georgian Guideliner]

suicide, they said. [Orbasm]

no one knows shit. just like the moon landing, except pavlov was not as good a publicity whore. [PensaMann]

i remember that egghead movie...was a kid when it came out. had a blast with the script. me and my brother competing to memorize the most lines. knew it by heart. "greetings, earthlings!" [SkitzBoy]

yes! me too! still remember the opening "in the near future, mysterious phenomena begin to emerge in an unhinged world..." [japi verdei]

4 me, de most memorable line was when Bezos addressed the IRS. "Moving to Mars! Tax THAT, assholes!" [niagaraDrop]

just found this bit of news from back then: "BREAKING: After a mysterious three-month absence from the public sphere, Jeff Bezos has reappeared in the most threatening way possible for the rest of humanity. 'Greetings, earthlings,' he posted on his AmaGram™ account. 'Just to let you know I'm on my way to my compound on Mars with my team and everything we'll need for the next singularity! In other words, we no longer need you! All the Amazon shipping boxes you've kept have been designed to detonate at my command, embedded with fissile material. Also, if you think you can be quick enough to destroy your shipping boxes, I've thought of that. It won't make any difference. My Millennium Clock in Texas was designed to send massive low-frequency electromagnetic waves to the earth's core—enough to disintegrate the planet. In other words, you're fucked!'" [mermoladi]

of course, nothing happened, which should have been a hint that the whole mars thing was a hoax. [me enchanted]

best part of the movie was the hot chick who played the spaceship captain. [lower than low]

and girlfriend [giantDear]

after the movie, she changed her name to alexa, thinking it would give her leverage to be cast in the sequel. [Bahtiyar Basar]

ha! little did she know there'd be no sequel! [chick fillette]

another pathological liar, that actress. during the movie's promo tour, called herself a former paratrooper in the jungles of siberia. [Ranter8811]

that, right there, was how she let you know that the movie was baloney. she was just winking at you, saying "this is shit" [Bottom Feeder19]

how do you know? ever been to siberia? [Gerbil Treadmiller]

for all we know, it's all jungle and humid heat there. can't be sure about anything until you experience it yourself. [Lana Borelo]

all education is a form of brainwashing. [bar-coded for life]

learning has come a long way—from a quest for knowledge to a vapid means of social reconditioning [Rustic Shakespeare] and let's not forget that the moon landing was a hoax, too. the chinese were the first to expose it. [POS employee]

and then india. dont forget india. decades of american boasting about giant step for mankind bullshit. if it were not for the indian space program, which found nothing on the moon when landing there, the american lie would have never come out. [TengoTango]

shut up about indians already. it was the chinese who found no trace other than laser reflectors on the surface, deposited remotely because there was absolutely no evidence of any human there. and it was after THAT reveal that the indianauts arrived to confirm it. [KeepBuying So]

Whatever. We Indians landed in America. Indian immigrants who came here by the hundreds of millions to refresh the gene pool—the tired, spent American Empire was in need of a jump-start. [SutraSutra Mama]

ha! so jump-started, we're about to experience the collapse of the american rupee [fattyMart chapati]

the chinese retreated to their own, improved empire [Big E at the 222]

better have the chinese in china and not here becoming dangerous s-e-p-a-r-a-tists, like the indians [morning sick-o]

BREAKING: Far-East-Asian-American 4th graders in Nebraska are being rounded up and fined for cultural appropriation. "These children have no right to be playing music from 18th Century European composers," said the state's chief prosecutor, Vilas Temporary. "It's culturally insensitive to have an ethnic group that does not belong to the European tradition appropriate the cultural heritage of Europeans," und added. Authorities have already issued a Cease & Desist Order to the youngsters, accompanied by a warning that if they insist on stealing European heritage, they will "definitely do time in jail." Sign up to #MyCultureMyMusic for regular updates on this important cultural-rights case.

i play a knockoff stradi [TeeVee grrrl]

u uropeean? [roxee lizt]

nope [TeeVee grrrl]

shame on you [roxee lizt]

PUBLICITY: Start earning immediately! The U.S. Department of Defense Corporation™ is hiring! Become your neighborhood's Senior Monitor for Terrorist Chatter Specialist! Report suspicious activity to the DODC—and here's the best part—anonymously! Health insurance, retirement plan, and personal loans included with your employment offer, along with a $10,000 hiring bonus! Start earning now! Yell "NEIGHBORHOOD MONITOR!" at your listening device now! Start monitoring today! And find out whether YOUR neighbors are tampering with THEIR listening devices! Serve your country by reporting your neighbors!

made good money doing this for a while but ended up having to move because all my neighbors found out and hated me. [falcon amapolus]

The personal loans is what did me in with the DODC. Really high interest rates. I owed THEM money by the time they fired me. [roberta george]

same here. making more on unemployment now than what they paid. it's a scam. [entschuldigung?]

BREAKING: Secretary of State Raja McKenzee speaking live now, discussing how und is reserving unda's right to drone any undesirable, antisocial elements anywhere in the world, especially if undas are a threat to our national security. [Bart News Syndicate]

PUBLICITY: Are you suffering from postpartum oppression? Don't let the little critter get to you, or the sperm donor make a nuisance of undself. Protect your sanity with a daily dose of HappyMother Nectar™, the supplement-elixir formulated to keep you in control of your motherhood. Don't let ANYONE oppress you. HappyMother Nectar™ will liberate you. Gluten-free!

. . . iRiver Network™

LIVE TRANSCRIPT: Secretary of State Raja McKenzee

Reporter: Who authorizes you to kill humans without a proper discovery and trial process? You're not even the Secretary of Defense.

Raja McKenzee: We unilaterally have the right to act on behalf of our partners in all our multilateral agreements, as is the case here with our fellow nations in the Americas. And you don't have a say while WE are in office. Until you yourself are either elected or appointed by someone who has been elected, you're just a citizen. We don't need your input on how to keep our citizens safe, including you in your capacity as a citizen. If Belize is a threat, Belize is a threat, and we're going to deal with it.

my hero! [estonia carmicle]

give'em hell, raj! [lindsey locker]

Reporter: With that attitude, no one who disagrees with you will ever have a chance to get elected. You'll make sure to drone them dead, preemptively, in the name of national security. Your party is conflating national security with retaining political power forever.

Raja McKenzee: You don't have a say. Next!
[Brought to you by Global Transcription Services™]

BREAKING: First painting ever sold for nine billion dollars! A small Stanić piece, painted nearly a century ago, sold by Chandler Bartholomew Auctions for a bit over nine billion dollars, a new record in the art world, and certainly in the non-digital sector.

saw it on veloz's new midcentury campaign. totally mediocre. [adan schmitt]

chandler gave the painting the title "weird guy walking dog" cause d'artist didn't bother to name the thing. [proud bostonian]

figures [racist mexican]

ridiculous. non-digital art is way overrated. [fuKanvas]

it's all hype generated by chandler bartho and their ilk of geezer investors. [piko-pikazzo]

they hype all the oil on canvas crap just to get more money. [vortex666]

digital is so much more valuable now. [gora show]

and a solid investment to boot [arti$$$ta]

PUBLIC ANNOUNCEMENT: Wear yellow tomorrow to honor our immigrant population. Fines in effect for all who break the law and wear other colors. Rural areas exempt.

public fucking dictum: greet and thank our wonderful memeigrants. sample greetings: "glad to have you!" "welcome to mrka!" "love your culture!" [bullshit detector]

"glad to have you!" you can't have me, asshole! i've lived in this country longer than you've been alive. [chineseTalkative]

newbie here. why are rural areas exempt? [Bogdán Lopez]

low eye-cue folks dont understand dictums! or pretend not to, with their antisocial, backward way of life. [Miser-atti]

if you can't follow the rules, stay there in your rural hellhole, or move there already! [joseph left mary]

Truth is, we can't afford paramilitary police in sufficient numbers to enforce the dicta in rural areas. [mensa champion]

in an urban setting, swat teams can be on site in seconds. i saw a grandma person last month's yellow day stripped to her yellow panties to prove she was in compliance. was fined anyway by the six officers surrounding the person. the color's supposed to be VISIBLE TO ALL, not in your privates. [nube morada]

kant afford to send the swatters to rural bakcuntree. people there better handled with drones. [ekonomico27]

thats what u get when u refuse to kontribute to urban, civilized engagement. hermits, outcasts, privacy fetishists, and paranoid weirdos get whats coming to them, and most of them hide in rural. [lizard fix]

You're like a century out of date with your bias, sir. There's something called the Internet now, and we have it in all rural areas. We're as connected as any urban hipster you care to name. The only difference: we live in much nicer surroundings. I'm not forced to see your ugly forest of concrete, metal, or glass horrors out my window. [free countryman]

overrated, forests! [soul sidewalk]

still, a whole lotta inbreeding taking place in rural, on account of the low population density [lizard fix]

bullshit. found ma bride on internet. dated online for a while, then she moved to my turkey farm from new yolk. and she's russian, so instant diversity in my neck of the woods. [thanksgiving thanker]

We have a whole bunch of Indians where I live, from the refugee migration. The U.S. has the most diverse rural areas in the world. [alter bandida]

rurals are still clinging to the wrong end of politics, though, supporting candidates that suck in every possible way. it's like they live on another planet. [rudolph garcia]

PUBLIC ANNOUNCEMENT: The Federal Government™ will begin mailing ChromaPeau™ meters next week to all citizens. The meters are free of charge and must be used along with online Census Form CF-100 via wireless connectivity to transfer readings. The meters can measure one hundred shades of human skin to provide a numerical score from one to a hundred. Individuals MUST report their score on the annual census form and mail in their blood samples. "Anything under a score of 20 is considered *Blanche*," Secretary of Commerce Vance Rectohamm said.

a new effort in bullshit futility, monumental waste of resources. who cares anymore? [blando dificil]

another way to classify people. it failed last census, but it's better technology now. [franka child]

will fail again [75net human]

there'll be people tanning to get a higher score and avoid discrimination [shriveled pickleball]

feds are banning the use of tanning beds and devices until after the census. during winter, no natural tans, either [GuapaLuchadora]

the rich will just go on island vacations [Fred Reddy]

so tired of this skin color bullshit! [amaya basu]

anti-racism rules don't apply anymore. they were created for when whites were in charge and discriminated against all others. [disruptiveHarlot]

a well-known category of odious resentment [berkley rao]

whites a minority now, so rules don't apply, certainly not to indians discriminating against blacks, or blacks against mexicans, or whatever. we done wid dat. [Erdogan Bonilla]

All this palaver about discrimination. We have much more important things to do with our resources than worry about antiquated laws that should have been purged from the books long ago. [Elder Berry]

amen [greenGo marketable]

white guilt is not our concern. it belongs in the past and has nothing to do with our modern, dynamic amerika. [gorgeous adonis]

so i'm all sad 4 whitey...how und whines left n right bout how the kuntry was stole blah, blah, blah. its our turn to boss n rule now! [MeekBeau]

and . . . news flash! the world DOESN'T have it in for whitey! we the people don't even bother to think about whitey! that's the difference. we are just living our democracy. we don't make every action a race thing. [King Coolie]

there's no race and no skin color here. when i get that chromashit thing in the mail, its going right in the trash. [rockStar38]

solid anglo-sax creds here, and agree the chromapeau is just the white colonizer speaking, trying to keep control over which und has lost. [John Smith XIV]

it's par for the course. we took it, now you take it. sick and tired of whiny white babies. [boa konstrictor]

BREAKING: Only thirty-eight businesses were destroyed in last night's peaceful demonstrations in Tampa. Mayor Karim Acosta indicated that, among the affected businesses, there was "a halal-ethiopian-vietnamese-deplorable kosher deli, a hungarian-chinese-tongan-hindu sports goods store, and a cambodian-hasidic-guinean-siberian pizza bistro." All businesses have already filed their peaceful-demonstration insurance claims, Acosta added, "and they expect to reopen their doors within two months, except for a Korean convenience store, burned to the ground and unfortunately operating illegally without PD insurance." [News Factory Collective™]

. . . ClassyNet™

Warning: This portal is owned by the National-Security Intelligence Services Corporation™ of the United States of America. If you have no business being here, exit this logon screen IMMEDIATELY. All visitors without permission, even if no attempt is made to illegally log on, may be subject to cyber-terrorism charges that carry prison sentences from twenty years to life, plus fines.

Enter your network identifier: *******

Enter your biometric algorithm: ********

Enter your Dispatch PIN: ****

Enter your National Security Number: **-****-***

ClassyNet: Welcome to ClassyNet, and thank you for your patriotic service. Your classification is Alpha 2 Level 7. You are not allowed to post entries, but can read posts up to Clearance 7.

ClassyNet: Warning: No words or letters displayed here can be shared with anyone outside this network. Any unauthorized sharing will result in cyber-terrorism charges that carry prison sentences from twenty years to life, plus fines.

ClassyNet: All information displayed will be scrubbed within seconds.

ClassyNet: Beginning session . . . your ClassyNet session number is 030528 . . .

...Welcome, new recruit. (scrubbed)

...Your deposits will be wired monthly... (scrubbed)

...to the top-secret account set up for you. Only crypto withdrawals and untraceable transactions are allowed... (scrubbed)

...do not live ostentatiously. You are a lowly journalist... (scrubbed)

...your handlers will always contact you via Classy... (scrubbed)

...anything else is not a legitimate communication. (scrubbed)

...your first assignment... (scrubbed)

...write smear articles about candidate Eddie Gingerboast until October 31... (scrubbed)

...post one per day multilaterally and multiplataformly... (scrubbed)

...editors are waiting for your content... (scrubbed)

...operation peaceful landing (scrubbed)

...(abandoned)

. . . Switching to World-O-Pedia University™

"The Indian Diaspora in America," a recorded lecture with Professor Gupta Singh.

Now deceased, Professor Singh was a popular academic. His lectures, recorded for posterity because of their excellence, were profitable for the many universities that used them. Students from all corners of the world paid, watched, listened to, and read them.

Transcript by Professor Singh's student Salama Ver, for BotBard Dynamics™.

> *Singh: So, we're learning about the seminal period of the Indian diaspora in America. This lesson's title is "Beyond the Patel Motel," a racist term once used to describe Indian ownership of motels in America before the big wave of immigrants from the subcontinent changed everything.*

PUBLICITY: The 2062 NAB is out and available for purchase! This year's Non-Author Bestseller—written by the best Au-THOR.ai™ available to publishers this side of literature—is *Glamorous Hunter*, an Inspector ReedyRide™ thriller set in the abandoned, post-earthquake Ovation Hollywood Shopping Center, featuring globo-influencer™ Lici Mitchellus™ and a host of other popular literAIry™ characters. Be VERY afraid! *Glamorous Hunter* will hunt YOU down!

Singh: You saw Indian wives, mothers, husbands, even the children running those motels in small towns in America. Even if the husbands had been engineers in India, they made the investment in the hospitality industry to be their own bosses, to be with their families, working side by side with relatives instead of in an office where their skills could be exploited by hard-driving, racist, white American bosses.

One must remember that America was still a very racist society at the time. Perhaps not as bad as when the British were in the subcontinent a few generations earlier, but the fact that many non-Indians made fun of successful Indian families, just because those families ran a motel, showed how skewed social priorities were in American culture—how earning an honest living was derided if it was an immigrant family doing it, only because it was in the service industry, being solicitous to motel guests.

A few cases of bad apples were constantly used to smear the Indian diaspora in the motel business. One story I heard, repeated, again and again, in different small towns in America, was about some Patel family that had owned a motel and operated it very successfully for years.

Then, Mr. Patel had gone to the local bank to ask for a loan to do a major renovation, upgrade the guest rooms and the lobby, maybe repair the pool, and replace the road sign with a better one—a project worth a quarter million dollars or more. Not much money today, but a significant amount back then.

And because Mr. Patel had been such a good customer of the bank for years, he was given the loan with almost no questions asked. The funds were transferred to his account, and the renovation work began almost immediately. "Ah, but those wily Indians!" the story went. It was just a ruse. Mr. Patel had it all planned. His whole family—mother-in-law included—was "vacationing" in India, and he followed them in the middle of the night, never to return to America, swallowed up whole by the anonymity of Gujarat, where the small American bank could never reach him.

That was the basis of this scurrilous story. There were variations, but the moral was "Immoral Indians, cowardly stealing our money, not facing the consequences because of hiding in the remote places where they once came from."

That was the attitude towards Indian immigrants before the Great Wave. There were of course rock-star Hindus in America at the time, running prominent tech corporations that everyone knew, but those were brilliant individuals who were meant to succeed in any culture. The Indian diaspora was very good at producing such individuals, thanks to hard-driving parents who gave a great deal of importance to higher education and hard work. But that was lost on most Americans who only saw a dark, ethnic face; heard an accent; and drew their own conclusions.

All that changed with the incursion into American politics of the descendants of Indian immigrants. These were well educated, smart individuals who had mastered both cultures and were, more importantly, women. [Professor Singh spoke directly to the camera here, for emphasis — Salama Ver.]

Nikki and Tulsi were the pioneers—powerful American women of Indian descent who blazed a path in politics for the many girls that followed, like Avni Patel, who looked up to them and wished to imitate them. Getting elected was very easy back then. For one, the young women following in Nikki and Tulsi's footsteps were smart and educated. Their upbringing prepared them for anything that life could throw at them. They had fathers who saw the light and treated them as equals to their male siblings, providing them with the same opportunities, ignoring their gender. And, to top it all, they had physical appeal—the perfect mixture of qualities that make unstoppable political candidates.

Their most important quality, as politicians, was that they were 100% percent American. When campaigning, on podcasts and recorded ads, they sounded like the neighbor's daughter, a girl with dreams and ambition. They never mentioned their ethnic background because that wasn't important. They never discussed the fact that they were women, that they spoke more than one language fluently. They strongly believed in dropping identity politics to favor raw intellect. Their attitude was, "You don't like women? You don't like the successful children of immigrants? You don't like people with darker skin in your political neighborhood? Well, I'm going to ignore you. I'm here to serve the American people, and you don't exist. Anyone who insists on focusing on trivial aspects of a candidate's background deserves to be ignored. There are too many important issues to resolve and work on, as a country, to be wasting time on frivolity. Leave that to the celebrity media."

Avni, in particular, had been successful beyond the imagination of pundits and critics. Among a pool of 47 candidates in a presidential primary that was a circus worthy of Nero's Rome, she distinguished herself very early on by going against the grade. Her approach was to avoid pandering and to speak her mind with an intellectual honesty that had been missing from politicians for decades. She was very astute in reading the electorate's desire for someone who would call out, in a very public way, the hypocrisy and corruption that had become part and parcel of the Washington establishment. The voters were ready, and she rode the wave with ease.

"The American people don't have a clue about what is really going on in our economy," Avni said early on. "It's not because they are stupid but because they've never been told the truth. They've always been taught lies, from kindergarten on. Lies about the way the economy functions. Lies about historical events, about revered Americans who were in fact scoundrels. And, above all, lies about war. The amount of taxpayers' money, of looted treasure, spent on the machinery of war over the last century is twenty to thirty times what the GAO's cooked books show. All the gold looted from China in the first half of the twentieth century, for example, was taken over by YOUR government and hidden from you to pay for clandestine operations, to provoke and engineer the conditions that trigger political instability and wars. This is what decaying empires do. They see their economic might slipping away, so war is the easiest way to not only distract their populations but also to transfer wealth from their adversaries to the empire. I'll give you all the details once I'm in office, and you WILL finally be told the truth. If we don't stop the clandestine government that's running this country, the shadow government that's ignoring our Founding Fathers' ideals, we are doomed."

A serious tactical mistake was made by Avni Patel's opponents early in their campaigns. They considered her approach so dangerous to the status quo and to their mighty grip on the reins of power, they ordered not only one but three assassination attempts on her, with the painfully obvious results that such attempts would have on the electorate. They never thought their assassins would fail, so they didn't consider what would happen if she remained alive, a standing candidate. Her popularity soared. "Why are they trying to kill her?" people asked. There must be something to what she's campaigning about. Her unusual first name became a verb. To avni was to tell the truth when everyone else said that you were making things up, and when your opponents were trying to kill you for revealing those truths. She had her candidacy secured.

Her promise was—once elected president of the United States—to do a transparent, forensic audit of the country's finances and "cut all the lies and the pork." All secret and dark budgets and funds would be brought into the open. All the looted gold would be owned by the American people and not by the clandestine operations of the intelligence services. All war that was not chiefly defensive in nature, within the borders of the United States, would stop. All defense treaties would be abrogated, and military aid of any kind discontinued. That, she said, would provide enough money to fund the social programs, new infrastructure, health and education needs that Americans deserved. Whenever an opponent or hostile journalist assaulted her with a question regarding how she would pay for the myriad social programs she talked about, she quickly replied, "We have all the money we need. It's just in the wrong hands and hidden. And it belongs to the American people. I fully intend to give it back to them." End of discussion. And the fact was, she became so sure of herself and so credible, that she could say anything she wanted, make up any story, and people would believe it, because it was coming from her lips.

In short, she was unstoppable, the dream presidential candidate headed to an inevitable, landslide victory. And so it was.

But once in office, her festering wound, Pakistan, became quickly apparent. Any incident, no matter how insignificant, became a crisis. Accusations—most of which turned out to be false—were presented as factual threats to the national security of the United States of America, backed by supposedly reliable intelligence. Citizens could not confirm the intelligence sources because the sources were off limits to anyone outside the inner circle of the defense apparatus.

Again and again, Americans were asked to trust President Avni on Islamabad's imminent threat to our country's freedom and democracy. Media organizations happily provided the feedback loop to keep the narrative going.

Hardly any American had ever been to Pakistan or knew anything about the place, but their president and news sources and intelligence community were telling them NOT to trust "the Pakis," and to go along with retaliatory, "defensive" strikes that would make sure to contain the threat of terrorism.

The very few opponents to Avni's unraveling political circus, those who got to be heard above the "I'm not with Pakis" consensus, were members of an antiwar nonprofit that depended on media stunts to get their point across, like videos of volunteers approaching university students with a blank map of the political world.

"Can you please show me where Pakistan is?" the students were asked. On a fine spring day, on the Radcliffe Quad, forty-seven students were happy to give it a try, on camera. Eighty-five percent of them had heard that "England has problems with Pakis, too," so they were sure that "the breeding ground for terrorists" that President Avni told them about had to be around the former British Isles. And most of the students pointed to France! "Is that your final answer?" the volunteer asked. "Yes, pretty sure," the students replied.

One serious incident involved India's demand that Pakistan allow a million pilgrims a day to visit Kartarpur Sahib without having to pay any fees. "The Pakistani regime is interfering with the freedom of religion of these peace-loving pilgrims who are not allowed to practice their religion and are charged extortive amounts to cross the border from India into Pakistan daily to fulfill their spiritual duties," the American State Department said, again and again.

Pakistan, on the other hand, saw the pilgrimage as an invasion. "At the very least," officials noted, "they are tourists who should pay for a temporary visa to enter Pakistan. And we will never allow that high a number of visitors daily because many of them are Indian intelligence officers who come with the only purpose of gathering data and spying on Pakistanis. They don't give a damn about Bābā Nānak."

Indian Prime Minister Singh visited Washington to complain about Pakistan's "callous disregard for human life" after a convoy of transportation pods made its way to Kartarpur from Khasanwala, and two of the pods were destroyed by Pakistani terrorists, he said, killing all pilgrims inside.

Pakistan's defense minister, Barar Kahn, protested that Delhi had been warned. Any intelligence agents who entered Pakistan's sovereign territory in the guise of pilgrims would be executed. "Plus," he added, "in this case, our surveillance clearly showed that the transportation pods were accompanied by a swarm of bee-sized drones used by India to gather information. We were able to destroy one of these drones and capture two others, so we have proof." Kahn offered photographs and videos showing the electronic devices—tiny circuit boards painted light blue, with high-powered cameras and matte, transparent wings.

"Those are not spying drones," a statement from the Indian Association of Kartarpur Pilgrims, averred. "They accompany us on our pilgrimages to monitor the situation and protect our peaceful visitors to Kartarpur from Pakistani terrorists."

India admitted that its military had provided the American-made Honeybee Drones™ to the pilgrims, and it accused the Pakistanis of "blatant aggression and the willful destruction of Indian military assets, not to mention the murder of pilgrims."

"What were these Indian military assets doing in Pakistani air space, then?" Kahn asked.

"They were not performing a military task when you destroyed them," Singh replied. "They were merely escorting our pilgrims. You had no right to destroy expensive military *equipment belonging to a foreign power. That is an act of war, and the Indian government will not tolerate any action against its citizens and property from a regime that is known around the world to sponsor terrorism!"*

And so it went, the spark that triggered the eventual migration of nearly six hundred million Indian refugees to North America. President Avni did her best to stir additional animosity between the two countries by immediately sending thousands of American troops to the region, plus military aid to India, including "one billion Honeybee Drones™ to protect Indian citizens from Pakistani aggression. Kahn [the Pakistani defense minister] thinks he can destroy peaceful Honeybees with impunity. We'll see how he handles a billion of them," Avni added. "I have instructed my team to assist SecSys Corporation™ in stepping up production of these useful monitoring devices, which will be shipped to Northern India as soon as possible. A team of American military advisors are now on their way to set up the logistics and train the Indian military on how to deploy and manage the Honeybees."

Pakistan's first nuclear "test" detonation came soon after.

Avni lost the next election and was replaced by President Japleen Gupta.

. . . switching to The EavesDrop Portal™, Posting the World's Every Hack!

[Live Transcript - An Interview with Candidate Eddie Gingerboast - Channel888news], interviewed by veteran journalist Peter LaTournage

Peter LaTournage: Another letter has been discovered. Some guy in Paris. Got top dollar for it. At least that's what the feed says. Poor in details.

Eddie Gingerboast: I'm sure. There'll be letters emerging all the way until the election. We've turned into quite a nation of letter writers of late.

Peter LaTournage: The letter proves—without a doubt, the experts say—that Jefferson repeatedly raped Hemings and kept her locked up in a room for long periods of time. Not that the world needed this letter. The one discovered last year was enough to get the juices flowing—the protests and demands for justice, the removal of all public monuments raised to the man, the movement to turn Monticello into the "Museum of Victims of Gender Violence," which is practically a done deal, and the Jefferson Memorial on The National Mall now referred to as The Rotunda of Hope.

Eddie Gingerboast: Events of this nature have been orchestrated by various activist groups for years. They are meant to keep the masses distracted. Organizers know it has nothing to do with victims' rights, gender equality, social justice, or any other cause. It's so easy to come up with a hot-button issue to inflame the passions of the perpetually angry these days. Long checklists of hot buttons have been carefully assembled to fit the activists' goals and agendas. One week, it's a politician's alleged penchant for pedophilia, never proven and completely forgotten a week later, when new accusations of orgies in luxury hotel rooms emerge, targeting senators and their abuse of congressional interns.

Peter LaTournage: YOU, now an official candidate, are getting your share of accusations, too.

Eddie Gingerboast: Look, I'm a thinking man in a world where most people refuse to think. I don't get worked up about these things. Some exposé appears somewhere, I go for a walk in the woods. Watch the squirrels play. Take a mental break. It'll all go away soon enough. Things take care of themselves.

Peter LaTournage: But DO they?

Eddie Gingerboast: No. Smear campaigns continue to battle with hagiography for eternity. In the end, only the sociopaths win.

Peter LaTournage: Meaning?

Eddie Gingerboast: I'm a historian. There's nothing new about what's going on today with smear campaigns. Take a plantation owner and slaveholder in the Old South, as an example. He is an imperious man whose sole goal in life is to profit—obscenely—from the sale of as much tobacco as his thousands of acres can produce. The historical record shows that, without a doubt, he was a sociopath, completely detached from social norms and the respect for life and for his fellow human beings. To keep his slaves in check, he has no problem hiring a budding civil-rights activist of the colonial era. The goal: infiltrate the slaves and organize a revolt, with the objective of creating a Nat Turner, say, who kills a few whites and makes headlines, thus labeling ALL slaves as potentially dangerous and deserving of harsh treatment and the whip. In other words, the strategic manipulation of public opinion to serve the master's goals, with zero ethical considerations regarding what that type of action might do to society at large. Well, people like that slaveowner never went away—they never do. Their tools may have changed, but their goals are always the same. The hagiography endures until the smear campaign takes hold. Yesterday's patriotic heroes turn into today's pariahs, so what's new?

Peter LaTournage: You think it is harder today for someone to stand on that pedestal of the patriotic hero? Does every politician go straight to pariah without ever occupying the place of the hero or patriot these days?

Eddie Gingerboast: Today, we pay a professional forger hundreds of thousands of dollars to create a legitimate looking "historical document," like Jefferson's letter. Then we pick a dim professor in charge of a whatever-studies department at a respected university— if such a thing still exists—and give that department a million or ten to do "research" on the matter of the newly-discovered historical document, and the professor takes care of the rest—publishing a book or report or study that states, with absolute certainty, that historical figure so-and-so was really a such-and-such. Then, the helpful media picks up and publicizes the story, and soon everyone is talking about it. Multiply that one case by the hundreds and, voila, you have a new manufactured distraction every week, keeping the masses entertained and away from scrutinizing what really matters.

Peter LaTournage: Right, and how can you fight against that? How can any candidate escape it?

Eddie Gingerboast: One percent of the world's population is estimated to be wired this way—clinical sociopaths, even psychopaths. They are excellent at climbing the national-security and corporate-surveillance bandwagon, where government funding makes it a cinch to accumulate vast fortunes in a matter of months at the expense of society. In other words, the other 99% of us, we've become the slaves, and the 1% is constantly plotting to stay on top of things, with OUR money, the money that allows them to create hundreds of Nat Turner boogeymen, with the sociopaths and psychopaths ostensibly fighting to defend us 99 percenters from those very boogeymen, who are in reality being used by the psychopaths who don't care who dies in the process. That's where we are now.

PUBLICITY: Get your tube of Food Glue™ today! It's more than edible! The new and improved recipe makes dough REALLY stick together. Seal those samosas when you need them to STAY sealed, damn it! Food Glue™ them today!

BREAKING: Virtual influencer MeaiBot™ will be starring in the role of KayMurti™ in the new season of "Mindful Revenge™", dropping tomorrow everywhere. "No legacy above- or below-the-line talent was included in this production," said the AI network that produced the series. "It is no longer profitable to the Mindful Revenge™ franchise to deal with legacy actors," und added.

i'll tell you one thing. the chicks in mindful are a hell of a lot hotter than any flesh n bone actoress could ever be [Belgian Chocorunt]

specially the sex scenes [Nikolazza018]

thank god for ai and cgi [MuyMuy]

BREAKING: Eddie Gingerboast Caught With His Pants Down! The presidential candidate has denied wire transfers to his underage lover's offshore account. Stay tuned for details!

anonymous tip, again [ladygodiva]

they dont learn, the journos [Stanley Ferocious]

don't have to learn. the whole point is to destroy reputations. repeat it enough times, and people will start having doubts about the guy [shoot me tender]

i dont pay attention to the dribble anymore. if a male candidate, i'm voting against the bastard [menagerie girl]

same here. women much more intellectually capable than men these days, more efficient, better organized. they can manage a country or a company or an empire with delicious administrative precision [proud priestess]

But they lack the disposition—the master ingredient to make it all work. In other words, you don't hire the tidiest, smartest, best organized person to run the corporation. You hire the cutthroat bloke with no scruples to step all over the competition and utterly destroy it. [the madden hatter]

yeah. only men have that primal ingredient to aggressively fuck everything that stands in their way. [a yarn is a yarn]

By nature, we're arrogant bastards who want to fuck and destroy, just because. You know, creative destruction. That's what makes civilizations move forward. [the madden hatter]

that's how multiculturalism and globalism developed in the first place—males from one culture wanting to fuck other cultures. armies and pestilence sent to start the process afresh every few years, n'est ce pas? [barcode junky]

itza thing of beauty to behold. men were put on earth to spice things up, like curry. otherwise, life's a shit, tremendously boring, without a single fucking expectation [shantaram]

H.G. Wells didn't write about a future earthly paradise where everything was orderly and well administrated and equitable, with fair treatment for all, free medical care and education and other unrealistic nonsense. He wrote about some bastard extraterrestrials invading the earth and destroying humans and their unearned sense of superiority. One culture invading and trying to destroy another, to keep things moving along. Sign me up! [the madden hatter]

people like you make the world the shit hole it is [proud priestess]

It's called reality, baby. [the madden hatter]

the reality is women are in many ways reaching a level of independence where, soon, men won't be of much use. men have been emasculated by the technology that, for the most part, they created themselves. no longer needed for most of their "traditional roles" in primitive societies, for physical strength, in hunting, building shelters, and other activities that required brute force. now, we have access to technologies that provide that element and more, even technology playing the man's role in procreation. it's much easier to produce a sperm-delivery system than a human womb. [xx is best]

ouch! [ronny round da corner]

sayonara, xy losers! [secret admirer]

gingerboast's a dick. all sorts of reports appearing now about secret behavior. he's toast. [conscious cushion]

don't believe a word. all scripted [salty mango]

they all goondas [suni59023]

just like the reports on military exercises, described as "national security activities," complete with media scripts written far in advance, produced with video clips and phony interviews—all used to "report" the under-attack scenarios, as if they were actual events. [citizen ranter]

the journos against gingerboast spew scripted shit about the candidate, and the security agencies have a vast library of material to release to the media whenever it suits the government to do so. [ale of the species]

excuses to establish curfews, shutdowns and lockdowns [high achiever lying low]

the under-attack scenarios are real, though, but they're actually PRE-scenarios because, a few weeks after the fake ones are reported, the real ones take place. coincidence? think not. [digital gambler]

thats when the bits and pieces from the prepared scripts make their way out to news reporters who print them as fact. [arka quad245]

fictional reports that pakistan was behind the bioterrorism attack against the united states make the talking heads and politicians repeat the scripts given to them, without an ounce of evidence or reality behind them. [citizen ranter]

a former cia director is interviewed and asked to confirm the fiction as fact, and everyone runs with the lie. [digital gambler]

someone swore under oath that kahn was behind the attack, with the assistance of the russians and financing from china. gotta be some truth in there, no? [andromeda rising]

a paki defector was reported to have inside information, "an anonymous source said," followed by "a highly-placed intelligence officer who spoke on condition of anonymity" to provide more quotes and "evidence" from the fictional script developed weeks earlier in the scenario exercise. hilarious. [citizen ranter]

who's paying for this shit? [bubbly bookie]

YOU are! taxes! [heady cork]

BREAKING: A Marshall-Patel secret executive order has been leaked. Written in Washingtonese and requiring deciphering, it is reported to state: "I hereby command special forces 321A to produce a false-flag event that will result in a national increase of patriotic fervor, with the goal of creating the new Expedited Military Procurement Agency (EMPA), which will allow direct, discretionary funding to the Commander in Chief (CIC) to select any arms manufacturer to supply the United States Armed Forces with whatever equipment the CIC determines is needed for the enhancement of national security, so help me God. I also command that this secret executive order remain a classified document forever."

. . . The VoxPopuli Stream™

patriotic fervor. brainless nationalism. two sides of the same coin. [john_smith37921]

nationalists mostly care about keeping immigrants from being able to vote. [PolyZen Prostitute]

that's because, if they vote, they'll just vote for other immigrants. we don't want that. [mook palaver]

the great replacement. dont get me started [bruja justiciera]

too late! y'all been replaced already! [Dalit Rude Boy]

i dont apreciate u spredin ur fuckin genes all over the place, in MY country! [homecoming king]

Indians are dominant now, of course. Does that make US, immigrant Indians, the new American nationalists? [Balabang Rogers]

I don't think so. We founded the Plenty of Room movement, after all. We knew better than vestigial Americans. When we arrived as refugees and saw how depopulated this country was, we said, "Americans haven't been utilizing their huge country efficiently. Let's build a busy place here!" So, massive construction projects began, all led by us, enterprising Indians. All workers welcome! [DragonWing]

Go, Flori! [Ayeman Nays Now]

I bet General LaRose would love Marshall-Patel's secret executive order. Be in cahoots. [driven 2 politics]

Hope they all have strokes soon, like Malsain Smith and Oomajan. [barista raté]

they'll only be replaced by new warmongers. plenty of them being churned out by the infernal factories. [shinto pram]

BREAKING: Turkey has filed a reparations lawsuit in the Hague against the Vatican to address the long-lasting damage caused by the nefarious crusades, the first of which began in the year 1096 AD. The invasions were initiated and supported by the Latin Church, the predecessor of the Roman Catholic Church, which is, therefore, now liable for damages, according to the Turkish government. "This was long overdue," said Juan Carlos Kahn-Patel, president of the nonprofit Redress-4-All and principal force behind the lawsuit. "We have to show, not just tell, that crime doesn't pay," und added. "I won't sleep until all these crimes are punished."

finally [anatolian queen]

the international court of justice has no jurisdiction over this. even if it did, the statute of limitations is long past, non? [garment snatcher]

muslims did nothing to the dhimmi. it was just a land grab. [turcoman5-0]

not a land grab. just taking the land back that had been stolen. remember al-andalus and all that. for the crusaders, it was within the 'just war' concept, as developed by augustine. tit for tat. [garment snatcher]

you dont say [baby warrior]

fuck off, troll. go back to your mummy network. [tea drinker007]

serious shit being discussed here. anyone hear aloo man just purchased belize? he's said to be using it as a center of operations. the federal government gave him the place to set up pentagon server farms. [roger dat]

that explains the victory parade in dc this morning! raja mckenzee and marshall-patel spoke to large crowds, flags waving while all manner of military ordnance paraded in front of them—even the very drones used from a control booth in nevada to neutralize president zabaneh in belize. they destroyed his recently completed belmopan palace. poor bastard. [hot for words] neutralize meaning killed? [axial ager]

duh [Simpleton Fort]

that's NOT what happened. mckenzee said zabaneh "wantonly and aggressively forced american troops to take over the belizean central bank, to protect democracy." zabaneh's been sent to miami to be tried for high crimes and misdemeanors. [prosperous preposterous]

Up next: Suriname! And McKenzee already said the Pentagon is planning to invade Djibouti to "help them fix their government." [mantra addict]

so, aloo man "bought" belize? [hot for words]

they say hes gonna rename it freedomland. [roger dat]

belmopan's been saved, folks. [frankie falling]

potato head purchased the country at a discount, due to all the destruction from the american invasion. [neena_w64a]

it was a real-estate acquisition, paid for by the u.s. of a. [hot for words]

> INFOPOST: SOURCE: World-O-Pedia™: Aloo Man: Pejorative nickname given to Oscar Farouch, the controversial multi-trillionaire who started his financial empire growing potatoes in Nova Scotia (hence the word aloo). It has just been reported that Farouch "purchased Belize for a song" after American forces destroyed most of the country via a punitive bombing invasion.

. . . The EavesDrop Portal™, Posting the World's Every Hack!

[Transcript - SunnyNews Interview Show™, with host Albert Relayant]

Albert Relayant: We are back with Robert Gandhi, the only

candidate of the Real Peace Dividend Party. Mr. Gandhi is on the ballot in all 51 states.

Robert Gandhi: Ours is the only party with an aggressive antiwar platform. All other items on any party's platform—fiscal policy, decaying infrastructure, universal healthcare coverage, social services, crime and violence, education, the economy—every single one of those depends on funding that is being wasted on the military and on invasions abroad in the name of national security.

Albert Relayant: How much money IS being wasted, roughly?

Robert Gandhi: We have no idea.

Albert Relayant: But there are numbers published every year, a defense budget.

Robert Gandhi: That's the tip of the iceberg. The defense budget we are shown is a fraction of what our nation is really spending on military warfare—trillions upon trillions of dollars wasted over the years, not including the long-term costs of caring for veterans. There's no more painful realization than what so many veterans experience. When they get back to civilian life, they realize they were just pawns in the game played by the industrial national-security market. Here you were, brainwashed to believe you were helping your country, fighting an enemy, being patriotic—then you see the light. You were used and discarded, like a worn-out cog in the machinery of war. As a result, the Real Peace Dividend Party gets a great deal of support from the millions of veterans who have realized how the military scam works. The benefits they were promised are being cut because the country can't afford them.

Albert Relayant: But we know the number of recruits has decreased, replaced by bots and drones.

Robert Gandhi: True, but that's not the full picture. We're sending fewer soldiers abroad, but every robot and drone needs at least one human minder. We have millions out there. Beyond that, the flesh-and-blood soldiers who normally serve stateside, in ever larger numbers, do so because the national-security industry needs a standing army, always on standby, ready to be sent overseas to perform its international theater. It's the "boots-on-the-ground" threat. So, you have troops constantly coming and going, at a huge cost, to give the world this pretense of global domination and projection of power, when the reality of how unprepared these young people in uniform are—for ANY kind of battle, let alone a real war—is painfully obvious. They're just props in military costume. And when they come back from their horse-and-pony shows around the world, they are put back on duty in the Keep America Safe™ ranks, supposedly assisting local police departments across the nation to fight the threat of terrorism. In essence, they've turned the United States of America into a police state. And here we are, more than halfway through the twenty-first century, with our nation at the brink of bankruptcy, still enriching a handful of oligarchs via the politicians who keep manufacturing wars and conflict for them. It's the same movie played again and again throughout the history of the United States. The Real Peace Dividend Party aims to put an end to it.

Albert Relayant: Let's say it's the day after the presidential election and you have miraculously won. What next?

Robert Gandhi: It's not just me who has to win [smiles]. We need congressional support. RPD candidates must be elected at all levels of government. We'll start by banning the manufacturing of larger weapon systems, giving factories and owners tax breaks and incentives to retool their operations to manufacture something else. Affordable housing is a real problem in this country. Maybe they can figure out a way to pick up where pioneers in that industry, like Mr. Fuller, left off decades ago. Put a house together like a car, in a factory, instead of a bomb or a missile, and fly it to the customer's lot for hookup to on-site utilities. We forget that so much has been neglected for so long by diverting brain power and resources to the weapons industry. All those engineers and scientists, over the decades, obsessed with producing and designing weapons whose sole purpose is to cause harm to many and benefit very few. We'll start right there.

Albert Relayant: How do you defend the United States, then, if we stop building the weapons we need? There's China, Russia, India, Pakistan, Iran to contend with. Twenty years from now, they will have more advanced weapons. We'll be left behind, unarmed, defenseless.

Robert Gandhi: That's a fallacy. The moment the United States stops manufacturing arms, other countries will follow suit, because it makes economic sense. Everyone's already armed in this country. Any invading country will encounter vigorous resistance by our citizens. That's all it takes.

Albert Relayant: Right now, but twenty years from now, others may have some new space-age weapon, some kind of gamma ray that sweeps the skies and fries the brains of American citizens, on the spot, in five seconds.

Robert Gandhi: OK [laughs]. You want to talk fear-mongering science fiction.

Albert Relayant: Just saying.

Robert Gandhi: Word of such a weapon would get out. We can then think of ways to defend ourselves against it. And the key word here is "defend" our population, not go on the offensive by bombing over there or sending troops to occupy, or what have you. That's over with, in our administration.

Albert Relayant: Four years. That's the term of your administration. Let's say the American public doesn't like what you're doing, and you don't get reelected. Too many people losing their jobs from weapons factories and defense contractors being shut down. They vote you out of office come the next cycle.

Robert Gandhi: So be it. At least we tried. But I think that won't happen. The moment funds get diverted from weapons to much needed infrastructure, people will see the light. We can begin by repairing roads that are falling apart, building rail lines and pedestrian and bicycle paths—allowing our citizens to be truly free to move affordably without having to contend with burdensome monthly mobility payments, for example. Same with the cost of housing. There's no reason why anyone should have to pay sixty percent of their income on rent or a mortgage every month for thirty years. There's no reason why Americans should have to be forced to work thirty hours a week, doing jobs they don't like, just to be able to afford shelter, mobility, health, and a balanced diet. Our aim is to make all those basic necessities available to everyone at affordable prices. An individual will not have to work more than fifteen hours per week to afford these basics, and we can do it very easily if we finally wrest our economy from the clutches of the war machine. It's a very simple solution.

Thanks to the exposure given to Robert Gandhi by shows like Relayant's and others', his candidacy is beginning to get some real traction. Go, Gandhi! [lotus potus]

nonsense. world peace is as much science fiction as anything else proposed by this klown. [karma policier]

he's being invited to events with larger audiences, mostly thanks to the pressure put on the media by young people who began to boycott advertisers and corporations that ignored candidate gandhi and were keeping him out of the public debate. [serrated persona]

As und moves from fringe shows to more mainstream coverage, however, the opposition to unda's ideas will become more vocal. Manufactured attacks on unda's character will begin to circulate— about unda's lifestyle, unda's family, and activities at all stages of unda's life. [solarsingh8]

one report already had him punching a girl in the stomach when he was eight years old, with headlines screaming "not so peaceful gandhi!" and "a coward's past," even a meme song with changed lyrics like i punched a girl, and i liked it. [gummy pants]

it's all standard smear campaign shit, and us, young, well informed, and more than jaded, know exactly how to read between the lines. we're not about to let slick p.r. assholes tarnish our candidate with glossy ads and laughable slogans. [anna roy 50]

In the early days of unda's campaign, a full two years ago, the public's response was so overwhelmingly positive, und attracted thousands of new volunteers every week, and potential candidates for the RPD kept on joining the party. There IS hope. [solarsingh8]

Relayant can pretend to be all humble and honest, but the stats show this interview is being streamed by 4.3 billion devices, and some commenters are already starting to call this "The Birth of Gandhi." [sonia polt]

this election seems to be of great importance to nearly half the world's population. [marrytocracy pastor]

Robert Gandhi is a symbol of what America once was, a beacon of hope, and he is right that if he manages to make the United States give up its war machine, other nations will surely follow. [marble players]

people everywhere in the world feel it in their bones. this is a good candidate, an honest human being, a visionary. he has joined the race at a crucial moment in history. [chapati Mon]

[Live Transcript - World Forum Online's Political Candidates' Debate]

Recorded Voice: Candidates, welcome to the legendary Firehouse auditorium, home of the now bankrupt No Sprokets™ movie-theater chain. This is the perfect location to host these debates because we have enough seats to accommodate all candidates. Keep in mind that your comfortable bucket seats not only have cubbies on the arm rests, where you can fit your drinks and snacks, but you are also able to swivel them to speak directly to an opponent. This debate format, as you know, has no moderator. The idea is to let all candidates moderate themselves, be polite and let others speak, and give the public an idea of who you truly are. Please control your tempers, do not act aggressively, or become a sore loser. Ready? Set. Debate!

Senatrix Alg: I'm Senatrix Alg, from the American Progressive Party, the APP. Our healthcare system is broken. We don't have enough nurses. Tech companies can say all they want about how efficient bots are at drawing blood, sewing stitches, and performing surgery, but the reality is that most patients want the human touch. Also, the promise from tech giants was always that, with bots, the costs of medical care would come down to nothing for patients, but it hasn't happened. When an appendectomy still costs the equivalent of four years of rent payments for a modest three-bedroom home, we've gone over the edge.

Governor Richard Guerra: That's a total misrepresentation of how the system works, Senatrix, and you know it. I'm Richard Guerra, GOP candidate and current governor of the great State of Missouri. You know for a fact that absolutely no one pays those listed prices.

Senatrix Alg: Then why have them?

Governor Richard Guerra: It's like the menu at a fancy restaurant, Senatrix. You post it by the entrance to keep the riffraff out. If we posted cheap prices, like they still do in some parts of Asia, we'd have all manner of foreigners coming to America to use OUR medical facilities and overwhelm the system, which is really meant for Americans. We Americans are like members of the restaurant— we belong. It's like a country-club restaurant, Senatrix. We walk in, and there's a different menu for us, the one for members, the one for those who have American health insurance, which every common-sense American should have—by law, I must add. That menu has much lower prices, almost at cost. And our membership dues pay for our lunch, as it were, so we don't even have to pay the lower prices listed on our special menus. It's a beautiful system, one that other countries haven't figured out yet. We're decades ahead of everyone else on this.

Senatrix Alg: Yes, Governor, beautiful analogy, but not every American can afford to join your country club, so your party's policies are turning most Americans into the riffraff that you mention, having to travel to Asian countries to get affordable healthcare via medical vacations.

Governor Richard Guerra: I see those people as not being good Americans, Senatrix. If they are willingly becoming riffraff by not taking the responsibility to afford health insurance, then they don't deserve to live in this country. Let them go get their lower-standard healthcare overseas and, while they're at it, they can stay there in those happy lands, if they're so great compared to ours.

Robert Gandhi: If I may... I'm Robert Gandhi, candidate of the RPD party.

give 'em hell, Gandhi! [soaring e-gal]

make them eat their f***ing words! [volume shopper]

Robert Gandhi: We are hearing this back-and-forth between two totally disconnected realities. The food being served at this supposedly fancy restaurant that Governor Guerra is talking about is being produced mostly by the so-called riffraff.

Governor Richard Guerra: INcorrect! Mostly mechanically via the wonders of ingenious American technological innovation. We don't need people anymore, let alone the riffraff.

Robert Gandhi: In the meantime, the country club has been spending all its reserves on maintaining a vast acreage of golf courses, wasting trillions of dollars watering the evergreen lawns. And when the next water bill finally comes due, the club won't be able to pay it, so the fancy restaurant won't have any water. The health department will shut it down for having no water. No one will be able to eat at the fancy restaurant anymore. THAT is what we're talking about.

Lassi Channar: Here you go again, Gandhi. Hello, I'm Lassi Channar, candidate for the American Glorious Defense Party. Your broken record, Gandhi, about the military-industrial complex—we're more than tired of it, and the American people don't want to listen to it.

yes we do! [bat collector]

drag that channar wench to the dungeon! [rosie no rivets]

Robert Gandhi: It's far from broken, Ms. Channar. I'll keep on playing it until the arms of those covering their ears get tired and need to come down, forcing their owners to listen. Any argument about our healthcare system is an exercise in futility because the money that would fix it is being diverted to something else, something that both your parties support. The APP and Senatrix Alg claim to be progressive, to want all manner of social services offered to the population at very affordable levels. Yet, you insist on this idea that the country won't be safe until we spend a large chunk of our annual resources on newer and shinier weapons. You are insulting the people's intelligence, Senatrix Alg. At least Governor Guerra comes clean with his intention of cutting all social services in favor of a police state.

Governor Richard Guerra: Wait a moment, Gandhi. You put me in the awkward position of having to defend Senatrix Alg here, but I'll do it because this needs to be said. We know where you come from, your peace movement, your anti-militarism, and all that. It's a bunch of hooey. It's not a simple matter of scrapping the military and doing away with the defense budget. One thing these anti-war folks don't understand is that practice makes perfect. We must engage in continuous war, as it were, to be always prepared, good at it. Otherwise, we're doomed. It's not a question of philosophy, or religion, or morality. It's about survival, and about whether it's you or the other fellow who survives in the end. I'll give you the most likely scenario. We, right now, have agricultural food production that feeds most of the world, thanks to American ingenuity. Granted, there are pockets here and there that are missing out on this bounty. But, for the most part, humans are well fed, enough to survive and live long lives. Now, imagine that something bad takes place, a calamitous natural disaster—global change in weather patterns, what have you—that deeply affects agricultural output, with a significant scarcity of food brought on as a result. Then what? Anti-war activists fail to understand this. When the threat of starvation kicks in, we will ALL switch to survival mode, and it will be everyone for himself and God against all, as the saying goes. So, we MUST maintain our military superiority to be ready for this eventuality, which WILL come someday, for sure. If we don't engage in "warmongering," as you call it, if we don't keep ahead by developing new weapons, drones, warbots, etc., we'll be doomed when the world's agricultural production collapses. It's as simple as that. So, when I hear these peace activists clamoring for world peace and brotherly love, that's fine when there's enough food and potable water for everyone, but it's unrealistic to think abundant food production will go on forever, uninterrupted by periods of severe scarcity. So, in the meantime, we must stay vigilant, trained, and ready. Anything else is sheer folly.

Robert Gandhi: Your point is off the mark, Governor Guerra. I would accept it if we took profit away from the equation. If you leave the research, development, and manufacturing of weapons to a zero-profit entity, building everything at cost, at well-monitored prices, and with all employees engaged in the production being paid a minimum living wage, even the managers and higher-ups, then I might accept your party's argument. But that's not the case. My party's main target is war profiteering. Take the profits away, and we'll have no more wars.

that was what the old Green Party used to say, i think [asa pin]

they had an anti-war platform, but i dont know about the profits bit [tight drum playing]

greens went blue in the face waiting for godot, and disintegrated for lack of interest in their stupid platform that included all manner of nonsense. [cool cucumber]

yes, a bunch of low-lumen technocrats who didnt know how to market themselves. they were all over the place, promising cures to all ills. recipe for disaster [fartivist]

Not true. Greens ceased to exist because they were never given a chance to even get on the ring. The ultra-corrupt two-party system made sure no other voices were heard until the Hindu population became numerous enough to topple the status quo. One good thing about mass immigration. [meek intellectual bully] hurray for hindis! [loreno marcos]

Hindus [ravi karvajal]

all are just as corrupt. two parties, ten parties, makes no difference. gandhi doesnt stand a chance. just an innocent babe there, among the vipers. [Yuri Virulenko]

we'll see about that [too-tight ascot]

a fantasy. you can't take the weapons from those armed-to-the-teeth without using weapons yourself. And that, of course, would be a violation of your non-violence principles. [blue bambino]

catch 24! [extra tommy52]

20! [lingue8]

22, ignoramuses! it's catch 22. [15chariots]

whatever year that was, who cares! [indie flogger]

it's simple. you violate your principles until you disarm the bullies, then disarm yourself by destroying all weapons. [kondo fixer]

doesn't work like that. by the time you disarm your opponent, you take a liking to using those weapons, to having that power. you start thinking ... "maybe i should keep these things around, just in case." [blue bambino]

like i said. catch [extra tommy52]

that's not what you said [15chariots]

gandhi is supported mostly by women, so if he gains any traction, it will be a battle of the sexes. [horrorscoper]

dont know bout dat. wia girls will oppose him. no one's gonna take their weapons, their ammo, and grrrl power from em. they see gandhi as a wimp [virtual suzzy]

wimp or not, if the rpd gets enough votes in congress and the senate, he'll deliver. no one doubts that. [mountain rival]

BREAKING: Razzmatazz Collico, a person of visual impairment, has been awarded $1.2 billion in a discrimination lawsuit filed against the City of Rochester. The judgment confirms the city did not hire Collico to operate an excavator at public works sites because of unda's visual disability. "The safety of our employees and public must come before inclusivity in hiring," said Public Works director Selma Martinez, who was promptly fired for unda's comment and replaced by a commission that will investigate what led to this expensive litigation.

Robert Gandhi: War is a transfer-of-wealth scheme. Wealth is transferred from the population of the warrior empire at large to the small elite that's connected to the war machine. So, you have a country that grows wealthier and wealthier because its citizens are productive, frugal, industrious. There's all this wealth. And the schemers ask themselves, How do we get our hands on all this money? How can we steal all the wealth without being branded thieves? Easy, they answer. Let's start a war.

right said, bob [Palatina Marcussi]

war$ i$ 4 profit$ [Bruttanicus the Younger]

PUBLICITY: It's time to upgrade your Tongee™! Because achieving orgasms is the most important thing to your good health, our Tongee™ orgasmic device is an indispensable feature of the modern American bedroom. Our team of medico-engineers have vastly improved the new Tongee™, designed to raise the bar of the happiness quotient in your life. Ask your orgasmologist whether the new Tongee™ is the right choice for you. Covered by all health insurance policies approved by the Federal Medical Devices Industrial Association™. Financing available for the 98% of the cost not covered by insurance. Get your new and improved Tongee™

today!

stop pausing this shit! it's a live transcript. let the guy finish! [intelligent dodo]

if people keep on interrupting, i'm gonna copy and re-post the whole thing in one go, again and again. [taxi fascist]

if you want it all at once, go away and come back when reposted then. we like to comment and analyze gandhi's words as they stream. [Moonasa Fabrisi]

too much analysis! too much thinking going on. let the candidate speak! [Ferdinand the Gorgeous]

Robert Gandhi: The warmongering elites say: We can extract wealth from the masses at all levels of the scheme. First, we pick a target enemy and get ourselves hired to go attack that enemy and destroy their infrastructure. Oh, but how will they hire us? No one will hire a bunch of schemers to destroy another country. No problem! We create this corporation called The Armed Forces, Inc. We say the corporation is here to protect our national security, to protect all our citizens from being attacked. So, everyone must financially support this corporation to stay safe. And the corporation needs all these war toys—guns, bombs, tanks, airplanes, drones, bots, etc.—that we, the scheming elites ourselves, produce and sell to the corporation! And we make sure that everyone knows that supporting the corporation is patriotic, and that opposing it is treasonous, enemy-like behavior. So, we make a fortune selling all the war toys to the warring corporation that WE incorporated in the first place. We get paid to go destroy and attack far-away spots around the world. Then, once those places are destroyed, we get ourselves hired again to rebuild them! This is a foolproof scheme, folks!

Governor Richard Guerra: Our military is justified in going overseas to attack our enemies.

Robert Gandhi: Manufactured enemies, Governor Guerra. When there are no enemies, the military industrial complex creates them out of whole cloth. That's yet another way in which they make money. They create all the fear, rumors of such-and-such country scheming to attack us. Cyberattacks. Bombs. Terrorist attacks. You name it. They sell their pre-packaged national security services to us, so we feel safe and protected. Then, boom! A convenient terrorist attack, a false flag, and they have us—the poor, terrorized citizens—eating out of their hands. They now simply point at the fabricated enemy, country so-and-so, which is harboring those evil creatures who attacked us. At that point, all that our warmongers need to do is tell us, "Hire us. We'll take care of it. We'll make you safe." The whole scheme is as easy as 1, 2, 3. First, you false-flag, then you attack end destroy, then you, quote and quote, rebuild. When done, create another enemy. And that's how all the wealth in this country has been transferred from the very many to the very few.

Governor Richard Guerra: You don't know what you don't know, Gandhi. And you are way out of line. As an at-large and honorary member of the Intelligence Select Committee—a high-level position that was legislated in large part thanks to my initiative, by the way—I get to read the briefings. I know who the enemies of the United States are, and that they are everywhere, constantly trying to undermine our democracy. It's war by other means, their daily cyberattacks, their theft of intellectual property, their spying by any avenues in ways that you wouldn't believe. Frankly, you're not prepared to undertake the president's role as Commander-in-Chief because you don't have all the tools and knowledge required to be the national defense strategist that our president should be to protect the homeland 24/7/365. It's easy for you, as a candidate, to pontificate, to name-drop your surname as an oracle of peace and as some kind of political royalty.

the nerve! [boricua in sausalito]

guerra, the insider. thinks a few terms in office gives him the right to be there forever and keep others out. [kau meelker]

term limits for assholes! [taiwanese barber]

no need. he'll lose his seat when he loses the election.

[Stefannie2833823]

i am pissed, and i vote [Elderly Alfred]

piss away then. ur vote's worth shit. [bañado en colonia]

Robert Gandhi: Governor Guerra, the public may have elected you to office, but voters didn't elect you to the select-committee-of-whatever for you and a few others to have this special information that's not readily available to anyone else, even to most people currently in office. National Security has become a code phrase for "We Do Whatever We Please," with no oversight. As a candidate for the presidency, I'm proposing to do away with this nonsense.

Governor Richard Guerra: You cannot. It's part of our legislative process. The nation must have a select committee and other defense-related committees and groups to safeguard our democracy. Otherwise, we'll have hordes of domestic and foreign terrorists breaching the gates of the U.S. Capitol.

Robert Gandhi: Where in the U.S. Constitution or Bill of Rights does it say anything about select committees? Where does it say that a small group of senators and representatives can meet and share information coming from the national intelligence apparatus, information that no one else is allowed to see? What kind of democracy IS this? It's not democracy you are defending but your privilege to provide the national-defense industrial complex with the tools to enrich itself while you benefit from it by accepting their large political contributions. You take our citizens for idiots, Governor Guerra. Everyone knows your motives. Your party uses the Constitution as a sacred text when it's convenient, applying it selectively. But when it comes to pointing out the surveillance swamp in which we keep on sinking, not a peep from you about the Constitution. You are most definitely not defending democracy. You're defending a police state. And that's what we have become, a police state that has elections every four years to readjust the roles of the policemen, all in the name of a nebulous national security, which ceased to exist long ago thanks to the weekly mass shootings taking place around the country right now.

wow [boring housewife]

look at guerra's face! speechless now, asshole! [plug power]

gandhi has just won the election [diamond baramhaman]

just won the young vote. still an uphill battle with the rest. ways to go! [jazmin callahan]

we'll get there. #realconstitution #termlimitsforassholes [voter362]

PUBLICITY: The Term Limits for Assholes™ Foundation needs your financial contribution! You know you're awesome when you support a good cause, and this is the best cause around during these times of political upheaval. We'll put your money to good use. Our foundation is rated A1A on the Clinton Scale for Efficiency and Transparency™. Our only mission is to legislatively impose term limits on politicians who make holding public office a highly remunerative career. Donate now! You know you're awesome!

. . . The MeSez Network™

my census chromapeau meter arrived last week with the wrong national id number. sent it back. they sent the right one today via expedited drone! [KarloWang311]

me, too. i scored "blanche18". nonsense. [London Sarría]

rectohamm announced the meters are not accurate again? [Luxury Sex Doll]

they're planning to drop the skin color thing next year. replace it with a new citizen classification scheme—a, b, c scale type of thing. [zenaida burton-ruiz]

citizens "a" will pay the bulk of taxes, then lower rates for b, c, and d folks. [Big Bucks Bertha]

They're also planning a "POS" classification. POSs are encouraged to emigrate! [vegan rapunzel]

how do you get "a" or "b" or "c"? [luckymf52]

nobody knows. algorithms. [happily married spinster]

BREAKING: Polar Shift Hysteria! Experts urge the global citizenry to ignore all past scientific speculation about how so-called polar shifts are gradual and take thousands of years to occur. "This is no longer a crackpot theory," says physics professor Lyndon Gora at Guadalcanal Online University™. "We're looking at an impending cataclysm of global proportions. Earthquakes, tsunamis, drastic temperature shifts, famine, the death of billions of people in a matter of weeks. No one is safe." Gora's theory places the trigger for a polar shift not on internal mechanisms of the earth itself but on powerful forces initiated by our galaxy through cosmic rays acting as a switch to flip the earth's poles every few thousand years.

old news. same cosmic-egg theory that's been around forever. [Young Akkadian]

That's the navel of Vishnu [Marsa Bora]

lotus sprung from a navel [elenaLin5196]

what? [bleak prospector]

it's what the universe looks like, a four-dimensional lotus. [Ozaki Yuu]

same black-hole forces that created the universe are the ones that trigger polar shifts, duh. [Careena Shivganesh]

guadalcanal online. what do you expect? [carbonzitto]

at least the guy's right, just late to the game. [referendarii]

He is NOT right! Why don't they tell people the truth? Polar shifts are the result of too many people on the planet, making Mother Earth HEAVY, forcing her to tilt to a point of no return! We are DOOMED until we get rid of half or more of the current population [EcoMother]

shaking a few billion off is definitely needed. useless humans anyway [Frankfurt Beer Guzzler]

i know quite a few i can put on the list! [smell-a-Rackett]

so do i! [Montessoried]

PUBLICITY: Get ready for the SHIFT! Food rations packed in an easy-to-dispense way, in case of emergencies. With a shelf life of five years, you and your loved ones will be ready for whatever the polar shift brings to humanity. We recommend purchasing a five-year supply to be REALLY prepped! Financing available!

for those who believe in god, a polar shift is not a punishment, it's a natural occurrence. [Aika Chen428]

you mean like the great flood? [YadaYadaFuck]

built into the system. a polar shift is designed to refresh everything. [Disgruntled Taikonaut]

A polar shift is a feature of god's creation, not a punishment. We should welcome its potential to cause our extinction. [LordCardinals]

because . . . how do you evolve without first becoming extinct? [bocadillo de cama]

. . . The EavesDrop Portal™, Posting the World's Every Hack!

LIVE TRANSCRIPT: The Walsmart Science Show™ Weekend. A Panel Discussion on Topics That Affect Us All

Kumar Achaa: Welcome to the Walsmart Science Show™. I'm your host, Kumar Achaa. Tonight, we're talking polar shift, or p.s., considered the latest threat to our wellbeing. My guests are Alfredo Marqueza, author of the book "We Are Doomed: How to Enjoy the Polar Shift," and Dr. Alana Alsan, a cosmetologist—excuse me, cosmologist—at Cantonment University in Florida. Welcome to you both. Dr. Alsan, let me start with you. How soon is now? as the saying goes. Are we THAT close to global cataclysm?

Alana Alsan: Not really. Like everything in the news and in the marketplace, there are forces involved here that have a vested interest in spreading mass hysteria.

Kumar Achaa: But other scientists, your colleagues at Harvard and at NASA—not Cantonment—are openly questioning the data of the last hundred years.

Alana Alsan: The magnetic field around the earth is still very strong, too strong for a shift to take place. We've lost about thirty percent of it in the last three thousand years. No shift will occur until we've lost at least ninety percent.

Kumar Achaa: Alfredo, you don't agree.

Alfredo Marqueza: Absolutely not. Scientists simply don't know. They fake it as they go. In the next twenty years, we're looking at satellites failing, saying goodbye to autonomous vehicles, to drone deliveries, to bot surgery, to everything that we take for granted in our modern world.

Alana Alsan: Even if a pole reversal takes place, the process lasts a thousand years, giving humans enough time to adapt, to migrate, if necessary. It doesn't happen overnight.

Alfredo Marqueza: You're wrong, and you're hiding the evidence. A severely weakened magnetic field has already been detected by satellites for decades, and it's getting worse by the minute. The South Atlantic Anomaly, for example, also known as the SAA, is NOT a conspiracy. It's reality. That's why satellites over South America keep on experiencing electronic failure, and it's what's keeping that part of the world so behind in adopting modern technology. Come clean, Alana. Tell the public the TRUTH!

Alana Alsan: No need to shout, Alfredo.

Kumar Achaa: That's alright, Dr. Alsan. It's OK to let it all out. Science is not a polite undertaking. You must shout your findings to be heard and be convincing.

Alfredo Marqueza: My book explains it very clearly. Start by moving to South America as soon as you can. Any place will do. Northern Argentina, however, close to the coast, is best. So is Uruguay and parts of Paraguay, for that matter. All over the rest of the world, citizens will be made to wear electromagnetic collars to supposedly counter the magnetic shift. In Argentina, the collars won't work because satellites will fail to transfer people's personal data when crossing over the SAA.

Alana Alsan: That has already been addressed. You're thirty years behind on your research.

Alfredo Marqueza: My CURRENT research shows that the present magnetic field will decrease to ZERO in the next twenty years! By then, all collars are off! The Anomaly will be GLOBAL, and your tenure at Deliveranceville University won't help you any!

there goes dr lana. exit stage left. [half tourist]

love her red pumps! [gardenGnome24]

Alfredo Marqueza: So, she doesn't like the heat in the kitchen. I guess that leaves us the rest of the hour to talk about my book.

Kumar Achaa: Tell us about it. Now on sale everywhere, folks. "We Are Doomed: How to Enjoy the Polar Shift." Aside from moving to Argentina, what other advice do you offer your readers? I like the meal plans.

Alfredo Marqueza: Yes, I've been developing, and just started manufacturing, these delicious meal pellets that provide all the nutrients a human being needs to survive the coming famine. I recommend you hoard these in your basement, in your crawl space, your attic, in your gun safe—wherever your neighbors won't be able to get to them.

Kumar Achaa: How about the cosmic rays and cosmogenic isotopes that are supposed to bombard us before and after the sudden polar shift? How do we protect ourselves from them?

Alfredo Marqueza: That's easy. My company is manufacturing Faraday Cage Coveralls™ that buyers will be able to wear for protection. You'll have all bases covered if you purchase my We Are Doomed Survival Kit™.

ha, ha! this clown wants to make a buck to spend it where? [robertito fo]

argentina! [Ruler of All]

anyone been there lately? [Ychiko Nasseau]

sucks. guy's right. dark cloud over the continent makes satellites fail. [star geezer]

live videogaming with folks down there isnt possible anymore. lost all my "kommando yo mando" buddies there in the last two months. [HunterGal22]

mee too. playing with cambodian gamers now, but they arent as good. [noiko_B51]

BREAKING!: Candidate Robert Gandhi Dead! Mr. Gandhi suffered a heart attack while hiking during a short break between campaign stops. He was fifty years old and leaves his wife and two children, as well as millions of followers who had placed their hopes on his message of peace for America and the world. This is a developing story.

damn! [pear liquor boy]

RIP [bargo zambreezi]

rip [Jody Parasuvraman]

shame. only good candidate there was. [estella2045]

They're not reporting the truth. He was assassinated. [Swathy Trending]

He WAS assassinated, pure and simple. Induced heart attack with some form of injected pharmaceutical. [marianne fix]

the man who found gandhi's body, a member of his staff, said gandhi had a wound on his neck, with some blood smeared around it [fp in pjays]

gandhi was found with a small piece of metal in his hand that looked like a black fingernail clipping. the staff member is being ignored by the news media, which is bent on saying this was a heart attack. [bonanzo]

gandhi had received threats he hadnt reported [informed consenter]

The months leading to the election have been intense. Robert Gandhi took a day off from the campaign trail to meditate and be completely on his own. He had barely seen his family in weeks. Every day had been like being a celebrity on tour. [Nandita Evergreen, Robert Gandhi for President]

I was there, and I know what happened. Not there the moment he died, but waiting for him to return from his hike. We were a large crowd of supporters waiting for him. [Sonia Mercedes Ballanchin]

Millions had approached him to shake his hand and wish him well. His message was getting across, and it was mostly because he stayed on it. Defunding the military-national-security-industrial profiteers was all he talked about. When planted journalists asked him to talk about other topics or taunted him with false accusations, he ignored them and continued to hammer on the point—the elites bankrupting and dismantling what was once a glorious nation. "I'm for a moral America," he said when closing every one of his public appearances, "not a bankrupted one." [Nandita Evergreen, Robert Gandhi for President]

BREAKING: Conspiracy theorists are blaming Robert Gandhi's death on foul play. Hearsay evidence from a campaign worker who supposedly found Gandhi's body after the heart attack, is being disseminated as fact. "Nothing is true until an official investigation by the government has taken place," said new Secretary of Defense Peter "No Conflict of Interest" Marcciano. Stay tuned.

Robert Gandhi was with our team in West Virginia when he asked staff members to find an isolated state park or large landholding, up on the hills, where he could go for a hike for several hours and not run into anybody. The truth must come out. He was an avid hiker and liked to practice meditation when hiking alone. He . . . [Nandita Evergreen, Robert Gandhi for President]

BREAKING!: Massive earthquake in Memphis! Thousands reported dead, perhaps tens of thousands! Live transcript from reporter Beto Rao, who is at the scene:

Beto Rao: Everyone's being urged to keep calm. The neighborhood of New Kerala in south Memphis was especially affected. We can see residents already beginning to mourn their dead.

we can see nothing, asshole. reporting from a wristband camera. what a joke. [fugitive delinquent]

beto's a shill for the establishment. it's all gonna be tragic videos from south memphis from now on, drowning gandhi's murder out. [viktor thankyou]

we won't let them. keep on pushing gandhi's campaign worker's account. [abel henry]

Beto Rao: This section of town emerged just a couple of decades ago as waves of refugees arrived and settled a mostly Hindu community. They have gathered their most cherished possessions and taken to the roads that lead out of New Kerala, once again migrant refugees, only one or two generations removed from their ancestors who arrived in America under the same conditions. This time, Mother Nature is their enemy, displacing them from their land.

you can tell these videos are old and not live from his wristband. thinks he can get away with massive bullshit. [maus21]

quake porn. people will fall for it, again and again. [Suli Barak]

i'm in pretoria. can't do anything about these supposed quake victims, so what's the point of showing me the bloodied bodies of children being pulled out of the rubble? [Merki Farzahn]

staged videos [maus21]

Robert Gandhi needed to be completely on his own, alone with nature and zero distractions. That was the routine, as we, his campaign workers, knew it. Only on his own could he gradually shut off his mind and, while hiking, reach the transcendental state that turned into his spiritual compass. [Doug Vikram, Robert Gandhi for President]

Without access to meditation, he would have never made it this far on the campaign. The political system in the United States is designed to turn candidates into robots parroting the scripts written by their financial backers. Robert promised himself he would never do that, and to fulfill that promise, he needed his spiritual compass recharged, rejuvenated every few weeks. [Nandita Evergreen, Robert Gandhi for President]

This was a hot day, but with bearable temperatures at that altitude. Robert selected the trail that was recommended to him, and he was soon able to hear only his steps and other pleasant sounds from the natural world around him. He had a wristband with him for when he needed to find his way back to the starting point, but he had turned it off for now so he wouldn't be tempted to check the time. [Doug Vikram, Robert Gandhi for President]

He even placed the device in his pocket when he started the hike, so he could not see his face in the black mirror. [Nandita Evergreen, Robert Gandhi for President]

Beto Rao: Thousands DEAD in Memphis, folks! Stay with me!

don't see anything, and i'm in memphis. [liquid joy]

no ur not, troll [eli bananas]

Beto Rao: It's absolute devastation!

When Robert Gandhi hiked to clear his mind, he... [Doug Vikram, Robert Gandhi for President]

BREAKING!!!: Pop music sensation Bellorusso has fallen from grace! His house has suffered extensive damage from a mob of protesters who invaded the property while the singer-songwriter was away on tour. Earlier this week, the public became enraged by the release of Bellorusso's "Almond Eyes," a ballad about his late girlfriend. The song was immediately identified as racist "because of its reference to a certain shape of eyes that are predominant in certain ethnicities," said Varig Carrasco, President of the #Get-the-Racists™ online organization. Carrasco added, "Almond Eyes was immediately detected by Federal algorithms and confirmed to be racist by civil servants at the Federal Department of Non-Offensive Citizenship. We are recommending a $500,000 fine for Bellorusso along with thirty days in jail with two hots and a cot to cure unda's racism." Bellorusso, for his part, doubled down on his racist crusade by asking, "Aren't all eyes shaped like almonds?" That was the last straw that infuriated the public to "get organized and set things right," as one protester put it, breaking into Bellorusso's home and doing some "angry remodeling." Aside from two rooms in the house that were completely burned to a crisp, unconfirmed reports state that Bellorusso's beloved parrot, Gabby, ended up in the property's backyard pool—drowned.

that'll teach that belloracist! [RosaLuis Magullin]

the parrot was yelling racist shit. people got angry and let it have it, that's all [fast like jesus]

so tired of these racists! they all need to be exterminated for sure [je fais l'universe]

Don't forget: There's an important, not-to-be-missed, 2-hour special tonight about this whole Belloracist saga—From Pop Sensation to Pariah in One Racist Song—that's the title. Don't miss it! [wolverine fun]

heard producers are putting the special's final edit together, as we speak, comparing belloracist's almond eyes to the hateful racism level reached by taitú johanssen's my watermelon muncher, which destroyed unda's singing career in a matter of hours after that disgustingly hateful song was released [Hellas Mahalo]

good riddance all these racists! [Irfana Musa]

protesters shouda got his dog and other animals too. parrot too small a price to pay [Boris DeMerengue]

Speaking of racism, what about the obvious, hateful discrimination in cricket against players who're not of Indian descent? [Stevie Ranganathan]

it's obvious and racist! [ni modo]

When Robert Gandhi hiked to clear his mind, he... [Doug Vikram, Robert Gandhi for President]

name ONE player in the American New Indian Cricket League who doesn't have a South Asian surname. You can't, can you? [WikiWiki Mon]

and pakis dont count. we want other races playing the sport. [Wan

Zhen]

#cricket_too_Indian! [Rafaelish]

When Robert Gandhi hiked to clear his mind, he... [Doug Vikram, Robert Gandhi for President]

Beto Rao: Listen, folks, MEMPHIS! People are DYING!

if they really are, it's just thousands of invading subcontinentals. who cares? [Raunchy Intellectual]

When Robert Gandhi hiked to clear his mind, he started by imagining a dog resting in the woods, its belly expanding and contracting with every breath. Then his own lungs followed the rhythm. As he climbed, the regular supply of oxygen acted as a cleaning agent, a gas that sloshed around in his brain, rinsing away the contaminants that caused stress, ferrying the toxins out of his body in the form of sweat, out of every pore. [Doug Vikram, Robert Gandhi for President]

The sweat evaporated almost immediately in the pleasant breeze that bathed his body, and it turned again into purified oxygen that he took in to repeat the cycle. [Nandita Evergreen, Robert Gandhi for President]

Beto Rao: In a few minutes, I'll be interviewing a man who lost his whole family! He's in shock at the moment, but a neighbor assured me he's being helped to recover his voice to give me an exclusive within the hour. This is history in the making, folks! Through this victim, you will be able to comprehend the devastating effect this disaster is having on this community, this city, and the whole of America! Don't miss it!

Then, Robert began his mantra: "It's already broken. It's already broken. It's already broken." He repeated the mantra in his mind. He had trained himself to echo the words in his thoughts without their having any grammatical meaning, instilling in him a sense of wellbeing. The sentence came from a philosophy book he had read in his youth about the state of things in human consciousness. All of us—his campaign workers and volunteers—heard about it at some point. [Meredith Ledezma, Robert Gandhi for President]

The mantra was not the goal of his meditation, however, only a tool that he used in the process to reach the transcendental quiet that allowed him to have no thoughts. "It's already broken" meant there was nothing to worry about because, in the cosmic sense, the absolute worst had already happened. His children had died the most horrible, painful deaths. His wife had endured unbearable suffering. Natural disasters had killed billions. He had been assassinated. The economy had collapsed. [Doug Vikram, Robert Gandhi for President]

Everything was already broken. So, the beauty that surrounded him as he hiked through the woods was the most glorious sign of hope because, how could this pleasant moment still exist in the midst of all the chaos? [Nandita Evergreen, Robert Gandhi for President]

BREAKING!: Memphis earthquake—hundreds of thousands affected... You won't BELIEVE this: the ten most stupid things victims are doing to try to save their belongings. Check it out on the exclusive MemphisEarthquate Network™!

Because every human being can enjoy a pleasant, quiet moment in the woods, even though everything is already broken, life goes on. The precious crystal that has fallen off a hand and shattered to a million pieces, when hitting the floor, has ALWAYS been already broken. [Doug Vikram, Robert Gandhi for President]

Plates and bowls in the kitchen cupboards look intact and solid, ready to last a lifetime, but they also are already broken. It is just a matter of time. The plates and glasses our grandparents used are long gone, even if they are still in our cupboards. [Nandita Evergreen, Robert Gandhi for President]

We can be careful when handling them, using them, and washing them, but their fate was sealed from the moment they were manufactured. The box they came in when first purchased should have said, "Set of six plates and bowls. Already broken." [Doug Vikram, Robert Gandhi for President]

Everything that crosses our path should be labeled that way, Robert Gandhi reminded us. [Nandita Evergreen, Robert Gandhi for President]

Beto Rao: I will continue my live coverage after this commercial break. And remember, everything in life is better with Coal Mountain Rush™, the beer made with the purest water in the world, filtered for thousands of years by the coal seams of nature! Coal Mountain Rush™, a sponsor of this news report and many others.

Robert would let go of the mantra as he ascended the hill and reached a higher level of mindfulness. Joy to the gods of the cosmos. He was free. [Doug Vikram, Robert Gandhi for President]

His body stopped and sat down on a soft mound of leaves, his eyes closed. The breeze ran past the trees and over the summit. The warmth of the sun accompanied it. There was a hummingbird that joined the scenery. Air flowed into the lungs without any resistance. It remained there, still, a visitor to the millions of alveoli. [Meredith Ledezma, Robert Gandhi for President]

Then, it flowed out to be replaced by a new breath. "In," followed by a long pause, then "Out." Nothing else came into play, just the organic mechanism of breathing, nourishing a human entity that was completely at peace with the cosmos, flowing with it. Breathe In. Long pause. Out. In. Long pause. Out. [Doug Vikram, Robert Gandhi for President]

The violence of the interruption brought Robert back in seconds. The hummingbird had attacked his neck, and he instinctively moved his hand to slap it, as if he were killing a mosquito. [Nandita Evergreen, Robert Gandhi for President]

What his hand felt was not a mosquito nor a hummingbird. It was something in between, more like a wasp, and it felt cold and hard. It buzzed as loudly as a hummingbird as it struggled to set itself free from Robert's hand and neck. [Doug Vikram, Robert Gandhi for President]

But Robert held on to it, aware of where he was and what was happening. The object that was attached to his neck was man-made, a tiny helicopter attached to a mechanical sting. [Meredith Ledezma, Robert Gandhi for President]

He could feel the strength of his arm starting to vanish, and his consciousness beginning to ebb. He made a last, superhuman effort to squeeze the object and get it off his neck, and he seemed to have succeeded in breaking it, and a loud buzzing sound graced his ear. [Doug Vikram, Robert Gandhi for President]

but the autopsy said it was a heart attack, so your fictitious narrative doesn't hold. [bam-bam linker]

Autopsy and cremation in less than four hours? The Secret Service took over the body and didn't even allow the family to see it. The "earthquake" established an instant national emergency. Everything else was swept under the rug in a matter of minutes. This was murder. [Meredith Ledezma, Robert Gandhi for President]

Several geologists are saying the earthquake doesn't make sense. It was manufactured via induced telluric movements. [Nandita Evergreen, Robert Gandhi for President]

Through fracking. They forced the mining industry to abandon the practice long ago, but the military kept the process in its toolkit, to wage war with giant pumps and tankers at the ready to inject billions of gallons into the ground at extremely high pressure at geologic junctures known to be vulnerable in enemy territory. [Meredith Ledezma, Robert Gandhi for President]

This one was most definitely man-made, timed to coincide with the assassination. [Doug Vikram, Robert Gandhi for President]

u-all conspiracy theorists should find something better to do with your time, like going out, door to door, to collect food and clothing for the quake victims. [Proud Citizen Jimmy]

yur brain's a victim [relished avatar]

Their plan was to induce the earthquake first, then the heart attack. That way, no one would have noticed Robert's death at all until way after the fact. [Doug Vikram, Robert Gandhi for President]

But they miscalculated, and there was about an hour or so of news about his supposed heart attack before the earthquake. Now they're busy deleting all digital files from the record. So, anyone who has copies of reports, video, audio, or articles, please post them on indelible servers at several locations and provide view access to all. [Meredith Ledezma, Robert Gandhi for President]

A whistleblower associated with the company Drone Technology Werks™, in Pasadena, has described a miniature robotic wasp capable of face recognition that can target victims accurately with lethal doses of any kind of compound that its reservoir can hold, injecting it through a mechanical sting. [Doug Vikram, Robert Gandhi for President]

The device was perfected around fifteen years ago, the whistleblower said, and has already been used in several assassinations that were made to look like natural deaths, like President Varela's, for example, six years ago. [Meredith Ledezma, Robert Gandhi for President]

You can see campaign reporters lying through their teeth, particularly those who supposedly "happened" to be at the scene, just a couple of miles from where Robert was found—when no one, not even us, knew exactly where to find him. Those individuals were the drone's operators-turned-reporters who began the coverup. They were so eager to plant the heart-attack story, rushing to do it right before the earthquake news hit. [Doug Vikram, Robert Gandhi for President]

the earthquake that "comes once in a thousand years" happened to come when the most promising candidate for world peace had a heart attack while enjoying a walk in the woods. [Gim Youngjae]

all i'm saying is his death must be avenged [Aparna Gopal]

He was for peace but was murdered with violence. So, fuck peace for a while and hunt down the animals who killed him. [Clifton Yora]

we should develop our own set of mechanical insects to snuff out the fuckers! [arabesque16]

invisible insects [surviver bolt]

Forgive us, Robert Gandhi, for doing this in your name. Sometimes, there's no other way. Pestilence demands extermination. [failed adoptee]

virtual gandhi [Harry Lupin]

. . . The MeSez Network™

Friend, I am Voltaire Rodriguez from the Mighty State of Michigan, and I'm here to help. [Mighty Voltaire]

spare us [Deemo Beetsmith]

you won't get the nomination [carouseller of dreams]

True. The AHP will most likely not select ME as its candidate, so I'm campaigning concurrently as an independent from the Mighty State of Michigan! My Real American Party (RAP) is making waves! [Mighty Voltaire]

You're no Robert Gandhi [valiente24]

I don't claim to be, but my campaign is all about extending his legacy. I am talking to supporters in Ketchum today, in the Mighty State of Idaho, one of my many stops as I fly my Piesof™, which allows me quick takeoffs and landings, fifty or sixty miles apart, covering a great deal of terrain every day, between six and eight hundred miles a day, stopping at more than ten locations and gathering a great deal of interest from the voting public! That's me, here for the American people! All my stops are streamed and transcribed live on the Wellington Lederhosen Network™, and my Ketchum speech is about to begin! [Mighty Voltaire]

loser [mundi trompetus]

let the poor fuck dream he's electable [Cincinnati UTFer]

. . . The Wellington Lederhosen Network™

Voltaire Rodriguez: I feel your pain, Ketchumians. We are all in mourning in this country. Whether you think candidate Gandhi died of a heart attack or was killed by some secret society of rogues, the fact is he's dead, and I'll tell you that his cause will not die with him. He was fiercely antiwar, as am I. He was compassionate and peaceful, and so am I. It is all these wars that the United States has kept alive for decades—nearly half a century in Afghanistan and Iraq, even after the phony "pull-outs" of the 2020s! Wars that have deeply destabilized the world and brought us waves of migrants and refugees from those war zones. So now that Mr. Gandhi is gone, I'm making world peace part of my platform. World peace is the only effective way to stop the aimless migration of billions. They currently travel from country to country, trying to get in until someone accepts them. That someone usually ends up being the United States! Other countries got wise. They tightened their borders. They made it nearly impossible to get in. Argentina has gone as far as requiring every tourist entering the country to wear an electronic ankle bracelet, to make sure each one of those visitors is truly a visitor who leaves Argentina after a few days of touring and spending money in restaurants and hotels. America should do the same. Thank you, Argentina, for that great idea! No more tourist visas required, just a stylish bracelet during your stay.

pathetic opportunist. makes you wonder if even he himself killed gandhi to take this approach and get the antiwar vote. [noisy kat] fake as fake can get [barfi sweetsmaster]

he's just being resourceful. votes become available, he grabs em. better rodriguez than the ahp. [Bentley Ramirez]

rap rap rap that candidate! [fournis en feu]

Hope his Piesofshit crash-lands somewhere and puts a stop to this nonsense. [Kishimoto That's Me]

not a serious candidate [VargasGirl]

serious candidate = oxymoron [Horny Beast]

Voltaire Rodriguez: So, we're incarcerating thousands of arriving refugees. You, in Ketchum, know it, home to the largest and newest federal facility in the country. I'll dare call it a concentration camp— hundreds of acres surrounded by several layers of barbed wire and electronic surveillance. Yes, it provides a number of jobs to your community, but what kind of dysfunctional society makes a living from depriving other humans of their freedom? Popular culture will have you believe that every one of these souls being held captive in this type of facility deserves to be in it. They committed a crime and so are paying their debt to society. That's just a blatant lie, Ketchumians! Most people in jail in America today are there because of some minor infraction. An act that should be punishable with a week in jail, at most, turns into a two-year legal ordeal. And that two-year sentence, into a lifetime of disfunction because any kind of stay in one of these facilities turns YOU into a life-long, unemployable felon!

learning to speak felonese, clown voltaire [furball fan]

give da poliz some power and everything becomes a crime [pancho miranda23]

i served my country violently in the war against nicaragua, then served time in ketchum for "acting violently" in nola [marky marine] go figure [alicia child]

Voltaire Rodriguez: The penitentiary industry is selling this country
a bill of goods. These facilities cost billions of dollars to build and
operate. Bulletproof windows, doors, and walls. Tens of thousands
of dollars per door, folks. Who is going to be shooting inside these
buildings to require that every door be bulletproof? The refugees?
Those who arrive in our country and are taken directly, by the
busload, to facilities like these? Instead of being sent back
immediately to their points of origin? So, facility number 383 is full
and the penitentiary industry clamors for number 384. We're running
out of space! they say. We need to build more beds! Hand over the
money! And the government, the STUPID government, keeps on
giving it to them, OUR money! It also keeps on giving defense
contractors OUR money, to keep on manufacturing wars overseas to
supply the penitentiary industry here at home with a steady supply of
arriving refugee-residents. Why don't we just pay to build landing
strips right inside these facilities, so we can fly them in, directly,
without having to waste money on buses? It's the biggest racket in
history, folks, and this national-defense-penitentiary-industrial
complex is working 24/7/365, sticking its finger deeply into your
you know what. If I get on my Piesof™ after my speech here today,
and the thing is blown out of the sky by some alleged homegrown
loner terrorist, you'll KNOW I was targeted by the defense-
contractors-national-security-penitentiary profiteers!

now he's making sense [approved angel]

hope it happens. maybe a thorough investigation will finally reveal
the corrupt machinery behind these wars [Lindsey Rawls]

never gonna hapn. theyll produce a hapless unemployed loser right
out of that same jail and pin it on him. blame it on his meds, or
somethin. put him back in for another fifteen years. [out 2 get ya]

Voltaire Rodriguez: Trillions of dollars wasted on useless bullshit—
excuse my Spanish. The American people have been bombarded
with fear-mongering propaganda for decades. The message,
essentially, is "they're coming to get you!" whether it's criminals,

foreign armies, spies, priests, staged terrorist attacks, what have you. It's all a strategy to keep everyone living in constant fear and giving the government the task to "protect" us. All we need to do, they say, is give them our money, and they'll take care of the rest. Well, that's not the principle on which America was founded. The principle was: You take care of everything yourself. Today, you are just a victim, here in Ketchum, of the parasite creatures in Washington who hire some company that hires some other company that hires some soldiers and sends them far away across the globe to poke a hornets' nest. You are the victim because the poor people who live near that hornets' nest then rush to America to seek asylum. All the while, the parasites in Washington and the companies they hire profit handsomely from the arrangement. And YOU keep on paying the bills, providing that profit for them! It's come to that, folks. You, the voters, are just a bunch of IDIOTS, with the profiteers' fingers up your asses. And you keep on voting for them! It's you against them, and I'm going to give them a name—the Bloated Unified Bullshitters Bankrupting America, the BUBBAs. That's exactly what they're doing, bankrupting America, and YOU are complicit, because you're doing nothing about it. But now you can. Vote for me. I'm going to deal with the BUBBAs and all their armies of bottom feeders who profit from your hard work.

moron's playing with fire [randy andy33]

counting on the bubbas not doing anything this soon after gandhi's assassination [brucinda afterlife]

Nobody cares. Everything will be swept under a vortex of lies anyway. Whether this guy's offed or not before the election, he's not going to win. They have nothing to worry about. They have the electorate by the balls. [enola drowning]

hmm...more than half the electorate doesn't have ballz, last i checked [renata d'arby]

Gripped by their fears, then. Fear knows no gender. [enola drowning] i see this kandydate as just a distraction. enough is enough. gandhi was the real threat to the bubbas and power-hungry warmongers. by having him killed, they crossed a final line. there's no going back now. [citizened ayer]

Voltaire Rodriguez: Goodbye, Ketchum. I'm Voltaire Rodriguez from the Mighty State of Michigan! I approve this message, and I'm going to help YOU! On my way out of here, I'll fly my Piesof™ around and over the Ernest Hemingway Maximum Security Transitional Facility™, and throw candy out the window for the inmates! See how the BUBBAs deal with THAT! God bless, and see you at the polls!

i spy a swarm of mechanical insects fucking with his piesof [el ingeniero verde]

he'll be heart-attacked before morn [shelby madden]

Today, at 23:21 GMT, join us to intervene Valero Broco, CEO of Delfy Harvest Corporation, the world's largest manufacturer of cherry and cluster bombs. [The Virtual Collective]

BREAKING: Pro-Gandhi supporters violently demonstrating by the tens of thousands. Conspiracy theories have taken hold of a population that demands action. Live transcript from reporter Beto Rao, live from Anaheim:

Beto Rao: These are scenes of mayhem and devastation, folks, completely opposed to the nature of Robert Gandhi, the man these hooligans claim to be representing. A crowd just broke into the abandoned Disneyland Park, cut the chain-link fence at several locations, and now said to be on their way to torch the ruins of the Sleeping Beauty Castle.

wasn't beto at the earthquake in memphis? [val mobby]

fake earthquake you mean? [Colonial Modernist]

he's in high demand [fred rao]

---

fucking tool [MissO302]

always whoring for the skipper [virgil lila]

Beto Rao: I've asked my camera operator to focus on closeups of participants that we can provide to the FBI for face recognition. As you can see, some are wearing bandanas to hide themselves while they commit these heinous, un-American crimes.

. . . ClassyNet™

ClassyNet: Welcome to ClassyNet, and thank you for your patriotic service. Your classification is Alpha 3 Level 9. You can only post classified entries for internal communications with selected members up to Clearance 9.

ClassyNet: All information displayed will be scrubbed within seconds.

ClassyNet: Beginning session . . . your ClassyNet number is 080632 . . .

ClassyNet_080632: out for a ride this afternoon. had to smile at how easy it is to manipulate the rabble. (scrubbed)

ClassyNet_091588: should of seen them, driving their trucks around with flags and banners, spewing out their anger and extreme politics. exactly as we planned. (scrubbed)

ClassyNet_080632: and the opposition, right on cue, performing their part, pre-programmed. (scrubbed)

ClassyNet_091588: fucking brilliant! (scrubbed)

ClassyNet_080632: indeedy (scrubbed)

. . . iRiver™

LIVE TRANSCRIPT: City Council Meeting, City of New New Delhi, Indiana. Special session to discuss the passing of a resolution condemning Pakistan's occupation of Kashmir. Mayor Ravi Rao has just brought the meeting to order. Aside from members of the council and a bailiff, a large crowd has packed itself into the small hall. Let's listen in.

Mayor Rao: Order! Order! I demand absolute quiet during the proceedings. Council member Varig, from District Five, has the floor.

Marika Varig: I make a motion that we go into closed session to discuss the only item on the agenda.

Mayor Rao: Second! All in favor, say . . .

Citizen #44: Wait a moment! You can't go into a closed session to discuss or pass a resolution. This is a public meeting.

Mayor Rao: We very well can. It's within our power. If you want a say, you need to get yourself elected.

Citizen #44: Nonsense. Citizens can participate without getting elected. Robert's Rules. Closed sessions are for personnel matters or contract negotiations only.

BREAKING: Valero Broco, CEO of Delfy Harvest Corporation has suffered a debilitating stroke. Details coming.

Mayor Rao: Contract negotiations, personnel, AND matters of national security. Our resolution has to do with items important to the interests of the United States.

Citizen #44: No, it doesn't. We are in New New Delhi, Indiana. As far as I know, Kashmir is not part of this municipality or even this country.

there goes rao again, banging his gavel on the poor oak bench [kashmiri crybaby] his way to relieve stress [mama grande]

Mayor Rao: Who are you, anyway, trying to robertsrule our special meeting? Do you even live in New New Delhi? Only residents can speak at City Council meetings.

Citizen #44: My name is Farid Kahn. I live on B. R. Ambedkar Avenue, in New New Delhi, with full rights to be here, sir.

Mayor Rao: This is not a city for Pakis. You should move. In any case, do you see any Pakis on this council? I don't. We all remember Kashmir, and we have the right to condemn the atrocities that Paki Muslims are perpetrating in our territory.

Farid Kahn: Muslims are and have always been a majority in Kashmir, sir.

Mayor Rao: Very well, we'll discuss the resolution in the open. Councilman Rahash, please read the draft for consideration.

Steve Rahash: Yes, Mr. Mayor. I'm Steve Rahash, representing District 2, and, no, I don't need a microphone. Whereas members of the New New Delhi City Council are extremely concerned about the growing violence in Kashmir; Whereas terroristic elements in that most Indian Province have been at work for decades, killing innocents; Whereas decent human beings have the right to live in peace in their own country without foreign elements threatening them at every turn; Therefore, be it known that the New New Delhi City Council and citizens of this community strongly condemn the invasion of Kashmir by Muslim terrorists.

Farid Kahn: This is a gross lie. No Muslim has invaded Kashmir because all Muslims have been there to begin with, since before partition.

Mayor Rao: They're still terrorists and don't belong in India. Bailiff Patel, please unholster your service revolver and be prepared to deal with this disturbance.

Farid Kahn: Kashmir is not India.

Steve Rahash: That's what all Pakis keep on saying. We're not going to stand for it. We all—diaspora Indians—the hundreds of millions of us whose parents had to escape the terrorism perpetrated by Pakistan, to save our lives, we're not going to forget that. We'll pass thousands of resolutions, if necessary, to make up for your transgressions!

Farid Kahn: This is not germane to New New Delhi. The business of this council is to administer this city, to keep the streets clean, maintain the water and sewer systems, parks, streetlights. Why is Kashmir being rammed down our throats?

Mayor Rao: Oh, you have a vested interest in criticizing us. That's obvious. We are very concerned with what Pakistan is doing to Kashmir, and we'll exercise our free speech and first-amendment rights to express that concern at every one of our meetings, if we so desire. You are a nobody here, a minority. We've allowed you to have your say, and your first-amendment moment has now passed. So let us go on with our business.

Farid Kahn: I may be a minority here, but Muslims are a majority in Kashmir. They own Kashmir.

Mayor Rao: That's because your whore women keep on popping out babies to try to outnumber us Hindus!

ouch! rao's done it [Mormon Barista]

more power to him! [punjabi motelier]

come on, bailiff patel, pop the guy a few! [rolly pyrenees35]

fifty to one the kahn dude doesn't make it out of there alive [Umit Serif]

course not. he's a terrorist. hindus have a right to act in self-defense

[Bora Bora Boring]

fuck! kahn's grabbing rao's shirt! [Hao Yan]

there goes patel! [ladislao409]

go, go, go, go! [Rupa Mahal]

Tomorrow, at 19:32 GMT, join The Virtual Collective to intervene Lester Raghmaran, CEO and principal shareholder of TechVeck Solutions™, for war crimes committed under the guise of defense contracts signed with the state. [The Virtual Collective]

Mayor Rao: Order! Order!

wow. didn't shoot the bastard [vermin suspect]

a crowd's already dragged him out. [Mademoiselle La Mouche]

red patch on rao's right cheek. received a pretty good blow. [kwasabubu23]

Mayor Rao: Order! Let's get back to business. Councilman Rahash, please finish reading the resolution.

Steve Rahash: Yes, Mr. Mayor. The Council and citizens of this lovely small city strongly condemn the invasion of Kashmir by Muslim terrorists who have made it a goal to exterminate the Hindu faith in that most Indian province. The people of New New Delhi, Indiana, strongly support the good work the RSS is engaged in with its effort to free Kashmir from the foreign scourge. We also support candidate Jennifer Patel in her bid to lead this wonderful, welcoming nation. She has been a friend of Kashmir and a supporter of all Hindus around the world, and we, Amerihindus, want to see her in power to do good things.

Mayor Rao: Thank you, Councilman Rahash. Any discussion? Those in favor of adopting the resolution, say Aye. The Ayes have it. The resolution has been adopted unanimously.

. . . VoxPopuli Stream™

Tomorrow, at 18:52 GMT, join The Virtual Collective to intervene João Kalanga, former Minister of National Defence of the Republic of Angola. Kalanga has been instrumental in the importation of weapons manufactured in France, Germany, and the United States—arming the male population of Angola to incite genocide and mass murder via the orchestration of a civil/gender war in which millions have been murdered. [The Virtual Collective]

LIVE TRANSCRIPT: The Teddy Comstock Show. Join Teddy in a new edition of "Our Finest Hour," where you get to know the candidates while Teddy has a lively conversation with them. Today, candidates from The American Hindu Party, the AHP.

Teddy Comstock: Welcome! We'll jump right in after I tell you I had a deliciously enjoyable shower this morning, mainly because of this fantastic new shampoo that my wife ordered for me from the folks at Aquamente™. Flavored persimmon tamarind. Incredible!

shut up already [Bosco con Gamma]

next he'll be hawking ass soap [Boris4833]

anything to make a buck [Mindy Tucker]

millions [resolve951]

Teddy Comstock: Aquamente™ makes me feel like I have three times the volume of hair, even if you don't notice it on your screens. Highly recommend it. Aquamente™'s Persimmon-Tamarind Shampoo, for men, women, and others. So . . . the American Hindu Party is fielding many candidates in its primary debates. We have several of them here.

vote jenni! [Gursel Uslu]

Jankar! [leekan_moe]

Flori Jankar's not AHP [January Lesego]

Teddy Comstock: Let Me Win This, I'll start with you. You changed your name from Marcos Martinez to Let Me Win This Johnson right before launching your political career, joining the American Hindu Party, which tried to disqualify you because you are not a Hindu, nor do you have any Indian ancestors.

Let Me Win This Johnson: I've taken the AHP to court on this issue. The case is moving up the legal channels. It will get to the U.S. Supreme Court with lightning speed, since it deals with the crossroads of politics and religion, and the high court WILL find enough votes to affirm my First Amendment rights.

Teddy Comstock: The AHP is not happy about this, of course. They say the First Amendment does not apply to their party, because, and I quote, "Hinduism does not involve any churches, so the separation of church and state is a moot point here."

busted! [DeSousa Quiridi]

love it! [Tamari-Tamarind Soup]

Let Me Win This Johnson: Is this a joke? The Establishment Clause does not include the word church in it. No meddling with RELIGION, it says, and, in my view, vice versa.

Teddy Comstock: They also say that you have a zero chance of being nominated, so why go through this? They say the only goal of your candidacy is to openly discuss your chief political interest, which is immigration, particularly Hindu immigration.

Let Me Win This Johnson: I'd say 99% of the candidates running for office, any office, know they won't win anything and are only doing it for exposure—to get a book deal, job offers, marriage proposals, whatever. That's not me. I'm here to win, and my name is more than proof. So, whatever the AHP wants to say about me, they don't know what they're talking about.

go johnson! enough indians already! [Cuba Amerikan]

que nos quitaron todo el poder de un de repente, hijos de puta! basta ya! tejas pa' los tejanos! [mi raza es mi raza]

Teddy Comstock: Let me read you this from The Financial Summit Journal: "The Federal Reserve Corporation™ has been lowering and raising interest rates, cutting and raising income taxes, etc., in the last two years, in an unprecedented way. Some say that Fed Chairman CEO Suitsuit is playing ping pong or yo-yo with the economy, not allowing enough time for the markets to adjust before changing strategies." In your opinion, what is the proper monetary and/or fiscal policy to stabilize the American economy once and for all?

Let Me Win This Johnson: The question should be, "What should our government NOT do?" And the answer is quite easy. No more immigration. No more pretending that a foreign power, the nation of India, is going through some internal crisis that forces us to keep on taking in tens of millions of their so-called refugees every year. This is the New Great GREAT Replacement. Full-blown Americans like myself are being replaced by waves of refugees who not only speak no proper English and Spanish, but will never learn our two languages, because, why learn a new language when your whole community, your whole city already speaks what you speak?

says the 100% american marcos, son of mexican immigrants. [lolo8valeria]

ha ha. marcos martinez, full-blown american [bandana guru]

monolingualism is soooo boring [Mr. Melinda]

anglos stole tejas from us, then the hindus [mi raza es mi raza]

and where do native americans come in? first nations! [paster mac]

dinosaurs were here first. land rights for dinosaurs! [alicia vrim]

Tomorrow, at 6:55 GMT, join The Virtual Collective to intervene former Secretary of State Lusan Bailey for war crimes committed during her term. [The Virtual Collective]

Charlie Singh: The U.S. has no official language, Johnson. It's a free country, and people can speak whatever they want.

Teddy Comstock: Mr. Singh, you'll get your chance to speak. Please, let Mr. Johnson finish.

Let Me Win This Johnson: The economic crisis is really a humanitarian crisis. Too. Many. Humans, particularly in the bloated, overpopulated United States. Further immigration, of any type, should not be allowed, period. When I'm president, any Indian who's unemployed and not being productive will be shipped back to India. I don't care what his story is about being afraid of being killed back home and thus needing asylum. That's not OUR problem. You're not paying taxes? You're not contributing? You're outta here!

Jennifer Patel: If I may, Mr. Comstock. Let's not make this about Indians and Hindus. Mr. Johnson, you are right to call this a humanitarian issue, but it's not a crisis. It's human nature.

she's prepared for this [molly malone11]

here it comes. mother india speaking! [quality human]

she's the best, hands down [Zenaida Barbarosa]

hope she wins [Anna Mai6873]

gorgeous, too. that'll get her a few votes [Felipe Caruso]

beauty AND brains! [old clockster]

love her sari! [Blessed Leticia]

Jennifer Patel: Migration is what humans do, Mr. Johnson, and what we have been doing since the dawn of our existence. It's preposterous to even think that the United States, a country that is not even three hundred years old, can—by legislating a law, by signing executive orders or adopting acts, or writing any kind of constitution or amendment—stop the natural flow of migrants across the world.

> *INFOPOST: SOURCE: World-O-Pedia™: Jennifer Patel: Political candidate and founder of the new BJP-America, an offshoot of the American Hindu Party (AHP). Born in Gujarat, unda's family emigrated to the United States during the Pakistan Nuclear Troubles (2030-2031) thanks to the Haley-Gabbard Act, which generously opened American doors to Indian refugees. Patel is the author of "A Passage from India," in which und recounts unda's migrating experience. Und has been accused of having plagiarized or fabricated part of the personal story, but Patel stands behind the book as unda's own words and life. That controversy has died down since unda's sudden surge in popularity as the nation approaches the 2062 election, two years behind schedule thanks to the 2058-2060 pandemic.*

Jennifer Patel: This idea that certain groups of people have ever owned this geographic spot that we call America is nonsense. Nobody owns anything. So, what if it's the turn of Indians to populate this soil? They're going to keep on coming no matter what your rhetoric or physical barriers. You can't stop them because they have a very strong pull—their families and distant relatives who are here already. That's what humans do. If you live somewhere in the world, and you don't like it, and you hear from others that there's a better place that has more food, more room, fewer hurdles—you're going to move there, no matter what others who got there first say.

sounds like an english colonist talking to the other indians, in virginia, circa 1607 [ValiantThor]

we came, we saw, we conquered [machu pissed off]

---

we came, and we came, and kept on coming until we overwhelmed! [gateway druggie]

the patels are the smiths of the 21st century [mason of masons]

shut up, fuckers. she's a wonderful candidate who cares about america [fur trader]

can't be elected president. wasn't born in america. [Ms. Creant]

that's no longer a requirement. [fur trader]

PUBLICITY: The In-for-a-Treat Pet Network™ is now offering services nationwide! Grooming, spaying, neutering, and gendering services are our specialties! Bring us your loved one, and und will be in hands as caring as yours. Only Global Healthy Pet Insurance™ policies accepted. For everyone else, financing is available.

Jennifer Patel: I am a child of the American Freedom Fleet. My family left Mumbai on the "USS Mighty Freedom," which was part of the regular-duty fleet helping refugees.

> *INFOPOST: SOURCE: World-O-Pedia™: Pakistan Nuclear Troubles: Historical event hotly disputed depending on the historian or commentator describing the circumstances that brought on massive human migration from the subcontinent to the Americas, particularly to the United States and Canada. The minor blast that initiated the Nuclear Troubles in 2030 was detonated by Pakistan as more of a warning than an actual attack.*
>
> *"We don't care about your phony moral posturing," Pakistani Prime Minister Ali Khan III said at the time. "We will not be bullied by the Indian government and its pathetic sidekick, the United States." It was a test detonation, in the Thar Desert, just to show that Pakistan meant business.*
>
> *No one was killed, but the global condemnation and panic were swift. "They have crossed the red line," American*

President Japleen Gupta said from the newly created Guava Garden (just transitioned from the Rose Garden). "The United States will not stand idly while a terrorist state endangers the world's population. Even if this was not an act of war against the peaceful people of India, it constitutes a crime against humanity because of the clear risk of triggering a nuclear winter, not to mention a tit-for-tat nuclear exchange that would kill us all. Pakistan must be stopped! This sponsor of terror has gone global, intent on annihilating the human race."

The rhetoric coming out of the White House was widely criticized, particularly by physicists who confirmed that the nuclear detonation had been minor, estimated at a mere 7 kilotons, half of what the United States allegedly unleashed in Hiroshima. Most Americans accepted the physicists' point of view, and didn't take their president's words seriously, until media aggregators began netcasting from Delhi and Mumbai images of panicked masses—people storming airports, train stations, and ports—demanding to be moved to a safer geography.

"All of India is at risk," President Gupta said at a second press conference in the Guava Garden, where und often engaged the press wearing a sari and oversized bindi. Unda's detractors had started referring to the White House as the Krishna House, blasting the announced "transition of the garden from Rose to Guava because of climate change." President Gupta added, "We must come to the aid of our Indian brothers and sisters against their terrorist neighbor."

But weeks passed, and no military retaliation came either from India or the United States. The attacks were mostly verbal and coming from President Gupta. "As Commandress in Chief," und said, "I have instructed our armed services to be on the offensive, to position undselves in the Arabian Sea and around the Pakistani border with Iran and Afghanistan, helping Indian refugees transit to a safe place. My executive orders dictate the steps my Homeland Security office and the

U.S. State Department must take to ensure safe passage. We are thankful to the Tata family and Air IndiAmerica™ for their beneficial service to facilitate this process and save millions of Indian families from annihilation," und added.

An Intelligence Report made public by President Gupta indicated that Pakistan was "getting ready to hit a real target inside India" with a much more powerful nuclear weapon. "We have clear, incontestable intelligence," the report said, "that Pakistani generals are positioning their arsenals and aiming their missiles at Delhi, Mumbai, Bangalore, Chennai, Calcutta, and many other vulnerable population centers. This will result in the deaths of an estimated six-hundred million Indians, with radioactive fallout that will kill many more as it moves east, across the Bay of Bengal, the Andaman Sea, Southeast Asia, the South China Sea, the Pacific, and, eventually, hit the West Coast of the United States, engulfing California and Oregon and Washington residents with a toxic cloud of radioactivity that will spread cancers among the American population for decades to come."

The American media aggregators were helpful in showing the evidence, the satellite imagery that, in colorful detail, depicted narrow strips lined up like ants waiting for entry to a bountiful picnic. "Those are Paki missiles," an intelligence expert helpfully explained on camera. "We have evidence that they have been loaded with nuclear warheads and are being readied for launch within days, if not hours."

"That evidence is not worth the minds that made it up," Pakistani Prime Minister Kahn responded from the exclusive Gadani Beach Resort near Karachi, where he was vacationing with his family. "Our nuclear test was to show the world that our nuclear capability is still very much alive, and we are serious when we say that we will counter Indian-American aggression with equal force. The mountains of lies and phony reports coming out of the White House are not helpful. The threats are not helpful. The United States is

consciously creating an atmosphere of fear and hatred between Pakistan and its neighbours, with the express purpose of making our region explode in conflict and then financially benefit from the chaos created. Their goal is to sell weapons to India and others, to attack and steal our natural resources, and to acquire cheap real estate, even Indian real estate, not just Pakistani. Mark my words, within a year, Americans will own half of Mumbai because of this so-called threat from Pakistan. It's all manufactured panic included in the profit calculations of American corporations poised to benefit from it all. This is about making money at the expense of our people. It's like we've gone back two hundred years and we're in colonial times once more, being exploited by the whites who expertly turn all of us in this region against each other so whites can benefit, at our expense, by making it easy to plunder our land and enslave us."

"Nonsense," replied Gupta from the Guava Garden. "The United States will defend its interests and assets wherever in the world they happen to be, and it will defend our sister nation of India from terrorist attacks. Every missile launched by Pakistan will be promptly destroyed and countered with overwhelming force. Operation Indian Eagle is now in full-alert mode to act and engage any terrorist activity coming out of Pakistan, no matter how small. In the meantime, the United States is actively engaged in the peaceful passage of refugees from conflict zones inside India to a safe haven in the United States."

Jennifer Patel: Right after the Pakistani nuclear detonation, there was a massive cyberattack that spread across India like a tidal wave, shorting every electrical connection and shutting down the country's electrical grid.

that's a lie. everyone knows it never happened. [ammo click]

Jennifer Patel: It was sudden, as if God had switched a master switch to shut down the whole country at once. All Indians were submerged in immediate suffering created by this.

false flag! the first such accusation came from someone in sweden, with u.s. thumbprints all over it. no cyberattack ever took place, period [monsoon wedded]

it was all about dying imperial powers grasping at straws, yet again. [pedro virgo]

not a single believable word coming out of so-called "indians on the ground" [jockey641]

all viral reports were spewing out of langley, written by trolls while sipping bubble tea [yaya mo]

don't be a technology moron. most indian phones were communicating directly with western media outlets, through the satellite shield. as long as their phones had battery power remaining. victims could continue to post. their suffering was real, created by the fucking pakis, and it was taking place in ALL of india. [molten marble]

yes, and though it was nighttime in delhi, all those photos of panicked pedestrians walking from their homes, all perfectly visible by streetlights, when there was supposed to be no power . . . false flag city, totally orchestrated by the united states to blame kahn [apache indian]

it took like only a day for media organizations to start netcasting elaborate reports, rich with data and detailed maps showing where the binary flips had been purposely triggered by paki intelligence forces from a hideaway in the karakoram, etc, etc. utter bullshit. [yaya mo]

> INFOPOST: SOURCE: Whole World-O-Pedia™:
> Karakoram: Mountain range partly in Pakistan, famous for harboring the center of operations of state-sponsored Pakistani terrorist organizations. Known as the Pakistani Aggression Command Center, or PACC, the hideout was first

made public by U.S. President Japleen Gupta during a press conference at which und wore somber colors to address the American people and the world from the White House's Guava Garden. "We have unassailable evidence," und began, "that Pakistan is behind this terrorist attack against the people of India and all the expatriate community that lives in wonderful India. It's too early to know how many millions will end up dying because of this vile military action coming from a neighbor whose avowed purpose is to sponsor terror from its PACC in Karakoram. I have thus ordered immediate, in-kind retaliation. American intelligence services are, as we speak, shutting down Pakistan's electrical grid, and we'll see how the Pakistani government likes it."

"Will that evidence be shared with the American public?" a reporter asked President Gupta. "The Keep America Honest Act requires the White House to come clean when planning to use force. Your own administration submitted this bill." President Gupta responded that there was no use of force in the retaliation und had ordered. "We are not sending troops with weapons anywhere," und added. "We're not bombing Pakistani targets, although they well deserve it. This is purely tit for tat. No congressional action is required. I'll take care of it with the powers clearly vested in me. Plus, this is a matter of national security, so the KAHA doesn't apply." With that, und left the Guava Garden while scores of reporters shouted additional questions that went unanswered. "Read my posts!" Gupta yelled as und reentered the White House.

Within the hour, posts relating to what was happening in Pakistan began to appear, but they were not nearly as descriptive as what had been coming out of India.

An official post from the White House stated: "The U.S. Government is now focusing its attention and resources on helping the people of India deal with the situation. American engineers and software analysts are in place in the region, bringing solar and wind power plants back online first,

providing electricity to the most critical institutions—banks,
airports, rail service, ports, telecommunications services,
water-treatment infrastructure, and hospitals. Portable solar
generators will keep the population's phones and cell towers
charged and in contact with the rest of the world via the
Global Satellite Shield. We will be able to witness the more
damning evidence, the devastation that this wanton attack on
India has engendered for its people. We will be able to see,
with our own eyes, the photos and videos uploaded by
millions of ordinary Indians as they show the world what
violence has been directed at them by a callous adversary
who doesn't care about the suffering of innocent people. The
United States is already doing everything it can to help
Indian refugees. As soon as electricity is restored and
systems are brought back online, persecuted Indians will
continue to board our American Freedom Fleet aircraft and
vessels to be brought to safety in America."

BREAKING: CongressUnd Rallan Perrypull has introduced "The Fair Marriage" bill, as promised during unda's campaign in the 3rd District of Johnson County. The bill calls for marriage quotas and puts teeth into the fight against lingering prejudice regarding who can get married in churches, mosques, temples, and other places of worship. The quotas listed in the legislation indicate that 25% of marriages officiated in tax-exempt institutions of worship must be of same-gender partners; 38.5% must be mixed-race couples; 12.8% of mixed religions; 7.9% with at least one of the two parties having a registered disability; and the remainder open to legacy conventional couples. If the institutions fail to meet these quotas for more than two consecutive years, their tax-exempt status will be rescinded, and they will begin to be taxed the same as Level 4 For-Profit Corporations—that is, the highest level of taxation, equivalent to what applies to sin businesses like tobacco and recreational-drug peddlers, manufacturers of sex toys and alcoholic beverages, and producers of respectful pornography.

this will immediately go to the supreme court, of course, and lose [rich soil 4 poppies] the founders and the bill of rights did not intend for religious freedom to mean the freedom to be bigoted. your worldview is disgusting to me [let ME tell U]

When you have to regulate everything, all citizens become criminals, and enforcement is impossible. Better have a free-for-all. [paul revere]

whats next—a bill to force marriage between pedophiles and children under ten? [cherry kola]

that's different [born tomorrow]

Miscegenation was "different" 100 years ago. It's all about what the culture will tolerate. Just a short decade ago, it was illegal for an adult to engage in sexual relations with a 12-year-old. Societies change, and it takes legislation to make people finally open their minds. [full of life]

that's not open-minded. it's disgusting. let children be children. [tuesday is best]

whatever. the scotus will take care of this marriage quota bullshit. unconstitutional! [rich soil 4 poppies]

Jennifer Patel: I remember it vividly . . . the Singularity of Dharma.

Teddy Comstock: That's what the journey of so many Indians to America was called.

Jennifer Patel: Yes. It's all in my book, as taught in schools from fifth grade on. The Singularity of Dharma was a large undertaking. After the Pakistani attacks, President Gupta sent a fleet of aging Dreamliners to fetch us refugees. These planes were part of the American Freedom Fleet, which included aircraft as well as aircraft carriers and merchant ships.

prez gupt owned shares in boeing, setting up zero-interest federal loans to lease hundreds of ancient dreamliners with a capacity of around 350 passengers each. the planes were run as "the india express" charter airline, back and forth from delhi or mumbai and america's newer, larger airports in the hinterland. and guess who owned shares in that? [manni knows]

they ran old a380s, too, with sardine-like space for 800 immigrants a flight. [mindanao bubble boi]

dreamliner sounds better for her fabricated story, though. [Life is a typo]

Jennifer Patel: Settling the refugees from the inside of the country out towards the coasts was the American government's brilliant plan. Start in Kansas and spread out towards New York and California. Each plane brought a new community that started and was joined by additional arrivals of New Americans. Everything was very peaceful. The only act of violence in the migration was a mechanical malfunction that two of the Dreamliners suffered, killing several hundred passengers. That was towards the end of the mass migration, however, when the press started to dub the planes "the Ford Pintos of the airline industry," in reference to some forgotten car model made by a now bankrupted auto company acquired by Tata Motors. The Dreamliners also suffered from severe design faults that caused Boeing to abandon the manufacturing of commercial aircraft for the much more profitable development of weapons systems, but that's a topic for another book.

more bullshit from her bullshit factory. there were actually SEVEN dreamliners and airbuses that crashed, killing thousands of passengers in a matter of weeks. "one thing is to have military snafus," an ntsb official was reported as saying at the time, "but you don't fuck with civilians!" no one gave a shit, of course. "it's just indians," a reporter added. [manni knows]

sources, please [gardamon handbook]

the lying media did not report it. the ntsb buried the evidence and then made it disappear. do your own research. there's the memory hole rescue network to start with. [manni knows]

Jennifer Patel: My parents had packed two small suitcases under the beam of a flashlight in the middle of the night. "This is the call, Indira," my father said. Everyone in my family called me Indira then. "We're moving to America," he added. For several months, while India had been trading threats with Pakistan, rumors floated that if anything bad happened, America would step up and help refugees migrate to safety. Indians had been encouraged to register their travel documents and have an evacuation plan ready for every member of their immediate families. I had heard my parents discussing it, and they had told me to choose one toy and one book to take with me when the time came. Only one change of clothes, as well, that I would not get to wear until we arrived safely in the United States, after a very long journey.

my word! pass the kleenex! [mission creep]

is she serious? [lady ray]

it's all in her book [mother sandwich]

doesn't make any of it real [englander15]

the whole migration thing was staged. as it was taking place, posters on the net kept crying "false flag" all over, but no one was listening. [TalonAnvil]

yes. mumbai was a busy port, they said, receiving a steady stream of refugees fleeing even from kerala and as far as west bengal, manipur, and other locations. [manni knows]

they arrived by train to board the american freedom fleet in mumbai. the shitty aircraft and ships were already there, waiting, diverted from their regular duty patrolling the arabian sea and indian ocean. [TalonAnvil]

the aircraft carriers, for sure, came and went nonstop, like a regular ferry service to america. the dreamliners couldn't keep up, so it was the carriers that transported the bulk of the so-called refugees.

operation indian eagle, with the dreamliners, was always a minor element, so jenni patel doesn't know what she's talking about, and her book is shit. [manni knows]

Let Me Win This Johnson: So, you're proposing to keep our borders wide open until we suffocate with Indians? Because they're still coming in droves, you know, decades after the staged Pakistani attack. I'll tell you what human nature is. It is looking after one's own people and resources, particularly if those resources are becoming scarce because hordes of migrants are arriving from far away to take our food away from us. The migrants become our enemies, and we'll have to kill them, if that's necessary, for us to be able to eat.

Teddy Comstock: Mr. Johnson, no need to become melodramatic. There's enough food for everyone, and inciting violence against others is, frankly, not acceptable in a political debate.

Let Me Win This Johnson: No one's inciting anything. She brought up human nature. To fight for survival is just as human as to migrate. That's what migration is all about, isn't it? Survival. So, when too many humans pack into one corner of the world, to the point where it isn't possible to live well anymore, it's survival of the fittest. You can't get more human than that.

Vikram Bhama: I think we're getting away from the topic of the economy, which is what voters really want to hear about. It's the economy, idiot! You've had your say about immigration, Mr. Johnson. We all know what you think about the topic.

Let Me Win This Johnson: The PUBLIC doesn't know. It needs to be debated, in PUBLIC.

Vikram Bhama: But we're talking about the economy now. Monetary and fiscal policy, interest rates, money supply. Let's give the humanitarian humans of humanity a chance to rest, and let's talk economic theory instead.

PUBLIC SERVICE ANNOUNCEMENT: For the millions of

Americans who have suffered for years with testicular chafing, now there is hope. If your body has testicles, it's a matter of time before you start suffering from this terrible condition—if you haven't experienced it already. Velvet Slide Ointment™ was developed by the Federal Health Department Corporation™ to bring peace of mind to sufferers of testicular chafing. Velvet Slide Ointment™, the difference between sanity and a downward spiral to crotch-discomfort hell.

Jennifer Patel: The economy is helped by new arrivals. My story is a true example of successful economic development for America. Large numbers of refugees have populated what was once rural wasteland in the middle of the continent, the American hinterland that was said to be starving for a new infusion of humanity, since all its young people had been leaving rural America to favor urban centers along the East and West Coasts. In many cases, Indian refugees came with their advanced degrees—engineers, lawyers, doctors—and set up shop in small-town, Main Street America. That's what it's all about. So, getting back to my long journey, my family left our house at around three in the morning. Other families in the neighborhood were doing the same, but no one talked to each other. Under those conditions, everyone became a competitor. If the United States did not provide enough transportation to easily accommodate everyone registered to come here, there might be violent mobs at the ports, train stations, bus depots, and airports—families having to fight each other to get a seat to America.

is this still her non-fiction book? [BonkersDelinquent]

beginning to sound like a trashy novel. "in a world . . ." [frisky andrade]

you can tell she didnt write that book. her political handlers did [mercator909]

this is the performance she needs to get those votes in [northern larder]

BREAKING: A Memphis resident has been incarcerated and given a two-year sentence for refusing to declaim the New Pledge of Allegiance. Details at Ten EST.

Jennifer Patel: Some emergency lights were on along the streets leading to the highway. I could see the quiet crowd walking with me in the same direction. All vehicles had been disabled somehow, though we occasionally saw one moving past the crowds, "How come . . . ?" I started to ask my father. "It's of their own design, Indira," he replied. "Don't talk. Conserve your energy. We have a long walk." On foot, the airport was about four and a half hours away, he said. There would be daylight when we arrived, and several planes would be waiting for the tens of thousands of travelers streaming to the terminal. My father had paid extra, he said, to allow our family to use the new east entrance to the airport, where there would be a VIP checkpoint that was designed to expedite entry to the concourse.

elitist! [Sousa Cracker]

bringing that good old indian corruption to the new world, i see [poli-sci fiend]

VIP. Very Indian Politician [jamie kahn]

Jennifer Patel: I worried that my younger brother might get tired long before our arrival at the checkpoint, that he would delay the family enough to make us miss our flight. Some other family would take our seats. That would be a tragedy. Plenty of people wanted to make it to America, my father said.

every time she mentions her father, my gag reflex kicks in [kansas city pimpress]

with you, sis. phony boloney adulation of men. [ama royalle]

Jennifer Patel: When my little brother began to complain, my father sat him on the top of one of the suitcases and wheeled him on. The adults had thought of everything. I was excited that my family had been selected to migrate to America. At the dining table, we had discussed the trip for months, even before the nuclear threats from next door. "But don't tell anyone about it," my father warned. "This is just for us to know. It's not clear how many people have registered and how the whole process will work. When I registered, I was warned not to discuss it with anyone, to keep it to ourselves."

this doesn't make sense. if it really took place before the paki threats, how did they qualify as refugees? [ex azteca]

you forget they're vee eye peas who have their own refugee program to siphon talent and capital out of india and into america. long-standing program with these brahmin. also to the uk. [floored mariachi]

Jennifer Patel: My father had selected, as our destination, what was called "The Middle Region," but no one knew the exact state or city the label referred to. I had read as much as I could about all the potential destinations in that vast vertical swath of Middle America. I had virtually walked the streets of Des Moines and St. Louis on WhereONearthSmyPlace™, turning around to see all the houses in the neighborhoods where I imagined my family would take up residence. Maybe that house with the flowery bushes next to the entrance? Maybe that rancher with the green shutters? It wasn't far from the neighborhood's school, and I measured and timed the walk to school from that house as I virtually walked the streets, crossing Primrose Place, turning left on Howard Street, and finishing on the long, wide crosswalk on Independence Avenue that faced the school's parking lot.

oh, so sweet [barcelona44]

quintessential americana [ready2ride]

rag to riches [lysby33]

vote for me. wasn't born here, but the new constitution lets me be your prez anyway. [chelsea soap]

Jennifer Patel: Or what if our family ended up in that state called

Indiana? Wouldn't that be a funny thing to tell our relatives back in India? "Here we are, Indians from India living in Indiana!"

plagiarized that from an existing organization. no way she thought of it as a small girl. what a phony. [Vikram Rolando]

Jennifer Patel: On the maps online, I found a small town called Noblesville. I imagined the inside of the school there. My classroom would be the third one on the right, close to the entrance. A line of legacy lockers faced the door, which was green. The chairs for the students were not legacy at all. They were round and turned 360 degrees, and as I turned in one of them, a small desk opened from within it, like magic, with a charging station and a built-in digital portal. The cafeteria was huge, enough to accommodate three hundred students. I was looking forward to eating in a place like that—ordering Freedom Fries and hamburgers, pizza, buckets of chicken nuggets and American apple pie and other delicious things that American students got to eat daily. I would be a proud American when I got to my new home. My father had said that, as refugees, it would take no time to get my American documents, a new passport, national ID card, and be like everyone else in my school. I'd be welcomed with open arms in my neighborhood. Everyone would want to be my friend. Indians were appreciated in the United States, he said. They even had an Indian president there, the ultimate symbol of power and proof that a young girl—even if her. . ., if unda's parents were poor immigrants—could get to be the Commandress in Chief of the second most powerful army in the world.

ha! pile it on, jenni pee! [lanyard addict]

i don't remember anyone waiting for indians with open arms, do you? [LudwigVonMissus]

once that warmongering loony seized power, all bets were off [rhada skolar]

who u talking about? [filipa14]

gupta, of course [rhada skolar]

jenni's the same, a laughing hyena in a sheep's tuxedo
[soupaWhimp]

Jennifer Patel: Glimmers of light appeared in the horizon, and I was
able to see better—those who walked along with me and my family.
I knew some of them, from the same neighborhood and school. The
one thing all of us had in common was the set of only two small
suitcases. Any family that wanted to go to America, my father said,
needed to follow that rule. Only two small suitcases per family.
"They don't want us to take any unnecessary items to the United
States," he said. Our new country had everything we would need,
and the United States government would give it to us for free
because we were refugees. "And it's not a handout," my father
added. "We Indians are proud people. While we may be in need
now, accepting their help, we will work hard in the future to pay
them back their kindness, pay American taxes, and become loyal
citizens to advance their democracy and freedom, far away from the
threat of Pakistan and terrorism."

Let Me Win This Johnson: That's enough! This syrupy shit is getting
out of hand!

Teddy Comstock: You will soon get your chance to tell YOUR
story, Mr. Johnson.

Let Me Win This Johnson: It's already been told! People obsessing
about my having changed my name, and no one's questioning HER
shameful sleight of hand from Indira to Jenni!

Jennifer Patel: America had not been the target of a Paki terrorist
attack, ever, at the time. All Indians would be safe here, and that was
why President Gupta had so generously invited me, INDIRA, and
people like my family to join unda in America, land of the brave,
land of the free, land of enormous buckets of chicken nuggets at
every school lunch. I couldn't wait to be here!

let the mexican speak now! enough of this indian chick. [peruvian king]

stop being disrespectful towards our future president. she will win. [chandra alvassi]

No doubt about that. She has what it takes. Go, Jenni! [ORC in waiting]

Jennifer Patel: We could see the airport at a distance. There was the roar of airplanes taking off, like birds calling our attention to their song. And when I looked up at them, I noticed their navigation lights blinking. I imagined those lights were speaking a language, saying goodbye to India and all Indians.

yeah, and the airport had lights, too, while all of india was sunk in a dark nuclear winter. [moribundus]

they had generators [bourbon shot]

just for them, of course [Alex Cha]

Jennifer Patel: Everything was so well organized, even the approach of tens of thousands of people, on foot—a wave of humanity covering the width of the highway reaching the airport. There were hundreds of men, all wearing green and white "Air Passage to America" vests, directing the arriving crowds. "Only registered refugees this way," one of them said through a bullhorn. "If you are not registered and have no QR code to show the authorities, move to your right, please, to the parking lot next to the processing center. You must at least have your national identity card." I noticed that very few people around me were moving to their right. My group was prepared, holding the coded stickers in our hands or glued to our chests. One baby was wearing the code on unda's forehead!

aww, soooooooo cute! you notice how she so expertly adds a cute comment every few sentences? someone must be collecting them for a new book to hawk once she's in office. [Thinking Neanderthal]

being cute isn't an option when your face is out of whack [Lucy

Hierro]

Jennifer Patel: "No need to rush," another bullhorn announced. "There are plenty of planes waiting, and more will arrive as they return from America for more refugees. Keep a steady pace and don't push anybody." Then, another plane took off with a roar. I could see it clearly now, with the morning light. Large white and green stripes on it, with the letters "APtA" painted on them in bright orange. I had heard that each plane could carry eight-hundred refugees, with hundreds of flights taking off every week, all over India, until all refugees were saved from Pakistani aggression. The American Navy would be carrying many more from Indian ports. "Soon, there will be so many Indians in America," my father said, "that no one will dare discriminate against us. Racists will be outnumbered and made irrelevant!"

we still HERE, bitch! and, outnumbered and all, NOT irrelevant! [roll-a-stomp]

larger numbers dont mean indians can beat us. most of their men are engineers and doctors n shit, not willing to fight [telewisher]

yeah. one real american worth ten of em [Payne Garrhaloon]

a hundred. i'm not worried. [Pollo Frito]

bunch of racists, y'all. shut the fuck up and listen to our next prez! [gargler50]

BREAKING: Dr. Gary Forsahann, known for "Man Protector™," his ubiquitous video-stream show, has released his latest study. It reveals, in his words, "a massive conspiracy to effeminatize all males of the species, worldwide!" He accuses the seven corporations that control most of the planet's food supply of "secretly lacing the human diet with female-hormone mimickers that silently lower testosterone level in males, essentially castrating us all." The estrogen mimics, he adds, are everywhere, not just in foods. "Plastics are the main culprit," he says. "Toilet paper, shampoos, the U.S. water supply. It's all a grand plan to take away our masculinity!

Your days as a real man are numbered if you don't start your testosterone-recovery therapy today. Inform yourself, and learn how to be a man again, before they complete the process and turn you into a eunuch!" The doctor's treatment is vegan, gluten free, GMO free, free-range, fat free, humane, 100% organic, sugar free, low sodium, and BPA free. Check out Dr. Forsahann's testosterone-recovery protocol today! Whisper "Forsahann to Stay a Man™" to your listening device. Bot order-takers are standing by. Financing most manly available!

YOU MUST KNOW: 20 doctors tried our MentholSky SafeMind Enhancer™ for a week. Here's their surprising reaction!

Jennifer Patel: The crowd was quiet as it reached a funnel that forced people into a single line, like at the finish chute of a 5K race. I imagined my QR code was my running number. Indira Patel, arriving fourth in her age group, worthy of a medal. "Make sure your QR code is visible to the scanners," they said. "You want to walk slowly under the facial-recognition camera and code reader for verification. If your code does not match your face, you will be pulled aside for additional verification. If that's the case, move quickly so as not to disturb the flow." That's what I remember them saying. The message was clear. Not just anyone could go to America. The scanners had to be able to read your face.

and YOU, read my lips—go back to where you came from! [NoPatelsHere]

she's a legitimate candidate [Morena Maderios]

not in MY constitution, the one they trashed to allow this travesty. if you're not born here, you shouldn't be allowed to become president. period. [soylent puke]

Why not? What's so special about being born here? We're all here, breathing the same air, buying food from the same supply chain. Get over it. Your place of birth doesn't mean shit in our quest to serve humanity. [analeeze severo] my lord [98.7% Chimp]

Jennifer Patel: As I neared the small tent with the blinking red lights, I could hear beeps, one after another. It was also like a bird's song, coming from a flock of birds, all busy chirping away as people advanced. Occasionally, there was a different sound, and I saw that one or more people were moved out of the tent to the side instead of the front. I understood that they were the unlucky ones, and that everyone in my family needed to get a normal beep to be able to board one of those planes to America.

Teddy Comstock: Go on. This is fascinating!

sellout! this whole thing is rigged. [sour grapes 20]

has anyone noticed he hasn't gone into commercial mode for a while? [texas hottie]

no need for ad revenue when jenni's party is footing the bill. [purple smith]

Jennifer Patel: I was only ten meters from the tent now. Another plane took off with a deafening roar, like a rocket being launched to America. I imagined myself inside it, like Sunita Pandya, wearing my all-white astronaut suit, as white as the tent with the glowing red lights that I was approaching.

suspense! [bananero227]

plot point! will her family make it? [earth capo]

don't miss the next episode of "presidential freak fantasy" [Mussy Sim]

BREAKING: Today's list of celebrities that have announced their New Beginnings™: Rapper TKO33, singer Ashamasha, actor Le Barghanni, Senator L. P. LaGrand, "Pimp My Profession" contestant Rizzio Samuels, vlogger Gardenia, ScreenTuber™ Farci Cummins, chef Ro Lambdatta, and gold-medalist Barkley Lestermaker. Starting

Monday, they will initiate their hormone protocols to transition to their true genders! Join us at New Beginnings™ tonight for a sneak peek! #NewGendNewBeginnings

Jennifer Patel: My whole family was beeped through in seconds! We were on the other side and on our way to the terminal. The sign of relief on everyone's face was evident. We were now true, registered refugees, and everything was going smoothly. America had approved our boarding of an APtA Dreamliner. "It's like a dream," I thought. Dreamers dreaming on a Dreamliner! I love language and playing with words. Indians from India living in Indiana, I repeated to myself. That was SOOOO beautiful, and it made me smile.

Awwww, Jenni. Me, too! Indians from India Inundating Indiana. [kienSabe]

Polished Polish Porcelain™ [last_minute bot]

cut her off, comstock! [Mr.Suzanne he/she/it/they]

go elsewhere if you don't like her. it's her turn to speak! [sabrosa31]

ja, ja, ja! ya calla, canalla [loca locavore]

mark my words, you're gonna eat yours [PoisonedIvy]

Jennifer Patel: As we boarded the plane, we were told to go all the way to the back, take the farthest seats that were not occupied, and put away our two small suitcases in the overhead compartment. "Move along," someone in a military uniform instructed the passengers. "Seats are not assigned, so you move all the way to the back and quickly get out of the way of the passengers coming right behind you. Sit down quietly and cooperate so we can take off as soon as possible." The cabin was like something I had never seen— huge, like an endless bus that kept on going and going towards the back. My father indicated where I should sit, and I waited anxiously for the plane to fill up so it could take off and I could experience my first flight and being in the air, like a bird. The small screen in front of me was broken and dark, but the one to my right was playing a movie with my favorite Bollywood actors. No one in my family had earphones, however, so I couldn't connect to any of the screens to hear the songs.

that's the evidence right there. still clinging to bollywood, with no desire to embrace american culture [All-n-all4u]

don't be daft. bollywood produced way more movies than hollywood back then, just like today. only difference is bollywood movies are now made by indians in hollywood. how's that for a twist? [Yang O]

Jennifer Patel: "As soon as we're in the air and at cruising altitude," a voice said over the plane's loudspeakers, "we will be offering beverages to all passengers. This is a very long flight," the voice added, "so we highly recommend you have a Kool Bar NightCap™. It's a non-alcoholic drink that will let you enjoy a long nap so you can wake up refreshed just before we land in Kansas City." Oh! I looked up at my father. "Is that where we're going?" He shrugged and said, "I guess. They told me our destination would be announced once we were on the plane."

kansas city. oh, jenni, what a disappointment! [redpilled afrodiziac]

sorry you didn't get depuke [SourDog]

i'm from depue. don't knock it [eddieIzzard's ghost]

Jennifer Patel: Our phones still didn't have a signal, so I couldn't search Kansas City and learn more about it. But I knew, in my heart, that it wouldn't be far from Indiana. Maybe once there, we could take a train, or borrow bicycles, or even walk to reach the place I really wanted. Although my father insisted, "Any place they take us to will be fine. The important thing right now is to find work quickly and become productive citizens so you can go to a good school and continue your education without interruption. You will then be able to go to any of the best universities in the country once you graduate high school. That's what matters. Where they take us now is not important."

whole life planned for her, i see [lensee3]

future career, future husband, number of children [homoErected]

nonsense. her father never could have imagined she'd be president one day [existentialist bard]

right, because she wasn't born here, and he knew you couldn't be president if you weren't a real american [soylent puke]

43rd amendment made it possible. part of our new constitution, so there [sabrosa31]

subversive foreigners responsible for that fucking amendment and many others that should have never seen the light of day. letting her come here and pretend she can be president. [marcoPoloPlayer]

two-thirds ratified. what don't you understand about that? [sabrosa31]

two-thirds wrong [Kuro Banda]

Jennifer Patel: The men and women in military uniform walked along the aisles, making sure everyone had their seatbelt fastened. I noticed their uniforms were a different shade of olive green from the ones worn by soldiers in India, and I was certain these soldiers were not Indian. But they didn't look American, either. Not one of them was white or blond. They looked more like Indians who weren't Indian.

yup. occupiers. mercenaries suckling on uncle sam's financial titties. [Bertie DeCappo]

racist jenni judging people by their skin color [fortranPro]

Jennifer Patel: I was distracted with that thought about the strangeness of the soldiers when the plane began to move. There was a cheer from all the passengers. Outside, the sun was already out, so I couldn't tell whether power had been restored to the city. But, either way, I was glad to be leaving. Everyone on the plane seemed equally glad to move on to new lives.

BREAKING: Leaked conversation between terrorists planning to attack America. Stay tuned for the transcript—coming soon. Terrorists in Karachi threatening Americans. Don't miss it!

Jennifer Patel: As the plane taxied slowly towards the runway, announcements continued to play on the loudspeakers. "This is your Capitán Pedro Barrios speaking. Welcome to this special APtA flight. We will be departing just as soon as given permission by the control tower. I'd like to reassure you that although this aircraft is old and does not look in good shape or very clean inside, it has long seen service mobilizing American troops to conflict zones around the world. Its engines and fuel-storage capacity have been refurbished and modified to allow for longer-range flights such as this one. We can reach any point in the United States from here, and as one of our cabin personnel has indicated, we are headed to Kansas City, the Heart of America, where everyone will welcome you with open arms and the biggest hearts at the Hallmark Visitors Center. To make these flights possible and be able to turn around planes to carry the maximum number of refugees in the least number of weeks, we have had to cut our in-cabin services to the bare minimum. No food will be served throughout the flight. Despite what you see on your screens, the entertainment system is not working, so this will feel like a very long, boring flight, especially for the children on board. For this reason, I urge everyone to take the Kool Bar NightCap™ that our cabin crew will be offering soon. It's a delicious beverage that will allow you to enjoy the flight and dream all the way to America. If I didn't have to command this aircraft, I'd love to have one myself, to tell you the truth. But YOU can. So, on behalf of all of us at Air Passage to America, enjoy your flight." A few minutes later, the plane began to move faster, and I felt my body being pushed back against my seat, and butterflies in my stomach. I tried to see out the windows, but others were doing the same and blocking my view. The whole airplane was shaking like a bus going uphill on a dirt road near my cousin's farm in India. The shaking went on forever, and the plane still didn't seem to be in the air. "How long is this airport?" I asked my father, but his eyes were closed. He seemed to be lost in prayer. Finally, my stomach and the comments from other passengers told me the plane was in the air. All sorts of mechanical noises under our feet made the plane shake even more. I looked around for confirmation that this was normal. My mother also seemed to be praying, but most of the passengers were happily chatting and enjoying themselves. "Next time those tyres touch the earth," one of them said, "it will be American soil they'll be soiling, halfway across the world!"

Let Me Win This Johnson: This is supposed to be a debate, not a reading of "Stomping on India," or whatever her book's title is.

Teddy Comstock: This is not a debate, Mr. Johnson. It is a Get to Meet the Candidates™, and we're learning about Jennifer Patel's wonderful and productive life here.

Let Me Win This Johnson: Well, you're clearly biased, because we're only learning about HER fairytale life.

. . . Switching platform to ArchivePedia™ . . . The New Akashic Records™

Jennifer Patel's "A Passage from India" - Excerpts.

> *Thousands of similar flights followed in the coming months, not only by APtA but also by Air IndiAmerica™. "This is a humanitarian crisis," brave President Japleen Gupta kept on repeating at press conferences every evening from the Guava Garden, even in winter, from inside a heated tent. "We must act with swift determination and apply the values that have made America the greatest country in the world," und added. "We're a nation of immigrants, and our Founding Persons embedded the notion of our duty to save humanity in our*

Declaration of Independence and Constitution. America moves forward in service to undKind!"

Not everyone agreed. Despite a major effort by the U.S. military to keep the processing of new arrivals running smoothly, the situation in many ports of entry was chaotic. Housing was one of the main problems. "We are creating hundreds of thousands of jobs in the home-construction industry," President Gupta reported. "This is a huge boon to our economy. Unemployment is down to zero percent, something not seen in ANY world economy! We're also keeping down inflation by applying the correct fiscal and monetary policies. Even the refugees themselves are getting jobs just as soon as they arrive. This is a win-win-win for everyone! Made in America!"

The new American citizens numbered in the hundreds of millions at this point, and there was no clear indication that the flights, or the full aircraft carriers, for that matter, would stop operating anytime soon. In the hinterland, near the new airports that acted as processing bureaus nicknamed "Ellis Centers," vast tent cities were set up—row after row of temporary housing built of rugged white canvas, to be heated in winter and air conditioned in summer, with communal baths located in the middle of every block of fifty tents or so. "It's not an ideal situation," the President said, "but our refugees understand this is the price they have to pay for freedom, and to be orderly incorporated into the fabric of our nation."

It's clear we Indian immigrants have made America a much better place. Our arrival nipped the #iCanDoBetter movement in the bud! [Lulu Acharya]

indian traditional values saved marriage and saved america from its 93.8% divorce rate. [stevie purohit]

and saved us from our legacy politicians' daily acts of monumental hypocrisy [boom boom mehta]

LIVE TRANSCRIPT: The Teddy Comstock Show. Join Teddy in a new edition of "Our Finest Hour," where you get to know the candidates while Teddy has a lively conversation with them. Today, candidates from The American Hindu Party, the AHP.

Teddy Comstock: We have a caller. Go ahead, caller.

Caller #1: Ms. Jennifer likes to love the immigrant, because she is one herself. What about us, native-born Americans? This immigration fiasco, perpetrated by a former president, was clearly a plot against America. Pure false flag. An invasion orchestrated by our turncoat so-called former president and . . .

Teddy Comstock: Sounds like the caller has indigestion, not the typical listener of "Our Finest Hour." Let's go to Caller Number Two!

Caller #2: I'm not a racist, but it would help to hear the candidates' opinions about why they think America should have helped so many immigrants. Why didn't we help them solve their problems with Pakistan OVER THERE, instead of bringing them here to replace us white Americans, to make us even more of a minority than we already were?

Teddy Comstock: I hear you. In a little under a year, Americans saw schools overwhelmed, shopping malls filled to capacity, horrendous traffic—even in small towns in South Dakota. But you must understand, the end result has been fantastic! A much stronger economy with a much younger demographic that will be supporting our Social Security infrastructure by paying into the system while YOU enjoy the fruits of your retirement.

Caller #2: I'm not enjoying anything. Immigrants were given trillions of dollars' worth of digital food stamps, which allowed the newly arrived Indians to purchase anything they wanted, for free, online or anywhere, with OUR tax dollars, while the rest of us law-abiding citizens were left to struggle with our miserable incomes, having to compete with the Indians for the few crappy jobs that remained and paid pauper wages.

Teddy Comstock: I don't know what country you are calling from, Caller Number Two, but what you are describing is not America. We are the most prosperous nation in the world, with the strongest economy, the most powerful military, and a population so diverse, we are the envy of every country on the planet. Caller Number Three!

Caller #3: I agree with the previous caller. This must stop, not only be stopped, but reversed. Come Election Day, I want to see more candidates like Howard Belt, who's promising to send all these people back to India just as soon as he's inaugurated, by force if . . .

Teddy Comstock: Caller Number Four! Don't know what's going on. My staff is not screening these properly.

Caller #4: These people are not worthy of living in America. They're not smart. The federal government is hiding or doctoring the results of the IQ tests they are given on arrival. The medical tests, too. All sorts of diseases are being brought to us courtesy of new arrivals joining the old arrivals in a never-ending chain migration. It's a disgrace.

Teddy Comstock: Caller Number Five!

Caller #5: I don't think we TRUE Americans should sit and watch our country being invaded like this, being lied to by our government with the false-flag-humanitarian-crisis narrative of long ago, being used again under a different name. There was and there is NO crisis. This was manufactured in the mind of our former Hindu nationalist Indian-in-Chief in the White House. And now, they want to get another one in there!

sounds like call screeners will get the boot today! [gateway to pleasure] probably all hindus. plenty out there to replace them. [marvelous comic]

this was all a chinese plot—opening america's doors to hundreds of millions of indians while they allowed no foreign devils to enter china. [chica_loca22]

so we're fucked, while the chinese keep on reaping their profits. [niko francoise]

Teddy Comstock: We'll pause for a word from our sponsor and be right back!

PUBLICITY: America is in danger of a multi-faceted civil war! Join Bigot Spotters™ by sending your donation NOW! Join our large group of demonstrators next Tuesday, as we walk the streets of Washington DC bigot-spotting the bigots who give this country a bad name. We'll start at the Georgetown mansion of Barney "Divide and Conquer" Curicom, the legislator behind the bill that aims to add 571 (and counting) new citizen classifications to the census form. If the bill passes and becomes law, Curicom will have "possum wedders" in his pocket! Help Bigot Spotters™ stop him! Donate!

Teddy Comstock: Let's try our luck with Caller Number Six.

Caller #6: I am candidate Hipolito Warmer and have been unfairly kept from participating in presidential debates.

Teddy Comstock: OK, Mr. Warmer. No, you can't...

Caller #6: I am campaigning FOR war, unapologetic about destroying the enemy and all other assholes who hate America.

Teddy Comstock: OK. Caller Number Seven!

Caller #7: Yes. Thanks for taking my call. My name is Ravi Patel. I'm from India and a proud American. Indian-Americans who have been living in America a long time, we're engineers, doctors, educated people. But, I tell you, these additional waves coming now, it's just encouraging the Indian government to empty its jails and send us the filth that was living in them.

Let Me Win This Johnson: Well, Comstock, sounds like most of your listeners agree with me.

Teddy Comstock: Caller Number Eight!

Caller #8: Kudos to the previous caller. He gets it. If I moved to China for better job opportunities, I wouldn't want all the American riffraff to follow me there and make the Chinese resent me. That's what our current administration doesn't get. So, we had the insane waves of refugees arriving and settling in America, back when Jenni was a child. Fine. It doesn't mean we have to continue now. There's a limit to how many foreigners you can force on a country. That limit was reached a long, long time ago with Indians. What is Washington thinking? That we are going to just sit here and take it? I reserve the right, as a proud member of the N.R.A. and W.O.W., to defend myself and my family from this invasion, and damn what our leaders say. In my opinion, all candidates have disqualified themselves on this topic alone. Damn Congress, too. We the People are not allowing another Hindu cunt in OUR White House!

Teddy Comstock: Wait, wait, wait. Let me interrupt here to remind everyone that we don't use offensive language on this WideWorldCast™. We're walking a very fine line here and don't need to give those who disagree with us the opportunity to call Our Finest Hour™ a racist, white-supremacist show. Let me also remind you that the Banish All Racism Act makes it illegal for us to use such language, or any kind of racial slur, to target any member of society—be it refugee, immigrant, or native-born. We can make our cases calmly, using intellectual reasoning instead of profanity.

Jennifer Patel: The fact is, with the situation the country is already in, there's no doubt in my mind that the next election is ours to win. We'll get the right people elected to Congress, to state legislatures, to the White House, and literally CLEAN HOUSE!

Charlie Singh: It will be one executive order after another, setting things right once and for all. It may take a few years to restore America, OUR America, but it WILL happen!

Teddy Comstock: And with that thought, I'll leave you until our next WideWorldCast™. I'm Teddy Comstock, and remember: Aquamente™ makes you feel like you have three times the volume of hair. I highly recommend it—Aquamente™'s Persimmon-Tamarind Shampoo, for men, women, and others. Good night, and God bless the United States of America.

BREAKING: A date will be announced tomorrow for the sentencing of the so-called "Fab Five," the five teenagers accused of hate crimes for listening to songs by the banned Beatles catalog. The Incitement to Hate Crimes Act, made the law of the land four and a half years ago, clearly states that "the consumption of any material—in public or in private—of a physical or digital nature, artistic or otherwise, that has had any association with groups or individuals who have been found to engage in activities deemed to be friendly to hate crimes, will be guilty of a felony with a mandatory jail sentence of at least five years and $64,000+ dollars in fines." The so-called Fab Five face jail time for listening to songs by the old and discredited British band, whose members have all died but are considered crypto antisemites. At the height of their fame nearly a century ago, John Lennon, one of the band's members, was known to refer to their manager, a mild-mannered Jewish businessman, as a "rich fag Jew." Also, songs by the band titled Walrus, Piggies, etc.—when analyzed by academic experts—were found to have lyrics that clearly fit the definition of hate speech. As the U.S. Secretary of Artistic Output & Influences stated after the announcement of the Fab Five trial, "These Hitler Youths will simply have to listen to some other type of music, won't they? Banned groups and musicians are banned for a reason. My department will not tolerate our young citizens being exposed to filthy, indecent, hateful, and hurtful material."

. . . iRiver Network™

Tonight at 21:07 GMT, in about eight minutes, join The Virtual Collective to impeach Igor Ivmochenko, CEO of Alma Systems in Moscow, one of the largest manufacturers of LS2 bombs and war-related laser positioning systems. [The Virtual Collective]

> *INFOPOST: SOURCE: TodoPedia Complete™: The Virtual Collective: A shadowy network of anti-war activists whose unofficial motto is "Pacifying Warmongers by the Dozen." Not much is known about the group or how it operates. Their communication channels are built by decentralized blockchains that randomly post their messages to the iRiver Network™, MeSez Network™, EavesDrop™, and VoxPopuli Stream™, plus other less-used social grids like the Open Social Ether™, also known as The OSE and created by the Collective itself. It also goes by the name "Virtual Gandhi."*

. . . Switching Platforms to The Open Social Ether™

Ivmochenko countdown. [Virtual Gandhi]

yeah. gandhi that motherfucker already! [dickkie roberts]

this is a peaceful undertaking, yaar [Cosmic Dharma]

pacifying warmongers by the thousands! [linterna oscura]

shut up already and VISUALIZE [anatoli vermusen]

If you haven't participated in a Virtual Gandhi event before, here are the instructions: Sit comfortably in a quiet room, stabilize your breathing, and close your eyes. Then, visualize roadblocks placed inside the entity known as Igor Ivmochenko, CEO of Alma Systems in Moscow. The goal is NOT to kill the individual we are focusing on. We have no right to end a life we didn't create. But we can stop and block the paths that enable the individual to cause human suffering and end the lives of others. [The Virtual Collective]

this is just hippie nonsense [successful transhuman]

pure propaganda [676_billyBob]

this idea that human beings can come together in thought and have any kind of power to remotely direct an event or produce an outcome, ha! [decollettuce]

you don't know what you're talking about. there is a precedent for this kind of activity, and with the number of people participating now in the millions, we are starting to see a pattern. several warmongers have already been incapacitated and removed from their influential and powerful posts. those who dare replace them have been warned that the same fate awaits them. [mere observer]

It may seem like a miracle, but it's all done through the pineal gland, which connects all humans. It's undeniable that a collective can harness the power to influence an individual without the need to be in the presence of that person, and without lifting a finger. In fact, the quieter each participant is—immersed in a trance of meditation, focusing on the task at hand to affect change in the target entity—the better. [Melody Depender]

You can now switch your devices to Lecture Mode so you can hear the following passage read to you, while you keep your eyes closed. Take a deep breath and visualize the passage of liquids through a twisted network of very thin tubes. [The Virtual Collective]

hello from brighton, england! we have 34 participants gandhing here! [maarita roy]

Visualize those very thin tubes getting tired, narrowing their passages, and restricting the flow of that liquid. [The Virtual Collective]

. . . Switching Platforms to the iRiver Network™

> *INFOPOST: SOURCE: TodoPedia Complete™: Virtual Gandhi: Name given to the process advocated by* <u>The Virtual Collective</u>*. Early in the development of the process, the Collective informed the world of how "everyone's mind has been controlled and dimmed for generations." The pineal gland, the Collective claims, is in fact an antenna, designed to allow the human brain to connect to the ether and*

communicate mentally with other sentient beings. The Collective also claims that the enemies of human freedom searched for and found a way to disable the pineal gland by calcifying it. "A calcified pineal gland is a hardened organ that loses its ability to absorb and transmit electromagnetic waves," the Collective says. "So, those who seek to control human behavior by disabling brain connectivity," the group claims, "look for a way to effectively and easily calcify the pineal gland of as many human beings as possible."

That turned out to be very easy in the so-called "Western" cultures. To calcify the pineal gland, the Collective claims, fear and vanity were the weapons. Widespread calcification took several steps, but within a few generations, the mission was accomplished.

The consumption of sugar was introduced first, promoted by government subsidies to make it affordable. Food manufacturers made sugar an ingredient in almost everything they produced. It was no problem getting consumers hooked on sugar because sugar is naturally addictive. Once a baby is given a sugary treat, unda's palate becomes a slave to it. Sugar is more addictive than cocaine and other powerful narcotics, the Collective claims, adding, "if you don't believe us, try giving it up 100%."

Those behind the purposeful calcification of the pineal gland are very few, the Collective says. They are a secret society whose members have inherited its mission from generation to generation. They are masters of the sciences underpinning every aspect of human existence—physics, chemistry, mathematics, biology, neurology, psychology, etc.—and thus able to carefully plan their silent takeover of civilization over several centuries.

"Massive consumption of sugar created the need to do something about tooth decay," the Collective writes in what is believed to be its manifesto. "Popular culture has been injected with the notion that rotting teeth cause extreme pain.

Teeth that reach a level of decay must be extracted. Cartoons of suffering humans with a string attached to a rotten tooth, at one end, and a doorknob, at the other, are common in every culture and language."

The image of a human with rotting teeth, the Collective says, became that of a suffering human, a failed being. So, the merchants of vanity, also directed by the secret calcifying society, used vanity as a fifth column. Through art and literature, they manufactured a cultural standard of beauty that was not attainable by humans, unless significant meddling was introduced.

The Collective claims the vanity merchants started by targeting women, not because they were weaker of mind or vainer than men, but because their influence over children was critical. As mothers, they set the direction of their offspring. They were and are the ones who first nourish, who give toddlers their first taste of concentrated sugar, assisted by armies of pediatricians who dictate their recommendations on what a child should be fed.

It was a very effective way to gradually calcify everyone's pineal gland, including those of the men and women who unwittingly participated in the process—the professionals, the doctors, the fashion designers, musicians, actors, manufacturers, etc. They advanced the cause because of their greed to make a good living.

After widespread tooth decay set in, dentists were brought into the mix, the Collective writes. "That's how all efforts to control society work: Manufacture a problem, then offer the solution." Dentists and orthodontists were a wild success. Who wouldn't want to have perfect, white teeth, like the purveyors of vanity—the models, the fashion designers, the celebrities, and style influencers?

All throughout developed economies, dentists were in very high demand, and their profession became one of the most lucrative. "The bonanza began during the last two decades of the twentieth century," the Collective says, "when assembly-line dental offices became common, where patients waited in rooms along a corridor and the dentist moved from one room to the next, spending five to ten minutes with each patient while a dental hygienist did all the work. And that work emphasized the application of copious amounts of 'fluoride coating' to ostensibly protect the patients' teeth."

Decades earlier, a young dentist in Colorado discovered that groundwater naturally containing fluoride stained the teeth of those who drank it. But it also protected the same teeth. Thus, consuming so much sugar in the average western diet was not a problem, IF fluoridated water could be used against it.

Grand Rapids, Michigan, was the first municipality to fluoridate its drinking water, in 1945. Others across the world followed suit. The problem of where to acquire the massive amounts of fluoride needed to supply the growing number of cities and towns wishing to adhere to "health department recommendations" was easily solved. "Factories producing aluminum and phosphate fertilizers had a toxic byproduct they needed to get rid of," the Collective claims. "That byproduct was fluoride."

Artificially fluoridated public water makes the project to calcify everyone's pineal gland a very achievable proposition, the Collective says. If some people refuse to follow their dentists' recommendations to brush with fluoridated toothpaste at least twice a day, to absorb the fluoride into their bloodstream via their toothpaste, that's not a problem. They will get their fluoride doses via the water they drink, or the beer or soft drinks they drink, since any product that uses water in its manufacturing process adds fluoride to the product via the fluoridated water in it.

And "to make sure no one escapes," the Collective adds ominously, "the powers that be push government-subsidized fertilizers on the farmers who produce the fruits and vegetables we eat." Along the way, anyone who mentions this purposeful contamination of food with fluoride, says the Collective, is immediately labeled a conspiracy theorist spouting "dangerous nonsense undermining public health." Case closed.

Sugar and fluoride. The result of this long, still-ongoing process has been the gradual calcification of the pineal gland, the shutting down of this biological antenna that once kept all human minds connected, the Collective claims.

PUBLICITY: Hook your kids on the Global Food Factory™'s new Mid-Century Kosmic Cereal™! the perfect fuel to start every morning, so they can have that extra oomph they'll need to be extra assertive and successful ALL DAY! Mid-Century Kosmic Cereal™!, made with 100% natural sugar and 100% natural chemicals. Nothing artificial added!

For a Virtual Gandhi event to be successful, participants with functioning pineal glands must be present in very large numbers, across the globe. All they need to do, says The Virtual Collective, is, at the appointed time, sit quietly in a darkened room, wherever in the world they might be, and concentrate on "restricting the flow inside the thin tubes" of the target entity identified in the untraceable posts. Their pineal glands will take care of the rest, transmitting the force through the ether, where the Collective's wish finds its biological goal.

The campaign to DEcalcify enough pineal glands to make these efforts possible, says the Collective, took over a decade. Aside from weaning the public from artificial fluoridation of everything they consumed, there was the need to remove the massive amounts of fluoride that had already accumulated in their bodies, particularly in their pineal glands. It took a conscious effort to go through the process. Chelation therapies had to be adjusted to make them affordable and easy to follow. Iodine became a star element in the

Collective's effort. A halogen, like fluoride, iodine can help the human body get rid of accumulated fluoride.

Once there was a number large enough to participate in a Virtual Gandhi event, the Virtual Collective developed what it calls the Criminals Against Humanity Index (or CAHI), where the names of individuals who are deemed to be "in need of a Virtual Gandhi" are ranked by the public and members of the Collective.

The list of names—thrown into the ether as proposed candidates for a Virtual Gandhi—has grown quickly. Any member of the public can submit a name or names to the CAHI. Presumably, someone, or something (AI), somewhere, analyzes the proposed names and ranks them. When the index was made public, accessible to anyone on earth with a digital connection, the database was found to have thousands of names already.

It took no time for those who were denominated as "warmongers" on the CAHI Database to react. They were not going to sit idly waiting to be struck by a Virtual Gandhi. "We will halt these terrorist assaults against human enterprise," members of The American Consortium of Weapons Manufacturers said. "They can decalcify all they want," the targeted group added, "but their little game will be upended. They will be apprehended, prosecuted, and neutralized with the full force of the law."

One proposed way to save CAHI-listed individuals was to give them ADDITIONAL calcification via calcification therapy. "If the collective terrorists are indeed trying to communicate with OUR pineal glands," a spokesund for the defense industry said, "then we have the right to block their transmissions by calcifying the heck out of OUR pineals, so these terrorists won't be able to get to us. Better yet," the spokesund added, "we can have our glands completely REMOVED, and problem solved."

Neurologists and brain surgeons were consulted about establishing "pinealdectomy" procedures. "It's perfectly natural," said Sakrit Vandlanaa, a prominent brain-research scientist. "The pineal is a vestigial gland—useless, really. We pull out wisdom teeth, also vestigial, all the time. Same with appendices because they cause health risks that can be easily avoided with minor surgery. Removing the pineal, thus, is a simple solution for steering clear of these mental terrorists who seek to harm and disable innocent people with their so-called targeted, wireless transmissions."

But that was easier said than done. The first pinealdectomy was a disaster, with the patient dying on the operating table.

As more Virtual Gandhi victims are reported, those who are being targeted by the Collective are not giving up. Vast fortunes are being spent researching the brain's ability for ethereal communication. Around the world, congressional, legislative, and parliamentary bodies have approved emergency funding to escalate research efforts and find a solution. "It's a matter of national security," numerous governments have said. "More important than finding a cure for cancer."

But the concept of "national security" is reportedly laughable to the Virtual Collective, which has said that "There is no nation, no army—no matter how fabulously wealthy or powerful—that can protect warmongers from having a massive stroke induced by millions of people, acting together, the world over."

. . . Switching Platforms to The Open Social Ether™

ivmochenko is said to be broadcasting himself live! [Basili Patakas]

greetings from ufa, russia. watching this bastard get it [milyy bibliotekar]

LIVE TRANSCRIPT: From the European Medical Center in

Moscow (Европейский Медицинский Центр).

21:16 GMT - Igor Ivmochenko [Translated from Russian by GlobalTong™, courtesy of Nattie Foodz's SuperChoco Cozy Drink™]: As you can see, I have moved with my medical team to this luxurious hospital suite to document this farce by the so-called Gandhi group that pretends to be against violence while inflicting violence on innocent human beings. I am ready and have a team of neurologists who are monitoring all my vitals. It's past the hour indicated by the virtual terrorists, and I don't feel a thing yet. I should be feeling something by now, don't you think? I've read that it does not happen all of a sudden, that victims feel it coming. That they panic. That it is agonizing. Not me. So, their farce must be failing, no? I'm not panicking. My breathing is normal.

just u wait, mr ivmo. just u wait [bobkatze de klug]

it takes time for all participants around the world to focus their energy on your pineal, ivmo [Bhumi Panag]

even if ivmo's pineal is super calcified, it will still transmit if millions of people are focusing their energy on the transmission [memorable fantoche]

Next Tuesday, at 11:14 GMT, join the Virtual Collective to intervene Annetta VanHauser, CEO of the International Weapons Association™. [The Virtual Collective]

that's the IWA for ya, spewing the usual argument that weapons don't kill people. humans using the weapons do. So, arms manufacturers must be exonerated. [alivio blando]

same nra of old stance [sweating it]

trying to wrap my head round that one. nra was about the right to bear arms, citizens defending themselves against criminals who were already armed. how is that the same as selling weapons to foreign powers and dictators who can easily become our enemies and turn those weapons against us? [Clipper Weirds] sophisticated weapons have a back door. we design them, we sell them, we disable them whenever we want, just like any software operating system. [america gonzalez]

we dont design shit. its all made in bot sweatshops in the arctic [kool montevideo]

that's an awful lot of back doors—when you have french, russians, israelis, chinese, americans, indians, australians, etc., manufacturing high-level ordnance. a lot easier to just gandhi the top-level fuckers everywhere. make'em stop making the fucking things in the first place [Tomás Óregon]

the nra was america. the iwa's the whole world, and the whole world is now america [Gopi Singh]

the logic is profits. neither the nra nor the iwa is about defending oneself or defending a nation. forget the sloganeering nonsense and the manufactured narratives behind their lobbies. they're simply in the business to make money. more sales, more profit. they don't care who's buying or what the product does once it leaves the showroom. [sweating it]

are we flash-mobbing VanHauser's house? what's the address? the iwa deserves some intervention. [possum jumper]

no need. we're being invited to a collective meditation, a wish-upon-a-star kind of thing [sharming sharma]

ja, like a call to prayers—like praying for the victims of the 58 earthquake. [Diana Sen]

those who believe millions of minds focused on something at the same time can "intervene" that something, positively or negatively, are fooling themselves. stopping some evil dictator. saving a child from a terminal illness. nonsense. focus your minds away, people. utter bullshit. [NicoLander] so what r we sposd to do? [sayonarus50]

21:23 GMT - Igor Ivmochenko: Most people my age, if they have a stroke, it's always a mild one, when it's the first one. I've never had a stroke before. I've taken care of my diet. My cholesterol levels are normal. Even if the terrorists succeed in making me have a stroke, it won't be a devastating one. I'll recover easily. I'm determined. With access to the best doctors and intense sessions of physical and speech therapy, I'll be back in business in a few weeks. I'll be an inspiration to the world, an example of how to reject evil forces that have NO RIGHT to judge the actions of a productive human being. I'm a good man, a recipient of the international Person of Quality™ achievement award. Only God has the right to judge me and, until now, God has blessed me in every way. I have a presbyter here with me, silently praying to God to help me defeat this wanton terrorist attack and show the world that this is just a propaganda stunt by the collective.

show the world you deserve to be taken out, you criminal against humanity [Shawn Owusu]

igor is my uncle, and I can attest that he is a decent, caring chelovek [borisDgreat]

can't be decent while making a living blowing innocent people up [mucho macho]

he's a businessman, not a soldier. blame the soldiers for the killings. [iswarita]

21:28 GMT - Igor Ivmochenko: Those who work hard are rewarded by the heavens. The meek shall inherit the earth, while the terrorist collective boasts its arrogant schemes. All such boasting is evil.

he knows his bible! [freedom is priceless]

don't they all [margaux foo]

only god can judge me, while i have the right to kill millions with my company's products and live a life of luxury. [webbedKarola]

broadcasting this thing live from unda's hospital room is a risky proposition. unda's intention was to show the world that und is just a regular human being, someone deserving compassion. but the feed could also be a venue for members of the collective to further vilify unda, which is what's happening. [morning koffeed]

All the negative comments are being given an audience of billions. Free publicity for the Collective. The most public display of an act by these terrorists to date. Stupid Ivmo, giving them exactly what they want. [Orkine]

don't forget, though, he thought it was necessary to do this, to expose them, to turn world opinion against these agents of injustice. [leather44]

and he's succeeding, of course. nothing is happening to him [siva priya]

shlyukha kollektiv [khabib moimir]

21:33 GMT - Igor Ivmochenko: My factories and offices have created jobs for thousands. Those employees have been treated well. Their pay, their benefits and pensions are above average. Their families have had exceptional opportunities due to the income received from Alma. I may live in luxury, but I've shared a large percentage of my wealth by passing it on to my employees, whom I consider partners in the enterprise.

trying to pass the blame on to his workers [manchurian candy date]

my WORKERS put those bombs together, not ME! gandhi THOSE fuckers, i'm innocent!!! [gigolo jim]

ha ha ha ha. ivmoshitko, your sekonds r numbered! [yoko uno]

21:35 GMT - Transcription stopped. Lost feed.

---

wtf? [vegan hunter]

he out? [giorgio's nanny]

it may all be a trick. he getting ready to fake his instant recovery, using a double to take his place and claim that nothing happened. [señor mostaza]

show us the cripple! [victorMarkad]

he has drunk from the chalice of god's anger, and will never drink again. [Transatlantiker]

ALL POSTS TEMPORARILY SUSPENDED DUE TO EXTREMELY HIGH TRAFFIC VOLUME

. . . Switching to the iRiver Network™

BREAKING: The Open Social Ether™ (OSE) platform has temporarily shut down due to very high posting volumes, grid traffic sources report. Comments about targeted oligarch Igor Ivmochenko were so numerous, in the thousands per second, that it was impossible to keep up with any conversation. In fact, among the tsunami of chatter, everyone missed, at 21:36 GMT, a post from one of Ivmochenko's doctors, who stated, "It appears some kind of thrombotic event has taken place somewhere in the patient's circulatory system. It is inexplicable at the moment, but we are checking all monitoring devices and data generated by them to provide a professional analysis of this unfortunate incident. We'll follow up as results become available." A hospital nurse commented to embedded reporters, anonymously, that the team of doctors were thrown off by the frantic questions that, suddenly, Mr. Ivmochenko started asking, as they focused on their efforts to keep him calm about what was taking place.

sounds like it was stress that got him, not collective mumbo-jumbo bullshit [top-shelver]

stress was his worst enemy, the primary inducer of the master stroke he probably had. [delhi belly]

Neurologists are now saying stress is the whole strategy behind these Virtual Gandhis. When the Collective publishes a date and time for an induced stroke, and then cleverly doesn't strike the target right at the appointed time—21:07 GMT in Ivmochenko's case—it keeps the suspense going for almost thirty minutes, building up stress levels exponentially. That's how this works. Once the victim learns about unda's fate through the news, that induces acute levels of anxiety and incredibly high levels of stress that end up triggering a stroke. The stroke has nothing to do with any special powers that members of the Collective claim to have. [Dr. Roar]

Next Tuesday at 11:14 GMT, join the Virtual Collective to intervene Annetta VanHauser, CEO of the International Weapons Association™. [The Virtual Collective]

she's a nasty piece of work. worth a try. [desdemonus2k]

doesn't cost anything [gorky alone]

we're making it a party in my mum's basement, shrooming it while we stop annetta! [MitMaite]

who picked her? there's many others more deserving. [belgian hoarder]

propose, then. the cahi's open to everyone. [good_imani]

this is not an assassination. we're not killing anyone. not supposed to. the idea is to get vanhauser to stop what she's doing without killing her. we don't have the right to kill her. [augie knows]

bullshit. vanhosen deserves to get it good. give her a taste of what comes out of her own handiwork. [Akashi Kelly]

i propose salim djaborit, so-called president of free eritrea. corrupt to the core, with fingers on weapons and child trafficking and responsible for the starvation of hundreds of thousands. [omer bahati]

someone should start a new list [DaFungus]

no need. just submit the action form. they'll get a gandhi eventually.
[Tebogo Yanzee]

ACTION FORM: I propose [name], [position], [location], [activities
in which this warmonger participates]

i propose susan berkley, supreme leader of the world bank,
responsible for the starvation of hundreds of thousands via loans
meant to destroy local agricultural development. [Skyler Williams]

doesn't seem as bad as selling weapons [misplaced troyan]

the bank's goal is to use food imports as a political weapon, once the
local farmers can't afford to grow their own food [Skyler Williams]

brilliant! [jivey therapist]

berkley and many others at the wb more than deserve a gandhi,
pronto. [Skyler Williams]

i propose pedro whittaker [forward lurcher]

president barmel kubita [Karl Dove]

ravi sarafaman [yaffe york]

fabrice lamarkeenni [_$$minty]

attila the hunk! [great greta]

BREAKING: Russia has been accused, by a growing number of
scientists, of stealing the Earth's magnetic North Pole. The
accusation is based on the clear evidence that the pole is gradually
shifting TOWARDS Russia. "Leave it to Russians to engage in
nefarious behavior of this caliber," said Secretary of Defense and

CEO of the U.S. Department of Defense Corporation™ Peter "No Conflict of Interest" Marcciano. But another group of scientists, calling themselves "The Polar Shifters," have insisted that the phenomenon is completely natural. They say there's enough evidence showing that 42,000 years ago a similar polar shift was responsible for the extinction of Neanderthals. "It's the weakening of the world's magnetic field," said Ramsey Ayode, professor of Sustainability Science at Hawaii's Geodesic Celestial Institute™. "And it's all tied to changing weather patterns across the world," und added.

polar shifts are normal. no fear required. [eleven11]

they take hundreds of years to complete, so you have nothing to worry about. [Itai Humbert]

just a turf war among so-called scientists who know nothing about nothing. these guys say 42 thousand years ago was the last one. others say 780 thousand. that's quite a gap. [floridian in alaska]

a "new" study claims the south atlantic has been "acting up" ha! we'll let you know if thats something you ignoramuses should be worrying about. [inyene27]

Fear-mongering put out by the likes of AgitpropWombat™, to keep people distracted from what the government class is doing to us. [Arturo Donostia]

PUBLICITY: You have committed a DE-marriable offense. Now what? The worst mistake you can make is hiring a divorce lawyer. Instead, let an expert in DE-marriage assist you so YOU DON'T HAVE TO PAY A CENT! Argan D. Bornacho, Ph.D., has the number of cases under his belt to conclusively prove und is the best DE-marriage jurisprudential expert east of the Mississippi. Don't let a low-level divorce lawyer botch your easy path to DE-marriaged freedom. Ping %#DrArgan today! Financing available.

the polar-shift thingy is as old as the earth, so we're talking about very old news here. [gorgonzolo] bermuda was the north pole once, so what? if it happened millions of years ago and will happen again millions of years from now, it doesn't concern us. [viajero mental]

Our day-to-day struggle against corrupt government profiteers is what should matter to us now. [goofyJokster]

BREAKING: The notorious "EggPod Racial Profiling" case has begun in Seattle. The trial, which will be overseen by a JudgeBot™ robotic judge, will deal with the accusations of a South Indian rider who has filed a discrimination lawsuit against EggPod™—the driverless personal-transport giant. The plaintiff claims the company's software is "inherently biased and racist" for flagging unda's national ID number as "Temporarily Excluded." The pod's Rider-Rating Software (RRS) determined the plaintiff's ineligibility based on evidence (video footage) showing the plaintiff eating inside the vehicle, leaving curry stains on the seats; smoking hash inside the vehicle; AND spitting. "The sanitizing device used after the rider got out of the EggPod," the RRS stated, "could not handle the level of damage the rider caused, so und was flagged (first flag)." The second flag came from a complaint filed by the rider who attempted to use the same EggPod right after the plaintiff, but could not "because of the filthy conditions in the interior of the vehicle," the software added. The result: two flags turning into a two-month suspension. The South Indian rider claims the subsequent rider who flagged unda was a "white racist who saw me alight and was biased to give me an immediate racist review."

he pooped in the eggpod! [graham goa]

disgusting! [Xia Llanera]

not true. the guy was just hungry and had a meal thats all [eli chandan]

eating's against the law now? [pat borges]

against the algorithms [tito yu]

BREAKING: Celebrity couple StanLucie have filed a lawsuit against the Spring Flowers Birthing Clinic™ in Los Angeles. Speaking through their attorney, Bridgelo Frapitti III, StanLucie allege "endless emotional suffering" after a technician at the clinic refused to tell undahas the sex of undas' unborn infant. "We begged the man to tell us the gender of our child after the sonogram," StanLucie were quoted as saying. "We even offered to pay extra," undahas added, "but the man was arrogantly resolute in that he could not divulge the information," Frapitti said. The birthing clinic's employee is reported to have invoked the Americans Free of Gender Act, as und later confirmed to the ethermedia that "gendering a human being before the individual has reached aged zero is equal to child abuse and a felony under the Freedom to Choose Act and the Americans Free of Gender Act. I am NOT doing it, and I don't care how famous or rich StanLucie is," the clinic's employee added.

the nonsense of rich folks who have nothing better to do with their time [Freud2020]

and money! [ThorKemado]

my cousin was traumatized all unda's childhood for being called a boy by my aunt and uncle. When und turned 12, und turned UNDAS in to the police, and undas got five years and a huge fine. [StrayPuppy]

good 4 unda [cluster mill]

clinic should be given an award for following the law [virusJaguar]

send stanlucie to jail for trying to bribe the technician. [thereka]

this is so stupid. stanlucie can just get an amnio and see whats what with the xx or xy [Barton Funk]

that's a risky procedure. stanlucie aint stoopid. [jing chandra]

my opinion is that the child should be gender free [delany89054]

who eves a fck bout ur pinion? [mocco hung]

Tomorrow, at 11:14 GMT, join the Virtual Collective to intervene Annetta VanHauser, CEO of the International Weapons Association™. [The Virtual Collective]

yeh, yay! ima b der [gunning granny]

like the chenko russian dude, this ones gonna be live broadcast. news media cash cow, these virtual gandees. [manny_u] its like the tv executions of old. people love to see someone die in real time [marioMaría]

snuff news [00_born]

you sick puppies [theodora te adora]

they say vanhauser is prepping to dodge the bullet [wicked funster]

her house in amsterdam? [pancho villano]

the hague [Corda Hunt]

I'm a doctor. Anyone who believes that a human being can be forced to have a stroke by telepathy is a moron. [BorgMassaro2]

being a doctor doesn't make you an expert on what you know nothing about, so shut the fuck up [ayotunde hodgson]

any moron who starts to say something with "i'm a doctor" should be kicked out of the conversation. [ichiko murphy]

i'm a priest, and this idea that god decides who gets gandhied is mendacious blasphemy [father mckenzie]

Im an ARCHITECT and i declare garbage the lines on that building! [ducto reducto]

i'm a politician . . . [sought-after imbecile]

please! [Lita Oh]

BREAKING: Global communities everywhere are being warned about Australian citizens who are currently traveling outside Australia and acting as unwitting bioterrorists. Traveling Australians are said to be spreading a new variant of the KangarooPox™. Dr. Seldon Torn, a virologist with the International Medical Governing Institute, Inc., is taking the matter seriously. Und has issued a Level 2 Pandemic Instructional Guidance (PIG) regarding the threat. "With governments around the world, we're looking seriously into mandatory vaccines at a global level," Dr. Torn said. "And there's every indication that next season's WombatPox™ will be even more lethal than this current strain, so we're looking at a two-for-one jab that will take care of both threats," und added.

he forgot to throw in the tasmanian devil strain [true believer]

and don't forget the dingo pox! that one will surely get ya. [jelly plug]

those aussies sure know how to be superspreaders. bless'em all [mex pedrito]

BREAKING: Isadora Mongorov is testifying before Congress right now! See it live! Accused of "making the United States vulnerable to terrorist attacks," the dishonorably discharged former soldier is trying to state unda's case in a sea of accusations against unda's person. Tune in!

> INFOPOST: SOURCE: TodoPedia Complete™: Isadora Mongorov: Notorious whistleblower who joined the U.S. Marine Corps at age sixteen with the consent of unda's parents. The country's Armed Services were so desperate to person the hundreds of U.S. military bases around the world (bases ably administered by private-sector entities headed by former military officials under very lucrative contracts, we must say), that a constant stream of recruits was needed to keep the overseas presence visible. "A base without personnel doesn't do any good to the corporation running it," said former General Almagro Chestertone. "Such a base poses too much of a risk of being identified as unnecessary and deserving shutdown." Congress changed the law, as a result, to allow recruits as young as 14, with parental consent, which is easy to obtain because families with members in the armed services are showered with benefits, including free medical insurance, money for college for all children in the family, five years of food stamps with no questions asked, not to mention the regular visits from local

politicians to publicly honor their child in uniform and thank them for their service.

. . . The EavesDrop Portal™

LIVE TRANSCRIPT: Isadora Mongorov Hearing. Barbie Lemonderry reporting.

Lemonderry: At 19, Isadora Mongorov is a veteran in the full sense of the word, much older than the average uniformed soldier-person in the services. As we can see, und is wearing a bright yellow ValenschiaMe™ gingham that helps unda achieve a maternal, innocent look. Everyone in the courtroom is waiting for the former soldier to compose undself, after und burst into tears a few minutes ago. Some of the elected officials present have called unda a traitor. Und was dishonorably discharged, publicly tarred and feathered, and humiliated for unda's actions. But despite the seriousness of the crime, nothing much has happened to unda. To many observers, Mongorov is just a whistleblower, a victim of military corruption, "a nineteen-year-old child," as someone indicated. Plus, und is pregnant.

preggers? sheeza bout to pop! [lil bobby]

general knocked her up [eusebius hardy]

commanding officer, not general [freddy lebogan]

same difference. some dude pulled rank to seed the poor thing [ravi soon]

Lemonderry: Unda's belly is quite visible. It's said unda's defense lawyers forced unda to wear, quote, "something tight."

she was tight alright! [lil bobby]

Can the sophomoric teenagers here please leave the forum? This is a serious discussion, with the future of this young person on the balance. [Arushi Sethi] she's a traiter and deserves all she got and all she gets [ronnie unusual]

Lemonderry: Isadora seems to have composed undself. It's Senator Valero's turn.

Senator Valero: Please answer the question: When did Officer Largo first give you access to the classified information?

largo!!!! you can't make this stuff up! [eusebius hardy]

Isadora Mongorov: I don't remember.

Senator Valero: Speak up, please! Get closer to your microphone.

Isadora Mongorov: Like, a year and a half ago. He showed me . . . some videos he and other members of his platoon took. They were disturbing.

Senator Valero: The platoon members or the videos?

Isadora Mongorov: Videos. People being killed. Officer Largo said something about going on a hunt for terrorists, but the videos showed mostly women and children, like, in some village. They went into several houses, with their cameras recording everything. Villagers were terrified, didn't understand what the soldiers were screaming at them. And when one woman moved to protect her child, like, they just shot her. Then, gunfire everywhere, like fireworks, and blood, on the walls. One child's head was . . .

Senator Valero: I think we get the picture, Ms. Mongorov. What I don't understand is why you kept this to yourself for so long. You stole the video from Officer Largo's secured server, accessing it from the hotel room where the two of you were staying early on in your relationship. If you considered the video to be so disturbing, why did you keep it for so long before making it public? In my view, you were complicit. You released the video to get back at him for terminating the relationship, but you ended up incriminating yourself.

Senator Bardagharan: I'd like to point out—I'm Senator Bardagharan, from Idaho—that this video has not been proven to show that the platoon was doing anything wrong. By making public this property of the United States, you committed a crime, punishable by law. The details of this mission were a matter of national security, a training video on how to conduct raids. By releasing it, you have endangered the lives of ALL our soldiers, showing the enemy how our tactical procedures work. You have also given the world the opportunity to judge our persons in uniform, to call them violent, brutal, without having the details and context of what was really going on in that covert operation, where there were numerous terrorists hiding in those houses, and the women shown were part of the terrorist cell, using their children as shields. I want to make sure the American people understand this. These so-called victims were nothing more than targeted TERR-OR-ISTS who got what they deserved. As a member of our military at the time, you should have known better. You chose to break the law, Ms. Mongorov. And, as you try to defend your actions now, it is hard to understand how you may think that you deserve ANY sympathy. You were having disgusting sexual relations with Officer Largo during all those months, while he was cheating on his wife. You knew he was married. You chose to become pregnant with him in order to blackmail him and force him to leave his wife and family. Who does such a thing nowadays? And when he dumped you, only then did you decide to release the video you had stolen, to get back at him. And now, you expect us to believe anything you say? You, a broken, pregnant teenager who has been dishonorably discharged, who has broken the law, put our military in an awkward position, and helped all terrorists around the world who hate our freedom? I don't even know why we're wasting our time with you and this hearing here.

Lemonderry: Isadora has begun to sob quietly again.

Senator Bardagharan: Yes, yes. Cry me a river now. That won't get you any sympathy, Ms. Mongorov. Anyone who endangers the lives of our soldiers deserves ZERO pity.

Senatrix Sandra Alg: I beg to differ. The appropriate question here is why is this poor young woman testifying before us, as if she were a criminal, when it should be Officer Largo on the stand, the man who took advantage of her?

Senator Bardagharan: He has already denied her version. She made the whole thing up to justify her treasonous act.

Senatrix Alg: You don't make up a pregnancy, Senator Bardagharan.

Senator Bardagharan: But she made up the conditions of its conception. I'm surprised she hasn't accused the innocent man of rape yet. At any rate, an investigation is ongoing.

Senatrix Alg: Yes, and this hearing is part of that investigation, so we're not wasting our time. We are discovering who is responsible for this mess, and it's not the teenager in front of us. The senator from Wisconsin . . .

Senator Bardagharan: Idaho!

Senatrix Alg: . . . has done a fantastic job at revealing to the world the kind of human capital we now have as members of our military. He has taken the mask off this poorly educated teenager, made pregnant by her commanding officer, a pregnancy by which she saw an opportunity to extract a windfall—making accusations, going to trial, thinking it would be an easy win, like the mercenary that she is. AND we must ask: WHO hired this young woman as a mercenary? WE did, because, when our country starts numerous wars—and, I should say, invasions—with the dubious excuse of helping our allies, or allaying a humanitarian crisis, or fighting terrorism—all manufactured, immoral, and dishonorable reasons—how can we expect our hired mercenaries to somehow behave like ethical human beings? We PURCHASED them, like slaves, with a long-term promise of "we take care of our persons in uniform," and then, we don't deliver. There's nothing ethical about the military apparatus that our armed forces have become. Even if we go back more than a century, to World War II, to our so-called Greatest Generation. The only reason we think it was so "great" is that it has been whitewashed with the lies of victory. Our flag-waving war criminals, who immediately accuse anyone who does not support these invasions—invasions that waste trillions upon trillions of dollars every year—of not being patriotic, of being a traitor to America. . .

she's antiwar now? i thought robert gandhi had laid her hypocrisy out in the open. [malhechor007]

just trying to become electable [marble lee]

Senator Bardagharan: I do not accept this kind of odious talk in this chamber!

Lemonderry: Senator Bardagharan has stood abruptly.

Senator Bardagharan: You sound like a spokesperson for that insidious collective, spewing hatred and vitriol against America! This young woman is guilty of an intolerable act of aggression against our country, and I'm NOT going to sit here while one of my colleagues defends her and blames US for her treasonous actions!

Lemonderry: Senator Bardagharan has walked out of the chamber to the tune of muffled sobbing from Ms. Mongorov.

i saw a potential terrorist in my neighborhood this morning and reported unda to the eleven-eleven network. you never know when doing your bit can make a big impact in keeping all of us safe. use the 11:11 to report terrorists. it costs only $11 a call [george zambrano]

george zambrano's a bot. pay no attention to it. [elsa tru]

i reported the 11:11 to the 11:11! [merry weather]

zambrano too [working stiff]

Senatrix Alg: Person Chairperson, I'd like the record to show that Senator Bardagharan is not willing to serve on this committee.

BREAKING: Join Vita Rhalasi's World Affairs Revisited™ as und interviews Kumar Jahan, a recent victim of the Virtual Collective. Proudly brought to you by Broad Channel Global Broadcast™

. . . The iRiver Network™

World Affairs Revisited™: Live Transcript: Moderated by Vita Rhalasi. Sponsored by Testostedor™, the only long-term deodorant for individuals fiercely proud of their XY chromosomes.

Vita Rhalasi: Welcome to World Affairs Revisited™. I'm Vita Rhalasi. Our guest tonight is Mr. Kumar Jahan, CEO of BrahMos Aerospace Limited™, a key commercial enterprise in the development and manufacturing of weapons systems. These systems have served as an effective deterrent to war for decades. My assistants are now wheeling Mr. Jahan into the studio, even though he is perfectly well to do so himself through his onboard computer. Though gandhied by the Virtual Collective, Mr. Jahan—as he likes to inform us often through his newfound activism—is BACK!

Kumar Jahan [through computer-generated voice]: Thank you, Vita.

Vita Rhalasi: Among those known to have been gandhied so far, Mr. Jahan is remarkable in that he has fought back. He has not disappeared into a hospital room and never been heard of again. He is not feeling sorry for himself for being targeted. With every public appearance, he presents himself as an activist, as a survivor, as the voice of those victims of the Collective who have been silenced by a stroke, destroyed by the attacks that have ruined careers, families, and lives. As the hard-driven CEO he once was, Mr. Jahan has taken his new condition by the horns and worked doubly hard to make a comeback.

Kumar Jahan: I am quickly recovering . . . aggressively!

sounds like an idiot. computer voice doesn't help. [tattaBon]

impressive what mountains of money can do for a cripple. [infra meta]

He's not a cripple. Can't you just listen to the guy? He might teach you something. [sino_renoir]

Vita Rhalasi: Tell us, Kumar, what inspires you?

cue in the violins! [alexa fyre]

a man responsible for the deaths of hundreds of thousands of innocents. can't believe he's being given a platform to whine about his fate. [morocho15]

Kumar Jahan: After seeing important national-defense corporations with gutted chairmanships and gutted boards, with their remaining directors and shareholders unsure about what to do with their operations, I said to myself, after I was attacked by these coward terrorists, I said to myself, "No. This stops here, with me," and, with the assistance of my able wife, I prepared an elaborate plan to fight back, to save BrahMos. Investors around the world were getting the message from the Collective. They were beginning to dump their weapons-related stock. Vast fortunes collapsed in a matter of weeks, following the opposite curve that depicted the number of Virtual Gandhi attacks reported by the media. I was not going to sit there and see a bunch of mysterious terrorists ruin the world's technological achievements and the wealth those achievements had generated.

Vita Rhalasi: You are no longer CEO due to the time it has taken you to recover to this degree. However, BrahMos created the position of Chief Executive Advocate for you. It has given you a significant marketing budget to try to save not only the company's reputation but also the industry's, regaining its financial prominence in various stock markets.

Kumar Jahan: It's not just about the industry or the stock. This is a civilizational struggle here. I'm not talking only about national defense but also about how to deal with these terrorist attacks.

Vita Rhalasi: Tell us about that. Fascinating!

my lord, vita. how much u gettin paid by this war criminal to push his agenda? [smart noodle]

Kumar Jahan: My recovery regime has been brutal, Vita. Hours spent daily on physical therapy, experimental drugs, chelation procedures. My team of doctors and therapists have commandeered a whole wing in my hospital to document my recovery and develop a protocol for others to follow when struck by the Collective. Software and mechanical engineers have quickly perfectioned this YouGo Chair™ that allows me to control it via a chip embedded in the motor-command center of my brain. And while speech techno-pathologists are still trying to restore my ability to speak, they have, as a placeholder, created this SpokesPerson Tong™ software, developed by BrahMos, and working at a neural level, like the YouGo Chair™, to translate brain synapses into what passes for normal, if stilted, computer-assisted speech. The voice of my thoughts, as I like to call it.

stop thinking already! [JustPlainZeya]

why does the voice have a female pitch? [podemos33]

makes him look sexy [fred service]

gross [Aimee Abbot]

maybe that's what it sounded like before he lost it? [apricot karma]

no, it didn't. i worked at brahmos several years ago. this asshole was already there, assiduously climbing the corporate ladder, with the voice of an asshole to match. [no username]

Kumar Jahan: This voice goes with me everywhere, and I like to use it to describe how hard I have worked to be where I am today, able to participate in society, particularly in talk shows and interviews like this one, where I make the case, strongly, for the victims of this nefarious terrorist group.

Vita Rhalasi: Tell us something about your background. Why were you targeted?

Kumar Jahan: Throughout my career, I have served in numerous leadership positions. Chairman of the Security Systems Industry Association, a Fellow at the Royal Aeronautical Society, on the Board of Directors of the Wounded Warriors Foundation, Honorary Chairman of the U.S. Department of Sustainable Equitism Corporation™, Executive Vice President of the Global Sustainability Project, President and Chief Operating Officer of the Langley Group Limited, the American Workforce Council, the Board of Trustees of Gandhi University, Jindhal School of Business at the University of Texas, and numerous other academic institutions. That's who I am, not a low-life, do-nothing excuse of a human being like those who have openly celebrated the vicious attack on my person by that terrorist organization known as The Collective.

PUBLIC ANNOUNCEMENT: The U.S. Department of Sustainable Equitism Corporation™ has seven openings for professional faculty at Guadalcanal Online University™ (GOU). The seven selected professionals, who will become members of the Sustainable Equitism Department at GOU, will advance the goals set forth in the university's Comprehensive Educational Strategies Plan. They will develop additional, adaptable strategies for the implementation of visions, goals, actions, and tasks at an interdisciplinary academic level that respects a cohesive approach to implementation of the plan. All candidates must hold Ph.D. credentials from accredited organizations certified by the Federal Department of Education Corporation™. Two of the individuals will be appointed Chief Social Purpose Officer and Deputy Chief Social Purpose Officer, respectively, to establish a coherent interdisciplinary behavioral approach that will help GOU achieve its goals. Selected candidates will be expected to start immediately and sign sustainable equitism pledges and commit to advancing a philosophy of human harmony among humans as well as with all sentient beings in the metacosmological realm. To apply, whisper "I am a doctor committed to sustainable equitism" to your listening device.

Vita Rhalasi: Did you receive a warning? That you would be targeted, I mean.

Kumar Jahan: They post these things on the social ether, the day of or a few days earlier. I guess that can be called a warning— something completely devoid of ethics. It's like a police department and a judge calling you to say, "Oh, by the way, we are going to your home to arrest you today. Never mind the charges. You'll be tried, convicted, and jailed for life without parole—just because. And you DESERVE it." No due process. No proving that their accusations have any merit. No respect for justice and the sanctity of life.

ha! because brahmos weapons just ooze ethics and respect for the sanctity of life. what an asshole! [JustinWantin]

he's like an old grandpa, telling his life's story to his grandkids. even vita's studio is made to look like a stately living room, a place where powerful individuals transact their power and influence. [nigerian prince]

Vita the enabler, wearing the type of light-blue business suit fashionable among women in leadership positions. She's just totally pandering to this douche. [tony monero III]

Check out the "Coca-Cola," "Marskand," "Lockheed," and "BrahMos" logos embroidered on the front of her jacket. [Ñato Vanna]

totally biased [Yeah U]

primary sponsors of her show [shellGirl]

PUBLICITY: LavenDorx™ is rejuvenating America like never before. Highly recommended by the National Association of Pharmaceutical Prescription Doctors, LavenDorx™ helps you regain all the health you once lost. Ask your medical account executive whether LavenDorx™ is right for you. It's free of harmful vitamins A and D, and causes only a handful of side effects that most patients don't even notice. Just a spoonful of LavenDorx™ a day will get you back on track. Sweeter than sugar, healthier than apples. LavenDorx™.

Vita Rhalasi: What does it feel like, this artificial stroke, the moment it comes? Some victims who have experienced a natural stroke, and have also been victims of the Collective, have said that the latter begins more like someone cutting off your oxygen supply. Can you elaborate?

Kumar Jahan: Yes, but that may be entirely due to the high levels of anxiety created by the announcement of the impending attack. What I would like to see happen, and I wish I'd had the forethought, is to create a task force that can isolate the potential victim so und does not find out the exact time of the attack, or that there will be an attack at all. The most effective weapon in these terrorist attacks is the victim's high level of stress. If I had been completely ignorant that I was being targeted, this would have never happened. I'm certain of it. They turned my own adrenaline against my cardiovascular system.

Vita Rhalasi: But that has already been tried, Mr. Jahan...Kumar. Victims have gone to remote islands, hidden in caves deep in mountains. One, as you must know, even paid his way to be on a space station—all in vain. They all ended up having a stroke.

Kumar Jahan: They all knew it was coming. You, as a victim, need to be isolated before the news reaches you.

Vita Rhalasi: But is that realistic? If you're the leader of a country or a major corporation and, one morning, a group of friends approaches you to say, "Listen, Kumar, let's go on vacation. We found this great spot for you to enjoy a week of swimming in the ocean, massage sessions, relaxed dinners on a patio surrounded by palm trees, sun, and good friends"—I mean, your first thought would be, What's up with these guys? You would KNOW the Collective had posted something about you.

Kumar Jahan: You're right, Vita, but the use of a task force, or a group of friends, as you put it, would go hand-in-hand with a turn to secrecy. As our world evolves, the nature of leadership of a country or corporation will become secret. It will be a matter of national security, where intelligence agencies actively engage in keeping the public at large from knowing who is running BrahMos, for example, not only the name of its CEO but everyone on its board, executive positions, and upper management. That will force the Collective to start targeting the rank and file, the man on the factory floor, say. And when that happens, the whole of public opinion will turn against it. We force these terrorists to focus on the soldiers, the persons in uniform. No one cares about the generals. The public admires and respects those who make the ultimate sacrifice. Any terrorist organization or foreign army that dares to harm our soldiers receives the wrath and fury of the American people. That's how we deal with this. The State of Delaware, for example, has already moved to keep corporate filings secret, and FOIA is now kept from revealing the names of those who run a corporation. Several members of Congress, as you know, are working on legislation that will permit individuals running for office to use avatars and profiles that reveal only their political positions, leaving any personal information out of the equation. So, we'll have Candidate #1, Candidate #2, etc., on the ballot, and, once elected, the public official will be referred to by their title, like The President, The Senator, and so forth, in complete anonymity. This will go a long way towards disabling the efficiency of these terrorist groups.

Vita Rhalasi: With all due respect, Mr. Jahan, I think the American people, or citizens of any country, for that matter, will have a difficult time going along with this. For a people to stand behind a leader, there must be a name and a face there.

Kumar Jahan: Yes, an avatar. We'll give the avatars a name, too. Example: Anna Alcara was targeted by the Collective for allegedly "aiding and abetting warmongers with her reporting." If Ms. Alcara had adopted an avatar early on, called "Princess Truth," say, with pearly green eyes and solid blue hair, she would be home free now. As an avatar, you still get a salary. You still report the news. But people won't know anything about your personal life, your marital status, your name, where you live, whether you have children, what you look like, where you work—absolutely nothing. And you will be completely safe from collective terrorists.

dibs on princess truth! and i want a half million salary with it! [stimuli guru]

prince charming here. make my avatar as handsome as a beauty queen on aveed. [trust no one]

Vita Rhalasi: I guess that would be a tradeoff that we would all have to accept on a case-by-case basis. Some leaders or journalists might prefer to live with the risk of being fully human, exposed to the public, not a cartoon.

Kumar Jahan: Well, NO. We should ALL be coming together on this, to pull the Lord's chariot as a team. We have no choice. If someone like me is viciously attacked, no one is safe. I have not killed anyone. I am a religious man. I didn't choose my profession, just found a way to make a living, being creative, manufacturing something, and leading others because they accepted my leadership in the administration of this fabulous corporation, which has done a ton of good in the world, giving hundreds of thousands of people jobs that they can be proud of. That's the bottom line. And the Collective, in the name of so-called Peace and International Brotherhood, inflicts the most vicious violence on my person, with a terrorist act of war, after calling ME a warmonger. People need to understand how these cowards manipulate language. I provide jobs. They disable innocent individuals with targeted strokes. If they love peace so much, why are they acting so violently?

Vita Rhalasi: We'll be right back with Mr. Jahan, after a word from our sponsors.

PUBLICITY: Sisters, this is Lady GODiva, your Digital Clinical TherAIpist™. Get my new holographic video with instructions on how to reverse the sexual neglect inflicted on you by careless lovers. The Lady GODiva Holographic Video™ is guaranteed to work, or your money back. Holler "God-holo-video" to your listening device and order today!

BREAKING: Gender historian discovers "the insidious backroom negotiations that produced our nation's legacy 18th and 19th amendments." Arroseae Jaragone, Ph.D., has deciphered the secret negotiations that took place behind the legacy constitutional amendments that gave us Prohibition and Women's Suffrage. "No one saw it in this light before," Dr. Jaragone stated at unda's Georgetown University press conference, "but the two amendments were a negotiation, a quid pro quo, where one political camp got what it wanted in exchange for what the opposition wanted." Unda's research discovered journal and diary entries from several of the negotiators (all xy, it must be said) who agreed to a compromise. "In short," Dr. Jaragone summarized, "we'll liberate women by giving them the vote, but only if this newfound liberty of the weaker sex is kept in check by prohibiting the poor things from harloting themselves under the influence of alcoholic beverages," Dr. Jaragone explained. "So, the women's right to vote begat prohibition, and the culprits behind this travesty hid their deeds by prohibiting alcohol first, and then, a year and a half later, giving women the vote," Dr. Jaragone added. "They were not counting on my skills as a gender researcher to expose them." The discovery is causing renewed outrage at the "dead white men" behind the deal, with calls to "finally pass the ERA Plus™ and make the legacy 14th Amendment actually mean something," announced a Don't Touch My XX League™ spokesund. Also, demands are being circulated that call for the descendants of those who negotiated the 18th and 19th amendments to post their apologies on MeContrite™ and Contrition Net™ immediately. At the end of the press conference, Dr. Jaragone spoke of unda's intentions to depart academia to pursue political office in the upcoming election. "The ERA Plus™ will pass on DAY ONE of my administration," und said, "and you can take that to the bank!"

. . . ClassyNet™

Warning: This portal is owned by the National-Security Intelligence Services Corporation™ of the United States of America. If you have no business being here, exit this logon screen IMMEDIATELY. All visitors without permission, even if no attempt is made to illegally log on, may be subject to cyber-terrorism charges that carry prison sentences from twenty years to life, plus fines.

Enter your network identifier: *******

Enter your biometric algorithm: ********

Enter your Dispatch PIN: ****

Enter your National Security Number: **-****-***

ClassyNet: Welcome to ClassyNet, and thank you for your patriotic service. Your classification is Alpha 2 Level 4. You are not allowed to post entries but can read posts up to Clearance 4.

ClassyNet: Beginning session . . . your ClassyNet number is 218145 . . .

...Your target is journalist/writer Maria Zallebri (scrubbed)

...MZ has had access to highly secured data relevant to national-security issues that she has been openly sharing through articles and posts using various media. (scrubbed)

...The data MZ posts is remarkably accurate, so she must have an inside source feeding her the material. (scrubbed)

...The information pertains to weapons-systems production, distribution, and utilization. Names of manufacturers, agents, sellers, buyers, and end users. (scrubbed)

...Her writing also includes charts and maps where she ties the use of these systems to casualties in various hotspots around the world. (scrubbed)

...This information, once out in the open, is extremely damaging to our national security, utilized by our enemies to weaken our defenses. It invites terrorists and radicals to target us via cyber-attacks and other means, negatively affecting any entity that works towards keeping our country and citizens safe. (scrubbed)

...MZ must be stopped. No matter who her source or sources are, she is the mouthpiece that must be immediately discredited. (scrubbed)

...Get instructions from Operation Dogged Alphapen and activate your cell now. (scrubbed)

...end of ClassyNet clandestine dispatch. You have been logged off and scrubbed. . . switching you to . . .

. . . EavesDrop Portal™

Check out Sayaddan Temprano's live feed from deep inside his bunker at Morador Air Force Base, West Virginia! [recruiter 30416]

He's a badass military dude! And he's on his lunch break and about to do a real-time demonstration of his Remote-Command Pod™—or RCP, as they're commonly known among users. [recruiter 10129]

Sayaddan is in a large room that contains a few dozen RCPs assigned to different parts of the world. You, too, could be gaming with him! Join the National Security Defense Corporation™ today! Chances are, you'll be assigned to an RCP within weeks! Get a bonus of $10,000 or more just for applying! [recruiter 30416]

Designed and manufactured by Sentinel Security Werks™ in Nevada, the RCPs are self-contained units with access to highly classified intelligence. The information is used to select targets around the world. [recruiter 10129]

Sayaddan's job is to monitor the pod's actions and manually override any lethal attack, if necessary. For example, if it becomes obvious that the algorithms have made a mistake—by ordering the destruction of a bunker hidden in some jungle, when, in fact, it is a shack occupied by a grandma and several grandchildren—Sayaddan has it covered. [recruiter 95134]

The AI takes care of about 97% of the potential targets. The remaining 3% is referred to human operators like Sayaddan and unda's colleagues at Morador. [recruiter 30416]

There are about sixty operators at Morador, each one in a separate pod but communicating with a neighbor via wireless headphones during their shifts. [recruiter 10129]

Take it away, Sayaddan! [recruiter 30416]

Sayaddan Temprano: Thanks, guys. The pods seem very slow today.

Tom Vajat: Bad weather, and too many questionable targets. Where you at?

Recruiter 30416: That's Tom Vajat, a recent recruit from California.

Sayaddan Temprano: Rasada, on the Paki border.

Tom Vajat: Maybe a network thing. I'm in Chad, same thing.

Recruiter 30416: As you can see, the system works through a series of flowcharts that ask questions to the human operators. Then, it reacts based on their answers. If it isn't clear to the algorithm whether the drone should fire its missile and destroy the target in question, the flowchart kicks in, and Sayaddan's joystick takes over the decision-making.

Recruiter 10129: Yeah. At this point, it's more about his joystick and his gut feeling than about his seventeen-year-old brain. At the National Security Defense Corporation™, our soldiers are trained to be intuitive, always erring on the side of killing a terrorist enemy combatant, whether that enemy is in Lahore, Acapulco, or even Pompano Beach. No respite for bastard terrorists!

Sayaddan Temprano: I can't stand night shifts, though. Eight hours of deciding yes/no gets old quick, and it's tiring. I'm totally sleep-deprived right now, dude.

Tom Vajat: Hear ya, but we gotta do our work when it's daytime over there, man.

Recruiter 30416: As you can see, Tom is busy with unda's joystick, pressing the button to answer the flowchart's questions.

Recruiter 10129: Case Number P00A247985 has appeared on Sayaddan's screen, followed by a real-time video feed that shows a house in what appears to be a mountainous region without much vegetation. Near Rasada, it seems. The flowchart is asking him if there are any vehicles parked around the target.

Sayaddan Temprano: Yes.

Recruiter 10129: Trucks?

Sayaddan Temprano: Not sure. Request another pass.

Recruiter 30416: These new FuzzyBallz Drones™ are very maneuverable and can turn around in seconds while keeping their cameras trained on a target.

Recruiter 10129: That's right, 30416! These are not the old plane-like drones that could only fly in one direction. The latest iteration, dreamed up by engineering geniuses at SecDef Systems™, Inc., are more like giant insects weighing no more than a pound. They're kamikaze drones, too, acting . . .

Recruiter 30416: Can't use that word, 10129.

Recruiter 10129: Uh, right. They're self-destructive drones, acting as 360-degree monitoring devices AND missiles, all in one very small package. Once a decision is made to destroy a target, the fuzzy speeds through the air like a mad bumble bee on its way to stinging somebody's ass! Though, in the case of the fuzzy, it's a deadly explosion.

Recruiter 30416: Right said, Fred. But keep in mind that Central Command does not like its soldiers wasting fuzzys on faulty targets. A drone that is sent to destroy a house where terrorists turn out to be an illusion is a wasted drone.

Recruiter 10129: Yep! And an expensive proposition, not only because of the waste of a fuzzy, but also because, eventually, relatives of the civilian victims in that house will manage to file a claim with OUR federal government, demanding outrageous compensatory amounts.

Recruiter 30416: Armies of anti-American activists and their lawyers are out there, making a very good living filing such claims for foreigners. You don't want to give THEM a chance to make a killing, either. Oh, check this out! A new video angle has provided Sayaddan a closer look.

Recruiter 10129: Although this lower altitude and high-resolution camera give us the feeling of being right there, it is cloudy in the Rasada region, and the gloominess of the day, with a light drizzle, makes the decision less certain.

Recruiter 30416: It's clear now why the flowchart has kicked in. Remember, Sayaddan has answered Yes to the question about vehicles, and now und has identified a few trucks, one with a motorcycle on it, and a couple of other bikes on the ground.

Recruiter 10129: Any domesticated animals in view? the flowchart is asking. Apparently, No. Any children?

Sayaddan Temprano: No.

Recruiter 30416: The questions are coming fast now. After a few more that Sayaddan has already answered in the negative, the algorithm has determined that there IS cause, and gives instructions to engage the target.

Sayaddan Temprano: Fire!

Recruiter 30416: A nearby fuzzy has automatically taken over the video feed so we can see the moment of impact and the subsequent explosion that will engulf . . . there it is, folks, a brilliant white light that lasts but a few seconds, then flames. No one knows what SecDef puts in these fuzzies, but it sure is fun to watch them blow up this way!

Recruiter 10129: And remember, if you are watching this magic, YOU can be like Sayaddan and join this important work for the safety of our nation—right now. Contact the National Security Defense Corporation™ with your ZipPrint CV™ today and let them know how eager you are to serve your country.

Recruiter 30416: Tom Vajat, by the way, got to engage unda's own target almost at the same time as Sayaddan.

Tom Vajat: This technology can be used for all sorts of purposes. In the wrong hands, some guy who wants to get his friend's hot wife can, you know, tell the friend to meet him for a round of golf somewhere, not show up, and vaporize the golf cart from a safe distance.

Sayaddan Temprano: Then console the widow!

Recruiter 95134: Guys, cut it out. This is serious national-security business here.

Recruiter 30416: The next case has appeared on Sayaddan's screen.

Sayaddan Temprano: That's all you think about, Tom. It would be easier to get your own hot wife.

Tom Vajat: Boring, though.

Sayaddan Temprano: Guess what I'm doing after my shift today.

Tom Vajat: Shrooms?

Recruiter 30416: Boys will be boys.

Sayaddan Temprano: No, seriously. I'm having breakfast with Kathy. Gonna propose.

Tom Vajat: No shit! How OLD are you?

Sayaddan Temprano: Who cares? Been together long enough, and it's the right time.

Tom Vajat: Didn't know you were the type.

Recruiter 10129: Notice that even through their friendly chat, Tom and Sayaddan are concentrating on the task at hand. That's how fun it is to work as an RCP operator.

Recruiter 30416: Sayaddan's flowchart is asking whether the children are in motion. Terrorists have grown wise about avoiding their fate by using dummy children strategically placed around their hideaways. The chances of being killed are much lower if children are seen playing outside. Problem is, real children move a lot. They normally don't stand still in one place, like dummies.

Sayaddan Temprano: They ain't moving.

Recruiter 10129: The algorithm has instructed the operator to engage the target.

Tom Vajat: Hot?

Sayaddan Temprano: What?

Tom Vajat: Kelli, Kaity—whatever her name is.

Sayaddan Temprano: To me she is.

Recruiter 30416: See, just normal young men having a good time while serving their country. And you can, too. Contact the National Security Defense Corporation™ today! All you have to do is send your ZipPrint CV™ via text to us, and you're IN! Free medical insurance. Free higher education. A generous retirement package. You Can't Go Wrong Serving Your Country™!

Tom Vajat: Congratulations, man. I'm outta here.

Recruiter 95134: Tom Vajat's shift has ended earlier than the required eight hours. This is another benefit you can get at NSDC: shorter shifts. It is our policy that if a recruit reaches the set quota for engaged targets before the eight hours are up, und can leave early.

Recruiter 10129: Central Command has figured that the emotional toll might be too great after seeing more than a hundred homes blown away in one session, especially when body parts appear on the screen, which they often do.

Sayaddan Temprano: Shit, you got a hundred already?

Tom Vajat: Everyone's a terrorist in Chad, my friend. Like shooting fish in a barrel.

Recruiter 10129: Notice that Tom is being replaced by Marika Smith. Sayaddan doesn't know unda, but it's easy to make friends here.

Recruiter 30416: The familiar tune plays as Marika Smith logs on to unda's RCP account. It's much like a professional video game. All the pods at Morador are like an arcade, a bunch of young guys, gals, and others having a good time blowing shit up on video screens, adding points to their careers. Think of it as serving your country while earning a very good living and having loads of fun.

Recruiter 10129: The next case has appeared on Sayaddan's screen.

Sayaddan Temprano: What do you know? Chad!

Recruiter 10129: It's a large gathering of men, sitting around in some patio shaded by trees as the sun appears intermittently through fast moving dust clouds.

Sayaddan Temprano: Is it a wedding party?

Recruiter 30416: Could be. But that's another trick terrorists play these days, pretending to be at a wedding party in the open, while, in fact, it is nothing more than a training camp where terrorist leaders are sharing intelligence on future attacks.

Recruiter 10129: The flowchart is asking Sayaddan whether obvious women are in view.

Sayaddan Temprano: No, so I know where this is going.

Recruiter 10129: You can see the Fuzzy circling and panning now, expertly operated by Sayaddan, who received unda's training at NSDC and, in only six months, increased his salary fourfold!

Recruiter 30416: It's obvious these guys know they're being watched, careful with their hand movements and mannerisms, as if having a chat and playing dominoes at a central plaza in a small rural town.

Recruiter 10129: Now the women appear on the screen, separate from the men, but they aren't as many, and most are dressed completely in black.

Sayaddan Temprano: Maybe a funeral, though wearing black in that godawful heat is stupid.

Recruiter 30416: The flowchart is asking: Are there as many women visible as there are men? No.

Recruiter 10129: Do the women appear, in general, to be of the same average age and height as the group of men?

Sayaddan Temprano: No. Looks like a bunch of ancient grandmas.

Recruiter 30416: Are there any children visible?

Recruiter 10129: That question is usually the clincher.

Sayaddan Temprano: No.

Recruiter 10129: So, there it is. The "Engage the target" command.

Recruiter 30416: Love it! And that's the end-of-shift chime for Sayaddan, too! Und's reached the quota.

Marika Smith: Lucky you. Got extra points for guessing those women were actually men in drag.

Recruiter 30416: That's right. The system rewards keen operators. The AI has taken into account the number of male combatants sitting in that courtyard and given Sayaddan bonus points for every terrorist killed.

Sayaddan Temprano: Tom was right. Chad IS a terrorist-rich target.

Marika Smith: Nice meeting you.

Sayaddan Temprano: Yeah. I'm outta here, guys!

Recruiter 30416: Thank you for letting us look over your shoulder and show future recruits what it's like, Sayaddan. Now that you got a bonus and can cut your shift short, what are you planning to do with the extra free time?

Sayaddan Temprano: Make my way to my bunk to get some shuteye before taking leave to meet Kathy for breakfast and start shopping for our wedding.

Recruiter 10129: Congratulations! You deserve all the happiness you get!

Recruiter 30416: And this concludes our EtherCast™ and transcript of a fascinating peek inside Morador Air Force Base, brought to you by the National Security Defense Corporation™. Remember: You can also serve your country like Sayaddan, Tom, Marika, and many others. Join us now. There will be a $100,000 hiring bonus for all those who are selected within the next two hours! All you have to do is send your ZipPrint CV™ to us, and you're IN! Free medical insurance. Free higher education. A generous retirement package.

And that $100,000 bonus, if you act before the two-hour deadline. You Can't Go Wrong Serving Your Country™!

BREAKING!: Journalist Maria Zallebri Caught in the Dog House! The antiwar activist has been caught smooching the pooch! Leaked photos reveal Zallebri's disgusting private activities.

saw them. having sex with her great dane, guys! [victor lassi]

she's denied it [wingwham goo]

photos look authentic. i checked them with pixverify™ [zita omolin]

bullcrap. pixver's just another gimmick malware put out by the intelligence agencies. doesn't prove shit. [oatmeal sniffer]

> *INFOPOST: SOURCE: World-O-Pedia™: Maria Zallebri: Discredited journalist who once tried to claim the moral high ground by supposedly revealing that national-security activities were immoral and unethical. In fact, her lifestyle turned out to be more than immoral and unethical itself, exposed only when credible evidence was leaked by former lovers showing her engaging in sex acts with canines. "Utterly disgusting," stated Senator Bharat "Bam Bam" Veloscent, Chairman of the Strategic Armed Services Procurement Committee. "For this individual to invoke morality and ethics on matters of national defense, when she is found abusing defenseless animals in a disgusting way, without the animals' consent—just abominable acts, beyond the pale," Veloscent added. Zallebri switched immediately to damage-control mode by claiming in a news release that the evidence was false, that she has never had a dog because she is a cat person—a statement that was soon followed by leaked photographs showing her engaging in sex acts with cats. Besides, she added, "even if the photos are real, which they are not, bestiality is no longer a crime since the passage of the Americans Free to Love Act." Senator Veloscent responded that the AFLA was "an abomination passed by depraved liberals like Ms. Zallebri, and an abomination that*

I will work hard to eradicate beginning on day one of my presidential administration."

PUBLICITY: Raise funds for your nonprofit by reselling our cute Zallebri & Pets™ t-shirts, with adorable photos of the journalist lovingly hugging her Great Dane "Pete" and various feline friends! No need to order, package, or mail the shirts. We do all the work for you! Just sell them and receive your commission in less than an hour! Zallebri & Pets™

Hey, everyone, Zallebri is being bot-interviewed right now at the obscure Anything Goes Network™. [jelly castle]

. . . The AGN! - Anything Goes Network!™ - Live Transcript - Interview with discredited journalist Maria Zallebri.

Maria Zallebri: What is happening to me is exactly what I describe in my report. Anyone who tries to expose the multi-trillion-dollar backroom deals between politicians, the military, and defense-industry giants is immediately targeted, drowned by distraction while the American public gladly follows the attackers' lead, lapping up all the bullshit, all the made-up accusations while the military-intelligence-industrial complex continues to stick its fist up the rectum of every American.

who's still listening to this animal? she's been completely discredited. [foal fall]

She has the right to defend herself, moron. You sound brainwashed by your own propaganda. [gone forensic]

Maria Zallebri: I've had to go into hiding, in exile after one of my anonymous sources was murdered. It is simply mind-boggling that a whole country of hundreds of millions of people so willingly accepts this, people who KNOW what is going on but don't dare say a word for fear of being targeted.

PUBLICITY: Take Note: Starting next month, ALL Americans will be required by law to carry Polar Shift insurance. Protect your loved ones by signing up now for discounted premiums, while supplies last. Deluxe coverage is only available from the Federal Nationwide Insurance Marketplace Corporation™. Or you can get the highest discounts from the Federal PS Insurance Group™, Inc., the Federal Public Protection Insurance Corporation™, and the popular and affordable GovInsu™ LLC. Financing available. Avoid paying high fines and potential imprisonment for not carrying this vital insurance coverage. Sign up for your Polar Shift policy now!

BREAKING: Active Shooter in Valentine, Nebraska! Only 33 victims so far. Police are at the scene at Ecological Park, from where the wounded are being taken to nearby Cherry County Hospital. A spokesperson for the Heart City's Police Department indicated, about ten minutes ago, that "the situation is almost under control. We have a person of interest, possibly a suspect, or even the actual perpetrator and future convict." Further clarification, however, revealed that the suspect, described as a "corpulent grandma," has not been apprehended. The individual is still an active shooter.

nebraskans don't break the law [arduous striver]

they have a suspect, but they dont [vanilla rodent]

be my valentine! [kimberPowers32]

Yesterday's active shooter in Idaho worked undself up to 58 victims. [selectivator sal]

not there yet. [socially unrested gal]

the more immigrants, the higher the population, the more numerous the potential victims for these shooters everywhere. [tragaluces]

don't blame the shooters. people dont kill people. bullets do. [minor andromeda]

there's a class-action lawsuit making its way now to the supree against ammo manufacturers. the loved ones of hundreds of thousands of victims will soon get their day in court. [many lakhs bambino]

dream on [Ana Bijou]

hold it! . . . another active shooter just reported in tejas. [lincoln parker]

. . . The iRiver Network™

BREAKING: A disgruntled employee at an Odessa, Texas, funeral home has taken several hostages after shooting at least three employees dead and one police officer who rushed to the scene. A city official announced that professional negotiators are currently talking to the individual in hopes of ending the altercation peacefully.

the guy's already killed four people. how's that "peacefully"? [malik jones]

who said it's a guy? [Nico Falcone]

disgruntleds are always a guy [malik jones]

sexist claptrap [Nico Falcone]

AgitpropWombat™ published unda's manifesto this morning. Goes by the handle "Bolero Pistolero." Sounds like a guy to me. [bad samaritan]

The University of Chicago published a study last year that proves women are just as prone to violence as men. [omolawn37]

it wasn't a study, and the "findings" were just the opinions of some wannabe professor who never completed a doctoral dissertation. [Valentine Otho]

not true. i was there. in a class with the professor in question. [fyre inda belly]

98% of women fantasize about "being violent against the opposite sex," the study says. look it up. [Lord Lecher]

whatever [Valentine Otho]

BREAKING: A new Collective has been founded to capitalize on the new popularity of the word "collective," thanks to the mysterious group claiming responsibility for unexplained strokes suffered by targeted victims around the world. The new group is calling itself The Victims' Collective Troupe. Members have begun to stage "police-brutality tableaus" and other choreographed attacks to raise awareness and money for "the victims of out-of-control government forces," said Vini Barkode, a member of the VCT. "We are mostly unemployed actors," und added, "but our help for victims of police brutality doesn't end with staging reenactments. Our organization also, immediately following a PB event, sets up a $4nothing™ account, where a victim can receive donations and support for their victimhood." And it's not just police brutality, Barkode added. "Our troupe has several subcommittees addressing abuses by other government entities. We have a Justice for Flu Victims Committee, which is now in the process of filing a class-action lawsuit against government agencies, health departments, and non-profits that have done NOTHING to protect victims against the common flu."

who gives money to these clowns? [Bum in Greece]

$4nothing's the biggest scam [Samaki Kubwa]

this vini character has a budget to pay his actors. "it's not against the law to be paid for effective performances," he said in an interview last week. [unZooDarius]

so they're not really unemployed? [Black Eagle Enterpriser]

the troupe charges 30% of the donations received by the so-called victims via $4nothing™. [bloodsportsman]

sweet [monga manga]

their next class action is on behalf of victims of government-imposed building codes. the codes failed to withstand hurricane-force winds that "the government should have predicted," they say [jesus analytical]

BREAKING: The U.S. Senate has passed the America Sanctions Staring Act. "This is a godsend for people who are sick and tired of being objectified by improper stares that have only one thought in mind," said Senator J.W. Santander, who sponsored the bill.

how can you tell a stare is improper? [EmotionalRescuer]

if it makes you uncomfortable, it is. [Phyllis O'Neill]

another law for the growing book of nonsensical jurisprudence. it's a natural act, staring. how do you think sexual attraction and procreation work? [lypsinker]

you don't have the right to procreate with whoever you want to stare at. [Susana O]

it's a courtship thing. got to start somewhere. [tyro foam]

you could start by saying hello, being courteous, having a civilized conversation. no need to start a courtship and procreation event with a lascivious "i wanna fuck you" stare. [Reina Salpicante]

This legislation is part of the government's new Equitism Toolkit. The ASS Act is one of the many tools being adopted, as we find our way to full and total equitism and humanistic respect, finally. [Lenora Parker Bravo]

I applaud Senator Santander for unda's honor and courage. We look forward to unda's sponsoring of the next Equitism law in the toolkit—the much-anticipated Hot Privilege Training Act. Can't wait! [Altísima Miranda]

. . . The Bull-Free Network™ - "Nothing but the Real Truth™"

LIVE TRANSCRIPT: Reporter Chandler Montague Gonzalez III (a.k.a. CMG3) is at the scene in France, where a vigil is taking place for Fabrice Riccard, PDG of multinational ZHT Groupe, the largest French company supplying weapons to north and west African markets. Riccard is scheduled to be Gandhied within the hour, according to announcements by The Virtual Collective.

CMG3: . . . some of the Collective's victims, as we know, in anticipation of being attacked, prepare elaborate plans to "come back to power," as it were, once they recover. They set up trusts and teams of doctors and nurses to care for them while incapacitated, assigning legal deputies and representatives to fill their offices "while away," etc.

is that even legal? [porcus zu]

dont know bout france, but here in amerika a senator cant assign a seat warmer while und's out to lunch [Berenson Delgado]

PUBLICITY: The new and improved ZiggyMins2™ are finally here! Proven vitamins that get you in the right GenderMood™! Enhance the hormones YOU want by ordering today! New and improved formula!

CMG3: These mysterious attacks are becoming popularly known by various names. We have "Master Stroke" and the more common "Virtual Gandhi," or simply "Gandhi," used as a verb, like in "being gandhied." And, my personal favorite, "patatú," as in so-and-so had a patatú, which has spread like wildfire in Hispano-Castilian-speaking countries. Anyway, with the backdrop of this impending stroke, we're going to do something different today, having a global forum on the subject of these attacks, as I report from Paris and converse with Mia Launch, a budding musician from Lyon, who is in New York at the moment, and Indira Ghedi, a U.S. State Department whistleblower who has leaked several petabytes of classified material and is now in hiding. We will also be graced by the beautiful voice of V.J. Rangattan, moderator of the show "Konversations," which is being live-cast on iWNND in New New Delhi, Indiana, right outside Indianapolis. V.J. has himself several guests on his show today, among them the incomparable Hermione Vashti, the wise Balathan Roberts, plus many others.

what's the deal with annetta vanhauser's gandhing? wasnt she next? [Marky Billiard]

no. the guinean and this frog were announced first. [puro wally]

CMG3: So, what do we know about Fabrice Riccard? It's three in the morning here, and Riccard, or FR, as he's known in France, is still at his Paris office. Nothing unusual. His office is a luxury penthouse designed for the express purpose of spending nights when he works overtime. And over the last few years, during the meteoric rise of ZHT Groupe—in a crowded field of cutthroat competitors, I might add—he has spent many long days and nights in this penthouse, mostly on the phone, talking and talking to industry chiefs, lawmakers, foreign government officials, and clients. That's what it took. Before joining ZHT, Riccard spent a few years climbing the upper echelons of management at Alston, where he learned the art of combining the needs of corporations with those of ambitious government officials. "Manufacture what the government wants," he is said to have told not only himself but many of his proteges over the years.

booze for alkies! cigarettes for lung-cancered smokers! lethal weapons for warmongers! [Janvi O'Toole]

apples to oranges there, bud. we're allowed to have our mild vices. drinking a pint dont hurt nobody, while grenades sold to dictators kill thousands. [edward the 10th]

drunk drivers wiping out whole families on the world's highways don't hurt nobody? [marissa markina]

CMG3: FR said a few days ago that one of his clients, Patrick Bioko, the leader of Equatorial Guinea, kept him up all night. FR had not spoken to him but heard that Bioko had suffered a massive stroke. Bioko is young and energetic. His country's fountain of wealth, oil, has lost a great deal of value with the demise of the oil industry.

Everything that touches our lives today has been electrified. Economic giants like Bolivia emerged thanks to natural resources, in abundance, that happened to match the voracious needs of the power-storage industry. Equatorial Guinea's economy limped along as it hemorrhaged everything in it. To stay in power, the increasingly unpopular Bioko had no option but to turn to war. And with the dwindling resources he had access to, he developed a massive military, the envy of all of Africa, except for the Egyptian armed forces, and Bioko went on a shopping spree to build up an arsenal he could use against his own people as well as neighboring countries that might provide him with additional wealth. His gambit, if successful, was to expand borders to the south and east to include large swaths of the Congo, where vast mineral resources would restore his access to wealth and regional power.

bioko followed the warmonger's script [Alarmed No More]

who can guess what's next in cmg3's report? [nuclear-error22]

so fucking predictable [Vladimir Mehta]

"gentleman reporter" [horseshit factory]

CMG3: All the weapons Bioko purchased came from the ZHT Groupe.

bioko leaves a young widow, fanny, and seven children [abarrotero medicinal]

he didn't die [ain't slim'nough]

might as well have. the vultures in his family and government have already moved in to secure their share of the carcass. [Cinnamoon Mon]

CMG3: The most intriguing thing is how this could have happened. When The Virtual Collective announced Bioko's impending patatú, no one believed it. A young man with an active lifestyle, an avid mountaineer in the Alps and even a runner of marathons. There was no president in the world who could have been in better physical shape than Patrick Bioko. Medical experts have run numerous tests on him to try to determine how the blood flow through his brain suddenly stopped, temporarily, long enough to destroy neural connections and turn him into "almost a vegetable," as his wife, Fanny, said.

i thought this was about FR. next target, please! [islandia tate]

this type of entertainment will go on for years. no end to the number of warmongers. [valoglar algo]

leaders of the collective will be caught and executed long before they get to all the warmongers. [amiya price38]

You're missing the point. Hundreds of millions of people are members of the collective. It's our mental power, united, that is taking care of these violent bastards. [Santiago Ferrell]

no "leadership" will be executed because there is no leadership. it's all of us. [razo salieri]

you jokesters so pathetic. this virtual gandhi bullshit is a psyop, run by rogue intelligence agents who were fired and decided to start their own gig. [Lasama Arxuti]

agree. no one can tell who's in it. [Arnold Nixon28]

if a psyop, what's the motive? [Nina Nona None]

profits. say you are president x and get tired of your intelligence agencies doing whatever they please. they tell you everything is "national security," so you can't do anything about it. [Lasama Arxuti]

what? [Nina Nona None]

so you fire the agents causing all the trouble. [Lasama Arxuti] right, but when you fire them, they take all their toys with them, including the covert black funds used to pay for all their activities, and they start their own, privately-owned intelligence agencies. then, they sign trillion-dollar contracts with the agents who are still working for the president, and the president doesn't have a clue. [Arnold Nixon28]

all those agents who were terminated are now running thousands of "successful" companies that make nothing and do nothing, but their stock prices rise and rise, inexplicably. all a front and a con. [Lasama Arxuti]

if you're anti-paki, you're in, running covert operations, drawing a hefty salary on the taxpayers' back. doesn't matter if you're an "official" intelligence agent, working for the government or not. NOBODY KNOWS THE DIFFERENCE! it's all covert, and the kitty is not in the hands of any government. get it? [Arnold Nixon28]

CMG3: When Patrick Bioko was gandhied, that left ZHT's FR unable to sleep. The Collective announced that FR was next, one more victim in the long list of caring, decent human beings being vilified for choosing to supply the world—civilization—with one of its basic survival tools, a tool that has been part of humanity since prehistory: the means to defend ourselves. Someone must do the manufacturing and the supplying of the tools for self-defense, which is part of being human, after all. We cannot escape political conflicts, border disputes, wars, invasions. Shit happens, so weapons are needed to defend ourselves. Even for humanitarian causes, for us to help populations at risk that are unable to defend themselves.

the old bullcrap excuse. just let me defend your country by invading it and destroying it. [Exene Zola]

then we'll sell you the means to rebuild. low interest rates y'all! [koni lang]

CMG3: It is totally unfair. Other industries that negatively affect millions of people, like those that decimated the world's fisheries, get a free pass. Why aren't the CEOs of Japanese whalers being gandhied? Furthermore, whatever or whoever is behind the Collective has no right to play God by judging, prosecuting, and sentencing fellow human beings like poor Fabrice Riccard.

better this way, without the need for vigilante assassins getting rid of warmongers. there is no violence in simply disabling a few key figures who make war possible. [orquonellie]

it's not like anyone's been murdered [borra60]

small price to pay for huge civilizational benefits in return [icira mucai]

brilliant, providential! [juan carlos wing]

especially since they deserve worse [tapuri05]

getting off lightly, imho [trace zuniga]

y'all stupid. warmongers are NEEDED to start wars to kill people and keep the world's population in check. otherwise, we're ALL doomed! [isis seer]

CMG3: So, let's go to Mia Launch. Tell us, Mia, where are you and what are you doing during this vigil?

Mia Launch: Thank you, Chandler. Let me begin by saying that I don't agree with you on the fate of these individuals. When it comes to defending ourselves, let us do so on our terms, thank you very much. I don't need some warmonger CEO thousands of miles from my home to decide he needs to manufacture weapons to defend me. That's just an excuse. The real drive behind his efforts is profit. You can dress it any way you want, but weapons are a vehicle for profit, nothing else.

you go, mia! [delihla pacheco]

educate that snooty cmg3 bastard [imani choi]

Mia Launch: I am listening to music in my hotel room right now. I have a huge mug of coffee in my hands, with my tablet propped up on a table. Arrived in New York today and have my first gig in America tomorrow. We can hear police cars rushing through outside. Next to me is Peter, guitar in hand, singing.

Peter Kalimar: cheers!

Mia Launch: Peter's from South London. I met him at a music festival in Algiers, where both of us participated a couple of years ago. He's been quite successful as an activist, while I'm still making myself known. Peter...he's a master. His music's very catchy, danceable, instantly attracts a following. Music that's so good, fans can ignore the lyrics if they don't care about the message.

Peter Kalimar: Vouch for that, while Mia's female-power anthems are kind of difficult for male audiences, you know? One song, for example, is the popular "QomN ON rOP'Xllws doe xARErw rhw vAResa qhilw"—translates as "their dicks ain't between their legs, look between their ears." You KNOW douchebags will go ballistic when they hear it.

Mia Launch: So, I'm originally from Tunis but live in France. I'm interested in bringing down all lesser, violent men in our government and other high places.

that's one of her songs! "down, down you fall" love you mia! [salomé anniemahl]

got tickets for her show in austin next week [imamu52]

Peter Kalimar: Hard on her male fans, it is. She lives in Lyon, on her own, constantly having to keep a distance from the many men who try to woo her.

Mia Launch: Stop it.

Peter Kalimar: They find her attractive, you know? With her short and lean frame; long, straight black hair; fucking perfect, flawless skin; and a symmetrical face that's so photogenic, it's all they put on her videos. You don't see ME on the videos, do you? It's all beautiful Mia.

Mia Launch: So, it's a shame we're not in Paris to witness this in person, but we have my tablet on, live, and I see the crowds, all waiting for fucking FR to be gandhied. *Putain, j'adore !* They finally caught the bastard. You know, I have a song about him, one of my early ones. He's the pious merchant of war. France is a steady supplier of arms to African countries. Tunisia, of course. Libya. Algiers, Morocco. RCA. FR and his ilk have fueled conflict after conflict in the region for decades. A manufactured war was the reason my parents had to flee to France, and as I grew up learning history from textbooks with a distinctly French perspective—a perspective that explained the waves of refugees towards France from poorer countries as a result of France's, quote, "superior culture, stability, etc."—I could only manage my growing contempt for that blatant lie by writing songs objecting to it. Hundreds of songs filled my tablet. I wrote everywhere and at any time. And when I started putting music to the lyrics, playing and singing them in small bars in Lyon, Marseille, Aix—all over—my parents didn't agree with me. As immigrants, they told me, it was better to keep a low profile. "But, Dad," I replied, "You're so out of date. This is a country of immigrants, of refugees. We are the majority, and FrenchEuro citizenship means nothing if we still have a tiny minority of overlords in Paris and Brussels manufacturing wars. So, down, down, down with them, *tu sais ?* All the immigrant, ethnic candidates who have been elected, all the women in public office— it's all a charade. They have no power to change anything. They're celebrated for nothing because they can change nothing.

CMG3: Hold on, Mia. I'm going to have to interrupt you. We're told FR has begun to broadcast live—his point of view, or it could be a mea culpa. We'll insert his feed as we continue our programming live from all corners of the world!

Fabrice Riccard: Yes, all my thoughts have been spent on the fate of President Bioko and the many other victims I have met in person throughout my career.

why is he allowed to spew this nonsense? cut him off! [adromeda mirelle]

he's ethercasting through the ose. [chunco boss]

Fabrice Riccard: I have been carefully monitoring my health, exercising daily, playing racquetball, tennis, and following the instructions of my dietician, a wonderful woman I hired with the express directive of keeping me from having a stroke. I am taking blood thinners and anti-stress medication under the careful watch of my physician.

boooooring. pull his plug already! [featherEst]

CMG3: V.J., let's go to you with Konversations, live from iWNND in New New Delhi, Indiana.

V.J. Rangattan: Thank you, Chandler. Today's Konversations panel is discussing a mix of topics, from Pakistan, a perennial subject; to the recent student riots in Austin, Texas; to terrorist attacks; and the value of taxing luxury goods that have no purpose in living a meaningful life; etc. Robert Flargan, our youngest panelist today, has brought up the topic of Field Marshall Bioko, former president of Equatorial Guinea and a recent victim of the Virtual Collective, as we all know.

Robert Flargan: Bioko's fate fits with the concept of violence. Those taking responsibility for these so-called "celestial interventions" claim their attacks are for the good of humanity. First, let me say that no one has accepted that the so-called collective is truly behind these attacks. There has been no credible claimant to the mysterious power or technology that is being used to cause these strokes. Nobody really knows what is causing them. But that's beside the point. Are they moral interventions? I'd like to know. Who is playing God here, violently ending the careers of human beings by permanently disabling them?

V.J. Rangattan: Saji, what do you think?

Saji Valero: Yes. I'm Saji Valero, professor of Ultra-Modern Ethics at UCLA. I think the attacks fit with the concept of just war. Sending an army anywhere is, by nature, an act of violence, but what if that army is on a mission to save a victim population, a group that would be decimated by bad actors otherwise?

Menlo Riggling: Oh, here we go again—the eternal justification machine. I'm Menlo Riggling, a leading non-denominational thinker. Aquinas's three requirements were ONLY brought front and center in the twentieth century to assuage the guilt of Christians committing war atrocities. New technologies adopted by the participating armies caused millions of people to lose their lives before they even knew what hit them. It was all unadulterated war crimes—from ALL sides—during the war, and the winning side adopted the concept of Just War and Aquinas's three requirements to justify the many crimes that resulted in victory. The side that won the war, by inflicting the most human suffering, then got to paint its actions with a moral brush.

Raddi Ur: I agree, but for different reasons. Raddi Ur is my name, and I need no introduction. Just War, as a concept, is ridiculous and has been completely discredited, mainly because it tries to provide a moral framework for human actions. A framework that is fictional, illusory.

V.J. Rangattan: The whole purpose of philosophy is to discuss the morality of our actions.

Raddi Ur: There's no morality, V.J. It's a product of our imagination, of our consciousness. And, as numerous studies have already shown, consciousness is a BIOLOGICAL process in our brains, just as digestion is a biological activity in our stomachs and guts. We humans are obsessed with giving our thoughts and ideas a higher value than the acts of salivating or defecating. But "thinking," as a human activity, is just another aspect of our biology, something we do to survive through decades of life that would be somewhat meaningless otherwise. If we were REALLY smart, we would only allow our bodies to grow old enough to spawn the next generation, then die. That's our biological, evolutionary purpose anyway. But we insist on prolonging our lives, and, as a result, we have come up with "thinking," with "consciousness," with "good versus evil," with "values and morality and judgement" to keep us entertained, to keep us from thinking about how meaningless the whole of our existence truly is.

Hermione Vashti: Preposterous! What are you doing here, Raddi? If your thoughts are so meaningless to you, why on earth are you sharing them with us and the public?

V.J. Rangattan: Hermione Vashti speaking, folks. She is the chair at the Global Council on Human Interaction at the Oklahoma City Public School of Economics.

Raddi Ur: Typical argument of a desperate intellectual. There's no morality, Hermione. The fact that President Bioko killed half the population of his country does not figure into anything. So, he killed them. It's just like taking a piss, something that happens. No one, and nothing, has the right to pass judgement on anyone's actions. If I were a trillionaire giving away my trillions to cure Azuren's Disease, for example, that wouldn't make me a better human than Bioko. It's all just actions committed as we go through life. It is sickening to see people in the media celebrate Bioko's stroke, as if trying to associate themselves with a higher power administering the kind of justice that their penchant for judgement demands, as if saying, "Good job, God! The bastard had it coming to him!" Whoever thinks that way is totally disconnected from our biological reality.

V.J. Rangattan: But everything we do in life requires a decision, and every decision is a kind of judgement—isn't it?—a conscious act of our consciousness. So, whether it's a biological function, as you call it, akin to passing gas or REM sleep, it still requires a trigger, a dealing with a fork in the road of life that pushes one to go this way or that way, necessitating a decision, a choice—a moral choice.

Raddi Ur: So, if the fork in MY road says, "Do I kill 50 million people in THIS country or 50 million in THAT country? Do I nuke them or bury them alive? Hmm, what a dilemma!" That's a stupid argument, V.J. There is no morality in decision-making because morality doesn't exist.

Balathan Roberts: If I may add my two cents here. This is Balathan Roberts, a disciple of the Ullam Sect, and I am proud to be part of this Koversations panel. We all need to engage in various activities throughout life—whether we like them or not. We need to eat to stay alive. We need to have bowel movements to stay alive. We need to breathe to stay alive. Those may all be mere biological activities, but we need them. And if consciousness is indeed a biological activity that our brains perform, then we also must need it—or it wouldn't exist.

Raddi Ur: No, we don't. Hospitals can keep humans alive—hooked to respirators and feeders—for decades, without the patients' having an ounce of consciousness left in them.

you can't KNOW that, moron! not being one of those patients yourself. what if they're wildly conscious, at a different level, and you have no access to that? [desDEmono]

highly unlikely [fatty morgana]

Balathan Roberts: But you interrupted my point. Our brains need consciousness. They need to label everything they perceive. So, for example, if there is a terrorist attack, we HAVE to judge it. Take 9-11.

Raddi Ur: False flag!

V.J. Rangattan: Oh, not the false-flag argument again, Raddi.

Raddi Ur: No. No. This is important. In fact, it's a perfect example of how useless judgement is, of any kind. For decades, we have this supposedly evil act attributed to a handful of Saudis and a terrorist organization hiding in the mountains of Afghanistan. Talk about a solid judgement. Evil people doing evil things to good people. You can't get more Biblical than that. Then, God—America—went over there to punish the evildoers with fire and brimstone. Case closed. In the meantime, all those who said, "Wait a moment, there's something fishy here," were labeled conspiracy theorists, false-flag fetishists, traitors. And guess what? Three decades later, thanks to the dogged insistence of a few excellent investigators and whistleblowers, the truth finally came out. The Saudis had nothing to do with it. The whole thing was a production worthy of a Hollywood blockbuster. Pretty funny, isn't it, all those decades of pointing fingers, of judging the "evil" Muslims? That's why September 11 is officially False Flag Day today, so people don't forget how easily they can be duped and manipulated.

V.J. Rangattan: How does this apply to President Bioko? Is he the Saudis in this argument? Did he deserve a massive stroke, if in fact it was imposed on him by some virtual vigilantes blaming him of warmongering? Let's take a pause here for a word from our sponsors.

PUBLICITY: This weekend, don't miss the premiere of the eighth season of "First Child in the Colony"! Follow the fifty contesting couples as they spend the next ten months at a secret location swapping partners and racing to conceive and give birth to the First Child in the Colony! Explicit scenes you'll thoroughly enjoy! The happy parents giving birth first will receive five million dollars and a free college education for the lucky child! And don't miss rewatching Season Seven while you wait for the new season! Seven's finale was the best yet, with Tangier Dee and Alberto Lanzamoto, the winning parents—though they were not a couple at the beginning of the season!—giving birth to their child, live on camera, while everyone wondered, "Will und look Asian or North-Island Boricua?"

vaya, ¡qué episodio ése! al terminar, le dije a mi marido ¡quiero un bebé YA, carajo! [carroza de oro]

pues kebien kete inspiraron. yo, ya embarazada asta los senos, con parto la proxima semana [mujerzota moderna]

English! This is America! [alcoholic bartender]

i'm in costa rica, ásjol! [carroza de oro]

CMG3: Let's tune in, for a moment, to Fabrice Riccard's live feed, as he waits for The Virtual Collective to FAIL in its effort to do him harm.

Fabrice Riccard: People have judged me for having brought prostitutes to my office. Well, the very few I brought here weren't women I met in bars or the street. They were escort professionals I hired from agencies. Nothing wrong with that. I'm not a bad man. In the last two months, I have made arrangements, set aside what I think these young women might need without the monthly financial assistance I've been giving them.

what is he talking about? did he have the stroke already? [lucero333]

see that blue light in the background? his office looks kind of dark. [kimoraLewis]

it's a high-end coffee machine. [lao fonseca]

blue dot shimmering in the dark, like a distant planet. [Vizcay Anand]

calms him down [uninvited guest]

Whatever group of biological terrorists are causing these master strokes, they are insignificant in the large field of the cosmos. They have no real power beyond the psychological terror they have managed to spread among the ruling elites of the world. [Anthony Bhatt]

the elites, the doers, the manufacturers, the inventors, the people who matter [Sincere Rubio]

Yes. Like cowards, members of the Collective hide behind a mystery, judging others without knowing anything. [Rex Tomeric]

That distant blue dot is a testimony to the fact that all of us labor under the laws of an unknown destiny. Moral judgement of any kind is out of place. For all we know, FR's company's weapons have provided a valuable civilizational service—getting rid of violent people across the world, forcing them to fight against each other and kill each other, leaving us alone, in peace. [Barbareinos]

bravo, l'artiste ! j'adore ta bullshit poetry ! [Kanada Mayor]

BREAKING: American Federal Intelligence Services LLC™ has published a secret conversation among terrorists planning to attack the Homeland. The translated transcript (see below) emerged from a meeting of young men and their intelligence handlers in Karachi, Pakistan. It was leaked by an embedded agent in the name of transparency and as proof of ongoing terrorist activities that threaten ALL Americans, not just those of Indian descent.

> *BOT TRANSCRIPT [Edited for Clarity]:*
>
> *Komar: It worked! The instructions called for an old phone for the trigger, plus fertilizer and wires and a battery. Still, I was surprised by how powerful and loud the bomb turned out to be.*
>
> *Hashir: So, we're ready. We must avenge the murder of our martyred Yusef and his family.*
>
> *Komar: The Indian government immediately announced, after the killings, that Yusef and his family were planning a terrorist act.*
>
> *Hashir: A lie. His nine-year-old sister? His disabled mother?*
>
> *Komar: Yusef's father was working three jobs to keep his family fed. The only spare time he had was spent in bed, sleeping.*
>
> *Hashir: Yusef was the only potential terrorist in the family. Fifteen, without an education, unemployed. He spent his days with us, setting up fires to abandoned buildings, drinking*

alcohol when we could, smoking, talking. If that is what the Indian government calls planning a terrorist act, then most male teenagers in Pakistan are a target.

Komar: We have no choice but to avenge our martyred Yusef.

BOT REPORTER: American Federal Intelligence Services LLC ™ recorded the group chatting in the dark, around flames burning high in the night sky. People from the neighborhood were gathered around the exploded vehicle, as if it was a campground bonfire, before the group moved on to a café to continue the conversation. The entity named Komar said, "We made sure the car's tank was empty. Otherwise, even a larger explosion."

Hashir: The only problem is the amount of fertilizer needed. Not easy to steal and transport to the site of a target.

Komar: I have read about plastic explosives, something called PTB.

Arif: Why are we wasting so much time with this?

BOT REPORTER [Edited for Clarity]: That's Yusef's younger brother, Arif, his family's only survivor.

Arif: If we want to avenge my brother and my family, let's pick someone in the Indian government, kill him quickly, with a gun or a knife.

Komar: No one is going to make it that easy for us. Attacks must be planned.

little do they know their shit leaked! [boring con ganas]

terrorists are dumb, man [mister tinkerbell]

Hashir: Yusef wasn't planning anything, yet he was killed

with his family. Arif was just lucky to have to work that night. Otherwise, he would be martyred, too.

Arif: We must target government buildings, then. My whole family must be avenged, not just Yusef.

BOT REPORTER [Edited for Clarity]: The conversation was heard by Alouf, owner of the café where this part was recorded. Alouf is the father of one of the members of the terrorist gang. He didn't blame the group of young men for feeling the way they did, but he was worried about their actions. If word got out, they'd be punished with impunity, killed with their whole families. The café itself would be targeted. Alouf didn't want to get involved in their affairs, but it was his son, too, so it was better to find the group some guidance, instead of letting them stumble into a deadly trap.

hard to believe this came from an actual recording. sounds like a scripted, crappy video game. [rein in that deer!]

who uses fertilizer anymore? the bot made it all up! [chickens don't die]

BOT REPORTER [Edited for Clarity]: So Alouf signaled to a man who was sitting alone at a corner, finishing his coffee, and lighting a cigarette. The man approached the young men's table and introduced himself. He said he had decades of experience in the field of "correcting the unfair treatment of Pakistanis in the international arena. I can help you find a better way," he told them. "Your efforts are being wasted. All you will accomplish is getting yourselves killed. And then what? Dead men can't do anything to avenge others."

ha, ha! mr. mystery man! [rein in that deer!]

BOT REPORTER [Edited for Clarity]: The man was Ahmed Moslada. He took a seat and motioned Alouf for another coffee.

Ahmed Moslada: I'll tell you the difference between acting and reacting to an act of violence. Reaction NEVER wins. The bullies in India, and more to the point, in the United States, have lifetimes of practice pushing young people like you into corners. It's all part of their plan. They are MASTER terrorists, responsible for the deaths of hundreds of thousands of innocent people. Yet, when you react, YOU are the terrorists. They did nothing wrong in the eyes of the world. They control the narrative. Their actions are justified as promoting peace and prosperity, defending human rights, the will of the people, freedom, and democracy. And you, you are just violent thugs, frustrated young men with no education who will never accomplish anything in life, so you terrorize and target innocents with your pathetic explosions and suicide bombs.

Alouf: Listen to this man, son.

Ahmed Moslada: At present, you can be much more effective by doing almost nothing, by psychologically targeting those who are responsible for the conditions we live in. We've been given a gift from the Gods. I don't like the name Virtual Gandhi, to be honest, but what a wonderful, delicate weapon it is.

Komar: Did you invent it? Do you control who gets hit by it?

Ahmed Moslada: No. It's not our role to control it or use it, just take advantage of it while it lasts. If you listen to the news, you must have heard of Raja McKenzee, the Secretary of State of the United States. Like most of his predecessors, he is a master terrorist, very smooth, carefully manipulating his words and actions to paint a picture beloved by Indian nationalists everywhere—that Pakistan is the aggressor, that Pakistan is always scheming and looking for ways to attack the vulnerable everywhere because that is what we Pakistanis do, what our culture demands, and what the world expects from us.

BOT REPORTER [Edited for Clarity]: At that moment, Ahmed Moslada rotated the band on his wrist and moved it closer to the group of young men, offering them a digital viewer.

Ahmed Moslada: This recording was stolen. I have maybe a few hours to make use of it before destroying it. Watching this video will activate a tracking device somewhere in Delhi and Washington. It's not a video about how to make bombs or how to martyr yourselves, just a recording of a recent interview with a man called Ravi Narel.

BOT REPORTER [Edited for Clarity]: The interview is not secret or classified. It is available to anyone who wants to see it anywhere in the world. But it is Ahmed Moslada's way of presenting himself to these young men as someone with inside connections. He played the interview for them, and the young men leaned in to listen.

Ravi Narel: The United States will not tolerate this type of provocation. If you are a peace-loving person walking past a neighborhood, minding your own business, and some puny little dog comes out of nowhere and starts barking at you and threatening you, you're not going to put up with it. I will not. I'll kick the filthy, runty mutt with all my might to put an end to the nonsense. And if it persists and comes back after that, I'll take care of it permanently. THAT's how you deal with terrorists. You don't ask them politely. You don't wait for them to do harm to you. The only effective approach is to strike preemptively, with extreme prejudice, and exterminate the vermin before they act. The United States has over a century of experience in not only keeping Americans safe from extremism, but also the whole world safe from the nasty elements of society. We work tirelessly to keep the world a safe place for democracy, for fomenting respect and the development of free trade and the wellbeing of global citizens everywhere.

amen to dat [fresh cherry]

eye for an eye, before they open theirs [Carlo Chabra]

you warmongers all the same. want to make everyone blind.
[Raan2927]

shut it, chi-chi. we wear high-end goggles they can't afford in their
pathetic shoestring militaries [sargento garcia]

shoestring with nuclear weapons [troySoto]

> *BOT REPORTER [Edited for Clarity]: Slowly, the young
> men around the table recognize Narel's distinctive, high-
> pitched voice—the angry tone of his pronouncements, as if he
> were rushing through a script to get as much of it in before
> commercial announcements bring his sound bite to a close.*
>
> *Komar: I think I've heard from this Ravi man before.
> Everything he's saying is not true. It just makes me angrier.*
>
> *BOT REPORTER [Edited for Clarity]: The interviewer asks
> Narel whether the economic blockade and sanctions were
> backfiring.*
>
> *Ravi Narel: Absolutely not. Sanctions are the best way to
> deal with threats to our democracy. Every American should
> be vigilant about the evil plans of our enemies. We carefully
> monitor the terrorist chatter coming out of Pakistan, out of a
> regime whose only goal is to fund terrorist cells everywhere.
> The most effective way to shut off the spigot of funding is to
> make their economy scream. When citizens starve, they rise
> against the regime and replace it with a democratic one,
> without our having to intervene at all. So, yes, sanctions are
> incredibly effective, and we will keep them in place until they
> produce the desired results.*

making paki children starve will sure make them love our
democracy! [amberleaf]

they'll be so hungry, they'll vote for us! [88note]

This isn't a joke. People are dying. [galvanized joe]

it's a joke when we're so impotent, we can't do anything about it. [Bullish Inventor]

not anymore. now there's the virtual collective, and this asshole narel will get what's coming to him. [daily ripper]

> *BOT REPORTER [Edited for Clarity]: Narel's Interviewer: "The United States has sent thousands of troops to line Pakistan's borders with air defenses, drone launchers, and other military equipment that Pakistan has denounced as a deliberate provocation."*
>
> *Ravi Narel: Listen, let's go back to the mad-dog example. American troops are simply walking peacefully through the neighborhood. It's allowed. There's no international law against it. If the yappy little paki mutt comes out to try to bite us, we'll deal with it decisively. And let me be clear: We will swiftly take action to defend our assets in the region. The United States has the right to be anywhere in the world. Our Indian brothers and sisters have graciously offered to participate in joint exercises on THEIR territory. If those exercises happen to be near the Paki border, that's not Pakistan's business. Pakis are the ones provoking us with their constant terrorist attacks. We are there peacefully to promote democracy in the region.*
>
> *Ahmed Moslada: That's as far as you need to hear. Mr. Narel is the classic warmonger—impossible to tell whether he believes all the words that come out of his mouth or if this is just something he does to earn a good living. Either way, he's a master of twisting reality on its head, and there's almost nothing any of you can do about it. The civilized world out there believes him. They have seen the cinematic productions showing our young Pakistani men in London, in Paris, Berlin—everywhere—being violent and close-minded.*

That's all we are in their minds because that's how people like Narel have painted us, and so effectively. Pakistan has no beauty to offer, they say, no culture, no Shakespeare or Proust, no love—we're just troglodytes on a deserted landscape killing each other, mistreating our women, and planning our future terrorist acts on the so-called civilized world. In short, they have won.

Komar: Why are you telling us this?

Ahmed Moslada: Because you can do something about it, something that could have an impact without costing you anything if you do it correctly. I am thinking of a man who painted the streets of New York City some eighty or ninety years ago. I read about him somewhere but don't remember the details. He went out at night and created some kind of contraption that allowed him to look like a normal pedestrian while painting his footsteps on the streets and sidewalks that he walked on. He used purple paint, I think, and I don't remember what the symbolism of his steps were, or whether any text or message was added to the prints. But the important part is that he did it regularly and extensively. It was a form of protest. The soles of his shoes were made from foam, and he carried paint hidden in a bag under his jacket. As he walked, he was able to feed his shoes from the paint bag through tubes that ran down inside his pants to the shoes. He was able to turn the paint on and off in case he saw others approach. Every morning, the city would wake up to purple footsteps in different parts of town. I don't think he was ever caught. Then, a few years later, an artist in London started painting protest murals, also overnight, without being detected. The quality of his art was superior to mere footsteps. His murals were brilliant, depicting police brutality and other topics.

Komar: So, we turn into artists? Our friends get killed, and we're supposed to paint about it at night to make a statement?

Hashir: No. They kill one of us, we do one of theirs.

Ahmed Moslada: Except that the tit-for-tat approach is not effective. It may satisfy your young thirst for revenge, but in the long term, it doesn't do anything to save lives and punish the truly guilty, the leadership that sits safely at home planning and directing and administering the wars and the conflicts that make them wealthy. Your only weapon is to make them live in constant fear, and now you have an opportunity to do so, even if you have no idea of who or what is behind the collective.

BOT REPORTER [Edited for Clarity]: The young men remained quiet, perhaps thinking about the street painters Ahmed described, while Alouf serves them more coffee.

Ahmed Moslada: Electronic messages can be traced. So, let others spread the news while you concentrate on CREATING the message. Maybe something as simple as stencils and spray paint. Several days of "Who's Next?" all over Karachi, for example. Then, read the news. Find out who is out there, who the major players are, politicians and war profiteers heading the companies that produce, transport, and sell the weapons, the ammunition, the drones. "Who's Next?" Then, a few days later, you start naming names. "Ravi Narel." Just the name. Others will take photos of your work and spread it. Hopefully, here and abroad, you will generate an army of copycats who'll do the same— youngsters painting their own predictions of who's about to be gandhied, generating a long list of culprits to be disabled and stopped for what they are doing to the world.

Komar: That's already been done by many people.

Ahmed Moslada: Then join them. With additional luck, whoever is behind these mysterious interventions will begin targeting the people YOU name. And even if that doesn't happen, the mere broadcasting of these names around the world will make those named live in constant fear of suddenly having a seizure. It's about time the news media started covering the crimes against humanity of the politicians and industrialists who make it all possible, naming names of the perpetrators behind the killing of innocents. Since the news media is complicit, too, maybe their leadership itself should be named—the publishers, the heads of global networks, the Bollywood Studios that have chosen to spread lies and ignore the truth. They too deserve to be gandhied. You have the power to start all that. It may not seem that spray paint can have that much power, but the mere idea of a few simple words is how revolutions start. And, in this case, you're not looking to have your names become part of history books. Your goal is to remain anonymous, and alive.

Komar: And surveillance cameras everywhere? They're sure to catch one of us in the act of painting.

Ahmed Moslada: That's your problem to solve.

Hashir: How about General Sharif? No one knows him outside Pakistan or India, but he's done enough to get many young Pakistanis killed with his rhetoric.

Ahmed Moslada: National and international names. That will give your list more credibility. If this is to be a force for good—a revolution to stop the guilty—all must be named, known and unknown, local and remote. If they have a role and responsibility in the creation of chaos and suffering, they must be named. Start with the top leadership, the most responsible, and work your way down. I can assure you, you'll never run out of names.

and that, my friend, is unadulterated terrorism. [jonestowner]

young pakis planning something [gatewayJoe]

up to no good [giddy_lotus23]

punish, punish, punish the young terrorist thugs! [red lagoon]

done! café alouf is, as of right now, just a pile of rubble [deep purple supremacist]

thank you fuzzies! [red lagoon]

BREAKING: The American flag to fly at full height today for the first time in over eight months! "Old Glory will NOT be flown at half staff today," the Government Accounting Office announced, "as no mass shooting has taken place in the last 24 hours." "We thank God for this respite, and let's hope it holds," said Robby Hunt, Mayor of Boomtown, Indiana, where the latest second-amendment shooting, as und called it, took place two days ago. President Marshall-Patel will commemorate the event at 4:44 this afternoon in the Guava Garden, the release said, despite the 101 degrees expected on this breezy late-fall morning in Washington.

CMG3: We have a statement from Fabrice Riccard now. He is still doing OK, though leaked reports tell us he's been feeling pressure in his head and chest. Let's get his feed now.

Fabrice Riccard: . . . yes, I feel like punching someone to a pulp to get rid of my anger. I did not work this hard all these years to end up like a vegetable because some vigilantes don't like what I do for a living.

CMG3: His jaw is clenching, we can see. Two of his teeth have begun to throb, which causes even more pressure in his brain. It's looking like some kind of attack is beginning to take place, folks.

Fabrice Riccard: I am not going to be the next victim of this thing. I am NOT going to give them the satisfaction. This nonsense stops HERE!

CMG3: But Mr. Riccard's doctors tell us he is no longer in full control of himself. The room began to spin for him. He heard the low vibration on his eardrums, a thud or two that seemed to be coming from the ether. A rush of red and blue lights speeding towards him. I don't know how his doctors know all this, but let's trust them. A live feed claims that Riccard had a vision of his young wife, his current young wife, before they had children, when she was very young. She has appeared to him in his brain, they say, sitting on a sofa somewhere within his field of vision. Their children are there, too, as babies. His parents are still around in the vision, playing with him as he crawls, as a baby himself, on the floor of their living room. A waitress comes with a drink, and Riccard spills it. He calls out to get her to bring him another. Please. He says, "please," but she is not turning back. He feels a bitter, bitter taste in his mouth, and then everything goes black.

BREAKING: The City of New Kollam (formerly Miami, in the State of Florida) has abandoned its last-ditch efforts to save its canal network. "Sea-level rise has proven to be too much for the 217 gates of its Venetian-styled MOSE," Chief Engineer Mustave Singh said during an emergency press conference. "It was bound to happen," und added. "They couldn't save Venice, so New Kollam's gambit was always a risky proposition, even with the many more gates we installed here." The city of 12.8 million now begins the arduous task of abandoning all residential and commercial buildings—begin a mass migration to higher ground. "There aren't enough boats!" Mayor Mani Rodriguez-Rao told President Marshall-Patel in a call— a desperate cry to the Federal Government for immediate help. The President has promised more boats, even though critics have pointed out that New Kollam did not overwhelmingly vote for M-P in the last election. "Read my lips," Marshall-Patel said. "I don't play politics with my National Disaster Declarations. They'll get their boats in due course, after the National Guard completes its flood mitigation emergency management plan, after the election."

the most irritating thing about what never happens is . . . it never happens! [toi datta]

speak for yourself. my naanee never killed herself before having my mother. [darling lala]

so? [refuseNick]

so i'm here, and that's not irritating to me [darling lala]

it is to me [refuseNick]

prayers for the outmigrants of new kollam. they gonna need them. [Baldo Garg]

i hear oklahoma isn't flooding [kahf sultana]

BREAKING: Author John Smith XXIV has announced the publication of his controversial new book, "The Neo Untouchables: The Sad Fate of White Men in America."

i read the leaked manuscript. basically, a 500-page screed about "how they took our women." [iUsedToBeAGiant]

exactly. us white women got tired of insecure white men bitching about immigrants, so we chose the more manly indian boys instead [joanna bambi]

manly? what kind of rock are you living under? [astro$]

it's not about being "manly" but about taking responsibility. [silvia cupcake]

what the hell does that mean? [sayHello]

accepting that you are a man and accepting that you are defeated. [silvia cupcake]

PUBLIC SERVICE ANNOUNCEMENT: This year, all citizens are commanded to complete and update their FL42 forms. The newly designed FL42s, used by citizens to officially register their preferred gender designation with the federal authorities, are now available. As in past years, the FL42 has numerous versions—from FL42-01 through FL42-137—to include all possible gender designations registered under the U.S. Department of Health Corporation™. Complete your FL42 today. Obey the law. Avoid penalties.

anyone know what the FL42-15 is for? [midnight tiger]

that the one for boys painting their fingernails starting at age 7? [Aurora Kapoor]

no. according to the instructions: "Use FL42-15 if you were born XY but chose Virtual XX by age 9, with a switch to gender-appropriate apparel at age 10, followed by gender therapy beginning at age 13, with prescribed gender enhancers and counseling for reproductive organ reconfiguration surgery by age 15. If you did not get the enhancers and counseling, DO NOT use FL42-15. Use FL42-37 instead." [immigrant bandit 26]

the fingernail thingy is FL42-19, i think [pío bravo]

whatever. my gender stance doesn't fit any of the 137 options. [me highness]

you can submit a request to create FL42-138 [kanasakaV]

too much work. takes enough time and effort keeping it all shaved. [me highness]

who shaves anymore? take some FurricideMe™ tablets, and you're done! [jobQuitter]

. . . Switching to My NarciMe Network™ (bot-sorted and curated to make sense)

CELEBRITY FEED: Musician Clarissa Nob is on unda's way back from the "51 Festival" in New Mexico. Und shares the experience:

Clarissa Nob (celebrity creds authenticated): ... beginning to regret doing this journey by bus! broken down too many damn times to remember! my mind's, like, still affected by the noise, drinking, smoking, and filth that's the norm for a young and upcoming musician. i just remembered the dream i had, with a TRACTOR! it was right before leaving for the 51. what did it mean? strength? protection? the answer must be in my dream journal, so i should read it, right? ok. my wristband just beeped! notifications coming through! six in the morning!! shit!

INFOPOST: SOURCE: TodoPedia Complete™: The 51 Festival: Annual musical extravaganza named after the many attempts in the last few decades to find out what the U.S. Government was up to in a corner of New Mexico denominated Area 51, an area declared off limits to American citizens. Gradually, protests mobilized hundreds of thousands of angry citizens from across the country to demand access to the site.

At first, the reason given for the flash mobs was something of a joke—about extraterrestrials that the U.S. Government was holding captive in Area 51 and who needed to be liberated. The government mobilized thousands of National Guard personnel to the site to contain the crowds and keep them out of the restricted area.

The same news release was issued every year: "Our Armed Forces will do everything required to protect our national-security assets. Any trespassers will risk prosecution for attempting a terrorist act against the citizens and sovereignty of the United States of America. Breaching the restricted territory will result in charges of spying for foreign governments and of treason, punishable with a death sentence or life in prison."

But no one paid attention. Enterprising young musicians began several music festivals at key locations around Area 51—free events to anyone who attended, featuring hundreds of bands, famous and unknown, who donated their performances to the cause. Thousands of participants brought their own miniature drones, purchased anonymously, and flew them into Area 51 to broadcast live footage of whatever could be seen from an altitude of around 30 feet, before the military had a chance to destroy them.

"An intolerable act of spying," the military insisted through

daily announcements. "Serial numbers of downed devices will be traced to their owners who will be fully prosecuted under the law. Face-recognition technology has already provided us with the identity of over 98% of those attending these illegal gatherings. Every single one of them risks, at a minimum, life in prison if a connection can be made to a spying drone."

Several participants were eventually arrested and prosecuted, and made an example of, but that only made the public's anger grow, and, every year, the banners—showing photographs of the faces of those imprisoned for life for spying—were distributed by the thousands, with musicians reading, between songs, the names of the "political prisoners" to the gathered crowds, demanding their release.

"This gets more ridiculous every year," Leif Rodriguez, the lead singer of the band Anton's Bastard Children, *said to a cheering crowd of tens of thousands at the 20th Annual 51 Festival. "I spend more time reading names than playing music! So be it. If we have to extend the number of days we spend here so we can fit in all the names and all the music, we're willing to do it, if YOU are!"*

The reply was a deafening roar from the crowd. "This is not something we are going to give up easily," he went on, "especially young people. After the fake moon landing and 9-11 revelations came fully out, and the actual truth learned by all, how can anyone in the American Government, let alone the military, expect us to believe ANYTHING they say? Who gave them the right to restrict US access to anything? This country is OURS! It belongs to US! They make their laws from their Washington sewers, handing us the commandments of what we can and cannot do, as if they were some kind of god? Who ARE these people? They are psychopaths and sociopaths with huge egos, with an elevated opinion of themselves. But guess what. They are just people. Like us, they have to eat daily, drink water, survive. They have to shit and fuck like all other animals interested in the survival of their species. So, what's so special about THEM? They have no supernatural powers. They have no right to deny us access to Area 51 or any other corner of America— or the world, for that matter. So, fuck'em! We're Anton's Bastard Children, *and WE are going to fuck THEM!"*

And the band broke into the recognizable intro of one of their most popular songs, driving the crowd crazy.

this todopedia entry is pure fantasy laced with bullshit. the bastard children never fucked anybody. like most young people who don't have the advantage of the lessons of decades of life, they underestimated, and still underestimate, the resourcefulness of the psychopaths in power. [ribosome delinquent]

yeah. the annual flash protests became just another event in the cat-and-mouse game between protesters and warmongers. [Izabelle Navarro]

soldiers making a show of being "defeated" via more and more breaches into the restricted area every year, while secretly removing everything that might be discovered there. [exomaniac]

Area 51 is a shell of nothing now, an annual tourist attraction— another distraction to keep the masses occupied and away from what really matters to those in power. [uri van]

nothing but an ongoing false flag [olaf etarri]

bread and circuses [nashuZone]

porn and big macs. [luckymf22]

govagents infiltrate the festival every year. distribute free narcotics and mind-altering substances to participants, turning the event into an annual bacchanal of young people who completely discredited themselves as legitimate critics of the national-security-surveillance apparatus. [lady bomba] drugged out of their minds [Paul009]

warmongers win, yet again. [lord broom]

for all we know, clarissa is a govagent, too [marina milly9]

Clarissa Nob (celebrity creds authenticated): ... hey, guys! about that fantastic dream with the TRACTOR! i gotta read it to you, cause u know how much i love my fans, even though i haven't written a song about the little tractor yet.

spare us [micky lara]

only interested if itsa porn dream [inve$tigator]

Clarissa Nob (celebrity creds authenticated): first thing i saw, when i woke up from the dream, was the portrait of my grandfather, in military uniform, on the wall facing my bed.

ughh [rocksteady lorenzo]

Clarissa Nob (celebrity creds authenticated): i have long forgotten why it's there—lack of wall space, i guess! also, every morning, my grandfather seems to be saying, "in the army, we get up at five to shine boots," or shit like that! all in my imagination, of course!

BREAKING: Aaaaaand . . . He WALKS! Nashville Murderer Gets a Mere "Time-Served" Sentence for Killing Popular Local Politician. "It was not pre-meditated murder," the defendant's attorney, Barbarino Commazon, said at a Victory Park press conference in the city. "This is what the defense team argued all along. The defendant killed the victim BY MISTAKE. The person who died by the actions of the defendant simply looked like the intended target, so a sentence harsher than 'time served' was not warranted."

the scumbag still killed somebody. [boli woods]

that's just manslaughter, like running a granny over with a tractor trailer by mistake. [infamousMoi7] but the defendant intended to kill SOMEBODY. just because the actual victim happened to look like the would-be true target, it's still murder. [Bob Mukherjee]

doesn't work that way [Dr102]

slap o-the-wrist for this defendant [GreenEnvier]

why do you keep on calling him "defendant"? and the media, same thing. whenever it's some undesirable low-life, it's always "the defendant," instead of the true identity of the perp. just say it! the paki intended to kill somebody, and ended up killing a beloved politician instead. [Patti Sharma]

he's not a paki. get ur facts rite [britnee gee]

born in new india [punjabi roadster]

just cause theres a crime doesnt mean a paki did it [Horn Mallick]

thats whats wrong with y'all indoamerican pussies! wont name the undesirables by name cause its "too offensive." fuck that! y'all in need of attending masculinization camps. [Estrella Jha]

grow the balls already. punish guilty pakis now! [Patti Sharma]

Clarissa Nob (celebrity creds authenticated): i never met my grandfather. don't even know what type of uniform he's wearing. pilot, air force, for all i know, or some kind of sailor or marine! doesn't really interest me!

there you go, subliminal promotion of the armed forces again by this celeb, claiming disinterest [Maverick Lampost]

Clarissa Nob (celebrity creds authenticated): so, days before i left for the 51, i was really tired when i woke up from the dream, saw my grandfather, then i saw my dream journal next to my bed, and i knew i had to use it or forget my dream forever! ever since i decided to follow the advice of the virtual collective and detox and eliminate fluoride from my diet, i've noticed my dreams becoming more vivid, u know? growing in color and detail!

whaaat? [eddy amin]

another lost, flaky fairy [bubba george]

Clarissa Nob (celebrity creds authenticated): my dream journal is already starting to run out of pages! it's like a spiritual experience, all these dreams. they describe strange incidents that feel absolutely LIVED, no matter how bizarre, if u know what i mean!

her obsession with dreams, insufferable. [rex el único]

brings it up every time. broken record. broken songs. [hormone of choice]

dream porn [Figurehead Kombative]

war porn [fellow more6]

stop it with the porn, already! you must be adolescent males, always sexualizing everything [Nata$ha]

no one's talking about sex, missy. [Rolando Robando]

condescending asshole! who said i was female? [Nata$ha]

war porn, for your information, is the dissemination of war casualties, the public's fascination with seeing gruesome images of people with legs blown off by landmines, etc. [fellow more6]

nothing to do with sex, MISSY! [Rolando Robando]

that's the wrong definition. war porn is luring recruits—mostly young men—with the promise of sexual exploits while in the military. [Yohan Kumar] the old-time pillaging and raping approach—known today as "liberating the oppressed with democracy" [dr. scum]

war porn uses pornography and other suggestive "assets" to give rubes a hard on for violence. [Jodo Collins]

like rosie the riveter back in the dark ages, better known as hortense the whore today—all in the service of war [dr. scum]

don't call these women whores. they're actors, getting paid to pose like sexually starved creatures to entice enemy soldiers. [bathroomSuspicious]

they probably don't even know their videos end up being projected or distributed in remote corners of the world as a weapon. [Alicia Caur]

i don't get it [gommer pyled]

bosnia 1992: posters, magazines dropped in the war zone. today: disposable screens. horny freedom fighters lap the stuff up. never seen women act that way in their culture. [learned the smart way]

even today? hard to believe. [gommer pyled]

gangbangs, amazons, aggressive nymphos—their commanders seen it, but rank-and-files been brainwashed since childhood by religious morality [dr. scum]

chad [taurux]

malaika more [Big Investor]

our hortenses enrage them, but they can't take their eyes off the action. they spend hours watching the stuff instead of maintaining their weapons or cleaning latrines or planning the next attack, get it? [Barely Stormy]

demoralizes them, too, knowing that what they're doing, watching porn, is a sin in their religion and culture [Vanus Sabralle]

but the stuff keeps on COMING! tens of thousands of disposable tablets loaded with porn dropped from the skies. [periwinkle mafioso]

cheaper than bombs! [Big Investor]

loaded with cartoons too, i hear. sodomized soldiers n stuff. all taboo and highly offensive over there. drives em crazy [Vanus Sabralle]

like i said, war porn [fellow more6]

there's a big difference between a whore and someone who's only acting like one [estellaris firmamenta]

MODERATOR: Off topic [meModerator]

not a moderator. ignore. just using the word. this forum does NOT have a moderator other than the algo [Raj Alvarado]

who's rosie riveter? never heard [928terko]

where u been? r u even american? [Samarth Mangal]

as american as curried rice, yaar [928terko]

i just looked up rosie. not showing much flesh there. [11exploiter]

butch, she is [kapuche copuchento]

"we can do it!" looks more like "ima fist u ma whole arm!" very aggressive and menacing fee-male. [11exploiter]

show dem boobs! [spitting image]

takes a lot more than boobs these days [kapuche copuchento]

portugal 1974 [Cinderello]

classic [Rubicon Marxist]

> *INFOPOST: SOURCE: TodoPedia Complete™: Portugal*
> *1974: The Carnation Revolution in April of 1974 removed*
> *the right-wing Roman Catholic regime of Marcelo Caetano.*
> *It liberated the masses of oppressed citizens who could now*
> *enjoy freedoms that had been absent in Portugal for nearly*
> *half a century. An "outburst of porn" was one of those new*
> *freedoms, which many considered a plot by right-wing*
> *forces, "sponsored by the CIA to sap the revolutionaries of*
> *their power to concentrate on what really mattered." Even*
> *left-leaning Prime Minister Vasco dos Santos Gonçalves*
> *called on citizens to fight "pseudo-leftists and anarchists*
> *instead of going to see the pornography that is around*
> *everywhere."*

theres a film shows how effective porn was in that portugal conflict
[herring falls]

coup [youthful reluctant]

whatever [herring falls]

stupid young men fighting for they dont know what [mic moth]

for the porn, of course [herring falls]

wake up, people! can't you see this is all orchestrated? arguing about
stupid porn while the rigged election is being STOLEN by Jenni
Patel! [Paul de Astute]

election? [mindy nguyen]

when IS the election? [carnival barker]

already happened! they are "counting" the votes! [Paul de Astute]

BREAKING: Three-way Tie Too Close to Call. All three top

candidates are claiming victory, and Baby Henderson, the former child actor, has gone as far as to threaten that if the votes are not "counted correctly," in unda's favor, California will declare Baby Henderson the victor anyway, and call a referendum for California to secede. Baby Henderson would then become the first President of the Republic of California.

NEED TO KNOW: 108 toothpaste ingredients you must avoid.

Clarissa Nob (celebrity creds authenticated): so, my tractor dream takes place in the large backyard of my parents' home. don't know if they are still alive in the dream because the house looks . . .

BREAKING: Cafe Chat Hall™ has uncovered a massive public-opinion manipulation campaign via bot trolls to influence social interactions among flesh-and-bone users!

i am a robot. men are shit. [top modeled]

the long patriarchal line of abuse stops here! [otto parts]

honey, the baby's crying upstairs. go check on und. [oral master]

Go check on UNDA! Proper pronouns, PLEASE! [Lindsey Barrans]

the whole of AFGA was a patriarchal effort to further subjugate women. all the ridiculous insistence on replacing pronouns by fiat is just one more bullshit activity dictated by men. [Zoya Smith]

if i want to call my girlfriend a she, and she likes it, who the fuck has the right to force me to refer to her as und? [starBullied]

fuck afga [22 de julio]

You are all despicable men, obviously. AFGA is about people being treated with respect, not a dark plot to control your behavior. Be a little flexible, please. [Lindsey Barrans]

respect is overrated. much better to be open and upfront with assholes you don't like. [Baby Methuselah]

if you don't like hearing me calling my girlfriend a she, don't listen. [starBullied]

it's a backlash thing. like more and more women choosing to be called whores, even, just because it's assertive and masculine to do so. [Baby Methuselah]

my girlfriend: i ORDER you to call me a whore! [Halston Goswami]

PUBLICITY: The Barbed Wire Defense Corporation™ strongly condemns the wanton use of bot trolls to manipulate public opinion, CEO Brandy Borges announced at a press conference today at the company's headquarters in Michigan. "We pledge to donate and support social-impact programs fighting bot trolls and other antisocial behavior. In partnership with our consultants, we will be coaching and mentoring the victims of trolls so they can have access to loans to pay for treating their trauma. We at Barbed Wire Defense Corporation™ always want to make a difference. We give back to our community, donating to our local food bank as well as providing, free of charge, tens of miles of our best barbed-wire products to local ranchers and correctional facilities.

Clarissa Nob (celebrity creds authenticated): . . . don't know if they are still alive in the dream because the house looks abandoned. all sorts of junk in the yard. like old toys strewn around. broken doors piled up next to a fence. two large metal drums filled with used motor oil. empty cigarette packets whose colors and lettering faded long ago. there's also the tractor! painted olive green, and where the paint is peeling, i can see the bright orange of its original color. my parents never owned a tractor, u know, so what the fuck?

. . . The iRiver Network™

BREAKING: Reporting live from various corners of the world. Virtual Gandhying has become a news-media sensation! Don't miss a minute of it!

Charlie Sobamor (reporting from the Hague): Yes, my loving fans, we're approaching zero hour for the Virtual Collective to intervene Annetta VanHauser, CEO of the International Weapons Association™. I'm outside the hospital where VanHauser has been taken. A parade of reporters is here with me, providing their versions of the event, including how they met the distraught wife of the victim and their children.

Avitta Hassan (SomaPress™, Amsterdam): This has been devastating for our community, the worst form of cyberbullying perpetrated against a peaceful individual. Prime Minister Uba Samatar told us earlier today that und means to put a stop to it. We're told that others named in the so-called CAHI database are taking measures to isolate themselves and hide their whereabouts. Members of their staffs have been told to keep a low profile and reveal nothing about their daily movements or those of family members. They're treating this as a terrorist act.

Charlie Sobamor (reporting from the Hague): Although the majority of the world's population is still skeptical that a relatively small number of people can meditate to cause a stroke from a distance, the novelty of the idea has drawn a great deal of attention, tantamount to a first landing on Mars by humans. However, it's too much like science fiction, some say. On the other hand, over the last few years, various reports have revealed that covert intelligence agencies have been responsible for rapidly metastasizing Stage 8 cancers that have killed their hosts in a matter of hours. Such events evolved from being considered conspiracy theories, to being plausible, then probable, and, finally, actual reality. Everything is possible!

Avitta Hassan (SomaPress™, Amsterdam): Too many world leaders have been affected by fulminating cancers to ignore the evidence. Generalissimo Cedric LaPlace, for example, playing golf in Santo Domingo—tanned, looking like the smiling trillionaire he was, surrounded by beautiful women at every photo-op arranged by his staff. And then, four hours later, agonizing in a hospital bed with tumors riddling his deformed body until he became just a dead blob. "Cancer to everything," his doctors pronounced. "No autopsy will be possible."

Charlie Sobamor (reporting from the Hague): Investigative reporters focused more on the political causes. "Another General Offed by the Powers That Be" is a far more believable headline than "Hippies Get Together to Cause Harm with Their Collective Meditation."

Avitta Hassan (SomaPress™, Amsterdam): The CIA and analogue intelligence agencies are known to have developed clandestine methods to surreptitiously inject malign cells in a human body. Nobody knows how Generalissimo LaPlace caught the bug that killed him—perhaps a golf ball nicked his pinky?—but there is no doubt that his terminal cancer did not come from his own genes.

Charlie Sobamor (reporting from the Hague): There are thousands of people gathered outside this hospital now, most of them waiting to broadcast THEIR versions of the event via ImHereRightNow™ livestream. Holding up the polished faces of their wristbands to record what they see, the crowd resembles a rookery in Patagonia— thousands of penguins chattering away to their wristbands and themselves, and all of them opening their broadcasts with the requisite "I'm here, right now" that allows them to use the app for free. Let's listen to some of them:

"I'm here, right now, and things seem pretty quiet outside this hospital for the rich."

"I'm here, right now, with a few juicy bits to share with ya."

"I'm here, right now. Just got word that VanHauser is in her hospital room, eating her just desserts!"

"I'm here, right now, and you're NOT!"

Charlie Sobamor (reporting from the Hague): Thousands of one-way conversations murmuring the day away. The better informed, with personal ties to doctors, nurses, and the hospital's janitorial staff, can provide a few relevant details. "Ms. VanHauser's daughter arrived with her husband and two children just a few minutes ago," one man said to his wristband. They came from Brussels as soon as they could, and their arrival set a somber tone because they were all wearing black, even the young ones. No official word from doctors yet, but anonymous hospital staff are telling us Ms. VanHauser is already "in a vegetable state," hooked up to medical equipment to stabilize her breathing and vitals until the medical team can assess the damage. Certainly, no one was expecting this to happen. The police are investigating the matter, believing there might be foul play, that the public actions by the so-called Collective are just a distraction, a cover, while a direct attack, perhaps with some kind of injection, a nano-syringe, is what actually causes a victim's massive stroke. Please check my VideoTrawler™ feed to see photos and video clips where VanHauser and her wife appear with their family over the years. Citizen reporters are aggregating their VideoTrawler™ feeds, too, and we can see images of VanHauser and family on a yacht, enjoying a vacation in the Indian Ocean and arriving at Eden Island Marina in the Seychelles—quite a contrast to all the relatives wearing black now.

on vacation with the happy family while her handiwork dismembers other people's children in southern somalia [former royal]

ding, dong, the witch's almost dead! [waitrex]

did they just call that monster a victim? [Alabama squirrel]

hope someone fills her position quickly and gets the same treatment, the lot of them. [sacerdotado]

No one has the right to judge, let alone punish, another human being. Let God do what He does best. [wisdomizer]

no ones judgin. this monsters responsible for the deaths of tens of thousands, prhaps hundreds of thousands, and no one even killed her yet, just stopping her from continuin to do what shes been doin, which is kill people. plus, gods been awol for a long time now. left us to do his job. [Guatemalan Cosmonaut]

amen! amen! [filipino chiguagua]

Pearl Tang (OZview Down Under™, Bondi Beach): It's 11:00 GMT and ImHereRightNow™ folks are reporting that the Gandhying of VanHauser already happened, ahead of time? We suspect they don't know what they're broadcasting. We have a huge crowd here, all getting ready to start their meditation at 11:14 GMT sharp. My fellow Australians have opted to make this a beach party, something to experience as a group, though most people around the world are taking this event more like a spiritual calling that must be practiced alone, in a darkened room, at home, as if saying a prayer.

Ana Benetto (Vocero Azul de La Plata™, Buenos Aires): That is certainly my impression. I talked to a young woman earlier today by the name of Rosa Martinez, who said she was going to be alone in her apartment in Buenos Aires. Her brother was killed by a TAB nine-millimeter automatic, manufactured by Vivram™, an active member of the International Weapons Association™. Rosa told me she would be lighting an aromatic candle and sitting on the edge of her bed, closing her eyes, and gradually slowing down her breathing. That's how the Virtual Collective has suggested participants begin their imagining of the labyrinth, of tubes carrying a liquid, a liquid that is hot and flowing slowly, like melted wax from a candle. "So that no other human being ends up like my brother Alfonso," Rosa told me, "the liquid's progress has to be frozen. Alfonso is dead, of course. He is not suffering. But I, and my parents and siblings, and Alfonso's widow and children—their torment never ends, even though our tragedy happened more than ten years ago." Rosa added that a low-life criminal with a stolen TAB had gone on a mugging spree, demanding whatever he could take from his victims before he shot them in the head. Absolutely senseless. There was no explanation. When caught, the killer said he just liked the sound the gun's mechanism made when he pulled the trigger. "It's very metallic," he said, "and all guns today are, like, plastic, so this one had something really nice going for it."

BREAKING: 11:05 GMT. Millions or billions around the world setting their minds to the frequency of one location in the Hague, switching to the image of VanHauser's brain, of thin tubes filled with slow-moving, melted wax. In their minds, it's winter—cold outside, cold inside. Without power and heating. The rooms of the hospital can't be kept warm. As the tubes get colder, the wax flowing inside them starts to solidify, very slowly. The inside diameter of the tubes becomes smaller and smaller, headed to a place where each will be a mere orifice, a pinhole, plugged shut by the thickening wax.

Pearl Tang (OZview Down Under™, Bondi Beach): 11:10 GMT. This is SO beautiful—out of this world. Thousands of candles in front of thousands of people sitting on the sand in the Lotus position while a single, harmonious voice is heard over a PA system. "Now you are at the start of the long, hollow spaghetti," the voice is saying. "Imagine how pleasant this place is, and how relaxed you are to be here, helping the crew of angels connect their celestial pipe to the spaghetti. Soon, the sand that flows inside the celestial pipe begins to fill the spaghetti. It's the same sand that you have under yourselves right now, mixed with olive oil and tar to create a viscous material that can flow but only with a great deal of pressure. At some point, we know that the tar sands will either jam up the works and completely stop the flow, or the thin walls of the spaghetti tube will burst, unable to handle the pressure. Don't lose track of the spaghetti strands you're inside of."

this is DISGUSTING! armies of self-righteous, self-appointed accusers, judges, and executioners directing their aggression at a single, defenseless human being! How can this be considered non-violent? The real Gandhi would be appalled. [Penn Dutch]

because it's better to have ONE person (VanHauser) being the accuser, judge, and executioner of HUNDREDS OF THOUSANDS of innocents? [Buenos Aires Belle]

no one is executing this entity here, just blocking her spaghetti. [1000miler]

Sylviane Richard (Echos Doba™, Chad): We've reached 11:12 GMT. I am whispering because I am in the Doba living room of Minikit Yaya, as she prays for her loved ones—her husband, son, and four daughters killed less than a year ago by a ChickadeePax Drone™ manufactured by Peaceful Bird Technologies™. Minikit should have died with them. But, on the day of the attack, she was away from her home at a clinic nearby to get medicine for her ailing one-year-old infant. Her husband had been a terrorist, she was told, and that was why her home had been targeted. Some foreign country—France, America, England, she doesn't know—decided her whole family had to be killed. And they were mistaken. She knew her husband. He had never done anything wrong, too busy trying to earn enough to keep his family safe, healthy, and fed. He had, on purpose, avoided getting involved with the various factions fighting to control Lai, the Logone River, and the region surrounding both. Accusing and targeting his family was a lie, she says.

Landa Martinelli (Le Mont Savant™, Montreal): It's a carnival at the summit of Mont Real as we reach 11:13:50 GMT. There's a petite woman wearing a sari and whispering through a bullhorn, "Ten, nine, eight . . .," a countdown to the coordination, they say. Everyone suddenly stands quietly, with their eyes closed and faces turned to the east. "Five, four," she continues, "now is the time when humanity has said ENOUGH. This bad human, this gleeful entity who has insisted her actions don't cause any damage, will not be able to continue her harmful activities. Yes, she will be replaced by another immoral individual to keep fueling the war machinery, but the world will deal with anyone who follows in Annetta VanHauser's footsteps. There's a higher power to answer to, and we, all together, across the world, are harnessing that power to disable those who wish us harm, and we will continue to do this until there is no one willing to step up to continue to lead the effort to turn brother against brother, sister against sister, human against human. VanHauser thought she was invincible in her wealth and power, but she was just a cog, a hired gun to tell the rest of us that her employers had nothing to do with nothing, that weapons don't kill people, that war is natural, like foxes and rabbits. But enough is enough! And, to you—Person-Somebody-Whoever Replacing VanHauser—we're waiting for you."

Sylviane Richard (Echos Doba™, Chad): Minikit heard about this movement of peace that hoped to punish those responsible for unjust acts of war. She learned from relatives in Doba about the time when everyone would come together in mind, across the world, to send a bad omen to the people responsible for fueling the violence in her town. She doesn't know who VanHauser is, exactly, but she was told VanHauser was a boss in a big city overseeing the production of many of the bombs and weapons that ended up maiming and killing people in Chad. She wanted this to stop. So, in her mind, she is imagining being inside VanHauser's brain, seeing how it works, like a complicated machine in a huge factory that makes a loud, disturbing noise that must be stopped, if only to have quiet and peace come back to Minikit's surroundings. The machine was described to her as having many tubes that carry fuel, and that the way to stop the infernal noise is to imagine that fuel suddenly stopping, blocked by some paste that God put there to help Minikit achieve her goal, the goal of humanity. "God bless my beloved husband and children," she whispered to me at the beginning of this session, then lost herself in the vision of forcing that unstoppable, infernal machine to come to a full stop.

BREAKING: International Weapons Association™ Executive Suffers Stroke. As predicted by the masses of "virtual lynchers," as some have called the mobs following the Virtual Collective's directives, Annetta VanHauser, the respected leader who took the IWA from a disorganized club a few years ago to the powerful lobby it is today, appears to have been disabled by a cardiovascular event. Doctors have already dismissed the notion that this medical incident was caused by collective-telepathy efforts undertaken by activists around the world. "Preposterous!" said Leeander Farmworth, a foreign policy expert in Washington. "To exert hurtful psychological pressure on targeted individuals, blaming them of supposed crimes against humanity that they NEVER committed," und added, "that's just . . . not right."

right. poor annetta's just making a living, pure and simple [Sandra Bo]

was [Feeling JamesBondie]

she was a virus that has been inoculated. with this action, the collective has literally stopped the deaths of millions of innocents in the coming months [gargles18] how's that good for our overpopulation problem? [taxMon]

The goal of the IWA is not national self-defense but profit. They use flags and propaganda, catchphrases that work their opium on the brains of simpletons. Hundreds of military bases all over the world have nothing to do with self-defense. [Susan Morelos]

but her wife is being punished, not her. the wife will have to wheel annetta around now. [indecently proposed]

she enjoyed the fruits of annetta's profits and did nothing to stop her. the least she can do now is push that adult stroller. [river oaks]

They'll be hiring more maids to take care of the wheeling and feeding and bathing. The wife will either divorce her or get a new captain of industry for her yacht. [chowTimer247]

BREAKING: Very Active Shooter (VAS) currently engaged in a Second Amendment Event (SAE) in Northern California. Reporter Erasmus Ciao is at the scene, FingerTipz™-reporting what's on the ground.

Erasmus Ciao: Yes. It's been confirmed. The VAS is wearing a MyJolieCamo™ deep-green bandolier that matches unda's StyroSuper Clogs™. This SAE, unlike those reported yesterday, is at a posh resort, and the VAS is using a more exclusive and very expensive AR-178 automatic.

sorry, bud, but this SAE cannot be blamed on the AR-178 self-defense device. [hunter perry]

absolutely not. AR-178s don't kill people. it's the psycho VAS who's killing people, not the AR-178, which was NOT designed for this purpose! [queerilla in charge]

All we can hope for is that tomorrow's SAEs won't be as gruesome as today's, and that Obsolete Americans stop being so angry at the world that they feel the need to become VASes. [d. key slasher] who said this vaser is an obsolete american? plenty of new indians misuse self-defense devices, too [queerilla in charge]

"I'm here, right now! Missus VanHauser is interviewing her new yacht crew! They all look awful young and super fit!"

borderline off topic [imperial pill pusher]

so what? [BigGirl Pollster]

this is not a topic forum. let the immature males speak their oversexualized minds. [shenaz tamang]

This is CongressUnd Vigar Rao. I represent the 5th congressional district of Indiana. Tomorrow, I will be introducing a bill that will make so-called Gandhing illegal and punishable by life in prison. Any individual who participates, either materially or mentally, in this form of cyber-lynching will be prosecuted as a terrorist and face charges not only of terrorism but also of crimes against humanity. Intentionally causing someone to have a stroke is not acceptable behavior in a democracy, no matter how many people are engaged in the activity. Our Armed Forces, National Guard, and local law-enforcement agencies across the country will be monitoring social forums like this one, op-eds, and any other public communications technology with the goal of identifying those who are behind these terrorist attacks, as well as those who are—even casually, from a distance—participating in them or celebrating them. We now have the capacity to incarcerate millions of criminals and terrorists, and the United States of America is not afraid to put its vast penitentiary infrastructure to good use. [Vigar Rao, CongressUnd]

I nominate CongressUnd Vigar Rao to the CAHI [MeNo]

aye [ipan ip]

eye [Rashid Lim]

send him to the U.S. Department of Castration already!

[altermann38a]

no one really knows if the tens of thousands of names added to the index so far will ever be considered as targets, though. [bad gifter]

the process works mysteriously [Santi Carr]

it's an algorithm, obviously. what would we do without these handy software bits that process so much info? [Semper Fifi]

not a single individual has been gandhied so far who was not on the cahi. so, even if we personally have no control over who gets gandhied, the public is certainly doing its bit by nominating perps. [ZeD Tarasyuk]

what's cahi? [mali chase]

criminals against humanity index [Elmo Rhamma]

VanHauser's been the only one gandhied so far. [zayo242]

she's the first one everyone knows about because of the crazy media attention. several others before her got their just desserts less sensationally. [sofia venezia]

but adding your neighbor to the cahi, just because—how does that work? [barfo baby]

that's where the algorithm comes in, to determine who scores the highest. . . [Semper Fifi]

hard to take the list seriously. they don't purge it. if someone adds your grandmà, who hasn't hurt a fly, there's no process to exonerate her and remove her name from the list. [summer koala]

No need to purge or exonerate. The algo takes care of sorting the wheat from the chaff. [Monica Stunning]

you just THINK you know your grandma. und has a long past for a reason. [millicent mora]

how do we know an intervention's legit, then? [sammyFletch11]

Once posted, check the target's score on the CAHI. If it's up there, it's legit, and you can go and put it on your calendar :} [Monica Stunning]

Weapons manufacturers and their associates like VanHauser should be given priority. [Carla Opel]

you can't dictate to the collective what to do. the algorithm seems to go by the number of victims. politicians can be just as lethal as those manufacturing weapons. and religious leaders—don't leave them out. [abbie byss]

RIP VanHauser [Borna Horkdell]

she's not dead [surgeonMD]

Retired In Perpetuum [Borna Horkdell]

PUBLICITY: Don't miss Episode #348 of "The Vaya & Ithia Vidcast™," where curious minds ask, "Where have all the male influencers gone?" In this episode, Vaya and Ithia explore why—all over the world—untold millions of sensitive boys in their 30s, 40s, and 50s never became the men they were supposed to become. Vaya proposes a "MeToo2" movement as a cure for male infantilism. "Can't find a reliable partner to have and raise children with?" und asks. "They're all too busy staying children themselves," replies Ithia. "It's a high-magnitude crisis!" Don't miss this important episode! Drop time for #348 is 17:42 GMT tomorrow!

sponsored by the U.S. Department of Castration [altermann38a]

. . . The EavesDrop Portal™

LIVE TRANSCRIPT: Interview with Sarah Sadchee, CEO of Women in Arms™.

sarah's pissed because they're having a man interview her [Sushmita Gangurde]

did it on purpose. foxtrot's an asshole. [glittersmith]

she's worked tirelessly to empower women around the world, being called "The Feminist CEO" and the "CEO Activist," and they send airhead foxtrot to ask her stupid questions. [allie fowler]

is sadchee being gandhied? [antarticoid bikini]

someone nominated her. not clear if it was the collective or some douche who hates powerful womyn. [Rolf Too Furious]

Like VanHauser, Sadchee has lobbied for weapons manufacturers who are responsible for the proliferation of millions of firearms, mostly in developing countries, distributed clandestinely to women, in the guise of empowering them and keeping them safe. [kandy de la buena]

Radisson Foxtrot: We'll get the best view if you lie down in the hammock, Ms. Sadchee. My crew is setting up the camera and lights to provide a compelling view.

Sarah Sadchee: That seems rather informal, doesn't it?

Radisson Foxtrot: My point. You've had a terrorist organization target you, vilify you for your efforts to protect vulnerable FEmales—so an informal approach will humanize you. You're not an evil corporate boss pulling emotional levers for a profit. You are a human being—FEmale, nonetheless—taking a break on your porch from your demanding schedule to set the record straight. Do you have a dog or a cat you could caress during the interview?

Sarah Sadchee: No time for pets.

Radisson Foxtrot: Maybe a grandchild who could come out to say hello while we do the interview, give her a hug, or something?

Look at her! KILL the jerk with that stare! [tropical congelado]

Radisson Foxtrot: Okay, then. Let's just start. I'm Radisson Foxtrot, bringing you an exclusive interview with Sarah Sadchee, the well-regarded CEO of Women in Arms™, an organization that's done so much to empower women around the world by providing them the tools to defend and liberate themselves. Sarah, as you know, has been targeted by the so-called Virtual Collective, the mysterious terrorist organization that, without evidence, without following the proper channels, has acted as accuser, prosecutor, and judge to condemn hundreds if not thousands of human beings, reducing their lives to total dependency on others. Ms. Sadchee, they say, has been nominated for a Virtual Gandhi—a virtual stroke or master stroke, or whatever new names they have come up with for these vicious attacks on peaceful citizens. We all know what that means for her and her family—and our goal here is to tell HER story, to let the world know, and to allow her to fight this baseless accusation. So, Sarah Sadchee, welcome to The Cozy With Foxtrot™. I have to ask, where were you when you found out about the nomination?

why is he placed so high? looks like foxtrot's talking down to her. [Marcela Tolle]

while she shifts uncomfortably in that hammock. [arabella838]

bastards! [Leeza Joyce]

they want to make her look like she's someone to pity, a few notches down from foxtrot's station. [Ms. Placed]

Sarah Sadchee: If you must know, I was in the bathroom. I was reading the news about the crisis in Angola, and a message from a friend popped up with a ridiculous "You've been nominated!" I didn't know what she was talking about. Nominated for what? I've received so many awards from women's groups everywhere, such messages have become an annoyance to me. The backlash in Angola. I was deep in thought, reading about the crisis for women in that suffering country, and here was some moron interrupting my deep thoughts about it.

Radisson Foxtrot: In the bathroom...mmm...but it wasn't for an award, was it? You didn't catch on, at first. You never dreamed...

Sarah Sadchee: Of course not. I get up every morning with a sense of purpose. I've accomplished a great deal in my life. What we do as an organization matters. It's as if you were a religious person all your life, doing the right thing, helping humanity, trying your best to do good, and then God splashes your face with a bucket of cold water and tells you you're going to Hell, without any explanation.

Raddison Foxtrot: A male God.

Sarah Sadchee: Whatever. I've done nothing to deserve this.

Radisson Foxtrot: So, let's talk about Angola, since you brought it up. It's a prime example of what your work has been since you founded Women in Arms™. Give us the background.

Sarah Sadchee: Like in most countries, it starts with a long history of male chauvinism, abuse, and disregard for women's rights—the usual crap that women have had to put up with for millennia. The citizens of Angola said enough was enough by electing Sonia Silva to the presidency. We supported her candidacy, of course. And as soon as she was in office, we worked with her to empower all Angolan women to...

Radisson Foxtrot: You mean you ARMED them, provided weapons to them.

Sarah Sadchee: Not just that. We have a program. We train the women. We work with legislatures to amend laws that provide equal rights to women and girls—in education, reproductive rights, self-defense.

Radisson Foxtrot: So, as it were, you WEAPONIZED Angolan women to take charge.

Sarah Sadchee: I wouldn't use that word. That's the whole misconception. This is not just about arms.

Radisson Foxtrot: But your critics, the Collective, say that's what your organization is all about. In fact, that's your name: Women. In. ARMS.

Sarah Sadchee: No. It's an obvious tag line, like MEN. AT. WORK. It's a catch-all phrase for women coming together to defend themselves, to form an army of love that looks after their interests.

Radisson Foxtrot: Yes, an ARMY, and WIA works with ARMS manufacturers. It takes a cut from profits generated by weapons sales to women around the world. In the case of Angola, for example, after Silva was elected, shipments of arms to the country reached unprecedented levels. These weapons were stored in armories at the Port of Luanda and distributed only to women through subsidiaries of WIA. Many of the women who received a firearm had never used one before, let alone owned one.

Sarah Sadchee: That's not an accurate description. No firearm was distributed without the recipient's undergoing an intensive training course that included certification and hours of practice at a firing range. Our goal is to help these women defend themselves effectively from male aggression. If you just give them the weapon without the training, you end up with a disaster.

Radisson Foxtrot: And that's what critics say happened in Angola. You brought the weapons in, you trained the women, and when the women went back to their towns, cities, and villages, the men not only confiscated the pistols and revolvers but also used them against the women and committed all sorts of OTHER crimes, even massacres.

Sarah Sadchee: Those were just a few cases that have been sensationalized by the media.

Radisson Foxtrot: Well, maybe, but there's more. WIA has managed to create a sort of civil war in Angola, with women on one side and men on the other, and the continuing importation of firearms is effectively arming both sides, encouraging the carnage.

Sarah Sadchee: We are helping women defend themselves, period. You can spin it any way you want, but the fact is, on the ground, men are attacking women, trying to kill them. And the fact that the women have access to weapons now—something they never had before—is leveling the playing field.

Radisson Foxtrot: So, there's an African saying or proverb I heard once. I don't know where it came from or if I'm paraphrasing, but it's something like this: "When the elephants fight, it's the grass that suffers." Wouldn't you say that WIA is, in a way, grooming the elephants, facilitating their fight, and that the grass is represented by the children of Angola and society at large?

Sarah Sadchee: Again, not an applicable analogy, Radisson. We're not talking poetry and verse here. Or, if you prefer, it's two MALE elephants out there, stomping on women and children. Men are the warmongers. We are merely helping the women hunt down some savage elephants until there's no more fighting. Matriarchal societies are not violent. They don't engage in war. If we keep on arming women around the world, we will have more matriarchal communities, and that will serve to gradually do away with the need for firearms.

Radisson Foxtrot: I'm sorry, but that's a ludicrous statement. You're saying that by manufacturing more and more firearms, giving them to women around the world, to half the population on the planet, that that will eventually lead to NOT needing those billions of weapons that will already be out there? So, basically, you're leading Women in Arms™ towards becoming an obsolete organization?

Sarah Sadchee: More than half the world's population. Women are a majority now, thus primed to shape societies after their worldview.

Radisson Foxtrot: Which is?

Sarah Sadchee: Matriarchal. Less violent. More nurturing.

Radisson Foxtrot: With weapons. Less violent and more nurturing by dint of a handgun and rifle for every FEmale. That's the talk of a marketing executive, Ms. Sadchee—one who's only worried about sales. There may be a good reason why we have so few matriarchal communities around the world. From an evolutionary point of view, without that kernel of male aggression, matriarchies may just not work, being unable to strike a balance between survival of the fittest and control of nature.

my word! the troglodyte foxtrot coming out of his cave now! [Narcissist Raté]

typical male gonzo. when confronted by a female more intelligent than him, he resorts to rules-of-evolution crap. [Margo Fleet]

BREAKING: Three of today's Second Amendment Events have been neutralized by Keep America Safe™ forces! Stay tuned for details.

Sarah Sadchee: I thought this interview was about how a terrorist organization has targeted me, an individual, a woman who has been working for decades to empower women. You are instead pouring fuel on The Collective's fire, Radisson, coming up with reasons why it's okay for them to ruin my life, as if I deserved it.

Radisson Foxtrot: Don't worry about it. This is just a conversation. It's not live. I'll be editing the material before I post it.

NOT! Doesn't he know about EavesDrop? What kind of media moron is he? [sapiens sapiens sapiens]

Radisson Foxtrot: I'm just trying to get passionate replies out of you so the world can hear your plight. Tell me about your childhood, Ms. Sadchee. Were you always this vocal and aware of women's rights?

Sarah Sadchee: No. I remember a few things in the early years in a remote Australian outpost, a former sheep station. I never found out why my father took us there. Looking for opportunity a long way from home, I guess. By the time I was ten, we ended up in London, closer to relatives from Pakistan who had also moved there.

Radisson Foxtrot: That's where you were radicalized, as it were.

Sarah Sadchee: A loaded term, that one. That's where I became aware that women were second-class citizens, especially among my community.

Radisson Foxtrot: The Pakistani community in London, you mean.

Sarah Sadchee: Yes.

Radisson Foxtrot: But Pakistan has had a female prime minister, even a long time ago.

Sarah Sadchee: Who was assassinated, Radisson. By males. Let's not forget that. And this is not about Pakistan. It's about London, about the world at large, about women being targeted, as I now am a target by, essentially, a call to end my life as I know it.

Radisson Foxtrot: So, we don't know much about The Collective, or how they work their magic, or the selection process of who's eventually awarded a Gandhi from a list of hundreds of thousands nominated by the public. And you got one—a Gandhi nomination—and, overnight, became a celebrity. Very few people knew or were aware of you before this, and now you're being interviewed, you have a platform. A blessing in disguise, perhaps? The world can hear your voice. The matriarchal queendoms-in-waiting are getting the final push they needed to make it to their thrones, thanks to you. Doesn't that give you some comfort? The FEmale Unitas in Angola are ready to take control.

Sarah Sadchee: That was not my calling. I didn't ask for this. My mission is simply the distribution of the tools women need to defend themselves. I never signed up to be a martyr.

Radisson Foxtrot: And, on that note, we'll conclude this pleasant chat. Thank you, Sarah Sadchee, CEO of Women in Arms™. We wish you the best of luck in your upcoming battle. This is Radisson Foxtrot, and you just enjoyed another excellent episode of The Cozy With Foxtrot™.

. . . My NarciMe Network™

Clarissa Nob (celebrity creds authenticated): . . . not far from the tractor, there's a pit about a foot deep. it's like someone's building the backyard pool i wanted as a child but my parents refused me. "you're our only child," they told me. "what if we build that pool and then you, like, drown in it? how do you think that would make us feel? we're not going to put ourselves in that situation. end of discussion, young lady," or some bullshit like that.

who cares! [kandid kandidate]

BREAKING: JudgeBot™ has delivered a decision on the notorious EggPod Racial Profiling case. The software's decision: "There's too much evidence against the plaintiff to allow unda to pull the race card. Just because a rider wants to board a clean EggPod doesn't make unda a racist. Two-month suspension sustained. This case has no merit, and the plaintiff will pay a $50,000 Nuisance & Frivolity Fee to the court within ten days. Case closed."

Clarissa Nob (celebrity creds authenticated): . . . then . . . the large arm of an excavator approaches the house. on the field beyond the fence. gets as close as possible, sticking its arm over the fence. can't see who is operating it. slowly, the arm comes down to excavate the hole for my pool. the operator takes the soil and dumps it around the area. at one point, the machine advances and breaks a section of the fence, turns it into a plank, splintered under the weight of the machine. very violent shit. the dude inside is wearing a helmet and sunglasses. doesn't smile. an asshole, obviously. his job is to finish the excavation as soon as possible. he has many other holes to excavate, the asshole, and he isn't going to waste time smiling.

BREAKING: Recently appointed Secretary of Defense Peter "No Conflict of Interest" Marcciano has been tagged as "coming up next" by the mysterious Virtual Collective. Marcciano, also the CEO and largest shareholder of the U.S. Department of Defense Corporation™, caused controversy when President Marshall-Patel named unda Secretary of Defense. Marcciano and Marshall-Patel insist there is no conflict of interest in the appointment. That insistence seems to have precipitated Marcciano's change in status from "nominated" to "next" in the so-called Criminals Against Humanity Index, better known as the CAHI. "This is a travesty," President Marshall-Patel posted on unda's MeSez™ account. "Here we have a terrorist organization threatening a cherished public servant. It is illegal, immoral, and totally against our American values of compassion and truthfulness. I will not let this stand, so I have ordered my team to prepare Air Force One to take flight with Secretary Marcciano half an hour before the attack against unda's person, and we will show the world how powerless this so-called collective of violence is when their targeted victim is under the protection of the United States of America, 30,000 feet above earth!"

ha! wont do any good. president m-p still doesnt understand his goose is cooked. [adele vanhulli]

he's lost all credibility now that he lost the election to jenny patel. no relation, thank god. [Dani Ket]

the collective will just have to continue gandhying these arseholes round the world until they get the message [Martha 33 Vidana]

BREAKING: A hearing date has been set for John Smith, the avowed leader of the so-called Environmental Justicers Group, responsible for the dumping of a combined total of 143.7 tons of garbage in wealthy neighborhoods across the country. "I don't apologize for a second," Smith said at a news conference this morning. "The rich have been fouling poor peoples' living spaces for centuries. It's time to pay them back with the same coin." But residents of the Tony Green Meadows™ development in Scottsdale, Arizona, one of the victim communities, disagree. "This is a gross misrepresentation of reality," resident Chester Barrington III said. "To blame our community for other people's filthy living conditions is unconscionable. This is how gated communities are forced into existence, and we are filing all the necessary paperwork to own our roads and become an official gated community, isolated from other people's garbage," he added. Hal Robbelot, a psychology professor who taught John Smith at nearby New Stock Market Community College, has provided a free psychological profile of the accused: "What's ironic," Robbelot said, "is that Johnny Smith grew up in a gated community himself. He's a rich kid, and he clearly evinces the pattern of a self-hating young man who has joined a neo-radical movement just to get back at his parents and his class. This is pure class-struggle signaling," Robbelot added. A Tony Green Meadows™ neighbor has accused Smith of emptying a dumpster "stolen from a smelly ethnic restaurant" on her front lawn. The act resulted in the coating of a viscous, oily liquid that permeated the whole neighborhood with an unbearable stench for weeks. "That's environmental justice from us Justicers," Smith replied. "And I don't apologize for a second."

Clarissa Nob (celebrity creds authenticated): . . . in the meantime, three other men in coveralls enter the yard through the opening made by the excavator. they get busy attaching heavy chains to the tractor, which seems small now, next to the other machine moving dirt from one place to another. the men are talking, but their voices are muffled, and i can't get what they're saying. the noise from the excavator is muffled, too. i am, like, in the yard with them, but my ears are three hundred meters away. there's some discussion on how the chains should be attached to the tractor, it seems. the men point at different parts of the frame and the wheels. one man, the asshole, is obviously upset that the other two don't agree with him and takes a cigarette break in one corner of the yard, like a wounded animal.

BREAKING!: President Marshall-Patel has refused to concede the election to Jennifer Patel and is threatening "drastic actions if the votes are not counted properly to show the real results," und posted on unda's MeSez™ account. By attacking Jennifer Patel's American Hindu Party/BJP-America candidacy, Marshall-Patel completely ignores the other candidates also contesting the election, including Fartho Savage, of the America on Top Party™. Each of the many self-declared presidents has engaged in dueling posts on MeSez™, claiming their superior allegiance to the United States Armed Forces. "I pledge $54 trillion in the next three quarters to end the systemic underfunding of our awesome military!" Savage posted. In the name of national security, und added, "our persons in uniform, our HEROfolks in uniform, should ALWAYS be funded at a level that allows us to fight against every other nation in the world AT THE SAME TIME, if necessary. America and Americans deserve nothing less than to be on top of EVERYONE and EVERYTHING!" President Marshall-Patel countered with "I am still the President, and I decide to immediately give our herofolks in uniform $80 trillion in the next year of my administration to plan for the defense of our citizens against virtual-gandhi terrorism and other threats. I will also, if the votes are NOT counted properly before my inauguration, give a presidential pardon to every person incarcerated in America. I will empty all prisons as a warning, to show what happens to a democracy when the rightful candidate—the people's choice—is not given the White House." Marshall-Patel has referred to this option as "Mariel 2.0," in reference to a massive emptying of jails in the Caribbean island of Cuba, some eighty years ago, with most of those prisoners shipped to the State of Florida.

that's stupid. isn't cuba a county in florida? [compravergüenzas]

wasn't back then. they had their own country, with a person in uniform in charge. castral, or something like that. [Karl Jalapeño Popper]

they were communist and poor back then. today, habana is the largest city in florida, glitzier and more prosperous than sad sack miami (new kollam), which is drowning in high tides and daily floods and being abandoned as we speak. it was our military that liberated those poor people in habana, of course. [Rot-a-rian]

That's why we need Marshall-Patel to stay in charge of our kick-ass military! [MuchoMásMejor!]

m-p didn't liberate cuba. that was whats her name . . . basilica or something, before i was born. [retro mentalist]

fartho savage is the man for the job [juicer88]

what job? [ElderBrute]

liberatin—we need to do more liberatin round here! [spinach ice]

i hear brasils ripe for liberation. lots of natural resources down there. [Aster Candy]

they still have some virgin forest that hasn't been raped. [Nikeetah]

jenni patel, our rightful, elected president, will not engage in any raping, thank you very much. [solariz infernum]

yay. a leader without cojones! just what this cuntry needs. [Marcelo Plaza]

Clarissa Nob (celebrity creds authenticated): . . . when the excavator's done, the hole's much smaller and deeper than what i want for my pool, so wtf? but i soon realize the THREE assholes are not laboring for MY pleasure. suddenly, the long arm of the excavator becomes a crane, and the non-smiling asshole operator moves it into place above the tractor, and the rest of the crew hitches the chains to it.

BREAKING: Vache & Cow Johnson™, the dynamic duo and mayoresses of Minneapolis and Saint Paul, are splitting. The two changed their names when they ran for office and won their respective elections seven years ago. "Not only do we love and admire these sacred animals," Vache said at their combined inaugurations party, "but also because our new names gave us heaps of publicity, and it worked!" The inevitable memes have begun to make the rounds now, like "Who's getting the milk?" and "Moooove out of my house!" And it's everyone's guess what the split will mean for the sister cities, politically, now that Vache has announced that unda's administration will no longer contribute to their combined, all-women police department. As a result, Chief Policetress Anna Valmoran has announced unda's resignation.

moooocho to do about nothing [peggy all-zoned]

best celebrity couple ever. too bad. [yuko knows you]

cow and vache rip [Kaija Naughton]

selling all my stock in butter n cheese companies. [Marisol Wang]

the whole dairy thing is toast, financially and otherwise [me ruler of U]

don't forget lactic galactic. just the name did it in, plunging 38% this morning alone [Vero Ahmau]

moooove on, please. theres more important shit taking place in the world [mystery guest #5]

Clarissa Nob (celebrity creds authenticated): . . . the crane's lifting the tractor kind of viciously, you know? to about four feet off the ground, then moves it to the hole. the bastard assholes are going to BURY it! this causes a sudden, unexplainable level of distress in me, as if they're burying the child i'm never going to have. NO! i yell. stop! don't do this! but, to the assholes, i am nothing. i'm not even there. they're just doing their jobs at some abandoned property.

BREAKING: There is an alarming "Reproductive Hesitancy" among young Americans these days. Child-bearing persons are simply not bothering with birth. A SmartDollars Polling Corporation™ survey—taken by sixteen thousand potential American child-bearers between the ages of 12 and 54—has revealed that undas are "not into it," according to Head of Research Margarita Child, a potential bearer undself. "We need young people to be born so they can keep the economy humming," added economist Ronald Suitsuit, Chairman and CEO of the Federal Reserve Corporation™, in a news release after the poll's results came out. "Young people are the engine of the economy. They borrow money to be able to afford the products that America imports," und said. "Everyone wins when young people engage the American financial services that make possible the high living standards that all of us enjoy today."

i'm xy. don't blame me for not bearing. it's the xx bearers that are to blame. [Patel-Guterra]

we men play no role in this bearing crisis. women say too few good candidates to father a child with, but that excuse no longer sticks. any woman can spermbank it anytime she wants. [Lord Baron IV]

and with all the government subsidies to single-parent sperm-banked bambinos, who can complain? [Ramoney Crickey]

all banks in america now offer financing for daycare, education, medical expenses, toys, and such. so, no excuse. [pancho arya]

like i said, we're out of it. stop blaming us and let us play our video games in peace. [Lord Baron IV]

yes, yes, you lord of the hikikomoris and tang pings. we hear you! [Avril Murillo]

why even bother with men? use your own dna. [Mars Mama]

not everyone can afford designer lab eggs. a fuck with a stranger costs nothing. [Ana Rosa Lupin]

PUBLICITY: The Divine Intervention Clinic™ is here to help you where others have failed! We specialize in de-gendering surgery, and that's ALL.WE.DO. We at DIC are not distracted by the endless arguments and politics of gender identity and inaccurate labels. It's time you stop giving all the haters a chance to define who YOU are. The Divine Intervention Clinic™ will successfully de-gender you once and for all, and that will be the end of it—free at last to be who you are. Call us if you've had enough of the nonsense and are ready for a successful intervention! Generous loan terms available only to those who call within the next 52 minutes. Don't miss this chance. Holler "DIC me right!" to your listening device now. We're serious about this!

Clarissa Nob (celebrity creds authenticated): . . . the tractor's at the bottom of the hole now, and the crew climbs down the crane's arm to release the chains. i'm beside myself, of course, looking around me, searching for other witnesses. and there's this young girl standing next to the house, looking at me. why are they doing this? i ask her, but there's no reply. the excavator's arm pushes soil back into the hole, filling the gaps around the tractor first, then on top. it's a crime, i tell the girl. it wouldn't take much to fix this tractor—an oil change and a couple of new parts, right? it would be as good as new. do you know that a tractor like this can be used to plant crops in countries where poor people have no money to buy a piece of farming equipment like it? no reply.

BREAKING: Now that Fabrice Riccard has been gandhied, a number of activists in France and West Africa are calling for the expropriation of Riccard's assets, all of which, it is claimed, were provided by the ZHT Groupe, the multinational Riccard headed until und was forced to abandon unda's post as PDG.

putain ! j'adore ! [Zuleika Das]

just desserts for the amoral asshole [Reina Esparza]

profited from the deaths of millions of innocents through his weapons contracts. [paidScreeder]

unda's family should not be punished for what und did. the spouse and children should be left with some money to survive and care for unda in unda's disability. [Marquise011]

wife deserves no compassion. she enabled him in his criminal activity. [RoboJohn]

i'm writing a song about this, folks! the refrain goes, "What a wonderful world this will be, when a few more join cad Fabrice!" [MiaMusic]

PUBLIC SERVICE ANNOUNCEMENT: Cyberterrorism alert from the Government of the United States of New India, keeping our citizens well-informed and safe. All citizens must become aware that our beloved cyber-greenback, our legal tender for nearly a quarter century, HAS BEEN COMPROMISED by nefarious Pakistani hacker terrorists who have purposely destabilised the most powerful currency in the world, to the point of spreading panic among investors. For this reason, the United States of New India has officially ordered an immediate move to a new, safe digital currency for the masses, denominated the *drupee* (pronounced "drew" "pee", for those who still haven't mastered the Mother Tongue). Remember, "d" for "dollar" plus "rupee" for "rupee" will become the digital currency of the land. And, beginning January 1, 2068, the old paper greenback U.S. dollar will become a legacy currency worth nothing other than as a collector's item. Start exchanging any paper-based dollars you may still have under your mattress into drupees right now. Digital accounts will be converted automatically at the rate of one drupee for every ten cyber-greenbacks. "The drupee will make everything much more efficient," said economist Ronald Suitsuit, Chairman and CEO of the Federal Reserve Corporation™.

just another power grab by the masters of the universe [Dads NOT Cads]

as if they didn't have enough power already [chamacus escuinclum]

Clarissa Nob (celebrity creds authenticated): . . . the tractor's buried. . . . when i woke up, i realized the tractor represented time, passing time—MY life's time—and the whole dream was meant to be a warning, like "you're wasting your life, clarissa!" ok, thank you guys for reading this. i'm writing a song about it, called the orange in the green, about life changes and personal fulfillment . . .

everyone writing fucking songs now? [hiddenCannon]

dysfunctional societies are uber creative, dont ya know? [Artur Basharov]

you've been had. typical pseudo intellectual songwriting bullshit generated by ai. clarissas clearly a bot [danny moi da 4th]

change's a-coming, toto, but we still in fucking kansas! [Monkey Smart] kansas? [lucky lal]

How old are you? New Telangana used to be called Kansas. Toto I don't know. [ramachandra96]

how old are YOU? toto's the name of the sidekick character in some ancient tv show. masked cowboy vigilante. rode a white horse. silverado. they making a new bollywood musical about it! [Arshi Shantari]

wasn't that tonto? i thought toto was a dog. [Gaurik the Handsome]

tonto means fool, tonto. it was toto. [rafaeli zúñiga]

BREAKING: A Social Services office in Grand Island, Nebraska, is under lockdown. A disgruntled client with an assault weapon killed 32 other clients waiting to be served, plus 3 staff members, before taking several others hostage. Initial reports indicate the suspect was unhappy with the amount und was receiving in monthly assistance, especially after und compared the amount with what unda's neighbor was getting. The disgruntled client published a manifesto on MeSez™ before the shooting took place. The manifesto provides calculations and formulas to show how und was being "cheated, marginalized, and discriminated against by callous, corrupt public servants who care only about themselves," und wrote.

notice they don't mention the ethnicity of the perp [R.Baker]

can't say it. when i worked as a reporter, my editor always redacted whatever i filed. orders from the publisher, he'd say. paki-on-hindu crime was okay to name names, and you could mention the perp was paki. but hindu on white, never. Hindu on black, only if the victim was gendered xy and darker than the killer, and so forth. tamils got a free pass most of the time. pakis, never. [Alberto Chopra]

crazy [Ammandah]

those are still the rules, from up high. [Alberto Chopra]

where'd u work? [R.Baker]

AgitpropWombat™, but they're the same everywhere [Alberto Chopra]

where does an ethical journalist get unda's stuff published, then? [TestarBijon]

funny!!! LOL LOL! no such thing as an ethical journalist, my friend. they went the way of ethical lawyers and ethical politicians. [Wayne Robinson]

some alternative networks still report full details, though [777boeing]

but they're full of harmful hate speech :)) can't trust their motives [Rey Krawller]

truth = hate [offenda_gahn]

. . . The EavesDrop Portal™

BREAKING: The terrorism trial of Francisco Cobarrubias has taken an unexpected turn. The accused has produced several documents that appear to show an elaborate government scheme of entrapment. Judge Elmer Losiewhot tried to make the documents classified, but Cobarrubias rushed them to EavesDrop™ and other open-info networks. The documents show that American intelligence agencies are actively "encouraging and orchestrating terrorist attacks to justify and even increase their budgets and power," Cobarrubias declared in his deposition and in court. He added that he "took out an insurance policy of sorts" by making a video months before he made himself available to the intelligence-agency handlers, who egged him on in planning the terrorist attack. "The agents even provided me with the materials necessary for a deadly explosion," he added.

now everyone claims to be taking out insurance on this or that. [Waldo Disappeared] next thing we know, there'll be a real paki terrorist, caught with his hands in the grenade jar, in flagrante delicto, claiming he's being set up by the fbi and the intelligence community—and he has the video to prove it! [world-made jammer]

same video all terrorists are making before future attacks, to be used exactly in this manner and claim entrapment. [parker poly]

to hell with'em. a terrorist is a terrorist is a terrorist. making a pre-video doesn't mean shit [porty chunso]

if you're not a real terrorist, when intelligence agents invite you to blow something up, you refuse. period. [OhLiNa]

100% agree. if you accept their invitation, even if it IS entrapment, then you're a terrorist. case closed. [Roman Dostál]

i'm confused. is this cobarrubias a paki? [Brendan Ayer]

no. who cares? [taro_lung50]

just like a defense attorney arguing stupid points. is he a paki? is he not a paki? that's NOT the point! he's a terrorist, y punto! [esteban mir]

BREAKING: Today's list of celebrities announcing their new beginnings: Musician Markool™, movie star Sushmita Lodha, tennis ace Rocket, cricketer Moss, senator Legard Borgianni, and authoress Vilas Thosh. On Monday, they will initiate their hormone protocols to transition to their true genders. Their Celebration of New Life™ will be broadcast live on Sunday at 20 hours EST. Join the joyous occasion!

is it me, or are these announcements coming out by the hundreds every week? [pet detective]

over-the-counter hormonal genderizing is the new thing, like pubic hair exposure a few years ago. [pinpunk gorilla] artificial meddling's what it is. [Cristobal Vassili]

playing god [ree anne kaluga]

travesty [primo cienfuegos]

god doesn't exist! [quest4truth]

Say you're born black—a deep, beautiful ebony skin enveloping
your perfectly gorgeous body. But you don't "feel" black, you say.
At age five, you start telling people you are white. You spend every
waking moment thinking in the first person, obsessed with the idea
you were born "wrong." Your mind's on Repeat: "I am white. I am
white. I am white." What kind of pathetic life is that? Appreciate
who you are as you were born! [Firestone Elganno II]

speak for yuself. if women are allowed to have abortions, they have
abortions. if i wanna change my gender, i change my gender. [pot
pourri]

from an evolutionary perspective, gender transition is just a blip in
the eons of time. let them mutilate their bodies with hormones and
surgeries any way they see fit. gender-switched individuals are likely
not to procreate. once they die, they're gone and forgotten. no
influence whatsoever on future generations. problem solved. [axial
ager]

u r just one of the haters, aren't u? [skin deep montes]

BREAKING: After almost twenty years of lawsuits and legal
challenges, the U.S. Department of Energy Corporation™ went live
with its energy-monitoring system exactly twelve months ago today.
As we all know, the system relies on warning lights to display
energy consumption at every 911 address in the country. "The red
bulbs go on whenever a household is out of compliance," the then
newly appointed Commissar of Energy, Tritus Musa, explained at
the program's unveiling. "The red light will provide a very clear
message to the neighborhood that ENERGY WHORES LIVE

HERE" und added, "so the whole community, the whole country, will know." Now, a year later, the initiative has backfired. Red lights outside homes and businesses have become a status symbol, with wealthy neighborhoods all over the country turning into Neo Red Light Districts to signal their wealth and the fact they can waste energy to their hearts' content. So, Commissar Musa has just announced stiffer penalties and even full disconnection of power supplies and/or forced confiscation and removal of independent energy-production equipment, such as solar panels and chemical fuel cells, for those who insist on "red-boasting their energy degeneracy," as Commissar Musa put it.

. . . The Bull-Free Network™ - "Nothing But the Real Truth"

LIVE TRANSCRIPT: Reporter Chandler Montague Gonzalez III (a.k.a. CMG3) interviews Indira Ghedi, a U.S. State Department whistleblower who has leaked several petabytes of classified material and is now in hiding.

CMG3: So, let's continue our chat with Indira, who once reviewed government data with the assistance of analytical software that provided policy recommendations to key government officials—anything from immigration quotas to the number of years of incarceration required for criminals to "maintain the peace," as they say. The data also include the number of agricultural incentives needed to produce the raw materials of a stable national diet that can support the nearly one-billion population of the United States, "our Land of Plenty and True Peace," as our new national anthem goes.

this guy's insufferable [Tara McMaster]

like a pimple on my dick. extremely annoying, but ultimately temporary and inconsequential [neil the butcher]

some southerners still insist on flying old glory, even if officially shunned by a majority of american new indians as a symbol of racism. [agenda domini]

The flag's colors mean something else to them, that's all.

[LicardoRo]

congresistas dont care anyway. in washington, the "let them fly it" attitude is almost unanimous. what damage can the old stars and stripes do, after all, when your political parties control all the levers of power and all the wealth? [canine immigrant]

well-crafted multi-party charade—all the same flavor of ice cream with different names. [gilcrest roselló]

let the stars and stripes live on! [eagle thumbs upper]

yeah, sure, along with the racism it represents. no, thanks. red is for blood of the oppressed. white for the whites oppressing everyone. [ege orr-choi]

blue for the blue-chip stocks owned only by the whites [hazel yates]

white's banned now? can't use the color anymore? [travis kombs]

it's not a color. white is the LACK of color. [LitzyCantrell52]

that was the point behind the #WhiteHouseTooWhite movement. [Maeek Frigo]

House of the People. Logon ka Ghar. That's a much better name, a win-win for all citizens. [Kerry Jo Patel]

de ke la kagaron, sí ke la kagaron. poor white house—completely soiled by hindus. [fernandito kahn]

And Rose Garden to Guava Garden? What was wrong with ROSE as a colour? [Und of a Beach]

don't be dense. nothing to do with color. roses were dying. guavas grow much better in washington now. [Papillon2042]

CMG3: Indira was concerned about certain indicators in the data. In fact, the software TOLD her to be concerned. These days, governing the American masses has become so complex, politicians and public officials have gradually ceded control and begun to fully trust the algorithms, which, in a few words, always call for maintaining the peace and the population's quality of life—with generous universal basic incomes, annual citizen bonuses, and what have you—not only for this country alone, but for the world at large and....

Indira Ghedi: One of the software's brilliant recommendations, over a decade ago, was to legally limit the implementation of automation. It was the most sensible and obvious policy for a country with a fast-growing population. At first, with the rush of immigrants and refugees, there was chaos. Among the many who had not been able to set up their own businesses in the informal sector, the demand for social services, food stamps, and SSI had been too great. The federal government was forced to subsidize the experiment to the tune of trillions of dollars a week, and even then, the demand could not be sustained.

CMG3: That's right, Indira. Thank you for interrupting me. So, the software's solution, you said, was to cut down drastically on automation and to encourage the creation of millions of well-paid, manual-labor jobs. Street sweepers and trash collectors received a living wage. The population density increased drastically, in cities and rural areas, but the country was cleaner than ever. There was no graffiti to be seen. Landscapers added color with new varieties of flowers brought in from India, where it had become too hot to grow them and is now perfect in the U.S.

Indira Ghedi: There was a tremendous sense of pride of place brought home by our new Americans. They showed their appreciation for being invited to become part of a new nation by taking care of their surroundings, and the Job Corps Project™ and Do It Ourselves Initiative™ made it all work—by showing a new appreciation for human capital. It was deeply ironic that it had been a machine that had come up with the idea to implement this successful social program, one that quickly stabilized the economy and avoided the inevitable riots and unrest that would have come for certain if automation had been allowed to go on unchecked, while our new Americans were being absorbed into the population.

unbelievable. who do these two think they're fooling? the whole country is fucked, and has been fucked for decades! [feta-cheesed]

automation WAS the answer! If they had allowed full automation, in everything—including health, education, and the construction sectors—the cost of living would have dropped to nothing. [Morelialist]

and there wouldn't be a need for street sweepers and supermarket clerks to be paid ridiculously high "basic" salaries that have only led to rampant inflation. [Rufus Romano]

PUBLIC SERVICE ANNOUNCEMENT: Citizens are mandated to take their ciprofloxacin doses starting tomorrow. Remember, November is the most likely month for anthrax terrorist attacks. Be smart. Be safe. Remember November!™ and take your cipro now! Citizens who cannot afford their doses can opt for generous financial options from the Federal Reserve Corporation™. Pay for your cipro in ten easy installments with low, nominal interest rates. Remember November!™

CMG3: Our social historians have pointed it all out, haven't they? While the immigrants absorbed the existing American population into a new, hybrid culture, we saw—literally—millions of immigrants become instant, productive Americans. Kumar Pardeeh is one of them. A systems engineer, he was assigned to sweep streets in downtown Omaha as a member of a crew of hundreds of downtown sweepers receiving a living wage of $17,000 a month. That amount was worth more back then than it is today, of course, but the point is, it allowed him to live a comfortable life. As he swept the streets, he noticed the numerous minor accidents that vehicles had daily in downtown Omaha. For years, several struggling car companies had been unsuccessful at making the switch from human-driven cars to autonomous vehicles. Kumar quickly realized that the problem was not in the engineering or the technology but in a weak federal government that didn't just DEMAND adoption of the technology and set a deadline for its implementation.

Indira Ghedi: Yes, but that didn't mean that drivers had to be removed from all vehicles at gunpoint, overnight. Pardeeh understood it would take a generation to make the switch, in the way that horses and carriages had gradually been replaced by automobiles, with an overlap period of years, when both needed to coexist.

CMG3: Brilliant! So, in the evenings, after sweeping streets all day, Kumar designed an inexpensive set of sensors and accompanying wireless transmitters that could be installed in any human-driven vehicle. Because nearly all the daily accidents were caused by human drivers who were aggressive towards the autonomous vehicles, the data gathered would allow the government to predict BAD human behavior! If every vehicle fed data to a central mobility database, Kumar thought, there would soon be petabytes of drivers' patterns to inform every smart vehicle on the road. He envisioned a coalition of governments worldwide establishing a global standard for traffic data, open-sourced, and shared by all vehicle manufacturers worldwide, in real time, free of charge, with governments everywhere forcing every legacy vehicle to install these sensors and technology to provide data to the system, at the very least, if not also to control the brakes, accelerators, and steering wheels—until all the legacy vehicles disappeared from the roads!

Indira Ghedi: You're absolutely right, Chandler. And because Pardeeh had relatives in Washington, he was able to sell his idea at the Federal level, and the United States became a global leader in pushing for a global standard, a free technology that could benefit billions of people across the globe, saving millions of lives every year with the resulting avoidance of vehicular accidents.

CMG3: And, for that, Kumar became a prime example of an immigrant who started sweeping the streets of Omaha, working hard during the day and harder at night to become a productive citizen of his new country, to contribute to society and towards a peaceful global community. His invention was so obvious that no government had bothered to implement it, and it was what finally allowed autonomous vehicles to succeed and show their true value to society and the environment. And for the millions of humans who lost their jobs as drivers, as a result, the algorithms found solutions with either new or revived legacy manual labor for them, being paid a living wage of at least $17,000 per month. And it was all made possible by an Indian immigrant!

this is the "whistleblowing" this woman promised us? [Disco Owner]

shut up. you dont get to define whistleblowing. [Scholastique Amorosa]

you missed it. from the recondite depths of the federal government and its department of misinformation, the definition of whistleblowing was changed to "good tellings and singing the praises of the wonderful deeds of the righteous." [prophezional spelsheker]

BREAKING: It has been revealed that Bimbi Bam's Celebrity Manifesto, published on MeSez™ two years ago, was ghosted by a high-school dropout and not written by Bimbi Bam at all! "Not only ghosted," said investigative reporter Alex Chu, "but the dropout writer actually PLAGIARIZED the story from an AI criminal element in the slums of DC that goes by the name Horatia Algerina!" Several members of Congress are calling for a thorough investigation of celebrity manifestos being published daily, to establish the veracity of the claims made by public figures. Stay tuned!

CMG3: Let us now go to V.J. Rangattan at his iWNND studios in New New Delhi, Indiana, a suburb of Indianapolis that has grown so fast, it swallowed the city whole and became a major metropolitan region in less than twenty years. NND, as the city is commonly known, has become the new intellectual capital of the United States, a city with the largest number of think tanks and cultural headquarters. Indiana University has a massive campus with 830,000 students, give or take. The concentration of wealth from intellectual property generated by the university is such that the institution can afford to employ an army of philosophers and other intellectuals.

And it requires every student to take at least four philosophy courses throughout their many years of higher education. Thus, the quality of its graduates and its reputation for minting world-class citizens. So, V.J., Konversations is a live-cast program on iWNND with an interview-panel format that has a moderator and a series of rotating panels, with all participants being well-known intellectuals who stop by your studio for a fireside chat with the hostPerson™, whoever that may be.

V.J. Rangattan: Correct, Chandler, and thank you for having me. Participants in my show change throughout the day because the program is cast to the world 24/7/365. At the moment, I'm the moderator.

CMG3: Before we go live with your guests, why don't you tell us something about yourself?

V.J. Rangattan: Alright, thank you! I have a divinity degree from Harvard and my specialty is morals and ethics in the generation of capital. My most famous book, early in my career, was "Does GDP Stand for God Doesn't Participate?" which argues that the once-popular method of measuring economic growth should be abandoned immediately and changed to one that favors the wellbeing of the population, the quality of life of the people, as opposed to the quantity of growth, which only comes with over-consumption. In the book, I argue that endless economic growth is unsustainable, and that economies must serve the people, not the shareholders.

bullshit. that book's been written a thousand times by a thousand holier-than-thou hypocrites. [aarohi51]

i bet vj has all the money he made from that book in stocks from money-making corporations. [johnny moneda]

there was a report on this guy, released on the eavesdrop portal, and you're right. all his money invested that way, the hypocrite. he's lost all credibility. harvard divinity school like intellectual toilet paper. [faquemoz]

CMG3: After publishing that book, you were accused of being a neo-communist, naive and dangerous, etc., but many economists took heed, and influential professors of economics began to implement your philosophy in their teaching, particularly at I.U. Now in your forties, you continue your campaign to make people aware of what their actions and preferences mean to society at large, always focusing on the big picture—the big, spiritual, and philosophical picture. That is truly commendable, V.J.

BREAKING!: News from Air Force One. "It isn't good," a spokesperson for President Marshall-Patel told the news media, following the flight where Secretary of Defense and American oligarch Peter "No Conflict of Interest" Marcciano was meant to be kept out of reach, at 30,000 feet, from the manipulating minds of the Virtual Collective.

word is his arteries popped like balloons in a cacti garden! [accidental MISO]

ARRE YAAR! they wasted all that taxpayer $$$ flying him around for nothing! [Payaseen]

no one can escape the collective! [the victimizer]

i don't think it's right. if people don't like his style, they should remove him from office at the ballot box. [dulce de lúpulo]

no one elected marcciano. he was appointed. [InSoLenta]

then remove the administration that appointed him. [dulce de lúpulo]

yes! gandhi all the bastards out of office already! [Theophrastus Bombastus]

that's not what i meant. marcciano is a good guy. i'm baffled by the so many good and dedicated civil servants who have been gandhied. why are well-meaning individuals at the forefront of making the world a better place for ALL humanity being targeted by these terrorists? [dulce de lúpulo]

I agree. It's bizarre, and without explanation about what makes them a deserving target. The list grows and grows with all sorts of good names added to it—the founders of The Better World for All Foundation™, for example, and Humans United for a Caring and Loving Planet™, and several similar organizations—all struck down like flies. [karina-ko]

what don't you get? these are all wealthy individuals (usually trillionaires and even a few tetrallionaires), their "well-meaning actions" clearly a well-crafted movie clip of mendacities. [philippic master]

technology and media titans who dress their profit-seeking in sheep's clothing. [Proud Fattu]

behind their goody-goody curtains, they're always asking . . . how can i make my corporation more profitable? how can i remove the human element from sharing my profits and instead turn them into long-term rent payers? [Kristoval Kilombo]

And how can we do it all while, at the same time, making the masses feel they're in control of their destinies and wallets? [What the Hector?]

BREAKING: Argentina Going Through Yet Another Cycle of Corruption. The regime in Buenos Aires has again proven that American/New Indian electoral monitors are necessary to keep foreign political leaders honest. President George Marshall-Patel has offered to send a delegation of New Indian experts to instruct Argentine president Felixa Pascuale on how to govern properly. "It's something we New Indians do naturally," Secretary of State Raja McKenzee stated, in reference to the effective management of corruption. "As a world leader and the most advanced and developed society in the world," und added, "we like to help our allies from time to time so they can get it right."

modest macca at it again [overserved dandy]

why hasn't HE been gandhied? [mark my pasos]

he's right, though. we the best, and shithole cuntrees are shitholes because they are—and will never come to our level. [darling spoon]

Because you've been to Buenos Aires and know, via first-hand experience, it is the "shithole" capital of a "shithole" country? [pancho marplatense]

i don't need to go. it's all there, for all to see on SnoopCartho™—all of latin america a dump of favelas, the whole cuntree a shithole. [darling spoon]

you mean like shithole los angeles? abandoned, as it was, by millions after the earthquake, with neither the feds nor the cali governor lifting a fucking finger to save and restore the city? [rudy milovic]

SnoopCartho™ is known to take money from intelligence agencies to misrepresent reality and show various corners of the world in a bad light whenever it suits their narrative. [33juan razo]

that delegation that marshall-patel is getting ready to send to buenos aires has its marching orders, and snoopcartho's cranking up the fake aerials of shanties and rundown infrastructure down there to match mckenzee's cartoonish representations. [Flavio Jugaad]

better see the place with your own eyes. virtual mapping has been compromised for decades. [Norman Delighted]

BREAKING: Important news just posted on Contrition Net™, Where Wrongdoers Set Things Right™: "We regret that poor judgement contaminated our restaurant when preparing food for our clients. Our beloved 'Menu Item #5' has been deemed a racist dish in a lawsuit by a client who found we had been negligent in the amount of curry utilized to prepare it. This was dishonest on our part, hurtful, and racist. We disrespected a well-known cultural recipe. We promise to do better in the future and respect customers whose cultural backgrounds demand an authentic, non-racist menu offer. [Paul Guru, President, The Spicy American Masala Joint]"

i'm sure as hell not eating in a place where racists are preparing my food! [junkfood gourmand]

looks like nobody cares about your comment. try again in all caps. [Lazy Feline]

I DON'T LIKE "INDIAN" FOOD MADE BY NON-INDIANS! [Loud N Proud]

BREAKING: The number of Virtual Collective victims is so large, news analysts say they can no longer keep track of those affected. "Impossible to report on everyone who's been struck down," Ladislao Ibarrux stated about victims in Europe alone. News aggregators are currently setting up a list of recently gandhied individuals in various countries, to keep up with the negative effects of this cardiovascular pandemic.

A startup in Ethiopia just created a wristband with a screen that flashes alerts whenever someone is gandhied anywhere in the world. [bic bam]

saw it. posts include photos of the victims [epic burger]

more like a mug shot, with vivid magenta background [starDust25]

in most cases, it's a completely unknown individual. [Rishabha Pande]

The intense glow of the wristband announces there's been a new and successful intervention by the Virtual Collective. [hot pataka]

Channel 666 News™ talked to influUser™ Chenna Viri to get an idea of what's coming up next with this fascinating technology. We caught up with Chenna on the way to the hospital, where she influences as an AI-nursie™. . . [Channel 666 News™]

. . . The iRiver Network™

Channel 666 News™ TRANSCRIPT: "I've been fascinated by how these massive strokes are being triggered," Chenna Viri told us, in her bright-pink, form-shaping nurse's uniform made by garmentoGoldenrod™, available at all gG™ virtual stores— financing available. Viri's education and nursing practice are based on pure science, so it has been difficult for her to believe that "long-distance mental vibrations," as they have been called, can be harnessed to suddenly change the medical condition of a single individual somewhere in the world, especially when the individual is healthy and has taken care to avoid all the practices that are known to lead to having a stroke, including recreational lypthro-fractal surgery, she said.

When Viri last became aware of the magenta glow on her wrist, just a few seconds ago, she squinted to clear up her eyes and read the piece of news. A member of parliament in Germany. Large shareholder in a firm specializing in training security personnel hired by governments to plan and administer counter-intelligence operations. After the mug shot, the victim was shown in the typical expression of sudden disability, in a wheelchair, with a blanket on his lap and tubes attached to his nose and other parts of his body, presumably a few hours after he was gandhied.

These "magenta reports" are now so common, no one bothers to read them. The main interest from the public's point of view is in seeing the victim's face and the location in the world where the strike (stroke, rather) took place. Most of the time, it's the victim's country of origin. But, sometimes, those gandhied are on vacation or somehow trying to escape their fate by quickly moving from one place to the next, with the goal, in their minds, of confusing the Collective.

One executive from a munitions firm in Seattle climbed on his corporate jet the moment the Collective announced the time and day of his stroke, and began a marathon of flights, to Sydney, then Durban, Rome, etc., thinking that staying in the air, in an unknown location at the scheduled time, might make the Collective fail. All for naught. The magenta report came as expected, and the man was wheeled off the jet, a corporate privilege that was no longer his to enjoy since the corporation's shareholders immediately announced his replacement.

As we talked to Ms. Viri, there was another mugshot on her wristband that did not have the telltale magenta around the target's head and shoulders. This time, she turned up the volume to get the details. "Mr. Blair, born in the UK but a resident of Australia for the last fifteen years," the reporter said, "had not been targeted by the Collective but was fully expecting it, given his line of business. He told associates he was being proactive, engaging a personal trainer, a dietitian, and a physician to look after his health. And he had been popping a massive dose of blood thinners, as a family member said, to stave off the stroke."

A short interview followed with a cardiovascular expert on the matter. "This approach," the expert said, "is becoming very popular among people in positions of power who can be easily accused of being instrumental in acts of war. It's a trend where hundreds, if not thousands, of personal physicians have found work administering a diet of blood thinners. In this case, however, Mr. Blair did not trust that his physician was doing enough, so he self-administered additional doses of warfarin, or whatever he could get his hands on, and the results were to be expected."

Despite being careful, Mr. Blair tripped and fell while walking his Belgian poodle, slightly gracing his forehead with the sidewalk. He quickly suffered a brain hemorrhage that resulted in death. "In a way," the expert said, "Mr. Blair was also a victim of the Collective." But no magenta background for him, critics said, because the man had "cheated," trying to avoid the responsibility of his professional actions.

BREAKING: Citizens are mandated to report any sightings of spotted lanternfly colonies. "It's a well-known Chinese bioweapon," said Department of Agriculture head Best L. Tapao. "It aims to destroy our freedoms. Lanternfly larvae were surreptitiously introduced to our sphere of influence, inside the egg cartons with eggs that our agricultural producers imported from China," und added.

weren't those cartons made in paki? [No 1 in Particular]

china owns all the paki industrial base, so same thing [belles & weasels]

YOU MUST KNOW THIS: We asked fifteen doctors to rate the healthiest Porc-a-Square™ sandwiches. Here's what they said.

PUBLICITY: Join Brave Homeland Community College, Inc.™ and earn your Ph.D. in only one year! Be like Reggi Bam. At Brave Homeland, Reggi has just completed unda's end-of-semester evaluation. "It was not difficult at all," und admitted. The test was "open tablet and connected."

Every evaluation at Brave Homeland Community College, Inc.™ gives the test taker a second or third chance, until each question receives a nod with the correct multiple-choice answer. *At Brave Homeland, No One Fails™.*

One of Reggi's recent courses was "Sagacity in Conflict," packed full of useful information that applies to all aspects of a scholar's life. Our students build their careers on defense studies, practicing daily by reporting, to the FBI and other government agencies, activities that threaten our national security.

Before we tell you how YOU can get financing with a free application to get this important Ph.D. certificate, let's answer some of those FAQs brought up by the valiant men, women, and others seeking to join our academic programs!

Q: Will I have to finance 100% of earning my Ph.D. certificate, or are there grants that will cover part of the cost?

A: The U.S. Military Corporation™, under the right conditions, can pay for a substantial part of your education at Brave Homeland Community College, Inc.™ The annual defense budget that is not subject to public scrutiny includes funds to pay for the higher education of all high school graduates in the country, in exchange for the standard six years of service in the military. You can earn your doctorate while you serve your country! In fact, the transfer from high school to college is AUTOMATIC! You are GUARANTEED high school graduation when you sign up for the BHCC Ph.D. Certificate Program, no matter your grades!

Q: There are numerous critics of the law that established this system of free higher education through the military, accusing us students of being "mercenaries hired to do the dirty work of cowardly politicians who have a penchant for war," etc. How do we reply?

A: Very soon, you won't have to! Congress is getting ready to vote on free higher education for everyone, along with compulsory military service that will allow our armed forces to get all the recruits our various branches want and need, without having to pay them any benefits.

Q: Won't there be demonstrations and riots if this law is enacted?

A: No. It will be codified in the 51st Amendment to the new Constitution of the new United States of New India, and the Department of Education will fix any potential discontent by creating fast-track Ph.D. programs, like ours, that will allow students to earn a doctorate certificate in one year!

Q: Critics of the amendment have said the Army will be "the institution where all recruits are Ph.D. candidates but no one ever graduates." How do I respond to that?

A: In fact, the only ones who won't graduate, for obvious reasons, will be those who die on duty, though there are strong indications that Ph.Ds. may end up being awarded posthumously to those candidates, too. The rest are expected to become armies of doctors who will flood the American New Indian labor market with good and useful knowledge that will make our exceptional country even more so!

This is why Reggi Bam is the first person in unda's family to earn a

Ph.D., and this will give unda bragging rights for the rest of unda's life!

So, whatever walk of life Reggi strolls in after unda's six years of duty, und will find undself being introduced as "Dr. Bam" to friends and strangers alike!

"Sagacity in Conflict" Course - sample evaluation question:

What is the most common definition of sagacity?

Multiple-choice options. Select . . .

1 - the scarcity of valor
2 - the practice of intuitive guessing
3 - failed municipal planning
4 - all of the above

You guessed correctly! Be like Reggi and get your Ph.D. certificate now! And, before we go, we'll let you meet one of our stellar instructors, Colonel Wesley "Wars on All Fronts" Alvarex. Let's visit him as he paces the front end of his lecture hall at the Center for Defense Strategies Think-o-tank™ outside Alexandria, Virginia, one of the main campuses of Brave Homeland Community College, Inc.™ Let's take a peek!

> *FULL OMNISCIENT JournoBOT™ TRANSCRIPT: Colonel Wesley Alvarex is pacing the front of the lecture hall. His audience is a group of over one hundred future Ph.D. officers visiting from West Point, Annapolis, and Colorado Springs. The young men, women, and NGDBCPs have been given a tour of the Pentagon earlier today, shown the corridors of power within its inner core, as well as tours at Langley, NSA, and other classified locations.*
>
> *Colonel Wesley Alvarex: So, you're finally here. This is an informal chat—a very important one, though. We asked you to disable your embedded microchips and leave your electronic wristbands and all other electronic devices at the*

door because we want you to be 100% with ME, right here, right now—thinking about what I have to say. This may be the most important seminar of your military careers.

FUN FACT: Colonel Alvarex is the author of the runaway bestseller *How to Safely and Responsibly Use Weapons of Mass Destruction™*

Colonel Wesley Alvarex: As you saw outside, we call this lecture The Fox and the Bunny Conundrum™, *and many of you have probably heard it. That's why there's a Fox & Bunny Cafe a couple of blocks from this hall, set up by a former intelligence officer, and a similarly named dining hall on The Hill. It's a well-known concept and philosophy among those who graduate with distinction and serve with even more distinction in the government of the United States . . . of New India, be it in the Military, the Executive Branch . . . and . . . and . . . the legislative and judicial folks, of course. We're all in this together. American exceptionalism demands nothing less of us—to understand that the use of power is a privilege, that we must use it effectively and with compassion, and to kill only those who deserve to be killed.*

JournoBOT™ DESCRIPTION: A wave of laughter crosses the hall. Alvarex is not amused.

Colonel Wesley Alvarex: No laughing matter, damn it! The power given to you by nature is a matter of great responsibility. Laughter is for losers! You don't see foxes laughing, do you? You are too young to know about a long-ago, forgotten manga character called Bugs Bunny—a stupid cartoon of a bunny who laughed a lot. We didn't have a Bugs Foxy manga back then. No, the fox is known to be only engaged in serious business, the serious business of survival of the fittest, concentrated in the role assigned to him by evolution. You laugh, you lose. Simple as that.

JournoBOT™: With this statement, lights are dimmed, and a video clip begins at the front end of the hall. "We hold these truths to be self-evident" appears on the screen in white letters over a black background, followed by a waving "Interim New Glory" flag. Then, a fox appears moving slowly through woods, its head standing high and its pelt a beautiful orange of various intensities. The fox steps cautiously, reaching an old gravel driveway, then crossing it to enter a field planted with corn. The stalks are about eight feet tall, perfectly spaced, and of a deep green that almost looks artificial and contrasts fabulously with the animal's lean, orange shape.

JournoBOT™: The camera follows the fox into the forest of cornstalks at the fox's eye level. We can see the back of this magnificent animal.

Colonel Wesley Alvarex: The fox is an animal of instincts. It knows its place in the world.

JournoBOT™: The camera goes past the thick, green stalks, turns left, then right, then, at a faster pace, advances to what appears to be a different location within the same corn forest, where a bunny is gracing. Most of the students in the audience gasp.

JournoBOT™: The bunny, a smaller animal, is equally attractive in its natural beauty. It has the requisite fluffy, white tail and floppy ears. "Peter Rabbit!" someone whispers in the audience, to a few chuckles that darken the Colonel's mood.

how long is this publicity shit going to take? [farouk mehlee]

paid for by the military industrial complex. they have the money to make it last as long as they need to. [vortex antonio]

what the fuck are they selling? [Mico Valencia]

patriotism. warrior pride. [11hoursSharp]

i just signed up for my phd certificate [soldiering franky]

good for you. hope you enjoy your expensive toilet paper. all you can do with it is wipe. [SoulSearcher]

wise career move, good on ur cv [vernacularist]

yeah, when everyone and their spouses' lovers have one too. so useful. [Jimmy Potente]

i graduated from pre-k cum laude. have the certificate to prove it. i'm clever. [bijouxRO]

dont come to me when you need protectin from the enemy, jerk. we phds will ignore your desperate cries for help [soldiering franky]

no need for you to come in my defense. already armed and ready for whatever comes my way, even for the moron phds who think they're above us. [bijouxRO]

> *JournoBOT™: The bunny sniffs the base of the stalk and eats whatever else might be sprouting from the ground around it. The music that accompanies the video conveys the pastoral idyl of a peaceful stroll and enjoyment of life.*

> *JournoBOT™: A baby bunny appears next to the first one, and the young officers in the audience react with a louder gasp. They know what's coming, especially when the fox returns to the screen and reacts to something in the air, looking around as he quickens his pace. The soundtrack follows suit with a faster beat. The stalks grow blurry. The fox goes past them like a spacecraft at the speed of light. Then, suddenly, a literal shower of red sprays the screen with a desperate screech and the last breath of the baby bunny as the fox tears it apart in a frenzy. The reaction from the audience is as expected. The camera focuses on the bloody limbs hanging by a thread from the predator's mouth, the facial expression of the dead bunny, seemingly frozen in agony, and the repetitive shrill from the score that imitates the victim's last cry.*

Colonel Wesley Alvarex: To some of you, this video seems unnecessarily gory, but that is its desired effect. We trainers want it to be memorable, and the Department of Defense Corporation™ regularly updates it to a new level of gore that is appropriate to contemporary sensibilities and perceptions of violence.

JournoBOT™: The lights go up again, and Colonel Alvarex appears to have a faint smile on his lips.

Colonel Wesley Alvarex: So, the bunny—don't feel sorry for the bunny. You were hungry. You HAD to have lunch. It's the natural order of things. When you're thirsty, you drink, right? You don't think twice about it. You just do it, do what's natural and needed and required. The bunny, too, fulfills its destiny. It has a role to play, just like the fox. Did anyone notice the fox hesitating about what it needed to do in this situation? NO. There was no room for that. He ran into a scenario, he sniffed something, and he reacted. As simple as that. YOU are the foxes! And when you run into terrorist bunnies, you're going to tear them apart because that's what YOU do, what your instincts call for. You are not going to hesitate—ask yourselves, oh, is it really a terrorist bunny? NO! You will KNOW it's a terrorist bunny, and you will DESTROY it! We all know there are soft characters among our politicians, among our leaders, even in the military. They like to HESITATE, to consider the rights of the bunny, the possibility of its innocence. NO! The bunny is NOT innocent! It's a FUCKING BUNNY! Our role is to ignore those soft characters. Our goal is to act with DETERMINATION in the name of national security, and to avoid casualties among our own. Ladies and gentlemen officers—and NGDBCPs—the bunny is GUILTY, no matter how cute. Get rid of it before it causes you harm, before it kills ALL of us. Our defense forces are run with precision. There is no room for error. We must constantly deal with a civilian population that is soft and doesn't know how to defend itself, that doesn't know the real nature of bunnies. Most people are clueless, but they are

OUR clueless—our idiot citizens—so we must take care of them with effective campaigns that keep them occupied while we do the important tasks, the duties of the fox. This goes a long way back. The military is not only composed of soldiers and warriors. We also have armies of psychologists and marketing experts who assist in getting the civilian population OUT OF THE WAY and engaged in busywork that gives them purpose. Go back about a hundred and twenty years and think of the so-called Victory Gardens. For those of you who may not know, Victory Gardens were introduced with the stated purpose of helping feed the population in times of war. Stupid, right? But it was sold as a way for people to contribute, to do their bit to win the war. A brilliant bit of psychology because it ain't going to do you a lick of good to have a head of lettuce growing in your fucking backyard when the terrorist goons storm your house, spray your family with bullets, and rape everything in sight! It's the fox inside you that's going to save you. The Victory Garden is just a dumb idea for dumb people who are fucking clueless! Let the civies believe in their gardens. The idea was developed for them. Let them feel important. You concentrate on being the fox that you are and were meant to be. Now, go out to the world and tear up some rabbit!

JournoBOT™: So, all you need to do to become like Reggi Bam is sign up to get your Ph.D. certificate now! And . . . before we go, let's hear from Lazo Rangel, who signed up and is having a fantastic experience right now!

enough already! [farouk mehlee]

JournoBOT™: Before Lazo joined, he noticed our billboards everywhere. They showed our soldiers in action, lying on their bellies, dressed in crisp camo uniforms, shooting at the enemy.

Lazo Rangel: The top of every screen said, "The Thrill of Serving Your Country!" I wanted to serve. "Only those who join have the privilege to experience the LIFE!" One photo after another, a young recruit shown going through basic training, in battle, being decorated for his valor, being awarded a higher-education diploma with a smile on his face, a Ph.D. certificate, then growing older, with a large family, receiving special attention at a state-of-the-art Veterans Hospital, and being forever honored in numerous parades as his hair grew gray and he had a ton of grandchildren! To me, that was the life. My teachers had humiliated me in school, you know, giving me shit grades, insisting I would never amount to nothing if I didn't apply myself to my studies, blah, blah, blah. But the joke's on them! I have a Ph.D., and I know how I can be a great soldier, defend my country against terrorism while earning a very good living, far more money than any useless teacher ever earned.

i just checked iriver and mesez. they're all streaming this same shit. how can they do this? monopolize all networks to puke out their military vomit on us? nobody wants it. [MercatorView]

some people do. [Émerson Moreira]

some actually NEED it [37onwards]

warrior porn's what it is [Sanket Reddy]

military castration [Bo Dixit]

patriot porn [Amira Ramani]

reeks of condescension. calling us softies and civies. they'd be nothing without us programmers and network developers. [hanibal rao]

exactly. you, for a paycheck, have been enabling these soldier boyz and grrrls playing fox and bunny snafu war games for decades, so stfu [bates motelier]

Lazo Rangel: "Become One of Our Saviors," the ads

announced on my school tablet. "You're destined for great things." "We Need You." "You Can Help." "Secure Your Financial Future." I was really moved. The series of quick statements appeared on my screen, one after another. Right above them, the "Apply Now" button showed up. "Your Family Will Also Benefit Greatly," it said. "Apply Now. Serving Your Country is the Highest Honor." "Apply Now. Battle the Forces of Evil During the Summer . . . earn your Ph.D., free of charge, while on leave the rest of the year." "Apply Now." It made me think of the Bible, you know? "I delight in weaknesses, in insults, in hardships, in persecutions, in difficulties. For when I am weak, then I am strong. 2 Corinthians 12:10," *you know? "Free Two-Week Vacation in Hawaii to every recruit who signs up within the next 15 minutes!" "Apply Now. Free Medical Insurance for Life, including coverage for plastic surgery and other personal-enhancement therapies." "Apply Now. Discounted ammunition for all your weapons for as long as you remain on active duty, even in the reserves. Apply Now." And, you know what? I was so, so moved, that I took the plunge. I applied. I didn't need to see anything else. I clicked on the button and began my application. Two-week vacation in Hawaii!*

what a simpleton [rocarlio conejon]

50-50 chance he'll get blown up in some shithole thousands of miles from home. [Minotaur Cardoso]

> *JournoBOT™: Let's follow Lazo's application process so you can see how EASY it is to serve your country and earn a Ph.D.*
>
> *Question #1: Are you under 18? No problem. You can be as young as 15 when you apply. If you can drive, you can protect your nation! Just be aware you'll need parental consent if you are under 18. Complete the application, then forward it to your parents for their electronic signature!*

JournoBOT™: The application is short but contains ten psychological-profile questions that are tricky. Lazo had heard that if you didn't get those right, the army would reject you. He didn't want that to happen. Luckily, Lazo knew someone in school who could ace the profile for him, for a fee. Lazo completed the basic section of the application and saved it, then messaged Roger, a known "school nerd," for help.

Lazo: need hlp w hawaii vac app. user lazo2044%21 password doingthisshit

Roger: k pay 1st

JournoBOT™: Lazo replied with the money, including the extra amount everyone knows Roger charges to expedite the response. Roger has done so many of these, he has the answers stored somewhere and only needs to paste them in the application. It doesn't take but a minute or two. Definitely worth the money, though. Lazo didn't feel like wasting an hour answering trick questions that could keep him from serving his country if not answered correctly. Lazo smiled at the thought.

Roger: got it . will tell u when rdy

JournoBOT™: While he waited, Lazo did some research on Hawaii. He read how military facilities in Honolulu have expanded their footprint thanks to large increases in the defense budget starting in the early 2040s. The Navy and Marine Corps have been acquiring land and buildings and redeveloping the coast southeast of Kaka'ako, including several hotels and high-rise residential buildings in Waikiki, where recruits can spend their leave whenever they earn enough points to have the Air Force fly them there. "Another option," the article said, "is to get vouchers with commercial airlines flying from Los Angeles or Seattle, or, if you're stationed in Japan, from Osaka. Aloha to all our new recruits! We can't wait to get you lei'd on the beach in

Waikiki!"

Roger: k done

Lazo: u submit it?

Roger: duh

Lazo: sweet. dont forget my math tst nxt wk

Roger: pay 1st

Lazo: will do

JournoBOT™: In less than a minute, Lazo receives a message from The Commander in Chief of the United States of America/New India! "Dear Lazo, the country is in receipt of your application to join the Armed Forces of our Department of Defense Corporation™, the mightiest and most advanced military machine in the world, deployed to serve and protect humanity. I am honored to have citizens like you under my command, individuals who are willing to give their all to defend the homeland from terrorism and make America/New India safe forever. My staff is thrilled to be reviewing your application right now. They will soon respond with an offer we know you won't want to refuse. There are very high honors in serving your nation, and there are also many benefits that will help you get ahead in life. Data clearly shows that young people like you, who join the Armed Forces, do much better once they reach their thirties, definitely better than average citizens who opt for civilian life. You can earn a doctorate on us, have access to the best universities in the country, the best hospitals through our comprehensive 'Veterans for Life' health insurance, VIP transportation passes to anywhere in the world, the best legal representation backed by our military's legal department in Washington, where a literal army of lawyers will be working for YOU in case you run into any trouble during and after your service. And don't forget the paid vacations in the most exotic locales that our military bases can offer—from beaches in the Caribbean, to private islands in the South Pacific, to mountaintop retreats in Nepal, the Andes, or the Alps. This is your moment to shine, and we're looking forward to your accepting our offer and becoming a productive part of our family. Thank you for your service!"

JournoBOT™: While he waits for the offer, Lazo imagines himself on a tropical island already. He switches the tablet's screen to the gaming store and searches for a game that fits his mood. There is one called "Death in Hawaii" that intrigues him. Soldiers on a beautiful beach that seems deserted at first, but a keen eye can soon spy subversives hiding behind palm trees. He switches to POV mode and begins the hunt, also hiding behind a palm tree at first, with the muzzle of his M16z in view, ready to aim its laser pointer in the direction of his targets. "Intelligence," he says to the tablet, and a pleasant female voice immediately starts briefing him: "Subversive forces are numerous. They've been trying to take the beaches of Waikiki and are already in control of the Ala Moana Center. Be careful, these are not just locals trying to force American soldiers to vacate the city and give it back to civilians and tourism. These are hardened terrorists trained in the jungles of the Philippines, directed by extremists based in Indonesia bent on toppling democratic governments in the region that the United States of New India has solemnly promised to defend through treaties and numerous executive orders. The peace-loving people of Hawaii must be saved from this scourge. Your mission: Defend our military assets on the island and neutralize as many terrorists as possible in the process. You have your orders, Platoon Leader Lazo."

JournoBOT™: Almost immediately, Lazo starts shooting at what appears to be some kind of turban behind a palm tree. "Don't know who'd wear a turb in this tropical heat," he says, "but not for long." He keeps on shooting and moving from tree to tree, slowly advancing toward the Ala Moana Center and a new Medal of Honor for his virtual medal collection.

PUBLICITY: UFO Pizza Pies™, drone-delivered in minutes! Try our new toppings today! Aardvark. Horse. Or rabbit! Or the traditional 15 Cheesestravaganza! Pay for it in installments (full disclosure: loan compounds every minute, so you know exactly how much you owe whenever you ask your listening device to give you the balance!). Start by ordering your favorite size and toppings. Tell your listening device to deliver a UFO Pizza Pies™ to your Me+ Coordinates™ right now! Bots are waiting for your order! UFO Pizza Pies™...making your taste buds euphorian™!

Tomorrow at 11:09 GMT, join us to intervene Dr. Ellesian Verduranna, Health Director of the Federal Institute for National Health Corporation™. Verduranna is responsible for causing the deaths of hundreds of thousands of citizens who unwittingly followed health directives issued by the FINHC. The directives were intentionally designed to cause widespread fatalities while enriching Verduranna via secret commissions from the Planned Healthcare for All Initiative™. [Virtual Collective]

BREAKING: The world is on high alert. Global military units are being dispatched to protect individuals targeted by the so-called Collective. Individuals in high places. Politicians. Captains of industry. High-court judges. Heads of media and health corporations. Anyone who has made the CAHI and is responsible, according to the mysterious Collective, for promoting war, violence, and suffering among human beings. Military units are giving protective priority to those already scheduled to be gandhied.

they'll be needing more bodyguards [Daisy Chain Mambo]

the cahi is a great learning tool. [kora wade]

4 sure. often, when a name is announced, most people have never heard of the person, and millions of us across the world begin our research on the new target. [mocoso from morocco]

verduranna. who would of thought? [cholulaloid]

love the vast, revealing biographies, published online in a matter of minutes. [gonzo priest]

the cahi parade [Jonali Minor]

unknowns becoming instant celebrities, just when they're about to be hit by the cosmos. love it. [RangeMatsunaga]

BREAKING: CAHI-nominated individuals around the world have begun to announce they will be changing their ways to see if they can avoid being gandhied. The CAHI list, whose acronym stands for Criminals Against Humanity Index, has accumulated thousands of names nominated to be "intervened" by the mysterious Virtual Collective. The interventions consist of remotely instigated strokes in the vascular systems of the targeted individuals. Now, CEO Lester Remmington IV, of Remington Strategic Properties™ (RSP), who has been duly nominated to the CAHI, has promised to change the focus of his corporation—from the manufacturing of human-tracking devices to sustainable transportation and housing. "It will take us a couple of years to complete our transition," und said at a press conference in Belize, "but I promise we'll work hard to better the human condition." RSP stock plummeted immediately after the announcement. Angry shareholders have moved to initiate a hostile takeover, their spokesperson, Sando Baraqué, meme-said later that evening. "Our other option, if a takeover fails," und added, "is to go the class-action route. We shall not be transitioned!"

bout time. ceos getting scared shitless [felipe hines]

cant gandhi all shareholders tho [Tony Jabillo]

says who? [elenaMorena]

it seems artificial...to "pacify" all these people via the fear of getting gandhied [Tony Jabillo]

only way [elenaMorena]

otherwise they won't listen [felipe hines]

that's what all the totalitarian shits in all of human history have said, believing their grandiose ideas must be adopted, by force, by everyone, or else [Gabriel Gyllenhaal]

totalitarian shits versus murderous empires...hmm [Lilly Chandra]

same shit [elenaMorena]

if we have to go by the sheer number of victims and human suffering, it seems to me empires win the shit contest, hands down. [felipe hines]

PUBLICITY: Attention! Your financial and medical wellbeing could be at risk if you don't act now! If your health insurance does not include Fried Rice Syndrome (FRS) coverage, chances are you could be seriously injured—for life—if FRS strikes your household. Don't delay adding FRS coverage to your policy now! Bot-operators are standing by. And, as always, Peace of Mind Health Wellbeing Corporation™ offers generous financing to its policyholders.

PUBLICITY: Is your cat behaving strangely? Anxious? Barely eating? These are serious signs that your beloved companion may no longer be a cat and is ready to transition to life as a dog! We are here to help your pet in this important step towards self-determination. Contact us on the cloud at PeTrans™, the world's foremost authority on transspecies journeys and species-affirming surgery. We are here to help!

BREAKING: The Supreme Court has once more agreed to weigh in on gender discrimination in sports, accepting to hear the case "Trans Badminton League v. American Cricketers Association." The suit was filed by TBL players to "correct the wrongs of being paid a fraction of what cricketers earn."

buncha bullshit. no one watches or cares about rackets hitting shuttlecocks. [apexShark] why should badmin players be paid as much as world-famous cricketers who generate tremendous revenue for their clubs and leagues? [drunk teetotaler]

u. r. just bigoted against trans athletes. [balmy333]

oh. i apologize. i went to an all-boys school [drunk teetotaler]

freak [rainbow warrior]

badmintoners are just doing it for the attention, like that influencer who pulled a disnot fake disappearance to gain market share for unda's account. classic move. [OsoBear]

how else are people going to ever hear about boring badmin? [Jules Jiang]

BREAKING!: The referendum for the Mexican annexation of Texas has American New Indians furious. Governors from all neighboring states have threatened to "send additional citizens to Texas" before the vote and "nip this seditious act in the bud," said Louisiana Governor Roon Agrait. "We will activate our REpopulation campaign," und added. "We will send waves of new citizens to repopulate the Texas territory and correct the inefficiencies of the past. From now on, there will be an appropriate distribution of subject citizens in Texas, living where they belong, and voting the New Indian way."

this is against international law. you can't send "new citizens" to a state to influence a referendum. [magdalena peck]

mexico's not having it. [yolanda your panda]

i'm texmex and tired of all the new indians in my state. we prefer to be part of mexico, not new india. [angel cruz]

BREAKING: Scientists in China, Europe, and the United States of New India are sounding the alarm of a potential shift in the earth's magnetic polarity that will be nothing like what's been expected.

"We've been taught for decades that a magnetic-field reversal would take 22,000 years to complete," said NOAA polarshiftologist Neal Readywork. "That estimate went down to 9,000 years, then to 4,000, then 1,000—but the data we're looking at now indicate it could take as little as six months, so the next shift is long overdue and should have started back on June 6, 2033."

so-called scientists keep on predicting the unpredictable. been doing so for hundreds of years now, and nothing ever comes. [javamar]

Fear-mongering worthy of AgitpropWombat™, this. Solar activity has not been higher or lower than usual. All sorts of sensors show this, so whatever NOAA's Readywork is getting out of his data is wishful thinking. [beenDemoted]

the last p.s. took place some 41,000 years ago. nobody knows anything with certainty about this. [Melita Sharma]

get ready for all that beryllium-10 bombardment! [Mao Tu]

it would kill most everything on the surface of the earth. [Joep Sanders]

start digging those underground shelters, baby! [hairy auntie]

useless. no food would grow. prepare to die. [c4u]

we'll all know when it's about to arrive. the human brain is capable of sensing magnetic shifts. [brassNipples]

all the tiring nonsense about this p.s. bullshit. shut up already. [yellerNchief]

they're just using polar shifts as a distraction. [oskar barinas]

who they? [ergo et borum]

The p.s. is a switch controlled by extra-terrestrials. They flip it whenever they see the need to reset the big game they're playing.

We are the clueless participants in their game, which they call Global Dysfunction™, and when it gets to its natural conclusion, i.e., where we are now—a completely dysfunctional species and failed civilization—they reset the whole thing by flipping the switch, activating a polar shift, to start from zero once more. [switched@birth]

does that mean the ETs are sore losers? who wins the game then? [dr sue me]

BREAKING: StageShield Plex, LLC™, has filed for bankruptcy. The bulletproof plexiglass company endured years of revenue losses after the Federal Government ordered the mandatory sedation of audience members at public performances. "Once the meds kicked in," CEO Ferdinand Farnsworth explained at the bankruptcy reveal event, "there was no longer a need to have a protective barrier between performers and their audiences. Since the feds started administering pre-event sedation," und added, "it's been a whole new ballgame." The reveal took shareholders by surprise, even though the writing had been on the wall for over three years, according to some analysts. "And now," Farnsworth added, "with the approval of new additives like FunnyBonz Pharma™, administered at all comedy specials, audiences have become so cooperative with their riotous laughter, there is no need to worry about attendees becoming belligerent and shooting the performers. Ergo, stage shields are no longer needed, and we're out of business."

glad i bought the dip of funnybonz when it crashed last year. loling all the way to the bank now! [the sinister canister man]

kicking myself for missing this. convinced the attacks on performers were all staged for publicity, extending their 15 minutes with apologies, then outcry, then self-righteous demands to have the aggressor publicly shamed, and so on. should have bought funnybonz shares and dumped plex. [armando botchi]

BREAKING: Congressund Jordi Ballon has been indicted for corruption—charges that, und says, are baseless because there's no evidence. "You are NOT a criminal if your crimes are committed in secret and no one knows about them," und added.

surprised they caught the bastard [mojo kon mocca]

indictment means nothing. all for show. [lesserSeed4124]

corruption of minors, was it? [amanda start]

no. just plain ole korruption. [kora mohiuddin]

some kind of embezzlement. [blade rivas]

hardly a crime [el juez botero]

next! [crepped out]

PUBLICITY: Millions of New Indian Americans suffer quietly of pre-stage hormonal cancer without ever knowing it. Our biotech startup is the only therapeutics-oriented firm in the world tackling this ugly pre-disease. Though our patented cure has not yet been approved by the FDGA, you can become a shareholder and receive direct treatment from our team. Doctor-Broker-Operators are standing by, and our financing department can make our stock affordable to you via our twenty-year monthly installment plan. You don't have to suffer from early-stage hormonal pre-cancer anymore. Let us nip that nasty illness in the pre-bud! Talk to your Doctor-Broker today. Look us up.

BREAKING: First Virtual Gandhi victim to fully recover from gandhian incapacitation. Joao de Sousa, former CEO of Brazilian cluster-bomb manufacturer Rosella Mella™, has regained most of unda's functions and has filed several lawsuits to try to get unda's former position as chief executive back. Joachime DaSilva, who took the risk of being gandhied undself by replacing de Sousa at Rosella Mella™, is not budging, however. "This is not the Brazilian Government," DaSilva said at a news conference. "We don't keep private-sector jobs for those who've left the building on a stretcher and on life support."

BREAKING: Dysfunctional Taiwan a Basket Case! Ever since the Taiwanese decided to rejoin their long-lost cousins on Mainland China, corruption levels on the island have gone to the stratosphere! A Xiza-Lorca™ poll reveals that four in six Taiwanese would like to move to America, "where corruption is very low compared to my country," one Manxi Sonu Li said to polling NGO agents. "This is why China cannot be trusted," added newly minted U.S. of New India Secretary of State Russell LaFurquette, who replaced Raja McKenzee after McKenzee's Virtual Gandhi event.

Chinese are all alike, backstabbing everyone and helping Kashmiri terrorist with intel. [alfonso patel]

mind your manners [mercredi cai]

sino-haters are all alike [Pan4Yu]

everything ur wearing is made by chinese-employed southern europeans [vikram leo]

your wife's sex toys were assembled by poor europeans given menial jobs by the chinese [misplaced addonia]

That's an insult to the honor of my diseased wife, sir! Step outside to the cyber-fight room, right now, if you are a man! [alfonso patel]

check under your bed, dude. toys still there, probably [misplaced addonia]

cyber-fight NOW! [alfonso patel]

they left? [mercredi cai]

what they fighting with? [Xtra Sharp Cheesehead]

Ringo DuelKraft™, or something. go check for yourself and cheer them on. kind of gory, though [missura-ko]

nah. probably just a kid who'll easily beat the dead wife guy. [karma carmelo]

since when are sex toys an insult? [iudina]

they aren't. just some old guy, or religious [early arrival]

this has nothing to do with china. just a publicity stunt to claim there's no korruption in america [koffi lada]

lol lol LOL! [rEal me]

my corruption is way mo' better than YOUR corruption [ClubHouse Bambi]

BREAKING: Artificial Intelligence Reaches Tipping Point, finally. "We are at the threshold where universal basic income doesn't make sense anymore," tech trillionaire Jimmy Cardumen said in an hour-long interview with Purpura World News™. "Pragmatic leaders are asking themselves, 'Why are so many people still alive when they're no longer needed?'" und added. "The simple fact is that UBI has plagued world economies for nearly three decades now, and the only result has been inflation, inflation, and more inflation. I'll be damned if I'll let MY trillions be devalued into billions because rampant inflation keeps on diminishing all currencies."

BREAKING!: Jenni Patel one step closer to being declared winner of the New Indian Presidential race! Her three closest, sore-loser opponents are in no way ready to concede.

More like closer to being PROCLAIMED president by the puppeteers. "Oh, what type of puppet should we use this time? The mixed-race child of African immigrants? The Roma rags-to-riches sensation, ivy-educated or self-made? Oh, how about the Indian chick? That would be a good segue, no?" [intelligent zevo]

ok. sit down, children. the show's about to begin. the puppets are ready to perform for ya. [khalistani orphan]

jenni's the most qualified and deserves to win. she's a doctor.

[Miranda Purohit]

is she? [peteBlando]

of course [Miranda Purohit]

docs make great leaders, just because [peteBlando]

at least they're educated and save lives [Miranda Purohit]

here's jenni's most circulated quote: "just because you sneezed today doesn't mean you'll be ruling the world tomorrow." a nonsensical statement beyond words. that's how "educated" she is. [new-market smoker]

back in my caribbean studies ph.d., we learned about some old president in haiti. doctor, he was. didn't turn out well for the haitians, as i recall. [Gardenio Pascal]

that was then. hispaniola has one of the highest GDPs in the caribbean now. [Patty Burton]

while more than half of its people starve. gdp means shit. bunch of robots on the island assembling drones, it's all. [peteBlando]

profits syphoned away by the ruling class and tech elites. [iNmature Crusher]

V.J. Rangattan covered AI on his Konversations cast recently. didn't say what to do about all the obsolete humans, though. [AzureGrrrl2044]

the political leadership IS doing something about it, disinfertilizing folks with so-called vaccines against phony viruses. [poolitzer medalist]

i think "sterilizing" is the word you're looking for there [greenEnvy]

whatever. that's the long-term plan, to have the earth only populated by the rich and their robots doing everything for them. all others phased out. [poolitzer medalist]

and jenni patel is in on it. keeps on harping about public health and free vaccines to keep the poor healthy n shit. [Cliche Trader]

the reality is they can't wait for us turd humans to die off, without progeny, out of the way. [poolitzer medalist]

the sooner you understand this, the easier your life will be: some humans think of themselves as lions and consider everyone else a gazelle. they don't care how many gazelles die while satiating their lion appetites. [hot fire eater]

shun the lions, or you'll end up as their lunch [The Sergei General]

some professor in chicago is pushing for a "metered economy" to grind regular folks down until we all die of stress-induced illnesses. [astrid haldar]

heard that. everything to be subscription-based. we'll have to pay for "the right" to go outdoors—monthly payments to be able to do anything outside. [garga iyer]

every step you take on a sidewalk will be billed by the yard, folks. that's how the poor will die off, broke and infertile, without progeny. [mauricius39]

it's not just the poor. men are hardly needed anymore [grrrrl supremacist]

here we go again [thermal sex god]

thats fucked up. you need us to inseminate. women can have only one child at a time, while one of us can have hundreds in one year. just a matter of how many women a man can knock up. [marcado@home]

eggxactly my point. to begin with, nobody needs "hundreds," plus men cannot procreate without wombs. they need women, while we only need sperm. [grrrrl supremacist]

and sperm comes from ?? [Proud Curry Muncher]

sperm banks. artificial insemination with quality sperm is the way to go. [grrrrl supremacist]

quality. define, please. [marcado@home]

there's currently enough sperm stored in banks around the world to last forever, so all men could be killed today. it would make no difference to the survival of the species, even if all male infants are also offed at birth, to keep the planet femme. [Glirz]

that's if the grid doesn't falter. and the stored sperm doesn't thaw and go bad. quite a few ifs. [marcado@home]

artificial fertilized eggs made directly from dna. no sperm needed [grrrrl supremacist]

artificial babies as well, so wombs obsolete. [marcado@home]

you're all wrong! a diminishing population is a threat to our national security. we need millions more to defend the homeland! [USofI Armed Forces Corporation]

more doughpersons, please [coffee chopped]

doughpersons are legacy. bots is all the rich need. [eurasian commander]

like i said, the rich and their bots. [poolitzer medalist]

the robots will be in charge of making the rich people's babies, in a lab, while the "parents" go skiing in the alps or vacationing in the caribbean. back home from their holiday, there's the baby waiting for them, all clean and well fed and smelling like roses. everything clean and pristine, with no poor people to bother them or make them feel guilty. [esoteric everest]

sounds like a brochure [nuria hagen]

religious pamphlet [MundusGOL]

paradise on earth! [BigEyes4U]

PUBLICITY: Xrifet-N-dermitis—the rare skin disease you've never heard of that afflicts 1 in 10,000. Are you that one in 10,000 who has only 3 months to live? Don't just sit there waiting for this impending tragedy to strike you and your family. Let us scan every square inch of your body's largest organ to make sure, with 99.38% certainty, that you are danger-free. Don't risk being dead three months from now. Check with your doctor's health insurance corporation to get your Peau-2-Peau Scan™ today. Financing available.

BREAKING!: Jennifer Patel, AHP candidate, has won the presidential election in a "moderate landslide," pundits have decreed. President Patel, or P.P., as people are now calling unda, was advised by experts to say nothing in public about the activities of the Virtual Collective. But und has announced that, as soon as unda's accelerated inauguration takes place, und will order Keep America Safe™ troops to "patrol the streets of this good nation and protect our citizens from terrorist attacks and intimidation." In Washington and New York, und added, KAS forces will be deployed everywhere, wearing their distinctive maroon blazers and KAS-emblazoned helmets.

BREAKING: Voltaire Rodriguez has lost the election despite his superhuman efforts to pander to the Virtual Collective and assorted peace movements. His "4 Vs Movement," launched only a week before polls opened, inciting the population to "Vote Voltaire, Vanish Violence," utterly failed.

this is a pack of lies. voltaire was as much FOR the military and violence as fascist peepee is. [silkster]

4vs just a slogan. no conviction [Vittorio Goswami]

it was obvious there was a higher force acting in the background, forcing all candidates to toe the line, to go mum about foreign interventions and defense budgets. [megaStriker]

yup. "vanish violence" voltaire kept on saying "i'm not going to discuss it at this point," when asked about the role of the military in our democracy. it was all "i'll vanish violence," but never said how he was going to do it. [jamondo lang]

like saying "i'll stop natural disasters, earthquakes, and migrating animals." [Alien DNA]

well, if he doesn't win, and they give it to pee-pee, there IS going to be violence. [Saint Lucie]

yes, yes, bloodshed! [mintyMacho]

love it when people die. [casse-tête tais-toi]

sicko [dessertButler49]

gotta hit bottom to be able to reset [mintyMacho]

can't have tragedies without victims, folks. SOMEONE has to suffer and die. that's a fact. so, loving something and celebrating it are two different things. [casse-tête tais-toi]

whatever...sick [dessertButler49]

and the military lives on, with the fatter and fatter budget pipi is ready to give them. [DragonSpark]

she's already sicced the stormtroopers on the people. "i want everyone punished" she said today, lying bitch. [Yaar Bro]

Well, und is appreciated by those of us who voted for unda. President-elect Patel was the best candidate and has my blessing. [Simonetta Vespucci] go go jenni! [alana birdy]

you get what you deserve, then. pee-pee's gonna make ur life hell. [Yaar Bro]

OUR lives. wir ALL fucked! [SanFranCA]

BREAKING: The State of California has codified Hot Privilege Training, or HPT, making it compulsory as of March 1. HPT is meant to create awareness among people who are "excessively good looking"—to make them understand they are a tiny minority and not everyone around them is as handsome and attractive (popularly known as "being hot") as they are. "The Social Credit Scores of hot individuals who refuse to participate in the training will be severely penalized," California Governor Randolph Pillisweet™ indicated. "We will be methodical," und added at a press conference announcing the new law. "Modeling agencies have already been instructed to e-roll all their clients in sensitivity training to understand and empathize with the trials and tribulations of the less beautiful, those who don't have the privilege of being attractive. Independent models and actors who don't register will also have their wages garnished. HPT will be mandatory, period," und concluded. The National Association of InCels™ has enthusiastically supported the legislation, its strict enforcement, and the severe fines it calls for.

hotties can always slash their pretty faces and join the quasimodos, digo [cuerazo]

the only thing that's gonna happen with this nonsense is anyone hot will move elsewhere—like nebraska—and cali will be stuck with a super large army of fuglies. [coastal gigolo]

i vote for dat! [middyOmahan]

BREAKING: Teddy Comstock discusses the remaining candidates disputing election results—now that Marshall-Patel and Fartho Savage have been discredited and discarded. Teddy's exclusive interview with President-elect Jennifer Patel, live on iRiver!

. . . The iRiver Network™

PUBLICITY: Have you considered? When you enjoy a cold beer, a soft drink, or a milkshake—any drink you consume below room temperature—you could be exposing yourself to potentially harmful cryoindigestion. Ninety-eight million New Indians suffer daily from this condition. Order your one-month supply of Dr. Master's WarmGut Syrup™ to effectively deal with it. Free shipping when you pay for a one-year supply in advance! Financing available! Don't let cryoindigestion ruin your daily enjoyment of life.

Teddy Comstock: Let me repeat: This is unprecedented in the history of American and New Indian politics—three deluded, sore-loser candidates inciting insurrection and subversion to the legitimate winning of President-elect Jenni Patel, and trying to undermine our democratic institutions. I don't care what conspiracy theorists say. These three men, who are a shame to their gender, I must add, have started forming their own cabinets, promising money to the military, outdoing themselves in praise of the military, in fact, and appointing more and more hawkish secretaries of defense to immediately advance recognizance missions, space colonization, global democratic tutoring, etc. These men are not true New Indian Americans. In fact, they are the opposite of the patriots they say they are. They are hatriots.

as if pipi wasnt doin the same [ernesto el honesto]

there's already a complete media blackout on what peepee's up to, and she's not even in office yet. [cookie dipper]

cuckstock got his marching orders to distract the sheeple with the freak show of a contested election [ian mcmillan]

staged [non_ducor_duco]

while pipi quietly mobilizes the KAS to occupy key locations all over the country. [Ezequiel Soto] the only platform that appears to be uncensored is eavesdrop. allons-y! check parchita's report [geranium@44]

. . . The EavesDrop Portal™

Parchita Ghosh's live MeSez Network™ stream (bot-sorted and curated to make sense), reporting from a commuter train on its way to Washington from West Virginia.

Parchita Ghosh: Yes! I'm on my way to DC with a bunch of KAS boys, and I'll give you an idea of what's going on with this movement of troops.

being kept safe by our patriotic kas! [more_western]

Parchita Ghosh: Most of them are barely out of adolescence, with their stylish uniforms contrasting their very lethal sub-machine guns.

that's the bullet-spitter 58 special, parch, known commonly as the bs58 and very popular with police departments and small urban and suburban surveillance platoons. [joe is for joseph]

Parchita Ghosh: Their behavior is a bit immature, to say the least. I don't know how they can be trusted with their weapons. Typical young males, and they are mostly male in the KAS. Though, in this convoy, there is also a wagon-full of female soldiers, segregated to avoid sexual harassment by the KAS boys.

boys will be boys! [liliana machado]

do the girls have BS58s, too? [Zakiyya el-Nour]

no. the defense dept found most of them won't use it when a situation calls for it, so they were downgraded to automatic handhelds [fabian serafin]

easier to handle than the 58s [34@Ugarit]

BREAKING: Celebrity couple JoshAnna splitting! "The relationship is undergoing a fork," Anna Laioen-Smith told reporters via live worldcast. "A soft or hard fork?" reporters asked. "Hard, unfortunately," und replied in tears. Anna has moved all of unda's Borriko Token$™ to a new asset indexer decentralized from their common server. In other words, there's no going back.

who cares? where's parch? [duran babu]

Parchita Ghosh: A moment ago, the KAS soldiers near me were speculating about the sexual capabilities of President-elect Jenni Patel while they watched clips of her inaugural speech on their synchronized wristbands. Following standard practice, Jenni Patel's inaugural speech was recorded months before the election, and it was leaked last night.

she knew she'd win before she was born [johnny dara]

and her electorate hasn't been born yet. they cast their votes pre-conception. [lee can ride]

Parchita Ghosh: "Her mouth's good for something," one of the KAS boys said about President-elect Patel's famous red lips. "Turn the volume down," he added, "and watch what she's doing with it." Laughter. "Blowing the air!" More laughter.

ye, parch. im on this same train as you, with my kas buddies, and we're having a fucking good time! [live-N-learn]

Parchita Ghosh: "Let's sexyvoiceit," another soldier said. If you are not familiar with SexyVoiceIt™, it's an app that can turn any speech into what sounds like a lubricious come-on. For example, P.P. was saying, "My administration is inclusive. Everyone is welcome to my House of the People...," and one of the KAS youngsters ran the lines through the SVI app, and "My administration is inclusive" sounded like, well, an orgasm. Their laughter was so loud, it hurt my ears, and no passenger dared reprimand them.

why would they? the kas are armed [Chandika Lata]

Parchita Ghosh: They replayed it: "Everyone is welcome to my House...," and the soldiers exploded again, one of them falling to the floor, laying his weapon flat next to him, almost unable to breathe between guffaws. "Everyone is welcome to my FUCK house!" they mimicked and chanted. "Play it again, dude. That's so HOT!" they shouted in unison. One of them was clearly getting an erection, and he glanced, embarrassed, at the passengers, as he noticed their accusatory eyes.

if those stupid kas boys only knew how close they are to unemployment, they wouldnt be laughing [cannabised to heaven]

how's dat? [purple fiddler]

PUBLICITY: Real men wear Patriot Deodorant™, formulated to keep you dry even through the most challenging activities and situations of day-to-day life. Patriot Deodorant™, the choice of heroes. It will leave you smelling like a man who matters, who is willing to defend his nation, because it's the right thing to do.

BREAKING: REPORT: Parchita Ghosh, the popular, independent PerkyReporter™-nominated journalist, whose social media accounts are followed by hordes of under-20 enthusiasts, is being investigated for "inappropriate imagery." The evidence was reported by her electronic devices and service providers to the authorities.

knew it. exposing the kas boyz gets you exposed. [Barkley Kumar]

> *INFOPOST: SOURCE: World-O-Pedia™: Parchita Ghosh: A former software engineer and analyst at the Department of Commerce before und became a popular, free-agent PerkyReporter™-nominated journalist. Unda's analytical background gives unda significant insights into the workings of government agencies, and und knows that President-elect Jennifer Patel is not expected to make it past unda's first 100 days in office.*

parchita's economic and social algorithms tell us there's cause for concern [riverFork]

english, please [pato deisi]

impeachment's a-coming! [bonne nouveles randy]

search bots are, as we speak, combing through vast swaths of data, crunching the numbers, to find some cause or tool to use against pipi, to boot her ass out of the limelight [shellbum]

parch likes pipi, and voted for her [pillowTalker]

as a senatrix, jenni took the lead on many initiatives that deserve praise, like the committee for reconciliation and peace, which removed all statues and monuments erected to honor divisive legislation like the haley-gabbard act. [Ramona Gaete]

wouldn't call that divisive [mr.felicity]

Senator Bharat "Best in Show" Molli has been vocal in opposing the inexperienced president-elect's every move, particularly the way she is dealing with the mystery strokes affecting the country's manufacturing industry. [Arshi Bose]

best in show is bent on claiming more power and wealth for himself, no matter what is destroyed on his way to the bank. [sena nan]

fortunately, the collective will deal with most of the major disrupters, bozo molli included [stevie govyal]

molli was instrumental in changing the country's demographics. allowed candidates like pipi to easily win office, so there [newGujarati]

told a joke about baby formula once, he did. a complete NO NO. [military loved one]

the way it was done is considered shameful now, so it must be historically cleansed [elsewhere dreamer] wtf u tawking bout? [members only member]

Parchita is now talking about pipi's female predecessor, "the first
real woman elected president of the United States of America, who,
back then, was a tough negotiator, an excellent Commandress in
Chief," yada yada yada—all out of context. Parch often doesn't
know what's what. Should change encyclopedias, at the very least.
[noticieroAdicto]

she's just trying to explain how the former commandress provided
pipi, who was a youth at the time, the inspiration to become our new
commandress, that's all. [uma bhatta]

Parchita Ghosh: It was the heyday of our Shut-up-and-do-as-I-say
American diplomacy. Not her fault. But we CAN praise our former
Commandress-in-Chief for the legislative acts that supported and
favored Jenni Patel in her youth.

ordering swarms of drones—the commandress—to whatever remote
corner of the world needed to be taught a lesson. [retroIQ]

heyday's still here today [purebreeder]

never goes away [gorky perky]

attention, soldiers: you are reminded to loot, my-lai, pillage, abu-
ghraib, and rape responsibly! [quarles jr.]

the collective will take care of it once and for all [diamond day]

the commandress's confrontation with pakistan was the catalyst, of
course. [355locavore]

sent the swarm to karachi. pakis easily intercepted and destroyed
them. their retaliation, instead of being directed at the continental
united states, went southeast, to india [carlos shree]

way to go [GrandKamal]

completely irresponsible [chad hudson]

endangering the world with threats of nuclear annihilation, while the commandress washed her hands off the whole thing. [Cualxochitl]

with goat milk, they say [roberta robusta]

but nothing happened, folks. threats just threats, fortunately for us. [Lorenzo Fallaci]

either the gods were protecting the human race from assured destruction, or the nuclear programs of both countries were and still are complete shit. [doric columnist]

even so, one female indian nationalist presidenta was enough! now we're stuck with another! [duncan lucero]

Parchita Ghosh: The fact that nothing major happened didn't stop the beginning of what became the most massive migration in the history of the world.

it was the h-g act that pushed through the phony "emergency" legislation to welcome "desperate refugees fleeing pakistan's nuclear threats." [100% Natural Smith]

the "nuclear contamination" argument didn't hold scientific water, either. but millions of indians kept on coming every month, relabeled "climate change refugees" by the media, ostensibly fleeing "the treacherous monsoon flooding" of the subcontinent. more like a monsoon of immigrants overwhelming the continental u.s. [Horrorscope Writer]

we was duped, obeesly [écouteur]

high time to eradicate this invasive species, i say [Carlos Paleo]

Parchita Ghosh: In the ensuing chaos, generated by the swift implementation of new measures, the eventual "Passage From India" scandal became so overwhelming, there was no time to stanch the migratory flow that quickly swelled the U.S. population from around four-hundred million to just over a billion, in a matter of months, by dint of chartered Dreamliners, cruise ships, aircraft carriers, and whatever else could carry human beings from one side of the world to the other—all solidly packed with soon-to-be Americans.

check the feed! one of the kas boys is thrusting his hips against a pole! others drumming syncopated rhythms with their hands to jenni patel's speech for lyrics. fucking hilarious!! [gorging on mandy]

"everyone's welcome to MY house" throaty voice, while the kas boy makes love to the pole! [zeroBlaster]

ha! i love ALL americans! everyone welcome to MY house! [electroMan35]

Parchita Ghosh: I'm afraid our KAS contingent is getting a bit rowdy, laughing uncontainably. Some passengers are clapping to accompany the young man's performance, which is being broadcast by several wristbands live, so I'll take a pause here and let you judge for yourselves.

BREAKING: Roberto Zalmuero, the only holdout of the Memphis Four, who insists on shirking unda's patriotic duties, remains incarcerated for not pledging allegiance to the flag in a public gathering. The other three, after stiff fines, saw the error of their ways, apologized to the nation, and have returned to full compliance. President-elect Jenni Patel has already issued a full pardon for them. Now, Zalmuero is in the crosshairs.

Parchita Ghosh: OK. This is getting out of hand. The pole boy is holding a pretend mic, talking to an enthusiastic audience. Take a listen:

Billy Budd (KAS): Laydies and gentledudes, we're the KAS, keeping y'all safe on this train from terr-or-ISM! I'm Billy Budd, and these here are my buds—Roger, Danish, Logan, and Wash-ing-TON! The rest forgot their dog tags—at home, mind—so they

DON'T RE-MEM-BER who.they.ARE!

Roger (KAS): We're not just armed to pro-TECT you. We have talent to enterTAIN you.

Logan (KAS): KAS soldiers don't get paid much, so if you can spare some change, we'll appre-ciATE you!

Roger (KAS): damn right!

Billy Budd (KAS): Hey, Wash, walk the wagon with your wristband to collect these wonderful folks' e-donATIONS! Thank you, everyone, and let's hear it for P.P. and her endless love for America!

Parchita Ghosh: The one named Washington is exchanging screen taps with the donors. Everyone is giving something, while the band plays and all the KAS boys are getting off the train accompanied by raucous laughter.

BREAKING: A petition that began in an Ohio high school seventeen years ago, taken seriously by a local politician at the time, is growing in popularity and about to become a national referendum! According to the New Constitution, a national referendum needs only 26 states to ratify it, compared to the two-thirds required by America's former constitutional document. The petition calls for "the United States to remove its imperialist, Italo-Spanish fascist name (i.e., America) from the nation's identity, and replace it with the more accurate New India, which has in any case already been in use by the population at large for nearly a decade."

. . . The iRiver Network™

ONGOING . . . Jenni Patel's exclusive interview with Teddy Comstock, who is blasting the other three remaining candidates still contesting the election's results: Voltaire Rodriguez, Let Me Win This Johnson, and General LaRose.

what's wrong with them? jenni's the clear winner. und will bring back humane leadership, humane executions, and a more caring death penalty. [poliSage Strategist]

she will bring back responsible and humane waterboarding to paki terrorists rendered to new india. [Ben Kapadia]

for sure. i voted for p.p. cause she's the best choice for getting our house in order once and for all. [Luther Nancy]

the string of bozo presidents we've had these last few terms has not done us any favors. hurray for jenni! [Chambeli Seth]

BREAKING: Veteran and well-respected journalist Jul Parkerfoot has been summarily fired for using the dreaded IA epithet on a live broadcast. "We have zero tolerance for hate speech in our media division," said Fulsome Bambi, CEO of the SattyDome10™ multinational media conglomerate.

parkerfoot put his foot in it. clueless! [stonedWare charlie]

"Veteran" journalist means he's over 30, so obviously didn't know that "Indian Americans" is considered hate speech now. The correct term is AMOIDs, for Americans of Indian Descent. [interested47]

what? what's amoibs then? with a b? [lila arias]

americans of indian birth. desis, basically, born in india, came to america. [Rani Mistra]

a.k.a. amoebas [Boris Haldar]

another offensive asshole making fun of an ethnic group [Estrellita Naidu]

chill. amoebas rule the coop [Boris Haldar]

All of you are wrong. It's New Indians of Indian Descent, NIOIDs. [511 space traveler]

BREAKING: A posting-person for the New Indian Department of

Defense Corporation™ has posted that "New Indian military algorithms have conducted defensive, precision air strikes against rogue elements planning to destroy New Indian assets in the Far Pacific." Und added that the United States of New India "acted pursuant to its right to self-defense."

what are we self-defending this time? [softieViolento]

our self-esteem. feels good to bomb the shit out of some little country that can't fight back [ville@vélo]

civilians were killed, including children [Patti Kanda]

fuck kids. if a terrorist chooses to take kids on his evil ride, thats his own fault. [FTA Joe]

it's us or them [wo bai]

bullshit. it's their country. why would it be us or them OVER THERE? they've done nothing to us here. we invaded and destroyed their country. WE are over there! [Arjuna the Peaceful]

u sound like the assholes who hate our new indian freedom and democracy. if you like djibouti so much, why don't you move there already and shut the fuck up? [no speed limit]

that's really high up there on the intellectual scale, your comment. [Arjuna the Peaceful]

private first class patel, the drone operator, and no relation to our jenni, did the right thing. [marsu hunter]

celebrating the wanton murder of children. yeah, be real proud of that. [Olga Mercurio]

we dont need to apologize for Operation Spreading Freedom™. those dead kids ancestors will eventually thank us for liberating their country. [Carnero28] so true [legal&tender]

PUBLICITY: Renew your work license annually by taking your mandatory New Indian Worker Accreditation Courses at the Dullis Academy™. Remember, if you don't do the work, you can't work!™ The Dullis Academy™. Yell it to your listening device. Dullis, Dullis, Dullis!—and get to work! Financing available.

BREAKING: New Indian drone attacks have killed an estimated 3,215 civilians in the last twenty-four hours and . . .

BREAKING!!!: New India's National Flag Re-Design Contest™ has been won by six-year-old Lessie Vardento! The new flag, which will replace the Interim New Glory, is nicknamed "Ode to Peace." It sports a white square, "so no one gets offended," Vardento said. Critics immediately countered that the new flag is "too white, very offensive," so colors have been proposed. Vardento, who knows the old Star and Stripes was a symbol of oppression, has refused to compromise but indicated that, for a fee, und will consider "concentric, coloured circles to be added to the white space, if it comes to that." The statement prompted the Olympic Committee to immediately sue the U.S. of New India government, staking its claim to the concentric-circles design. Stay tuned.

BREAKING: A secret recording of a conversation between Ravi Narel and Senator Bharat "Bam Bam" Veloscent has been leaked. But while news media concentrate on Narel's misogynist comments about president-elect Jenni Patel, other groups are emphasizing unda's discussion of GeraTech™ and its Angelicus Missile™. Narel adds that Jenni Patel is inexperienced when it comes to national security. "You don't hire a girl selling samosas to run Tata Motors," und said. "The national security team she is putting together is laughable with a capital L. This is a critical moment for the United States of New India, and we need real leadership, not a samosa vendor."

fucking gandu, that narel [timmy goel]

jenni will deal with him [Alexandra Mehta]

BREAKING: Cyberattack on water-supply system in Iowa! Pakistani hackers are behind a vicious attack that aims to deprive New Indians of safe drinking water. As a result, the Logon ka Ghar (House of the People) is considering mandatory cyberterrorism insurance for all New Indians. Digital-banking cards of those who refuse to purchase the insurance will be disabled and blocked. For citizens who cannot afford the premiums, low-interest loans will be available, said a spokesperson from the New Indian Homeland Security Group LLC™.

BREAKING: Marcos Smith-Patel, the First Gentleman-elect, is taking his presidential spousal duties very seriously. "I am eager to start my Logon ka Ghar/Guava Garden duties as soon as possible," und said. "I will hit the ground marathoning, as it were, officially moving my inauguration up so I can launch my WOHM Project even before my wife signs unda's first executive order," und added. Asked what the acronym WOHM stood for, Smith-Patel wasted no time to explain, at length: "War on Hate-Mongers, of course. Me and the members of my First Gentleman's Cabinet will work tirelessly to eradicate the haters among us," und said. "We will ruthlessly stamp out emotional dissidents, and I will not tolerate any type of intolerance!"

marathoning. fucking klown. [catnip junky]

tsk tsk. i detect some hatin' in your tone? [rainbow dollar trader]

sounds like the first gent has already been emasculated [spoiler: the naukar did it]

BREAKING: Men's basketball has been banned for a year to create more equity in the sport. Gender-neutral teams have complained that males in basketball have been pocketing the bulk of the revenue for decades, and now it's the other teams' turn. The U.S. of New India Supreme Court has thus banned all male players and/or teams for a year in a carefully structured decision that allows for "revenue sharing in an equitable manner," the decision says. Activists are also celebrating another US-of-NI Supreme Court decision that mandates unisex public bathrooms—and only unisex—at all airports in the country. "This was a longtime coming," said London Bardissii, chief litigant for the #UniBath movement. Und added that, "multi-coed has always been the way to go. It will save airports heaps of money by standardizing cleaning of such public facilities."

house dat gonna work with de pervs? [Billy Rossetta]

the camera's your friend [funeral party animal]

all unibaths will have cameras in every stall, put there to discourage attempted rapes n such [irish time traveler]

someone's gonna be watching you take a dump? [kimo rainbow667]

what's the big deal? don't we all poo the same way? the camera's your friend [funeral party animal]

PUBLICITY: Earn your double doctorate in Strategic Defense Studies plus the subject of your choice in only ONE YEAR! Visit SDS University Online™ and sign up with your DigiKard™ in less than five minutes! Financing available with low interest rates helpfully compounded by the hour, so you don't have to pay too much!

BREAKING: The vigilante anti-war group calling itself The Virtual Collective has published classified documents that reveal secret dealings between members of the USofNI Armed Forces, elected officials, and foreign powers to . . .

PUBLICITY: Unhappy with your newborn's gender? Regretting that you didn't pay in advance for genetic gendering at conception? It isn't too late! The AdamEve Choice Clinic™ has locations across the country! We specialize in neonatal sex-change services and are here to help! Yell "NEONATAL SEX CHANGE!" at your listening device to find out where, how, and how much! Financing available!

got a couple of relatives who did this. botched. [Rooty Ma]

a scam. just surgery. chromosomes still xx or xy, whatever you were born with [tom-tom mariachi]

better than hormones, at least [Gabi Bañados]

not true. you still have to take them after the surgery [Buri Della]

shouldn't the babies be allowed to grow up and decide for themselves what they want to be? [conspicuous cypher]

I'm a mother, and I wanted a BOY, dammit! [BarbieSue24]

BREAKING: General Frankie "M16 Addict" Viscousson has lashed out at "the cowards who wish to tarnish my life's work," as he refers to the numerous individuals, xx and xy, who have accused him of sexual misconduct. "I have served my country well," he stated. "I'm the definition of a hero, and here we have these accusers, discredited lower-order citizens, patriotic failures, conspiracy theorists, spouting nonsense based on false, malignant evidence." Viscousson added he will fight "this vicious attack on my person until the enemy is crushed under the sheer weight of truth."

incredible what this country is coming to when a decorated soldier and hero gets attacked this way [Elaine Graham]

do you know the guy personally? how can you be sure he's not lying? [oily entrepreneur]

soldiers are honorable people. i don't have to know the man [Elaine Graham]

m16 addict for a reason. how many innocent civilians has he killed? [bizitza gozatzailea]

enemies are not innocent (Bodyguard of Lust)

civilians are [Kara Larga]

Viscousson stayed well within the non-combatant casualty cut-off value (a.k.a. NCCV). The number of innocent civilians he killed never reached the NCCV threshold to make him guilty of any crime. [Captain Bonaro]

so he turned to sexually abusing people instead [Skippy Flynn]

Operation Blue Sky Freedom™ had an NCCV of only 9 dead civilians. That's something we can be proud of. [Brandon Della]

as long as each attack stays under ten nccv, we're good. [4bogarded]

viscousson, the evidence shows, always stayed under ten. [Captain Bonaro]

i thought the military did away with the nccv, that it should always be zero, or the attack must be aborted [nav-lahar sainik]

That's for public consumption. You can't run an army with a zero NCCV. There are just too many civilians, and the drones can't avoid them all. [almohada celosa]

PUBLICITY: PornyPortraitz™ is in your neighborhood! It's time to schedule one of our professional photographers to visit your lair and get the alluring photos your family deserves! Solo and group photos that each member of your family will cherish for life. Our professional photographers will make each of you enhance your sex appeal AND self-esteem! Kids under fifteen FREE! Whisper "my greatest photos" to your listening device now!

BREAKING: The MediaFactory AI Consulting Group™ has received a multi-trillion-drupee contract to run the Pentagon's Truth Dies in Darkness™ campaign. Gano Butano, president and CEO of MFAICG is keeping the deal under wraps, stating, "Can't tell you more about it. It's classified." So far, all documents leaked about Truth Dies in Darkness™, even those posted on AgitpropWombat™, have been heavily redacted.

what a joke. everything shrouded in secrecy, paid for by us dummy taxpayers who cannot find out what we're paying for.

[euskeramerican]

because it's secret :) [Teddy the Toad]

In the meantime, Martha Bombastic (her true name, for real), who's the head of the Women in Charge Organization (WICO)™, is complaining that the deal only benefits men because the entire board of MFAICG is XY. [Carmelo Villa]

wico's wacko, that's all i can say [Aakarshak Rao]

bombastic purrs like a murderess [tony puri]

word is mfaicg will be moving its headquarters to washingtoon [Oliver Espeland]

of course! [25$egundos]

BREAKING!: The State of the District of Columbia is considering passing a new law called #DC4ME! that will prevent New Indians moving to the state from other states or countries. The MediaFactory AI Consulting Group™ and other "high hiring" companies that create tens of thousands of "in-person-only cybersecurity jobs" in DC are expected to trigger mass migrations towards the city-state to apply for those jobs. "These jobs are for us," DC resident Alberto Viamoto said while he considered applying for a highly coveted position at MFAICG. "No stinking Floridians needed here," a friend of Viamoto's added. "Go home, gator breaths! Go home, cheeseheads! Create your OWN jobs, your own economy, and stop stealing our resources."

unconstitutional! [lisaK12]

not with the new constitution. time to brush up on your civics, bud. [all corked up]

FEDERAL GOVERNMENT CIVIC REMINDER: From the Federal Register Today: "In accordance with the new-and-improved Federal Civil Rights Law and U.S. Department of Agriculture (USDA) Civil

Rights Regulations and Policies, the USDA, its Agencies, offices, and employees, and institutions participating in or administering USDA programs are prohibited from discriminating based on race, color, national origin, religion, sex, gender identity (including gender expression), sexual orientation, disability, age, marital status, family/parental status, wealth, health, social-media membership, citizenship, vaccination status, tax-payment delinquency status, income derived from a public assistance program, political beliefs, and reprisal or retaliation for prior civil-rights activity in any program or activity conducted or funded by USDA (not all bases apply to all programs, and citizens are encouraged to familiarize undselves with the law and inquire with the proper agency). Remedies and complaint-filing deadlines vary by program or incident."

we citizens of color got this! updated civil rights law would never have passed without us. [antarctic toddie]

but if your color is more colorful than mine, isn't that a type of discrimination? [cosmic benzendrine dealer]

PUBLIC ANNOUNCEMENT: Attention: Public sirens will start wailing at exactly 9:32 p.m. tonight to mark the official arrival of COVID-2063. Be prepared in your civic duty and take precautions as dictated by health officials.

BREAKING!!: Celebrity Trouple MoRoJo is breaking up! Morton, Robert, and John are no more, but the legal battle is just beginning, as Morton and Robert file for divorce and for custody of their lover John!

it's a-gonna get messy! [Prince of Princes]

both want custody of john [melinda rosario]

more like shared ownership [gupta4prez]

what does JOHN want? [forest dweller]

the money! [KookAidDenier]

ha! there's bound to be a prenup. johnny gets nothing! [georgina travels fast]

Morton wants him, at least. [space kadet 365]

robert, too. that's what will make this so fun to watch. [Marseille Chess Player]

i'm not selling my shares of morojo, though. in fact, i'm buying the dip as we speak! they'll bounce to the moon when the dust settles and people find out this was all a publicity stunt! [brilliant karma]

Happened before—with BeFiAn and MaLaCoSa. Celebrities always jockeying to get their shares to go up and cash out instead of doing real work. [Click Bait Professional]

The gift that keeps on giving! [KingUnbiased]

i'm in. just bought 480 morojos. my retirement! [leverage jockey]

Obey Jesus NOW, comma! [Jar o' Sweets]

The day after tomorrow, at 15:01 GMT, join The Virtual Collective to remove Declan Fountain from the helm of WIMP, the World Important Media Partnership™, due to Fountain's active role in refusing to cover real, important news and thus keeping the world in the dark. [The Virtual Collective]

they're already making this about the collective's threatening freedom of the press [mediaticom$1]

what freedom? [native tokenist]

freedom to constantly lie [Gastón Dickens]

it's not. see the live interview. dilip chhabria, on nowwhat [eagleCounter]

. . . The NowWhat? Social Network™, The Question of the New Generation™

Bot Reporter SandyNow™: We're back with anti-war activist Dilip Chhabria. Before our commercial break, Dilip said, "I'll be delighted and surprised if all I'm saying here makes it to the published version of this interview." Why, Dilip? Why that hostile attitude towards reporting professionals? It's the same attitude that has led terrorists to target our leader, Declan Fountain, who, as head of WIMP, is the exact opposite of what he's accused of. And this interview is evidence of it. Every single word you utter is being transcribed and offered to the masses, uncensored.

Dilip Chhabria: I say it because that's how journalism works nowadays. It concentrates on the trivial masquerading as the important and intellectual. In present-day journalism, there's zero intellectual coverage of anything that's truly important. Long articles and live reports will glibly cover politician so-and-so bickering with an opponent about nothing that matters—all staged performances, while, in the meantime, a fleet of the department of defense corporation's very expensive drones decimates a village in a remote corner of the world where hundreds of civilians die, and no one reports about it.

Bot Reporter SandyNow™: Well, Dilip, in many cases, it is not a matter of not reporting but of the sheer volume of news. The live-stream algorithms give the viewers and readers what they want. Some little village being blown up somewhere doesn't score high enough on the scale of what our viewers want.

Dilip Chhabria: And the money to manufacture that fleet of drones could have instead been invested in replacing ten bridges in this country or building hundreds of miles of bicycle lanes to substantially improve the quality of life for tens of thousands of us.

Bot Reporter SandyNow™: But the algorithm...

Dilip Chhabria: That's what journalists and reporters should be writing about. WIMP is being targeted for this very reason. Declan Fountain and his armies of newsbots provide business reasons for the lack of serious coverage, but it goes beyond that. There's active manipulation and censorship by the humans who are paid to curate what goes out. This interview's transcript may be published in full, but when it is written about later—and reported on—its final version will be unrecognizable. Your bot editor will start redacting and cutting, and if not your bot editor, then the editor's superior, the human curator, or the superior's superior, all the way up to the publisher, if necessary. And Declan Fountain, of course, because some politician will call his good buddy Declan to quietly cleanse or kill the piece. The CEO of some defense-national-security corporation will call the politician to complain that his company is being smeared by a nobody activist, that thousands of bot jobs are at stake in Dubuque, and, "May I remind you," the CEO will say to the politician, "my corporation has contributed handsomely to your re-election campaign and is gladly willing to continue to do so, but these smear campaigns..." So, the politician calls his buddy Declan, who takes care of the problem. That's the essence of journalism in the 21st century.

Bot Reporter SandyNow™: But that's not true, Dilip. We have the best schools of journalism in the world, the freest press in the world, we have the newly reopened Newseum in Washington that tells us how fair and balanced we are in our coverage, how true to the truth...

Dilip Chhabria: But zero reports on the wasteful military spending that has already bankrupted the country, destroyed the republic. We must genuflect in front of the mighty armed forces at our national-security altars. If you don't, you're accused of not being patriotic, by the media itself, or you're tracked and harassed for being a terrorist sympathizer. It's all completely upside down. This kind of twisted logic is what destroyed the Roman Republic, turned it into an empire, which doomed it. Every empire is doomed. We are in Emperor Maurice times here, and we don't have to go as far back as Byzantium. The United Kingdom is a more recent example. Look at what's left of it. They squandered it all, and that's where we're headed.

this reminds me of that chap disqualified in the presidential election—what's his face? [YesManchurian]

primus prideful [Jimmy72029]

He did not respect the flag on All Patriots Day. [benched]

bot-enforced, too [once+cinco]

can't say non-allegiance to the flag doesn't affect you. but if you go to military church, you're covered. [plus oskarizeé]

worshiping at the altar of patriotism [Virgin Rum & Coke]

turns people into sheeple, acting out their masters' orders. [world defender 169]

The easiest way for leaders to manipulate the masses is to give praise for being patriotic and accuse anyone who does not fall in line as someone who's not to be trusted. [Paki Troll]

i'm not to be trusted [Beta Cowboy]

pledge allegiance to your country, man! serve the small group of corporate shareholders who profit from your sacrifice. [Qualia333]

sacrifice for those who're bankrupting the country, destroying everything that serves the common good. [Citoyen25]

that's why declan's gotta go? he's just a businessman making a good living. why are you so jealous of him? [qualiaMan]

PUBLICITY: The Department of National Security Defense Corporation™ announces a $1 trillion New Indian drupee reward to anyone who convincingly and successfully sabotages the undemocratic government of New Thailand, with the goal of allowing New Indian investors to buy property and businesses in that wayward country.

BREAKING: Pakistani scientists have been accused of collusion with the Pakistan-Russia-Iran-China (PRIC) coalition to precipitate a polar shift and harm the United States of New India. The House of the People has issued a cease-and-desist order to the PRICs, threatening "immediate, massive, and overwhelming retaliation" if PRIC officials don't "surrender to New Indian troops being sent to the region as we speak."

. . . AgitpropWombat™, Where the Truth is Everything

Chakula Johnson, Professor of Astrophysics™ at 4Fordam University™, is convinced that a polar shift is imminent. "All the data point to an impending catastrophe," und said in a call conference with several members of Congress this morning. [The Political Lobby of Concerned Scientists]

bunk! [OrthoDump]

the enlightened are really starting to push this p.s. bullshit. they're desperate. [brainweaver]

hence the outrageous accusation that the prics are causing it [Tim Nguyen]

posts revealing who's actually behind this are already being censored, like on vox pop. [motorized democrat]

wouldn't surprise me if it happened here, on wombat, too. [Science Says]

it's all about peepee's new government trying to control us. do not let them install electronics in or on your body! once the polar shift collar is solidly around your neck, it's game over! [Mrs Danger]

won't be able to escape it. governments already announcing stiff fines and jail time for those who refuse to wear the p.s. collar. [Wilco Miyamoto]

The whole plot has been hacked out of ClassyNet users, like

ClassyNet scum #30343, who wrote that security forces are closing in on the Virtual Collective, ready to arrest and execute all who participate in the implementation of the mysterious strokes. [Ray Valiente]

the collective is fighting back by releasing the identities of classynetters. #30343 has been outed. his name is Barry Short (probably an alias), and his address is . . . [mercury mirror]

. . . ClassyNet™

Warning: This portal is owned by the National-Security Intelligence Services Corporation™ of the United States of New India. If you have no business being here, exit this logon screen IMMEDIATELY. All visitors without permission, even if no attempt is made to illegally log on, may be subject to cyber-terrorism charges that carry prison sentences from twenty years to life, plus fines.

Enter your network identifier: *******

Enter your biometric algorithm: ********

Enter your Dispatch PIN: ****

Enter your National Security Number: **-****-***

ClassyNet: Welcome to ClassyNet, and thank you for your patriotic service. Your classification is Alpha 4 Level 1, Clearance 1.

ClassyNet: Warning: No words or letters displayed here can be shared with anyone outside this network. Any unauthorized sharing will result in cyber-terrorism charges that carry prison sentences from twenty years to life, plus fines.

ClassyNet: All information displayed will be scrubbed within seconds.

ClassyNet: Beginning session . . . your ClassyNet session number is 072231 . . .

...Welcome, #30343. (scrubbed)

...You are advised to leave the country immediately... (scrubbed)

...Your personal information has been compromised... (scrubbed)

...Your new identity passport is waiting for you at P.O. Box 3148. The key to the box can be retrieved from P.O. Box 105 at the coordinates to be provided to you via secret courier ... (scrubbed)

...WARNING: Do not include any family members in your retreat. You are instructed to abandon all family members and, for their own safety, disown them... (scrubbed)

...WARNING: This is a national-security matter. Your non-compliance will result in serious repercussions for you and your family... (scrubbed)

. . . Switching to The Bull-Free Network™ - "Nothing But the Real Truth"

Bot Narrator: Folks, Larry Bandatan has seen the studio's red light go on. Und is now turning unda's face to the inimitable "Bandy" spotlight, flashing unda's trademark smile. Let's join unda!

Larry Bandatan: Welcome to What We Know™, being EtherShadowStreamed™, live, to your device by the power of Bestopol™, the detoxifying powder that cleans your bowels and rejuvenates them twenty years! Nothing brings more health to its user than Bestopol™. Our panelists today are Dr. Fardo Raskusso-Bam, an expert on neuropsychology; Sarah Lancaster, a journalist covering mass hysteria; and Mr. Bandervilt Hua, director of marketing at FamaFarma™, a leading manufacturer of pharmaceutical products headquartered in the Central African Republic and the largest supplier of over-the-counter opioids in the world. The so-called Collective has given Mr. Hua thirty-eight hours to live, accusing him of, quote, "fomenting addiction." Welcome, panelists. Dr. Raskusso-Bam, let's start with you. What DO we know about this?

Fardo Raskusso-Bam: Well, Larry, it's more than fascinating. Mr. Hua here—and others who have been sentenced and executed, in a manner of speaking—is the victim of what I would call a neuropsychological attack on his psyche. Everyone is acting as if these so-called attacks are something unexplainable and new, but the pattern has been obvious in parapsychology circles for ages, going back to ancient times.

Larry Bandatan: You mean the master strokes.

Fardo Raskusso-Bam: Yes. It's like those childhood games of yore in school playgrounds. A group of children would target one child among them that they didn't like. They would give the child a message, something along the lines of, say, "we're cursing you, and you and your parents are going to die!" It's the same thing with the Collective.

Larry Bandatan: Are you saying that the announcements by the Collective, stating that someone is going to be gandhied, are like bullying?

Fardo Raskusso-Bam: Exactly. The poor, targeted child goes back to class after recess, trembling, and spends the rest of the day, and that evening, and the next day, and the ensuing weeks, immersed in fear—fear that the curse is going to come true. From that point on, whatever happens to him, or his parents, is self-induced. You start thinking too much about what bad thing is going to happen to you, and, of course, it's GOING TO HAPPEN! Duh! It's the well-known C.U.R.S.E. effect, which stands for Curious Undermining Reflex Shame Escape, for those not familiar with it. That is the title of my latest DigiBuk™, by the way, which is now on sale for only six ninety-drupee installments, plus taxes and interest.

Larry Bandatan: So, this CURSE thing is what the so-called Collective is applying here?

Bandervilt Hua: Preposterous! Doctor Fardo is basically saying it's all in my head, and that all the victims who have succumbed so far—who have had their active lives taken from them—have willingly acted against their own interests. Preposterous, ridiculous, and WRONG! What kind of doctor are you—a military doctor?

Larry Bandatan: OK, Mr. Hua. Let's not go on arsehole mode yet. We're just starting the discussion. Let Dr. R-B answer the question.

Fardo Raskusso-Bam: I've said what I said. I'm not going to repeat myself. People can interpret the facts any way they want. If MY facts are not YOUR facts, then so be it. I'm the doctor here, and this is a medical enigma we are talking about. AND it is not an enigma at all but an act of self-sabotage induced by expert psychological manipulators.

Bandervilt Hua: MY theory is simpler. These are targeted kills by...

Fardo Raskusso-Bam: Not kills. No one's died from being gandhied!

Bandervilt Hua: OK, targeted incapacitations, then, by the government, to justify additional surveillance and intimidation of citizens.

Fardo Raskusso-Bam: Nonsense. We're more than surveilled already. And targeted individuals include mostly the elites, and politicians, plus this isn't a national issue but international.

Larry Bandatan: A global new, new, NEW World Order, some say, with an emerging elite that's getting rid of the old ruling class, vacating leadership posts that the new elites can easily step up to.

Fardo Raskusso-Bam: It's not so much an attack to vacate positions that can be filled by new applicants. It's an act of getting rid of the positions altogether. The whole point is to eliminate the Shivas.

Bandervilt Hua: It's not the natural order of things, then. You must have Shiva, whether you like it or not.

Fardo Raskusso-Bam: Says who? Maybe this is our real Dharma, and, after all, we're just discovering it. Hundreds, maybe thousands of people around the world have been gandhied in the last few months, resulting in an unprecedented peace dividend, with weapons and defense firms going bankrupt as investors switch their loyalties, taking the Good Path and avoiding destruction.

what are they going on about? is this guy a real doctor? [kissyLips2040]

god shiva, duh [staring@it]

doctor of something [LiHua938]

wouldn't let him operate on me with a ten-foot pole. [Alabama Camus]

is he saying dharma is some kind of psychosis? [Olympia_Patel22]

PUBLICITY: Dream BIG! Someday, your son may become a mother, inherit the family business, and grow it beyond your wildest dreams as a successful, preferred-status, female-owned enterprise! When that time comes, she'll need access to capital, and we, at Fluid Bank™, will be here and there to help her! Fluid Bank™, because life is fluid. Yell "Fluid!" at your listening device.

Bandervilt Hua: Why target ME? FamaFarma™ is not defense-related or playing an active role in national intelligence. Mine is just a good company making good products for the good health of the people.

Fardo Raskusso-Bam: Ha! Turning people into addicts via mass distribution of over-the-counter, no-prescription opiates! Drugs are Shiva, my friend. They're slowly killing those who take them. Bombs may be faster, but drugs are still weapons of mass destruction. You fit the profile. FamaFarma's stock is going DOWN, and we the people are getting a real peace dividend.

this ethercast is shit [Boludo Johnson]

move along, then [Unspoiled-N-Quito]

propaganda and distraction. all of them, actors hired to entertain the masses, divert our thoughts, and spread fear. [Spectral70]

so why you watching? turn yourself off. [4goodssake]

what they need to do is provide the bios of those who have been targeted, to reveal why they deserved to be gandhied [kabrakabrona]

Where have you been? It's called the CAHI. This Hua chap earned his crown. [Honey Rao]

he wants to feel superior. conspiracy theocratist. [purple canary]

peter castellon must be peeing his pants by now [Gavi Conrad]

no. hua is. look at him sweat [Pavo4to]

castellon has fewer hours left [Wanda Biscuitrock]

PUBLICITY: Protect yourself and your family against Dreaded B™, the silent illness that is costing hundreds of billions of drupees a year to families that FAIL to insure against it! Botulism, or Dreaded B™, is a REAL threat! It attacks when you least expect it! You are bound to be a victim of it sooner or later. If you don't insure against it, you are actively engaging in familial neglect and endangering the future of your own progeny! It is time to call your health-insurance practitioner and add this rider to your policy. The Federal government will not tolerate families that are an economic burden to our free society. Limited economic means is no excuse to lack Dreaded B™ insurance. Financing is available to ALL, offered by the Federal Affordable Loan Corporation™ and its affiliates in every state. Call now!

Larry Bandatan: Let's hear from Sarah. Ms. Lancaster, I'm always interested in the opinions of women.

Sarah Lancaster: The people's behavior has turned totalitarian.

We've seen this before, when most people are ignorant of what's really going on, they support the police state to do the dirty work for them.

Larry Bandatan: You're saying our honorable men and women in uniform are perpetrating these atrocities?

Sarah Lancaster: Was that what I said?

Fardo Raskusso-Bam: How DARE you?! I've spent my career in the Armed Forces of the United States of . . . New India, and there is NOTHING but honor in the hearts of our noble men and women and others in uniform! They deserve medals, and their free medical coverage for life, and their full retirement at age thirty, and every other reward they've earned for serving this country and risking their lives for us! And now you dare accuse THEM of terrorist acts?!

Sarah Lancaster: Was that what I said?

Larry Bandatan: Totalitarian states usually wear uniforms. That's how they can differentiate, us against them.

Fardo Raskusso-Bam: This is a travesty! I will not sit here while some third-rate journo insults the honorable patriotism of our soldiers!

and there he goes, his usual m.o., ripping the mic from his collar and rushing away from his seat before bandatan stops him. [Aliosha Dominguez]

if this isn't staged, i don't know what is [LunaristPHD]

Larry Bandatan: These things need to be discussed, Dr. Raskusso-Bam. If you leave now, you'll be conceding that Sarah is right. Let her finish what she has to say, and then you can have your turn.

Sarah Lancaster: Have I said anything?

raskulo-barm is a uniform-loving warmonger [kuai32]

i will not have our honourable ha ha ha! [Alain McWong]

i hear they switched brown shirts to black ones, to make them more honorable [Fred Barber]

Larry Bandatan: Please, let's get back to our topic. It's this CURSE thing. Mr. Hua, do you think you can fight it, beat it?

Bandervilt Hua: I have invited friends to my two-thousand-acre estate. We're having a party. It's at more than four hundred guests now. My staff is getting things ready. A cosmic-rock band will perform. We'll stream the whole thing live. The band will even play a countdown—the last one hundred seconds—and mock the whole thing. You see, if it is a mental vibration that these terrorists will be beaming at me, I will counter it with all the super positive goodwill of the hundreds who will be enjoying my party, wishing me well. Nothing will happen to me.

Sarah Lancaster: That's what Gunther Shroeder did in Germany. He was the CEO of Pfeilkiller Weltweit Konzern™, developer of high-grade, cyber-busting apps. His company claimed credit for overheating and destroying all power generators in Bolsonaria. Didn't work. His big, celebratory party, I mean. He still had a stroke.

Bandervilt Hua: Well, he didn't do it right.

he didn't have a cosmic rock band! [lolly-Lolita]

how do you get invited to these things? [Midnight BOZO]

if yur in california, just go. wear a happy face and load up on hua's opioids [Kalipali CafCaf]

Bandervilt Hua: In fact, just for sounding doubtful, Sarah, I'm disinviting you. My bodyguards will make sure you don't come near the place, full of that negativity of yours that nobody needs.

Sarah Lancaster: I'm a realist. I've covered hundreds of these things in the past few months. I've seen all sorts of approaches and novel ideas by condemned people trying to avoid their fates. As far as I can tell, in whatever way this thing works, it's foolproof, the closest I've ever seen to a judgement by God, to the application of the golden rule by unknown forces, to tit for tat.

Bandervilt Hua: There's been no tit here, missy! I've done NOTHING wrong! I've been targeted unfairly. My company is nothing but good for the world! We employ thousands of Africans whose lives have been improved incalculably by the generous salaries and benefits they earn from working for us. Whole armies of West Africans have joined the world's middle class thanks to FamaFarma™. I don't see any tit in this equation!

tat that! [CarrotNotStick]

throwing himself a stroke party with hundreds of guests and a live cosmic rock band and wants us to feel sorry for him? [Asan Wynaloon]

there's been no tits here and i dont deserve no tats. poor thing, hua [Pensant Petite]

just an innocent aspirin peddler [whacked mafioso]

my two mums became addicts to this guy's aspirin stuff. deserves to have his brains fried [Kaa Waetona]

violence begets violence, children. spare him his life [dim but not witted]

only way to stop the profiteering is to stop the captains steering the profit ships [UltraConservative]

o captain my captain! [Joseph Skilled]

take THAT, lancaster! [oftr66]

what the f. . . [Cammo Fedora]

hua just lunged at lancaster and punched her in the chest! [ZodiacMarbella]

angry at the tits! [1234@myBeach]

no. the tats! [Loza Soyaza]

bandatan's doing a poor job at defending her [Ravi Limogne]

not supposed to. all staged. [Screened4parasites]

studio crew's getting involved [journo amarillo]

man born of a woman... [Kumbayazo]

women are more peace-loving than men [Julieta Medina]

ha! that's what jenni patel would say [Soldat Raté]

BREAKING: The Surgeon General Field Marshall Commander of the United States of New India, General Dr. Armory V. Darling, has announced that the Scandinavian ferret pox pandemic has finally been eradicated in humans after years of "selective lockdowns and tactical vaccinations." But und warned New Indians not to feel too confident because "the Costa Rican iguana pox is right around the corner, and our pharmaceutical strategic partners are coincidentally working hard toward the discovery of a vaccine to eradicate this terrible threat to the human race." Subscriptions to the iguana pox shots go on sale early next month. Add your name to the list before prices go up, General Dr. Darling added. Don't get iguana-poxed! It may be lethal!

BREAKING: Mysterious, deadly earthquake just minutes ago where least expected! London in flames! ImHereRightNow™ folks reporting the tragedies live via iRiver feed!

. . . iRiver Network™, the world's never-ending stream of comment, opinion, and thought

"I'm here, right now, and it's the weirdest thing. Magnitude 10, or whatever, and a bunch of people dead—everywhere. Gruesome sights of severed limbs coming out of collapsed buildings. Debris turned blood red, folks."

"I'm here, right now, and London is hit by this polar-shift-induced earthquake without precedent or warning. Some say it's karma for karma's sake, because it doesn't make any sense, you know?"

i don't believe the videos and photos. the polar shift is not a thing. [ipso-factoid]

it sure is. i'm in birmingham, and we all felt it [alberka]

same here. leeds. [Kardboard Peppe]

dublin! [CUverdie]

won't believe it until i'm there and see the destruction and dead bodies with my own two eyes. [romantic@rest]

governments conspiring to push their citizens to purchase p.s. insurance. rotten to the core. no scientific basis whatsoever. [Rous Palanque]

stinks to high heaven [gorilla girrrl]

just like the dead bodies we're having to deal with all over london. morgues full. the office of the chief coroner is talking about digging mass graves in hyde park, "to accommodate". [insufferable poodle]

mass cremation's been discarded as well. too many victims. [5-eye Wonder]

PUBLIC ANNOUNCEMENT: Member states of the New Global United Nations™ are working out an agreement to arrest, prosecute, and punish anyone posting, promoting, or advocating virtual get-togethers that target individuals with a so-called "Virtual Gandhi" vascular event. Any person who is found to participate in such virtual gatherings will be prosecuted to the full extent of the NGUN's international law and charged with attempted murder.

is this a joke? [Lela Sunak]

chinese hackers posting fake shit [ShortNfatty]

has anyone noticed the very small number of chinese who've been gandhied? that's a clue right there. [Anna Karriola]

paki hackers, too. there's always a paki involved. [GuavaLander]

there are studies going on right now that prove that the virtual thing is just a hoax. victims are being injected with something beforehand, surreptitiously. then they claim it's the collective's mind that successfully intervened the poor bastards. [Mike Pencil]

studies are worthless. many of the already gandhied have expressly kept away from public places to avoid being inoculated in advance. your theory doesn't compute. [GooZahNoh]

pee-pee's ON it! already appointed, count them, SEVEN blue-ribbon commissions on this issue! [Clipper Varela]

including the Enemy Control Blue Ribbon Committee Commission Board. [a good boy]

a.k.a. Surveillance Thugs [Madeline DeJesus]

and she hasn't even taken office yet! [Delta8ter]

FEDERAL GOVERNMENT IMPORTANT ANNOUNCEMENT: President-elect Jenni Patel has unveiled the formation of the new Ministry of Correctness and Good Citizenship to "punish those among us who wish to do us harm," und said at a Reveal Ceremony in the Guava Garden this morning.

before the digital ink on her fraudulent ballots dried, she started giving edicts and threatening the population at large [_mysticLanai]

fucking clear we've been given a six for a nine. phony candidate-turned-dictator-politician. [choco-choko2000]

or worse [mega+omega]

That's why it's UNconstitutional to elect a woman president. Unlike all 99.9% of you citizen morons, I've read the constitution. Article 2, Section 1, clearly says, "The PERSON having the greatest Number of Votes shall be the President." It does not say "person with a vagina," and women were not considered persons when the constitution was adopted because they were not allowed to vote. Hence, they couldn't and can't be president, period. [Teeko León]

the 12th amendment updated that [Legal Turdster]

still says "person" in the 12th [inKspiller53]

all you constitutional connoisseurs are dead wrong. that's the LEGACY constitution and LEGACY amendment—both replaced by the 2052 "upgrade." [sortir de ça]

UN-constitutional upgrade, that was. [Capitan NATOstan]

BREAKING!!!: Pope Ernesto Azul IV of Padua has been exposed as a trans man who, protesters say, has no legal-biological right to become the head of the Catholic Church. "To say I'm outraged is an understatement," said Chan-Yeol, one of hundreds of thousands of protesters now occupying not only Piazza San Pietro but most of Vatican City. "That woman used subterfuge and mendacities to introduce herself in the sacred shrine of our religion," Chan-Yeol added. "She must go, and pronto!" The Pope, in the meantime, has denied the allegations and insists he is a biological man, with testicles. But the crowd is not appeased. Thousands of devout Catholics can be seen holding "Show us your penis!" signs, or "SUYP!" for short. "We will not allow our faith to be highjacked by freaks!" yelled Father Angélico Karabineri at a candlelight vigil at the Fontana dell'Aquilone.

BREAKING: Dr. Armando Ferragamo, the renown crypto-biologist, head of the Federal CDC Corporation™ and CEO of the multi-national Pharmentto BioSolutions™, has released his findings on the most recent coronavirus strain, better known as COVID-63.5. "This one's a doozy," Ferragamo said at a press conference in Atlanta. "A lot more lethal and contagious than last year's strain, so I'm afraid Pharmentto will have to significantly raise its vaccine prices to allow for the higher level of complexity that this novel coronavirus represents." At the same time Ferragamo spoke, a group calling itself Investigative Journalists at Large (IJAL) released a massive collection of medical documents that, they say, implicate Dr. Ferragamo in a price-fixing scheme in collusion with the CDC. "He's not going to get out of this one so easily," Verdie Ronn, president of IJAL, said. He added . . .

stoooooopid verdie ronn! [Warmermon Riscotti]

a stray dog in search of a speeding car's bumper, verdie is. [crazy stacie davenpurr]

BREAKING!!: COVID-63.5 vaccine EXTREMELY essential and effective, health officials say. "Not getting the jab on this one TODAY is tantamount to suicide," Dr. Armando Ferragamo, head of the Federal CDC Corporation™, said. Citizens are urged to ask their doctors and start applying for financing now because prices WILL go up.

PUBLICITY: Everyone's talking about our new Terrorist Burger™, Exploding with Flavor! Our food scientists at ZaBroza Rosa Corporation™ have developed the perfect recipe for a zero-carbon-footprint hamburger that will terrorize all your tastebuds with delight! From our labs to your palate. Order it at any food establishment that displays the ZaBroza Rosa™ logo, starting today!

disgusting. anything to make a buck. no respect for the victims. [Juanito Toyota]

what victims? culinary? [plaid pantaloons]

true terror victims, like those gandhied [Juanito Toyota]

BREAKING: The National Oxygen Equity Enforcement Committee (NOEEC) has announced its 2063 Fiscal Year budget to include $993 billion for the installation of tiny oxygen sensors throughout the country. The sensors will stream oxygen-level data wirelessly to the Federal Government for enforcement purposes. Localities that are found to be out of compliance with required oxygen levels will be fined, and their federal funding suspended immediately.

iRiver Network™ . . . compromised by hackers . . . YOUR FEED HAS BEEN INTERRUPTED (scrubbed)

. . . VoxPopuli Stream™

VoxPopuli has been compromised by cyber-hackers . . . YOUR FEED HAS BEEN INTERRUPTED (scrubbed) . . .

. . . and . . . WE'RE BACK!

BREAKING!!!: Pope Ernesto Azul IV of Padua has agreed to submit unda's biology to a medical examination undertaken by experts in gendering issues. Stay tuned for the reveal of the century!

like william shakespeare wrote in 1639, "don't believe anything you read on VoxPopuli Stream™ or the iRiver Network™." [william d. wonka IV]

BREAKING: 89% of the world's nations have slashed their military budgets due to fears of being struck by a so-called Virtual Gandhi. Unemployed veterans now number in the millions, and most governments don't know how to deal with them.

vets armed & angry [SaudaciousME]

not a good thing [KolMeMañana]

gravy-train retirements starting at 30 or 40 all been rescinded [See-thru Shady]

poor things [Morito Pim]

VoxPopuli Stream™: Retired General Bobby Rassarleco (42) is not having it. "This sets a dangerous precedent, concocted by Marxist terrorists hellbent on destroying Amer . . . New Indian supremacy," und said. "We must not be intimidated by some silly notion of attacks on our integrity. New Indians will ALWAYS bear arms! I urge president-elect Patel to immediately restore all defense contracts before it's too late," und added.

BREAKING!: PUBLIC HEALTH WARNING: Protect yourself against P.S.S. —Precocious Sciatica Syndrome—which costs New Indians billions of drupees in lost productivity and wages every year. Prepare for your onset of P.S.S. by getting the vaccine today and adding P.S.S. coverage to your health-insurance menu. Financing available. Ping "Safe_From_PSS" on your medical wristband now!

PUBLIC HEALTH ANNOUNCEMENT: Protect your toddler from the possibility of developing rampant deloccio-virus-induced-cancer by age 6! Bastondale Rx Labs™ has developed the vaccine against deloccio so you don't have to worry about it striking your family. Our vaccine is packed with health-boosting borquinas and rubalodic receptors. Ask your doctor about Bastondale's life-saving products today. Ping "Bastondale Rx Labs™" on your medical wristband now!

BREAKING: After nearly three decades of litigation, the airline industry has been legally forced to disable the reclining-position feature of airplane seats. "The buck stopped here," consumer advocate Margaretta Enllo said about the decision. "Passengers are finally free from being pinned by a reclining seat in front of them. They'll be able to breathe better and actually use the trays in front of them. Our #Get_Out_of_My_Space campaign was a decisive factor in the result of this litigation. We can say that now," Enllo added.

BREAKING: Opposition candidate Rusty English has been arrested by Federal Antiterrorism Forces, Inc™ (FAFI) thanks to a tip from

English's own LizDev™ listening device, which captured subversive vocabulary being spoken by English at unda's home in Pasadena, New Maharashtra. English has claimed und was merely reading aloud from a play for which und was cast at a local community theater. "I was learning my lines!" und protested, adding und was "nearly off-tablet" for the performance. FAFI's CEO has countered that "it will be for the courts to determine whether subversive vocabulary quoted from artistic material is eligible for a waiver. Our job," und added, "as stipulated in our contract with the New Indian government, is to detect subversive behavior and send in our swat teams to do their job. It's our contracted responsibility and duty to our shareholders and the federal government."

break a leg! [Yummee Brot]

broke the law, more likely [sister-f insult]

BREAKING!: Wonderful News! The United States of New India has landed (solared) a probe on the surface of the sun! With this historical feat, the probe has planted our flag and staked our claim on the sun.

this will make us very rich [Pig Swill]

the whole world will have to pay us sunlight royalties, or else! [Julie Gagarin]

drones already developed to enforce this. any nation that refuses to pay what's our due, our drones will swarm and totally darken their skies until they bring their accounts current [Demonic Avatar]

they'll be eclipsed :) [dineroTwit]

BREAKING: Global citizens are being urged to shelter in place and protect their assets from mysterious and deadly earthquakes that have been taking place around the world in cities where they are least expected. Last night's London Earthquake—following last week's telluric movements in Chicago and Paris—is expected to cost quatrillions of Digital Yuan in damages, with tens of millions of dead, including "a substantial number of hapless American/New Indian tourists," a report said, "who were in the city of lights." President-elect Jenni Patel has indicated earthquake insurance will be made mandatory for all New Indians in the coming weeks.

everyone, ignore this shit. it's all orchestrated. the polar shift is NOT real [Russian Dole]

earthquakes being induced [Sos un lucer]

there is very strong evidence that . . . [rosie cruzian]

BREAKING!: A country divided over a new medical device capable of turning an individual's xx chromosomes into xy, and vice-versa!

no one's divided. more like a country distracted by bullshit reports of made-up shit. [arthur yelling]

BREAKING!: ChromoSwap™, a device invented by brilliant scientist Lizzy Holms Avatar™, is attracting a great deal of interest from investors!

the virtual collective is the only entity that can keep the population focused on what's important. ignore all other manufactured controversy that's coming through. [Nakao Kohaku]

BREAKING! The controversial, patented ChromoSwap™ uses a blood-transfusion-like process that's too complicated for a layperson to comprehend, Dr. Holms Avatar™ explained. And it is very expensive. Tens of millions of Trans Americans are demanding that the Federal Government fund Dr. Holms Avatar™'s IPO. They also encourage all American New Indians to use MoolahGod™ to invest in this revolutionary technology that is the great hope of tens of millions of TransAms to finally get the long-promised equity they deserve.

moolahfraud™ more like it [YogheeBeard]

like the reports on the upcoming mars landings—all b.s. that will never happen [Monsieur Muttard]

but, by all means, invest your hard-earned savings, boys and girls! [UltraGetSum]

what savings? [barking swan]

tens of millions of transams? what planet are these people reporting from? [Remo824]

pay no attention. manufactured distraction [moosekrat]

BREAKING: Self-Gratification Awareness Month is right around the corner! Don't be caught without a new and upgraded set of toys while everyone else is pleasuring themselves with the latest models! Whisper GraToyz™ to your purchasing device now! Packages delivered with explicit photos of their contents on the outside, so your neighbors can turn green with envy at how happy your new GraToyz™ will make you 24/7/365!

BREAKING!!!: Several so-called "Green Bay Virtuals" have been arrested this morning. Self-identified as "a Midwest chapter of the Virtual Collective," these are hateful individuals better kept in a federal facility. They willingly participated in events meant to cause harm to fellow human beings targeted by the terrorist organization. The Green Bay Virtuals are not only being kept in a secured federal facility, but also inside Faraday cages, to make sure there is no way for them to mentally communicate. Their trial has been set for "as soon as the Federal Government deals with the global threat of the upcoming polar shift," an unidentified national security spokesperson said via a triple-factor-authentication communiqué.

so we know it's "official" [robin in the sun]

. . . YOUR FEED HAS BEEN INTERRUPTED (scrubbed) . . .

ClassyNet_091588: Operation V.G. is an abort, folks. (scrubbed)

ClassyNet_091588: Repeat: Abort Operation Virtual Gandhi.

(scrubbed)

ClassyNet_091588: Switching to Operation P.S., it seems. (scrubbed)

ClassyNet_091588: Not at all sure what's going on. There were unexpected telluric events all over the place. (scrubbed)

ClassyNet_091588: Repeat: Switching to Operation Polar Shift (scrubbed)

. . .

sálvese quien pueda! [princesa rebelde]

abandon equatorial regions now! they will ALL be flooded within hours! [pluto return]

for sale, cheap, caribbean island, landing strip included [phon caller911]

waat lag gayi! [yungYungRao]

un être humain est simplement un singe raté [carlitos dargüin]

the end of civilization, folks. nice knowin' ya! [aluud]

god save humanity! [dog al revés]

guinda'l postre [half tourist]

just repent, and god will take care of you [Gia Flowers]

rapture time! [roberts rules]

ghanta. too late [Alicia Gulati]

just desserts for a despicable species, n'est-ce pas? [Govi Ku4]

. . .

. . . YOUR FEED HAS BEEN INTERRUPTED (scrubbed) . . .

ClassyNet_30333: anyone in charge of this p.s. thing? (scrubbed)

ClassyNet_58932: mind your own business (scrubbed)

ClassyNet_22866: Attention: To all Operation Santa Romana personnel: CENCOM is calling for the immediate abandonment of Operation Superpatriot (scrubbed)

ClassyNet_22866: Repeat: Immediate abandonment of Operation Superpatriot (scrubbed)

ClassyNet_83941: Interest rates to be hiked to 28.35% without prior government announcement the day after tomorrow.

ClassyNet_22866: All active personnel to immediately switch to Operation Global Freedom. (scrubbed)

ClassyNet_05812: what? i thought it was ops p.s. now (scrubbed)

ClassyNet_22866: Repeat: Virtual vascular interferences should stop immediately in favor of geo-polar transitional staging events, a.k.a. Global Freedom. (scrubbed)

ClassyNet_65789: confusing. they told me wildfires first, then earthquakes. someone even mentioned the meteorite option. WTF? (scrubbed)

ClassyNet_88231: whatever they pick, it's supposed to be an act of god. you know, for public consumption (scrubbed)

ClassyNet_43793: so is it global freedom or polar shift? (scrubbed)

ClassyNet_22866: Same thing! Use the fucking guidelines! "All activities are to be referred to by their operation name, not the civilian tag line." (scrubbed)

ClassyNet_83941: The cost of gasoline, sodium, natural gas—all energy commodities, all scheduled to rise 953% in the next 21 days. Food shortages will happen concurrently. Plan and act accordingly. (scrubbed)

ClassyNet_03215: WTF? (scrubbed)

. . . VoxPopuli Stream™

everybody! polar shift's being orchestrated. false flag! [trusted scientist]

don't believe anything you read, hear or see about the earthquakes and other drastic events supposedly taking place around the world. it's all virtual zoetrope! [basketKäse35]

roger. impossible to tell who's behind all this bullshit [marra bombara]

obviously a small group . . . with very deep pockets and heaps of resources [estela solaris]

black money with access to endless power. they have no need to tax the population anymore because they have the authority to say, "let there be money..." and then buy whatever they want [Kimberly Lan]

vast armies of unsuspecting workers (us rubes, we the morons) receiving the funny money to do their bidding [morning petal]

all behind the shield of patriotism and national security. you were forewarned, folks, and . . . [blank-check charlie]

. . . YOUR FEED HAS BEEN . . . (scrubbed)

. . . YOUR FEED HAS BEEN TERMINATED (scrubbed)

p.s., i love you [blissed-out marionette]

. . .

. . .

. . . YOUR FEED HAS BEEN TERMINATED (scrubbed)

. . .

. . .

show us your penis! [uncle dorothy]

. . .

. . .

===

WAKING DOWN

===

ABOUT THE AUTHOR

Intrigued by how easily the world's chess masters distract, lie to, and abuse the peons of humanity, Krim Faustino (und/unda) has endeavored to produce a mirror—admittedly a small one—that aims to reflect the peons' cluelessness back at them. No word yet on whether the effort has been successful or even worth it. In the meantime, Faustino is back on the farm with unda's significant others, waiting for the call.